THE SPIRIT OF
WALLACE
PAINE

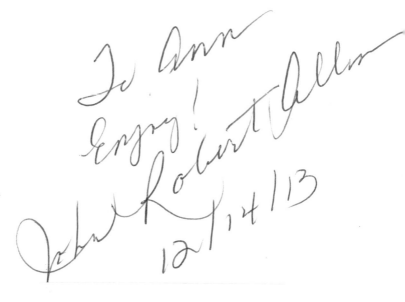

THE SPIRIT OF
WALLACE
PAINE

JOHN ROBERT ALLEN

authorHOUSE®

AuthorHouse™ LLC
1663 Liberty Drive
Bloomington, IN 47403
www.authorhouse.com
Phone: 1-800-839-8640

Published by AuthorHouse   08/29/2013

ISBN: 978-1-4918-1122-1 (sc)
ISBN: 978-1-4918-1121-4 (e)

Library of Congress Control Number: 2013915225

CONTENTS

CHAPTER 1

It was 1PM when the priest, officiating the funeral, called for everyone's attention. He asked Eveline if she wanted to say anything during the service. She looked at Rudolph and then at the priest and told them to get it over with. She had heard enough and wanted all this in her past. Rudolph was surprised when she was so irritable and direct about the service. The guests were moving into the large reception room. Winston, Wallace's lifelong friend, arrived and Rudolph caught Winston's eyes and realized he appeared as if he were crazy. He had hoped Winston would have settled down after his outburst yesterday. Rudolph sensed there was going to be trouble. Wallace had divulged more information to Rudolph before he died than he wanted to know. Now, Rudolph had a feeling Winston knew the story about Wallace Paine. Samuel, the family physician, and Rose his wife, was Eveline's closest friend. They stood near both sets of parents who were attempting to be civil to one another. Until that point, each group stood across the room from one another. Sable and Olitha, Eveline's domestic servants, remained in the back corner of the room. Sable overheard a woman say to her husband that Eveline did not seem to have any patience with the event. She told her husband that Eveline was already planning her life with that handsome man she was always seen with. Mrs. Preston overheard that remark and glanced at Sable before she quietly told the woman she was spreading vicious rumors. The woman reminded Mrs. Preston that Geneva was a small town where everyone knew what others were trying to hide. At that remark, Mr. Preston took his wife's arm and moved away. Sable nudged Olitha and told her there was going to be war soon. Olitha shook her head ever so slowly and said, "Weez gonna be part of dat war."

The priest began with a prayer and a short introduction of what Wallace meant to his family and what he had accomplished during his brief life. Alice began crying and Rose went to console her. Frank shook his head and told them he was going to leave if she did not quit the act. Samuel went to Frank and stood by him to keep him from creating a scene. Eveline glared at Frank as he stared at Wallace's casket. It was as if Frank had no connection to his dead son. At the same time, Eveline's mother, Mrs. Lounsberry, began fanning herself as if she appeared faint. Mr. Lounsberry, Eveline's father, told her she was acting like she did the day they went to Willard State Hospital to see Eveline. Mrs. Lounsberry sucked her teeth and continued fanning herself. Rudolph, Wallace's business associate and close friend, was observing the activity in the room and wondered why everyone acted like they were not at a funeral. The priest asked Rudolph to say a few words about Wallace. Eveline gave him a slight smile as he began his speech. He began by telling how they all met in Buffalo. When Winston heard this he cleared his throat and everyone turned to see who had done that. Rudolph explained how smart Wallace was with the ability to be a success in all he set out to do. He mentioned the fun they had and how everyone seemed to have a purpose in their relationship. Frank grumbled saying, "They sure had a purpose all right." Eveline saw Frank's gestures and lowered her left eye at him. He looked the other way when he saw her looking at him. Rudolph mentioned that Wallace had encountered many hurdles in his climb to success. Winston cleared his throat again. Sable told Olitha, "That boy gonna get us all in jail." Olitha made a queasy face. Rudolph complimented Eveline on the patience she had during all the time she was alone while Wallace was busy making his fortune. Eveline smiled and the woman that made the caustic remark to the Prestons told the man next to her that Rudolph and Eveline had been stirring up trouble in Seneca Falls. The man told her to be quiet. She motioned toward the front of the room and told him that he was probably as crooked as the whole lot of them. The man said nothing. Rudolph finished by telling the guests that Wallace was truly an amazing person who would be missed. There were sobs heard throughout the room. The priest ended the service with a blessing and a prayer. He explained that Wallace's burial would be at Mount Hope Cemetery in Rochester later in the day.

The guests were leaving while the horse drawn hearse pulled up to 775 South Main Street. Most of the people were discussing how tragic his death was at the young age of 39. The atmosphere was still dreary and gray for May 2, 1919. The rain and wind was worse than before. People were scrambling to their buggies and running down Main Street with their umbrellas facing into the wind. As the last guests left, the family discussed what the plan was for the rest of the day. Rudolph looked around and did not see Winston. Rose told Rudolph that Winston left through the servant's door. Eveline thought it strange but considered he had not behaved normally the last few days. The casket was being taken to the train station and would arrive in Rochester in two hours. The final service would be at 5PM at Wallace's burial plot at Mount Hope Cemetery. Everyone except Alice and Frank were going to Rochester in their own automobiles. Rudolph asked them if they would like to ride with them. Frank declined the offer. Alice looked like she was going to cry and Frank told her to stop being a baby. He told Rudolph they would go on the train with their son. When Eveline heard this, she said, "As if you even care or ever cared about you son. I never want to see you or hear from you after today. I don't give a damn how you get to Rochester." She looked at Alice and said, "You poor woman, when are you going to get rid of him?" Rudolph took Eveline's arm and walked toward the car. Alice and Frank trudged down the street with only their hats to fight off the driving rain.

CHAPTER 2

During the trip to Rochester, Rudolph and Eveline discussed the final details of the funeral. All Eveline could say was that she wanted the whole thing over. Rudolph asked her why she was so determined to put things in the past. She explained that she wanted to get on with a new life. She spent many hours trying to justify her life with Wallace. She always liked him and wanted the best, but he was too busy and she never felt part of his decisions. After all her work with the Women's Suffrage groups and liberation she felt like she was being hypocritical by allowing Wallace to operate in a secretive way. While she was telling Rudolph these things all he could think of was the TOE&TIC operation. How was she going to react if she ever found out that she was now the owner of such an operation? He hoped that Winston had not been told the truth when he went to New York because he could make life very difficult for Eveline and himself. Eveline continued to explain that she wanted to have a meeting with Rudolph in the near future to discuss the people, places, and businesses that Wallace was involved with. Rudolph became uneasy when she asked to do that. She asked him why he was so nervous. He made up an excuse that the funeral and all that was happening was more than he expected it to be. She shrugged her shoulders and said, "I'm just glad it is over." Rudolph wanted to question her attitude again but thought she might want more explanation than he was willing to discuss. He made an attempt to change the subject but she was determined to set up a meeting as quickly as all the people could be brought together. Rudolph explained that might be hard to do because there were many people involved from places other than Geneva and Rochester. She showed a different side of herself when she said, "Then we will go to them." Rudolph knew he was in for a difficult time with her. He thought that maybe he was not so happy to be trustee. He had a feeling they may all be in for trouble when Eveline found out about Wallace's past business operations.

Everyone agreed to meet at the train station in Rochester where a hearse would be waiting to take the casket to the cemetery. Eveline ended the conversation telling Rudolph that they would be speaking soon about the meetings. The train had arrived early and Frank was standing guard at the door of the train car where Wallace's casket was. Eveline sarcastically said, "Frank, are you afraid someone will steal your poor son." Even Alice thought Eveline was acting out of order. Frank calmly told everyone that Winston was on the train. Alice admitted she tried to talk with Winston but he refused to say anything except he wanted to tell about what he had heard in New York

City. Rudolph asked where he was on the train. Frank told him he was not sure. Mrs. Lounsberry took Eveline's arm but Eveline jerked her arm away and told her mother that she had done enough and to leave her alone. She asked her mother if she had apologized to Alice yet for her horrible accusations about her family and the reasons for having a brown baby. Mrs. Lounsberry stepped back while Alice stared at her and Eveline said, "Well, you can start now in front of everyone." At that, Eveline knew she was right when she said that her mother would never apologize for anything she did or said. Mr. Lounsberry looked at his wife and asked if things had been resolved. Alice shook her head and Mrs. Lounsberry moved aside as if to end the conversation. Then, Eveline said, "I'm so glad that funerals bring out everyone's true colors. That's why I can't wait for this to be over."

The funeral director and the pallbearers took the casket off the train and placed it in the hearse. They started the procession with Alice and Frank riding in the funeral car, while the other people followed in their automobiles. When Eveline saw Frank and Alice get in the car she told Rudolph, "That damn Frank has made it look like he was the one who cared and was in charge of everything. I'll put a stop to that." The procession went through downtown Rochester and up South Avenue to the entrance to Mount Hope Cemetery. There was only the family and a few friends that came from Geneva, so it took very little time gathering everyone at the gravesite. The priest from Christ Church was present for the final words. He offered to be present since the families belonged to the church and Eveline and Wallace had been married there. He completed the service and everyone put a rose on the casket as it was lowered into the ground. Everyone except Eveline shed a tear. Rudolph now knew why Eveline seemed so heartless. As Rudolph glanced around he saw Winston in an area that overlooked Wallace's grave. He appeared to be more upset than anyone else. He stood alone watching his most cherished friend being buried. Rudolph wanted to go to him but was not sure if he should. When the group began to go to their automobiles, the funeral director came to Eveline to give his final condolences. Eveline touched his shoulder and said, "By the way, give this bill to Frank Paine since he was the one who thought he was in charge." The funeral director looked at her then Rudolph and said with confusion, "Okay." Eveline wrote his address on a card and turned and walked to Wallace's flashy new car that now belonged to her.

Eveline decided that there would be no reception after the funeral, even though it was the proper thing to do. The families and friends went to the Seneca Powers Hotel for dinner. As they entered the dining room, Eveline mentioned how strange it seemed now that Wallace was gone along with Mr. Helfer and that old witch Hilda. Rudolph located the manager to ask for a private area for their dinner. While they were waiting to be seated, Alice mentioned to Eveline that she notified Miss Holleran, Wallace's school advisor and editor for his newspaper, of his passing. Alice hoped she might have shown up at the cemetery but she did not. Miss Holleran wanted Eveline to know how much she grieved Wallace's death. Eveline told Alice that they should have remembered, but in all the confusion, they forgot to invite her. Alice told her that she had her telephone number and could at least give her a call. When Alice spoke with Miss Holleran she was delighted to be included. The waiter seated everyone and Rudolph told him there would be a ninth person arriving. While they were waiting Rudolph was asked to come to the front of the restaurant. He went to the lobby and there was Winston. He appeared exhausted, confused, and wet. He began telling Rudolph how angry he was with the news from New York. He pleaded with Winston to put that aside. Winston broke down and sobbed about how he felt alone and scared. He had relied on Wallace as his guide, friend, and he loved him. Rudolph gave him a hug and told him that they could work all this out after everything settled down. Winston said he never got Wallace to admit how he felt and now life was not worth living. They had done so much together and he never got to say good-bye to him. Rudolph invited Winston for dinner and asked him to stay in the hotel that evening. Winston agreed to stay. The waiter gave Winston a jacket to wear for dinner because he looked like a hobo. Miss Holleran arrived. All she said was, "I am so sorry my boy is gone, but I see life has continued on. What are the choices?" For the first time everyone laughed in honor of Wallace.

CHAPTER 3

Everyone began to relax and talk with one another while the wait staff reorganized the table for ten people. Miss Holleran asked Winston why he looked so worn out. He explained he had been trying to get from New York City to Geneva before Wallace died. When Rudolph heard that conversation he told everyone that Winston was trying to find out some information about the trading company he had worked for. At that remark, Miss Holleran said, "I hope you are not involved in those companies that are smuggling things in to the United States. The law is trying to put a stop to that." When Winston heard this he appeared ready to speak up about what he had learned. In a nervous way, Rudolph motioned to the waiter to have people seated for dinner. Noticing that Rudolph had deliberately interrupted the conversation, Eveline looked at Rudolph in a quizzical way. It was as if he was trying to avoid a confrontation. The drinks had put everyone into a better state of mind with the group less tense and ready for dinner. Eveline positioned herself between Rudolph and Winston. It was a round table for ten people so everyone could be seen. Directly across from them were the two sets of parents. Eveline stared at Frank. Alice noticed her deliberate actions. Nothing was said even though it was very obvious Eveline was angry with Frank. This gathering was different than all the rest. This time the main player in the group was gone. How would things turn out without Wallace?

During dinner, Miss Holleran suggested that everyone tell something that they remembered about Wallace. No one expected such a thing might happen as they looked at one another. After some hesitation, Alice wanted to know if it should be funny or just anything about Wallace. Miss Holleran said, "I'm sure we can all think of a million things to say." When Frank heard this he said, "Are we ready to hear about all his underhanded and less than good behaviors?" To everyone's surprise, Mr. Lounsberry spoke up and said, "He may have only been my son-in-law but he was the best young man I have known and he made my Eveline happy." After that Frank remained quiet. Rudolph thought this was the first time Eveline's father had spoken up to settle a potential problem. Mrs. Lounsberry said nothing because of what Eveline thought of her behavior with Alice. Alice offered to tell about how Wallace had behaved when he was trying to find out where Eveline lived. She explained, in great detail, how love sick he was. She even told about the night he ran around in the rain searching for her house. As she spoke, she laughed and asked everyone, "What would he have done if he had found it." After that Frank laughed and explained how it looked to be lovesick. Eveline watched in a curious way when she heard the story. It was a part of Wallace's personality she never knew. Eveline laughed at that story and knew she wanted to tell about her first time with the group. Eyes went up when she began to talk about the New Year's Eve Party. Her parents did not know much about that occasion, nor did Rudolph. They looked at one another as the rest began making faces and ready to explode in laughter. She began by telling that she was allowed to go as long as Alice and Frank were there, since she was so young. She explained that what started out as an ordinary party turned in to a burlesque show. The Lounsberry's eyes went up when they heard the description of Miss Lemon Drop and Trixy Will Do. Alice looked at everyone and burst out laughing when she told Frank that he should not wait up for her that night. Mrs. Lounsberry, in a shocked way, asked why. Alice said, "Because I was taking lessons about multiple muscular movements by a man on stage." Laughter continued when Miss Holleran told them about how she would have ruined Miss Lemon Drop if she got a hold of her. More references to other people in the show helped to create a jovial discussion. Winston looked at Rudolph who seemed confused and said, "Good thing you weren't around, you would have loved Mr. Horseman. He was built like a stallion and entertained a newly married woman on stage." Mrs. Lounsberry asked Eveline what she experienced that night. Eveline told her that she did nothing but watch. She realized Wallace was an interesting and fun man to have created such a place and a good time for people. It was over fifteen years ago and people were still talking about it. Winston said, "Except Hilda, she was such a mess from her performance that she never spoke of it again." Eveline said, "That was probably the only fun the old witch had."

Samuel decided it was time to talk about a part of Wallace that some people did not know about. In an attempt to divert any possibility for disagreement, he directed his comments toward Wallace's commitment to Eveline. As he said this, questionable looks began going from one person to another. There were some who thought Wallace was not committed to Eveline. Samuel explained how glad Wallace was when Eveline and Rose became friends. It was like two women found their match. What one did not think of the other did. They kept themselves happy as long as Wallace and I paid the bills. Rudolph shook his head when he heard that. Wallace wanted Eveline to do everything she wanted and he never minded what it cost. Wallace was lost when Eveline was in Willard State Hospital. It was obvious to many people, he missed her around the house and in the midst of all the action she created. While he was telling his story, Eveline wondered why she was left out of so many things. Samuel continued to tell about how funny it was to see Rose and Eveline going to see the house being built during high winds and a dust storm. Even the workers thought the two women were lost. Eveline tried to defend herself but Samuel and Rudolph laughed her out of that by telling everyone they both wanted to be bossy. Eveline and Rose made the same face when they heard that remark. Everyone else laughed. Rose began talking about all the times they would go with Rudolph to the Women's Rights activities. Wallace never liked how "chummy" the three of us were. He felt like Rudolph was having all the fun while Wallace did all the work. Frank piped up and asked, "So how was it with two young women?" Alice was aghast but Rudolph told everyone it was the best trio ever. He hoped it would continue. Mrs. Lounsberry sat in amazement of what she was hearing about her daughter and began to realize that Eveline was involved in much more than she knew. Eveline could sense her mother's reaction and thought it was good that she heard about her daughter from other people. Mr. Lounsberry spoke up and asked, "When will you set me up with two beautiful women?" Mrs. Lounsberry glared at her husband while he ignored her gestures. Eveline informed everyone that times were changing and that women were going to start doing things for themselves without a man's permission. She announced, "The 1920's are going to be much livelier and freer than ever before and I can't wait." Rose held her glass up and cheered for Eveline. Rose said, "I want to be one of the first to be out there with her." Everyone shook their heads when they heard that. Eveline told them that they could sit home but Rose and she were going to be out on the town. She further explained that it was time for women to have as much freedom as men. Wallace would have allowed me to do anything I wanted. She did not mention her feelings about his death or any of the past. She looked at Rudolph and said, "We will find out about Wallace's past with the best yet to come."

Winston explained about their visit to the Pan-American Exposition. He talked about the thrills they had and how Wallace was so interested in taking notes for his future home. He mentioned how disgusted Wallace was with him because he was there to have fun. Winston told about Wallace riding on the jackass while everyone shared a laugh. He talked about Sybil Rose, the old woman they met, who was thrilled to see an entire city light up. He explained how terrified everyone was when President McKinley was shot and how Sybil pretended to be weak to get them all on the train back to Rochester. Winston also mentioned how much fun he and Wallace had sleeping in a single bed at the guesthouse in Buffalo and the reaction around the breakfast table with the butler and the guests. Winston finished by saying, "I have had so many experiences with Wallace that it would take me hours to tell them all. I miss his companionship and that he knew what to do no matter what." He sat down and wept. Eveline looked at him and said, "You still have us and you know what we've all done." With that remark, Winston perked up like he realized maybe he could go on without Wallace. As Miss Holleran said, "What are the choices?"

CHAPTER 4

Dinner was concluded with a cup of coffee and a liqueur. The parents were the first to excuse themselves and wanted to know when they would be seeing everyone again. Miss Holleran piped up and said, "I hope it won't be for another funeral right away." Heads shook back and forth in agreement. After they left, there stood Eveline, Rudolph, Winston, and the Haynes. Everyone had a hotel room for the night except Winston. Earlier in the evening, Alice offered for him to stay at their house, but Winston had refused. He was hoping for an invitation to stay at the hotel and return to Geneva the following day with the others. Rudolph told Winston he could stay in his room. Eveline stared at Rudolph upset with his offer to Winston. When Winston saw her reaction, he assured her that it was only for sleeping. With a questioning eye she said, "I'll bet." Rudolph did not make any attempt to intervene in the conversation. He was more concerned with what was going to happen when they returned to Geneva to meet with all of Wallace's associates. Samuel and Rose asked Eveline if she would like to take a walk before retiring for the evening. Eveline agreed that she needed some air and time to plan what she had to do with Wallace's estate.

Winston was quiet as he and Rudolph approached the door to the room. Rudolph was not certain what would be happening next. They went into the room and found it was a room with two single beds. Rudolph was relieved to see that. At least, there would be no discussion about the sleeping arrangements. Winston thanked Rudolph for offering the room to him for the night. He told Winston that it had been a long day and a good night's sleep would make the next day better. As Rudolph was dozing off he wondered why Winston did not confront him with his apparent news from New York City. Rudolph needed to be careful with his conversations with Winston until he knew what Winston found out; if anything. There was very little noise from Winston while he slept. Rudolph thought this was all very strange because earlier Winston was a madman and now complete silence.

During the night Winston awoke and left the room. Rudolph heard the door shut and wondered where Winston was going. Rudolph waited a minute then looked out the door and saw Winston knock on Eveline's door and go in. From a distance, it was like she was expecting him. Rudolph walked toward her door and tried to listen for any conversation. At first, all was quiet but then Eveline's voice could be heard. It sounded like she was lecturing Winston about his looks and behavior. Then

Winston could be heard saying something about the Waldorf. Rudolph hoped he was not telling anymore about the serial killings and Mr. Ling's behavior. Eveline could be heard saying that the Seneca Powers Hotel was considered the Waldorf of Western New York. It was as classy as the Astoria in New York City. Then Winston could be heard telling of his experiences in that hotel. Rudolph held his breath when the conversation continued about going back to Geneva. It was as if a switch was turned off when silence came from the room. All that could be heard were muffled sounds from Winston saying, "Oh please." Rudolph made a scary face when he heard that and went back to the room and waited for Winston to return. When Rudolph awoke in the morning there was no sign of Winston.

Everyone agreed to meet at the restaurant at 9AM for breakfast. Rudolph was inquisitive about Winston's whereabouts so he made sure to be first at the restaurant. He was seated at the table when Rose and Samuel arrived. They asked how it went with Winston last night. Rudolph ignored them so they did not push him for any further information. They thought it strange that Rudolph was not more conversational. As they were sipping their coffee, Eveline and Winston appeared at the entrance to the dining room. Rose looked first at Samuel and then Rudolph as they moved closer to the table. Eveline sat next to Rudolph and smiled at everyone as Winston sat on her other side. Rudolph got the impression that she enjoyed being in the middle of everything. Rose asked Eveline if she slept well. She hesitated and said, "Never better." All Winston did was smile at group. Nothing more was discussed except how they were getting back to Geneva. Rudolph made a point of asking Winston if he was riding with the Haynes or Eveline and him. Winston was quick to tell him that he wanted to take the train back to Geneva. He had some business to attend to in Rochester before he returned to Geneva. Rudolph said nothing and the Haynes continued drinking their coffee. Eveline looked at Rudolph and in a demanding tone said, "We have a lot to find out about don't we?" He shook his head up and down as the breakfast was being served.

When breakfast was finished Winston announced that he was leaving and would see everyone back in Geneva. Samuel and Rose had nothing much to say and said their good-byes. Rudolph, on the other hand, wanted to know why Winston was staying in Rochester. Winston stared at Rudolph and told him that everything was not his business. Eveline smiled politely at Rudolph. Winston looked at them both, excused himself, and left. Rose said, "I hope he changes those awful clothes soon. He looks like a hobo." Eveline assured her that he was going to change; it was only a matter of time. Rudolph began to wonder what the reason was for Winston's actions before Wallace died and all the behaviors during the funeral. Eveline sensed his discomfort and asked him if he had a problem. Rudolph told her no but he wondered why Winston was so different. She explained to Rudolph that he was relatively new to their group. He wanted to know what that meant. She finished by saying, "There are some things you will never know about us." At that, Rose and Samuel decided it was time to go. Eveline told Rose that Rudolph and she were scheduling some financial meetings but she still wanted her to go to a Women's Rights luncheon with her. Eveline told Rose that women were uniting against the limits that were imposed by men and what women could do about that. Rose said, "I thought they were over that." Eveline said that men were not over much of anything yet. The luncheon was a combined fashion show and a presentation about what the next decade was to bring for women. Rose laughed when Eveline said in a lecturing tone, "Men are not so eager about all the new freedoms for women."

While Rudolph and Eveline were on their way back to Geneva, the conversation was very strained. All Eveline discussed was getting rid of the house on 380 Washington Street. Rudolph asked if she wanted to reconsider and maybe move back there. Eveline yelled, "Under no circumstances am I ever going back there. I don't want to talk about it again." Rudolph felt like he was not a trustee but a servant to the estate. He was confused by the change in Eveline's attitude. Before all this happened she was sweet and receptive to Rudolph and appeared to like him. He now wondered if he mistook her personality for something else. Eveline told him that Rose always liked the house and she was offering it to them. They would have the first right of refusal. Rudolph asked what she was selling it for. She told him about $7000.00. She knew it was a deal but did not want to deal with the townspeople who would make fun of it or try to get it for nothing. Rudolph explained that maybe people were not eager to purchase such a property because it was complicated to maintain. She looked at Rudolph and told him to get rid of it or she would. He felt like saying, "Yes, Madame." He was sure that something had changed her ways. This was not the Eveline he knew. He only hoped that doctors were knowledgeable of her condition before she was released from Willard State Hospital. Maybe she was acting the whole thing out again to appear off her rocker. After their conversation, all

Eveline could talk about was how she could not wait to get on with her life.

Rudolph made an appointment with Samuel to discuss the purchase of 380 Washington Street. Samuel wanted to have Rose present at the showing of the house. They agreed to meet the next day. Rose was excited about the prospects of living in such a grand home. Samuel was afraid it might be too expensive for them. The price was set for $7000.00. Rose and Samuel met and without much deliberation, the offer was made. Rudolph would have the lawyer draw up the necessary papers. Rose could not wait to move into the house she had always wanted. Rudolph assured them that the house was empty and clean. Winston had been staying there but was informed that he would need to move. Everything had worked out as Eveline had hoped. She could use the money to grant Wallace's wishes to give each of his brothers, sisters, and parents $500.00. The rest was to go to Rudolph for payment as trustee. Rose asked Eveline if she was happy. Eveline assured her that she was beyond happy and hoped Rose did not have as much trouble and heart ache as she had in that house. Rose could never understand why Eveline disliked 380 Washington Street.

CHAPTER 5

Rudolph contacted Mr. Keyes, Wallace's attorney, to draw up the contract for the sale of 380 Washington Street from Eveline Paine to Dr. Samuel Haynes. Mr. Keyes suggested that Rudolph have her review the document before its final signing. Rudolph asked why he wanted Eveline to okay it. Mr. Keyes reminded Rudolph of the outbursts she had every time she signed a contract at the bank. Rudolph did not know of her outlandish behavior every time Wallace had her sign for property. The entire bank personnel knew there would be a show when Eveline entered the bank. All they would need was to have something wrong and Eveline would be a crazy person to deal with. Rudolph told him that he had already experienced that with her. Mr. Keyes reminded Rudolph that he needed to set up an appointment with the associates connected to Wallace's estate. Rudolph was surprised that Mr. Keyes knew this. He explained that was one of the first things Mrs. Paine requested they do after the burial. Mr. Keyes asked Rudolph, "Why is she in such a hurry to deal with all this?" Rudolph explained that she wanted to get on with her life. Mr. Keyes shook his head as he said, "Some woman."

Rudolph went to give Eveline the information about the contract. She was in the library looking out at the lake when he entered the room. She turned and with piercing eyes asked if he had done what she expected him to do. He explained that Mr. Keyes needed her approval for the contract. When she heard that she smiled and said, "Good Ruddy." When he heard her, all he could think of was how she had referred to Wallace when she was at Willard State Hospital. Now, he felt like Wallace used to and was wondering if she really was psychotic. As much as he thought he knew her, maybe he never did. She wanted to know if there was any mention of a meeting with the men involved with Wallace's businesses. Rudolph thought her tone was condescending and asked her why she was in such a hurry. With an impatient tone she asked him, "How many times do I need to tell you that I want to get on with my life? I have watched you and Wallace and all the business associates behave only for their own good. Now, it's my turn to take over and straighten things out. Women have now stepped up and the men are going to have to listen and take responsibility for all they started." By the time she finished with Rudolph she was pointing her finger in his face. He stood motionless as she demanded the date and time for the meeting. Rudolph politely told her that he would have it arranged as quickly as possible. Before he left, Eveline asked him if he was still interested in the Women's Rights issues. He was not sure why she would bring something up like that after the tone of the conversation. He explained that he still felt the need to be involved with the movement. He said that women would be bossing men around and making them their servants. Eveline then told him that he could resume his political interests after all the estate issues were resolved. She reminded him that she was paying for his personal services. She told him that Rose and she were doing very well now that women had more rights and may not need to have him involved.

One morning, while breakfast was being served, Olitha gave Eveline the newspaper. The front-page read: "Treaty of Versailles Being Signed Thursday Afternoon." The article detailed the points of the peace treaty that ended World War I. Below the article was the possibility of Prohibition in the United States. Eveline agreed that the issue of prohibiting the use of alcohol was appropriate. She knew that women were especially in favor of it. All too many women were injured and abused by drunken husbands or attacked in the streets. Then Olitha asked her, "Did you see that women were going to be able to vote in the next presidential election?" Eveline was elated to hear this. It was as if a rock hit her when she asked Olitha, "When did you learn to read?" Olitha smiled and told her she had been secretly teaching herself. Eveline was very proud of her and offered her any help she might need when reading. She hoped Rose had read the articles about voting and all the things giving women more chances to be in the forefront.

Rose telephoned Eveline to find out what time she would stop by. She asked if she had read the newspaper.

Rose told her that she had and that Samuel was happier about all the news than she expected. Since Wallace died Samuel had been withdrawn. According to Rose, she thought he was feeling blue about Wallace's death. Eveline told Rose that he would get over it soon enough. As she put it, "There are enough men in town to be friends with." Rose disagreed with Eveline and told her that there was a lot more to the friendship than they may know about. Eveline was puzzled and wondered what that was all about. She shook her head as she hung up the telephone.

While Eveline was walking down Main Street she saw Winston. He was cheerful when he came up to her. He asked her how she was doing. She explained about the things she wanted to accomplish and that Samuel and Rose were buying 380 Washington Street. He informed her that he had found a room to rent in downtown Geneva. Eveline told him he was welcome to visit any time he wanted to. Winston wanted to know if she needed any help with Wallace's affairs. She told him that Rudolph was in charge and she was waiting for him to organize the affairs for her approval. Winston stared at her when she explained Rudolph's role in the estate process. Winston looked at her with a questioning eye and said, "Be careful, Rudolph hasn't been around as much as we have. We were around when Wallace first began his empire." When Eveline heard the word empire she looked surprised at the enormity of such possibilities. She wanted to know what he knew. All he said was, "I'm afraid of what may happen when all is said and done." He told her he had to get to work at Goodwin Printing. He had not been at work in a few days. She told him they needed to spend time together like the other night in Rochester. Winston's eyes sparkled when he heard that. As Eveline walked down the street she wondered what Winston was talking about. Maybe if she had him visit her she could find out more information.

Rose was on the porch waiting for Eveline, when she saw her visiting with Winston. When Eveline came to the porch, Rose asked her what the conversation was about. Eveline told her that he cleaned the house for them to move into and that he mentioned something about Wallace's empire and to be careful of Rudolph. Rose seemed confused and said, "Rudolph is a very smart man and will do whatever is best." Eveline shook her head and said, "I hope he is the right one for the trusteeship." Rose laughed and reminded Eveline that he had to pass everything by her first. Eveline smiled and told her how she gave him his orders yesterday. Rose seemed surprised by her stern attitude. She wanted to know how Rudolph took to her orders. Eveline explained how sheepish he appeared and that she had him right where she wanted him. Rose shook her head and told Eveline that she was glad she was her friend and not her enemy. The ladies continued to the luncheon to hear the speech about what the 1920's were going to be like for women.

As Eveline and Rose were walking into the Seneca Hotel, they saw Mrs. Preston. She asked Eveline how she was doing after Wallace's funeral. Eveline told her she was doing fine and that there were many things to find out about. Mrs. Preston explained that ever since Wallace's death her husband had been behaving strangely. When Rose heard this she looked at Eveline and said, "Sounds like Samuel." Rose asked how Mr. Preston was acting. All Mrs. Preston mentioned was his worrisome behavior as if something was going to happen. "I have a feeling there is more to the businessmen and their rise to wealth than we really know. It should be an interesting time ahead." Eveline said. "Wait until we hear about what the 1920's are going to be like for us." said Mrs. Preston. There was an atmosphere of excitement during lunch as the women were anticipating what the speaker would be saying. A woman, who was at their table, asked if anyone knew how to find and hire a domestic servant. Rose jokingly told her that her servant was stolen away from her. When the word stolen was heard Mrs. Preston became uneasy. Eveline noticed and asked her if she was okay. Eveline told the woman that she needed another servant and offered her more money. All the women at the table laughed when Rose told them her husband was a doctor but too cheap to pay her servant more money so Eveline employed her. Eveline laughed and in a haughty tone said, "My dead husband would have paid for anything I wanted." No one knew what to say after that remark. The speaker had arrived from New York City and introduced the topic as: "The New Woman of the Twenties". She gave a brief introduction and began by asking, "What is the first thing you would change if you could?" Laughter broke out in the room. Most women yelled, "I'd get a new husband." More laughter was heard. Then Eveline told those around her that she did not have to worry about that anymore. Finally, the speaker was able to settle the group so she could explain the newest things happening in society. As part of her presentation, she discussed the hairstyles, clothing, dancing, job availability, and fewer restrictions on what and where women could go and do. One woman yelled out that she heard men and women were all going to try to look alike. The speaker agreed with her and added that partying and going out on the town was going to be for everyone. No longer did women need to wait for the husband. Eveline's table was in an uproar with plans and laughter. Another woman at the table told everyone that her husband would either kill her or lock the door and throw the key away. Eveline piped up and said, "That would be the day." The speaker ended her speech with this thought, "Everything is new, everything is equal, and everything is for those who want it." The audience cheered and acted as if it was going to be a contest to see who could have the best time. As they were leaving the hotel, Eveline saw Rudolph in the corner of the restaurant. She went to him and in a very businesslike manner asked, "What would be the first thing you would change if you could?" He looked at her and said, "I'd become a woman so I could be a better friend to you." For the first time, Eveline was speechless.

CHAPTER 6

Mr. Keyes notified Rudolph that the paperwork for the closing of 380 Washington Street was completed and ready for Mrs. Paine's approval. When Rudolph received the note he wondered what was going to happen if anything was not to her satisfaction. He took a deep breath and set out to see Eveline. As Rudolph was walking up to the front door, Sable opened it much to his surprise. She mentioned that Eveline had told her and Olitha that they needed to be more like real maids and not to be too friendly with the guests. All Olitha did was roll her eyes and shrug her shoulders as she showed him to the library. When he entered, Eveline was staring at Seneca Lake. She appeared to be in a trance. Rudolph politely said, "Good afternoon Eveline." She jumped and turned and with fire in her eyes said, "So, what do you have for me this time?" He gave her a strange look when he heard her tone. She said, "Well?" He told her about the appointment they had for the approval for the sale of 380 Washington Street. Eveline sighed and said, "Oh that place, haven't we gotten rid of it yet?" Rudolph ignored her remarks and told her they were to be at Mr. Keyes office in one hour. Eveline wanted to know why he did not ask if it was a good time for her to be at a meeting. He snapped back and said, "You are the one who wanted to be done with things and on with your life." She told him to be careful with his tongue. She mentioned hearing about people who had tongues cut out for lesser things. When he heard that he knew she must have some knowledge of what the trial and murders were about in New York City. She agreed that it was a good time to get on with the signing of the papers.

While they were walking down Main Street, Eveline was chattering about all the things that had to be finished up so she could get on with her life. Rudolph listened politely and asked her why she was in such a hurry. She stopped cold in her steps and reminded him that she had waited a long time and put up with being home alone for many years, now she wanted her own time to do as she pleased. She lectured Rudolph that he was now working for her and that she was paying him for his work as a trustee. Rudolph said nothing and wondered how long this behavior would last and what would happen next. They arrived at the attorney's office and Mr. Keyes was overly polite to Eveline. She soaked up all the attention. She sat quietly and said, "Well, how much money will I be getting?" Mr. Keyes' eyes went up when she said that. He asked if she was interested in the details of the sale. She looked at Rudolph and said, "I'm not interested in the little stuff. Rudolph is in charge of that and it better be good." Mr. Keyes continued as if nothing was unusual about her remarks. Rudolph did not care either because this seemed to be the new woman that he helped create with the Women's Rights Movement. Now, he wished he had never encouraged it. Mr. Keyes explained the monetary distributions of the sale. According to Wallace's wishes, his mother and father were to receive $500.00. His five brothers and sisters were each to receive $500.00. Rudolph was to receive an additional $500.00 as trustee. The funeral director was to be paid for services rendered which was nearly $1000.00. Eveline reminded him, "The bill should have been sent to Frank Paine for the funeral. Better yet, instead of sending him his $500.00, send him a bill for $1000.00 because he was supposed to have paid the funeral director." The remainder, which was a total of $2,300.00, was to be in an account for five years until all businesses were sold or liquidated. Rudolph watched Eveline's face turn scarlet as she listened to the financial restrictions on the money. She looked at Mr. Keyes and then at Rudolph and asked, "Whose idea was this and how can I change it. I don't want to wait five years for all this to be finished. I gave the funeral bill to Frank so that is not my responsibility." Mr. Keyes apologized and reminded her that these were her late husband's wishes and they could not be altered. She stood up and said, "We'll see about all of this." She told them that this meeting was over and walked out. Rudolph shook his head as he looked at Mr. Keyes and told him that they were in for a long road ahead with her.

Rose saw Eveline walk up the street from the attorney's office. She stopped and asked why she was not with Rudolph. Eveline snapped at her and told her about the delay in funds from the estate. Rose asked if she knew this before when Wallace first died. Eveline explained she knew about a hold on things but not for five years. She told Rose that Rudolph was in for a surprise when he met with her again. Rose asked why the sudden change in her attitude and behavior toward Rudolph. Eveline told her what Winston had said about being wise to what Rudolph was capable of doing. She began to figure out that the reason Rudolph was so close to Wallace was because they had more financial involvement than most knew about. Rose wanted to know how she found out. Eveline continued about Winston reminding her of the magnitude of the estate. Rose made a surprised face when she heard the word magnitude; just at it had affected Eveline when she heard it. She referred to the trial in New York City. She had been thinking about how coincidental it was that all of them were involved in the trial. Now it all began to seem fishy to her. Eveline thought that Winston was probably the one who was the most dedicated and honest of the three men and the most poorly dealt with. Rose jokingly said, "I'm glad Samuel isn't in that line up." Eveline smiled and told Rose she was glad they were friends and that she felt she could confide in her. Rose was happy to hear that and reminded Eveline that all the questions would be answered and put in the past.

Samuel and Rose had an appointment with Mr. Keyes to finalize the purchase of 380 Washington Street. Rose was excited that they would soon be the owners of such a grand home. She told Samuel that it was too bad that Eveline hated the place so much. Samuel was not as eager to enter in to the conversation about the reasons the Paine's did not care for the home. He reminded Rose of how much she had wanted him to build her a house like that. He told her that it was meant to be and to be glad it all worked out. Rose thought he was being abrupt with her but let it go. She had better things to think about. While they were signing the papers, Mr. Keyes suggested that they go through the house to make sure that all was well and ready to be moved into. After the appointment, they were walking home and saw Winston. He asked how the house closing went. They told him all went well and about the idea of walking through the house. Winston offered to go with them to show them all the gadgets and how to operate them. They agreed and were happy because he had lived there and knew more about the house.

Eveline stormed into the house and went to the library. She found a copy of the will. She sat down and began reading it more carefully. Now, she realized how much she had left up to Wallace and Rudolph. Olitha came in to see if she needed anything. Eveline told her that she was too upset to want anything but some answers. She asked Olitha, "Do you think I appeared disinterested in what happened at 380 Washington Street?" Olitha took a deep breath and thought she needed to be very careful of her answer. She did not want to be treated like Rudolph. She explained in a caring voice, "Honey you just bein a good wife. No man wants a woman to knows too much about all they do." Eveline was not sure that was the answer she was expecting but considered the source and the background domestic servants come from. Then Eveline asked her, "Did you know much about my baby before he died?" Just as the word baby came out, Sable walked into the room. She looked at Olitha with her huge brown eyes wide open. Sable asked, "What I hear about dat baby dyin?" Eveline looked at them and told them that she never really remembered too much about what happened to the baby. They looked at each other and shook their heads and said, "He dead." Eveline thought that was strange how they were responding but lately nothing seemed to be the way she thought it was.

Eveline decided to make some changes to Rudolph's reimbursements for time as a trustee. She figured if the will could not be altered then he would have to continue no matter what. She wrote a note to Mr. Keyes informing him that Rudolph would not be receiving his money for trusteeship services for five years. She felt it was only fair that everyone be treated equally. She made an exception for the attorney fees and stated his payments would be made when the services were rendered. Just as she was addressing the envelope and placing it on the table, Rudolph walked in. He told her he was concerned about her and hoped she understood the will and its execution. She glared at him and told him that was not all that was going to be executed. He asked why she was so difficult and seemed to be punishing him. She told him in a calm voice that she was finding things out that led her to believe that there was more involved to Wallace's past than she knew. He wanted to know how that involved him. She looked at him and reminded him of all the dealings he had in Buffalo and that his loyalty to Wallace was questioned then. She reminded him about their get togethers and all the unanswered questions about the trial in New York City. The more she talked the queasier Rudolph became. She wanted to know why he was so fidgety. He told her that he was tired of being treated like a servant. She spoke up and reminded him that she was paying him for his work as a trustee and friendship should not enter into business. She wanted him to understand that she was in charge and he was to listen and do what she expected. Then, she wanted to know how much longer she had to wait for the meeting of all the associates in Wallace's companies. Rudolph told her they were trying to find a few people. She laughed and wanted to know if they were taking off early before the storm hits. Rudolph asked why she thought something was awry. She gave him a look to kill when she reminded him about the import and export business. When he heard this he panicked with the thought that she may have heard Wallace's story the night he died. He told her she was trying to do too much and needed to take care of herself. Eveline glared at him and said, "I am taking better care of myself than even before. I am getting to the bottom of all the underhanded dealings." Then she decided to give it to Rudolph when she told him he was being treated as an equal now. He wanted to know what that meant. She explained that she had reduced his payment to half and that he would have to wait for five years to receive his payment for services as trustee. She pointed to the envelope on the table addressed to Mr. Keyes. She told him it was time for him to leave now. She was expecting Winston.

The next morning Winston met Rose and Samuel at the corner of Washington Street and Nursery Avenue. The house looked as regal as always. The summer foliage had begun to fill the property with privacy from the street. Rose and Samuel stared at how large the home appeared. Winston thought they should go through the front door way first. He was as excited as a child to show them the house. He demonstrated the speaking tube. Rose reminded him that they had all been there many times so such details were not necessary. They laughed at how funny it seemed to be going into the house that was now empty. Rose remarked how different it was without their friends and their furnishings. Samuel reminded her of how much she had spent on furniture that would soon fill up the place. Winston showed them the features in the kitchen. Rose asked Samuel if she could have some domestic servants. He told her only one. She did not need a personal assistant like Eveline had. Rose made a face but was happy to seek out a new servant. Winston pointed out gadgets in the garage and explained that they might need the telephone for the driver. Samuel thought it was a good idea saying, "If Rose can have a servant he could have a driver that would care for his automobile." Rose told him that the driver could manage the yard and the pond. Winston demonstrated the central vacuum system, which Rose was fascinated with. She laughed and remarked that she had never seen Eveline even touch it. Winston explained the basement items and reminded Samuel that the fish needed to be taken in at Halloween. As they went upstairs through the servant stairway Winston was telling them that the roof needed caring for on a regular basis. He had to clean it because the roof was built like a dome but had four feet perimeter flat roofs around the house. Those areas would collect debris and clog the drain system. Samuel thought maybe the driver could do that when he had spare time. Winston reminded them that a house such as this took a lot of care. They were interested in the attic. Winston explained that there was no attic only a crawl space. Samuel wanted to know how to get up to it. Winston took them to the bedroom closet where there was a small opening to the area above. Rose was disinterested but Winston insisted they see the tiny space above the second floor. Winston found a ladder and went up to the opening. As he was reaching to get higher in the opening he felt something. He came down from the ladder and looked like he had seen a ghost. Samuel asked what it felt like. Winston explained it had a sharp corner like a knife. Samuel thought he was dramatizing so he decided to go up to find out what was there. He reached into the dark. He too felt a sharp object. He grabbed it and a black tin box fell to the floor. Rose screamed from the sound as it hit the floor. Winston picked it up and found it locked. "Wallace Paine Personal," was written on the top. He shook the box and it sounded like papers and metal things were in it. Was this the answer to the questions about the magnitude of Wallace's estate?

CHAPTER 7

The Geneva Daily News had front-page headlines that World War I had officially come to an end on Thursday at 3:50PM. Germany signed the Treaty of Versailles. It was Friday, June 27, 1919 and President Wilson was returning from Paris to the United States. There was great hope that the world might never experience such devastation and corruption again. There were cheers and applauds throughout the country when the news was made public. The second major article was reporting about the possibility of Prohibition. It had been debated in Congress. Senator Volstead proposed that the country become alcohol free. There were groups that had been lobbying for its passage. The question was how dry would the country become? According to the paper, starting July 1, 1919, beer and wine would be the only alcohol-based beverage that could be sold. A slogan began to appear in New York State. It was "Good-bye Whiskey,

Hello Beer." Bitter fighting broke out in various places over such a harsh rule. Many groups began plans for smuggling alcohol into the country. People thought it was too early to become concerned about the prohibition of alcoholic beverages and most thought it would be temporary.

Winston saw an advertisement for a magic show. It was to be held in Geneva on Thursday, July 3, at the Strand Theatre on Seneca Street. The first person he thought to invite was Eveline. A few years ago he took Wallace to a show at the Smith Opera House. Now, he was dead and he was doing the same thing with Eveline. He could not help but wonder if there was some reason why all these things were happening. He laughed to himself and thought that Wallace was probably watching everyone and how they were behaving. He decided to go to Eveline's house to ask her to go to the magic show. As he walked to the front door, he thought about how much more he knew about Wallace's life than even Eveline was aware of. After what he and Wallace experienced in New York City, Buffalo, and Rochester he was sure all this had a reason. He knocked on the door and Sable answered it and said, "My, my, look what the cat done dragged in." When Eveline heard his voice she came to the door. She looked at Winston with a suggestive eye and told Sable he was much nicer than a cat. Winston was invited into the library. He explained about the show as Eveline studied his tight pants. He had not shaved or combed his hair because he was on his way home from work. Eveline complimented him on his rough appearance. He thought to himself that was what Wallace liked about me too. Sable stood at the door as she was instructed to do when there was company. As she listened, she rolled her eyes and motioned to Olitha to hear the conversation. Winston explained that, "The Great Blackstone" was the World's Greatest Magician. He was giving the greatest and most sensational magic show ever. He asked her if she wanted to go with him. She accepted the offer and thought it was about time she did something that was fun. Winston laughed in his deep tone and told her that he knew she would go. He bought the best seats in the theatre. They were 75 cents each.

Rudolph received a call from the manager at the Seneca Powers Hotel. He wanted to advise Rudolph that because of the new Prohibition law there needed to be an adjustment to the Hunting Room Bar in the hotel. Rudolph had been so busy in Geneva he had ignored the hotel. Rudolph knew that he would now operate the hotel with Eveline just as he used to with Wallace. Wallace and he used to enjoy their time together when they would meet in Rochester. Now he had to involve Eveline. He made a face when he thought of the differences there were with Eveline, especially her touchy disposition. He told the manager he would be in Rochester the next week with Mrs. Paine to discuss the changes in the hotel.

Samuel and Rose decided to deal with the black box. They told Winston that they would not tell Eveline that he was with them when they found it. In that way, he would not be implicated when they delivered it to her. Rose shook it and tried to figure out what made the rattling sound. She knew that whatever was in the box had to be important to Wallace. She said to Samuel, "Why didn't Wallace take the box when they moved?" Samuel was hesitant to say much until she demanded he tell anything he might know. Samuel admitted it was strange that it was left behind. He thought to himself that Wallace was smart enough to know that it may never be found, so anything that it may contain would not get him or anyone else in trouble. He redirected the conversation away from the "whys" to what they were going to do with it. Since Rose was Eveline's best friend she should deliver it to her. All she needed to do was say they found it in the crawl space. Samuel was relieved when she agreed to do it. He feared what the box was going to reveal about Wallace and his past.

When Winston arrived to pick up Eveline she answered the door in a flashy outfit of bloomers and a blouse. The best part was the size of the hat. Winston asked her if she was going to the races. She laughed and said, "No silly, I want everyone to see me and who I am with." Winston took that as a compliment. He was traveling with one of the most noticed woman in town. He was wearing his usual attire; the worker look and a bit dirty but appealing. Eveline was used to his way and was beginning to find him attractive. Every now and then he would ask himself why she was being so nice. She never disliked him but now she gave him the feeling she wanted to be closer friends. Their seats were in the front row at the center of the stage. As the show began, the lights dimmed and Winston nudged Eveline and said he wanted to be called up to the stage by the magician. He told her that he wanted to see if the magician could make him float in air. She laughed and said, "You're too big for him." The show was as good as the advertisement said it would be. At intermission, Winston began his little boy pouting because he had not been called to the stage. The second act began and the magician pointed to Winston to come up on the stage. Eveline and the audience were in hysterics when he fell up the steps to "The Great Blackstone". He asked Winston what he wanted to do or become. Winston told Blackstone that he wanted to float in air. Blackstone asked Winston who the pretty little lady was that he was sitting with. He said, "Eveline." Blackstone said that was a lovely name and he commented on her large hat. He invited her to come to the stage. He told the audience that, "This big boy might need two people to make him float. He is built like a stallion." Winston was complimented by the remark but blushed from the thought of the size of a stallion as the audience cheered him on. Blackstone did some waving of scarves and hoops to show that there were no ropes connected to Winston or the ceiling. There was dead silence as he began chanting and counting. Eveline was asked to pass a hoop back and forth to show the levitation. By this time, Winston was in a flat position. He was told to close his eyes and hold his breath for ten seconds. Blackstone spoke slowly and softly as Winston began rising up in the air. There were sounds of, "ooos and ahhhhs", from the audience. Eveline's mouth was open in astonishment. After the ten seconds Blackstone lowered Winston back to his original position. The audience went crazy and Eveline let out one of her piercing squeals. Blackstone laughed and asked her if she wanted to go on the road with him as audience noise. She made one of her cute faces and refused his offer. Winston, on the other hand, offered to go on the road as his stallion. Blackstone laughed and said, "You look like you might be more than I could handle." Winston told him that he would have a great time handling him. The audience cheered as they left the stage. Eveline and Winston were so enthralled with the show that they never saw Rudolph in the audience. He had a less expensive seat but could see all he needed to see to realize that there was a new relationship developing that he was not part of.

The next morning Rudolph went to tell Eveline about the hotel. Olitha answered the door and was hesitant to allow him to come inside. Rudolph wondered what the problem was now. Was he not allowed inside anymore? He stood in the foyer with Olitha as Winston came downstairs. Rudolph's eyes went up as Winston and he looked at one another. Rudolph asked him if he had fun last night. Winston replied, "What part; the show or here?" As they were trying to make some sense of the conversation, Eveline appeared in her sporty little tennis outfit. She informed them she was on her way to play tennis. Sable came in and told her that her instructor was coming very soon. Rudolph decided to speak about the hotel in private after Winston left. Eveline greeted Rudolph in a far better tone than usual. Rudolph told Eveline that they needed to go to Rochester for some hotel business. He wanted to know when she would be available. She looked shocked when he told her that it was up to her how the hotel was to be operated. For the first time, it appeared as if Eveline realized that she was in charge of not just the businesses in Geneva but a plush hotel in Rochester. She told him she would be available tomorrow. Rudolph thanked her for her quick and pleasant response. She gave him one of her sweet but sly smiles.

CHAPTER 8

Rudolph arrived at 8 AM. Eveline had finished her breakfast and was dressing. Rudolph waited in the library. She appeared with a snappy dress that she had purchased when she heard she needed to be in charge of the meeting. She told Rudolph that a good image is the best way to gain the respect of the subordinates. Rudolph laughed when he heard that but knew she was just the person to command that type of behavior. She informed Rudolph that they were taking Wallace's new car to Rochester. Since it was so flashy, and a good quality car, they needed to work it hard to keep it in good working order. She had notified James, her chauffeur, to be ready to escort them to Rochester. Rudolph thought he would drive, but Eveline told him they would be spending time in the back seat. After what he thought happened with Winston he did not think Eveline was interested in him. However, he was taken back when she put her arm around his waist and gave him a tickle. She said, "I have some ideas for you." Rudolph was even more confused with her personality shifts. He thought what she needed was more than one man to make her happy. His mind began to move to the thought of what it would be like if Winston, Eveline, and he were to spend time together. He felt a surge of excitement as he gave it further consideration. James appeared in the doorway and said that the car was ready. He asked, "Mrs. Paine, do you want the top up or down?" She looked at Rudolph and motioned for him to decide. He thought the top could be down because it was a lovely day. Eveline ran upstairs to get one of her wide brimmed hats with a pink ribbon that tied the hat so it would not blow away. Rudolph felt like it was the old Eveline returning. How much time would it take for her to return to the demanding woman she could be?

The ride to Rochester was enjoyable but the wind on their faces made it difficult to talk. Eveline kept putting her hand on Rudolph's leg. She commented on how muscular they were. She laughed and said, "I need to examine you again from top to bottom." Rudolph smiled and thought his dreams may be coming true. James pulled up to the front of the hotel. The doorman tipped his hat as James helped Mrs. Paine out of the car. Rudolph followed and tipped the doorman. When they entered the lobby everyone recognized them. They were treated like they were royalty. Eveline nudged Rudolph and wanted to know why they were behaving like that. He explained that was his policy and that all guests were to be treated with utmost respect. Rudolph said, "After all, they are the paying customers." Eveline laughed and told him she was not paying anything. Rudolph smiled but could sense the tone that she was the important one now. When they walked into the office, Eveline remembered how many times Wallace would come out of there and complain about Hilda. The office had been remodeled and there was no sign of Mr. Helfer or Hilda. For that matter, there was no sign of Wallace either. Rudolph did remind her that he and Wallace had their portraits in the lobby. Eveline sarcastically wanted to know when hers was being hung in the lobby. Just as Rudolph was going to answer her, the manager came out. He explained that because of the possibilities of prohibition, they were no longer in need of the bar in the restaurant. He asked what Mrs. Paine wanted to do with the area. She looked at both of them and without hesitation said, "I want it turned into a candy shop and bakery." The men were astonished at how quickly she had decided. Rudolph asked why that combination. Eveline explained that everyone loves to buy candy especially if it was a good quality. She also wanted to make sure that the bakery made the pastries and bread on the premises. She reminded them of how inviting it was to smell freshly baked cookies, cakes, and bread. She was emphatic about wanting fresh aromatic spices that would attract guests to the new addition of the hotel. The manager reminded her that they already baked the bread for the restaurant in the back kitchen. She looked at him and smiled sweetly but firmly and said, "Then change it." Rudolph said nothing but was impressed with her steadfast attitude. He thought that maybe they could come to terms about how things needed to operate. The manager wanted to know when she would like the changes to happen. Eveline looked at Rudolph and said, "He's such a nice man, but he will need to get to know me better. I am not Wallace as you can see. I want it done in two weeks." She explained that she was returning for the anniversary sale at B. Forman Company in two weeks and expected it to be complete. Rudolph smiled as she dramatized her explanation of why she wanted to make her trip to Rochester worthwhile for the hotel and her shopping. Then she asked Rudolph if he wanted to come with her. He wanted to know why. She told him that if he did not want to come, she was bringing Sable and Olitha and showing them a good time. She explained that they deserved some new clothes. The manager looked at her and thought a big change was in store for the Seneca Powers Hotel now that a woman was in charge.

The manager thanked them for coming from Geneva and told them he would keep them notified of the progress in the hotel. Eveline reminded Rudolph that he would be coming even if he did not want to. He shook his head and told her he did not need any new clothes. She smiled at the manager and said, "You boys can entertain yourselves with something else while the women shop." Eveline wanted to see some of the other parts of the hotel before she left. Rudolph thought that strange since they had been there for the night after Wallace's funeral. She told them that it was better to arrive unannounced to see how the employees work and how things operate on a daily basis. The manager's eyes were wide open with surprise. He thought everything was okay and had never had anything said to him like that before. Rudolph assured her that the hotel was operating at the highest level. She looked at him and said, "I'll be the judge of that." As Eveline and the men walked around the guestroom floors, she expressed the need for new carpeting and fresher looking flowers at the end of each hallway. While they were walking around,

Eveline wanted to know how the takeaways were going. The manager explained most people liked the free pens and pads but especially they liked the free umbrella policy. She was happy to hear that and said, "It may cost some money but it is good advertising for the Seneca Powers Hotel." Rudolph wanted to know how she knew about all these things. She shook her head and told him she was not as disconnected as everyone thought when Wallace was doing his work. Rudolph wondered what else she knew. The future was going to very interesting.

On the way back to Geneva, they talked about the appearance of the hotel. Eveline admitted she acted direct but wanted the manager to know who was in charge and that policies were going to change. Rudolph listened and compared her remarks to how he had been treated. Maybe he was mistaken about her trying to be more involved. Eveline had a way of making people feel they were not good enough, but maybe that was her own insecurity issue. Rudolph told Eveline he was proud of the way she handled the meeting and liked her ideas. She smiled and said, "I'm not as nasty as I sometimes appear." He shook his head as James stopped the car in front of 775 South Main Street. He walked Eveline to the door. Sable was there to open it and Eveline thanked Rudolph for his help. She admitted she was glad he was there. Rudolph bid his farewells to both women. As he was walking home, he thought about how the day had gone. He did not want to question too much but reminded himself that he was part owner of the hotel. Why would he not want to help when his interest was at stake?

Rudolph saw Winston on the street. They talked about what had been happening and Winston mentioned how much fun he had been having with Eveline. Rudolph listened and then asked if they had slept together. Winston admitted that they had spent a couple of nights together. Rudolph was remembering the night at the hotel in Rochester when Winston went to her room. Winston admitted she was much different than he expected. Rudolph wanted to know how different. Winston laughed and admitted he let her tie him up and have her way with him. Rudolph smiled and thought of the time when the men shared a room at the apartment on Washington Street. Winston laughed and told him about the time Wallace tied him up in the woods when he and Eveline went to a Sunday concert. Rudolph asked if that was the time when they used LeterBuck aphrodisiacs. Winston shook his head yes. Rudolph wanted to know what it was like to be tied up by a woman. He admitted it was not much different than when Wallace did it. Rudolph jokingly said, "You don't think Eveline is a female version of Wallace?" Winston laughed and told Rudolph that would be fine with him. Rudolph told Winston about what Eveline said on the way to Rochester about how she had forgotten how big he was and had such muscular legs. Winston smiled in a cute way and said, "I have kind of forgotten how big you are and your muscular legs too." Rudolph told him that Eveline thought the three of them should get together sometime. Winston thought that might be a good idea. He asked Rudolph what he was planning to do to him. Rudolph laughed and wondered what Eveline would do to both of them. While they were discussing all the possibilities, they were walking toward Rudolph's place. Rudolph stopped Winston and told him he was going to take him home so they could rehearse what they should do in front of Eveline. Winston agreed and hoped something would come of all this talk. They got into Rudolph's apartment and stripped their clothes off. They looked at each other and it was like they were on fire. They had not had a time like this in a long while. While they were handling each other, they talked about what Eveline would be doing right now. Winston thought she might be just watching but Rudolph thought she would probably be in the middle. They agreed they needed to find out soon. Winston said, "Right now I want to finish what we've started." He handed Rudolph the Leterbuck and watched the excitement grow.

Rose had been busy organizing their new house. She had not seen Eveline in some time. She was avoiding the time when she would have to give Eveline the black box. Rose justified it by telling herself that maybe she did not need to give it to her right away. She could wait for months because no one knew about it except Winston. She hid the box in the basement in hopes Samuel might forget it. She knew Winston would not admit to anything. After a while, it may never be important enough to admit finding it. Maybe she should throw it in the garbage. How was she going to act when she did see Eveline. She was her best friend and it would be deceitful not to give it to her. Rose wished she never knew about it. She had an uneasy feeling that the information in the box was going to reveal more than most people wanted to know. Eveline would kill her if something important was in that box and she never knew about it and found out she had it all the time. Rose got over the self-evaluation of her intentions and decided to give the box to Eveline the next day.

Samuel came home from the office and announced he was getting a new job. Rose wanted to know if it meant they had to move. He laughed and told her no. He had been appointed Chief Health Officer in Geneva. He proposed a program that outlined the city health program. He had been working on it and gave a speech to the Women's Club a few weeks ago. His main focus was how far behind Geneva was in improving and safeguarding public health. He proposed a higher budget from the health department. He made such an impression on the officials that they offered him the job of leader. He accepted the position and would begin immediately. Rose wanted to know what would happen to his practice. He would keep his current patients but would not accept new ones. While they were having dinner, Samuel asked Rose if she had seen Eveline yet. She told him not lately. Samuel thought it was time to give the box to her. She explained she was doing it the next day. Samuel agreed it was best to do it and get it over with. He wanted to know if the man he hired to be the driver and maintenance man for the property had been there yet. His name was Bob and he would be starting next week. Rose had not seen him but was glad they would have some help. She had not secured a domestic servant yet. Samuel said she should find one soon so she could get all the mess cleaned up. Rose made a face but agreed to see Mrs. Preston after she gave Eveline the box.

Samuel was getting ready for work while Rose prepared breakfast. She had the newspaper on the table for him to see the national news. There had been so much coverage about Armistice Day that other less important things had been left out of the papers. For the last few days, the country had been celebrating the one-year anniversary of the ending of the war. There had been large parties throughout the country. President Wilson had been less visible because he was suffering from exhaustion and stomach ailments. The part Rose thought would be of interest to Samuel had to do with Emma Goldman. As she was reading about it Samuel arrived for breakfast. He saw the headline that the government may deport Emma Goldman. It was brought to light after investigation that her citizenship was false. Samuel looked up at Rose and shook his head and said, "That was over eighteen years ago." He told her about the day President McKinley was shot at the Pan-American Exposition in the Temple of Music. The guy who shot him was a follower of Emma Goldman who was in favor of anarchy as a form of government. Samuel said Emma Goldman was not good for the country and hoped she would be deported. Rose told Samuel she was going to see Eveline that morning and ask Mrs. Preston what she knew about securing domestic servants. Samuel reminded her that there was to be only one servant. Rose made a face as Samuel turned his back.

Rose was nervous about going to Eveline's house. She knew she would not be implicated in anything but still felt like something was going to change. She decided to procrastinate and see Mrs. Preston first and then stop by with the box. Rose called Mrs. Preston to inquire if she was available. She told her she would be happy to see Rose and explained she had knowledge of quite a few women she may be interested in. Rose left and began walking down the street to the Preston's house. It was November and the day was gray and dreary. Most of the leaves had fallen from the trees. As Rose walked, she thought the day was similar to the day of Wallace's funeral. At least, it was not raining but was dismal and foreboding. Rose thought it was because she was carrying something that was personal to Wallace. She approached the Preston's just as Mr. Preston was leaving. He asked what was in the bag. Rose realized how obvious it looked. She told him it was a box they found in the house that must have been left when Wallace and Eveline moved. Rose went into the house and Mrs. Preston presented her with a list of four women that were suited for employment within a few days. Rose wanted to know why it would take a few days. She thought they were all women who lived in town. Mrs. Preston explained that these women were moving from a different responsibility. Rose thought it sounded terribly businesslike. She was assured that they would be good or they would not be working in Geneva. Rose thanked her for the information. It still sounded fishy to her but she was not about to examine the person who was helping her. As Rose was leaving she picked up the bag and her coat. Mrs. Preston looked in the bag and saw the lettering Wallace Paine Personal. She looked at Rose and inquired what that was all about. Rose explained in a calm manner that it was something left behind from when Wallace and Eveline moved to 775 South Main Street. Mrs. Preston became defensive and wanted to know why Eveline needed to have his personal things. Rose looked at her and was surprised she would even say such a thing. She asked Mrs. Preston if she would want her husband's stuff after his death. Mrs. Preston looked over the top of her glasses and said, "You have a lot to learn about what husbands do and what they actually tell you about. There are many things you may never want to know." Rose looked like she had just been reprimanded for doing a good deed for a friend. Rose told her that not every husband did underhanded things. Mrs. Preston looked at her and shook her head. She wished Rose good luck in finding a servant.

Rose left and started for Eveline's house. She was angry and confused about all she just heard from Mrs. Preston. Granted, she was much older, so maybe she had some bad experiences but not everyone had underhanded husbands. She hoped Samuel was not like the men she just heard about. She kept trying to figure out why this box was so mysterious. She arrived at Eveline's house and Olitha answered the door and was glad to see her. Rose asked for Eveline. Olitha said she would be right down and to have a seat in the library. As Rose sat in the library, the memories of Wallace's funeral rushed back to her mind. She looked out the window. The view was the same with the waves rolling in off the lake. She remembered Winston's outburst about not knowing the real Wallace Paine. She remembered Samuel telling him he was wrong. Then she remembered her telling Winston how he should be ashamed of his behavior. Maybe he was right and they were all wrong. Just then Eveline walked in. She was glad to see Rose. She wanted to know what was in the bag. Rose hesitated and reached into the bag and pulled out the black tin box. She handed it to Eveline. Eveline looked at the writing on the top. She looked at Rose and asked where she found it. Rose explained that Samuel found it in the crawl space above the second floor. Rose said, "Wallace must have forgotten to move it." Eveline stared at his writing on the box, "Wallace Paine Personal."

CHAPTER 9

Eveline stared at the box. Rose tried to explain that they would have never found the box unless Samuel had been looking in the crawl space. Eveline asked how long she had the box. Rose told her they had just found it the other day. Eveline appeared distrustful of that information. Rose assured her that it had all just happened. Eveline asked, "Why do you think Wallace put the box in the attic?" Rose was reluctant to say anything for fear of saying the wrong thing. Rose shrugged her shoulders and said, "Maybe he hoped no one would ever find it." She wanted to know where the key was. Rose told her that she and Samuel had no idea where the key was. Eveline shook the box and heard metal moving around among other items. Just as Eveline finished shaking the box Sable walked into the room. She stopped short when she saw the box in Eveline's hands. Sable asked, "What all da noises in dis room?" Eveline motioned to the box and Sable saw the name on the top. Sable's eyes grew wide open as if she had seen the box before. Eveline asked her, "Do you know anything about this box?" Sable froze just as Olitha came into the room. She said, "Oh my Lord, why everybody lookin like they seen a ghost?" Eveline raised the box up so the writing could be seen on the top. She said, "You can read. What does it say?" Olitha repeated what was written on the top. Sable said, "Oh no, the spirit of Wallace Paine. My mammy done told me to run from boxes that have dead people stuff in em." Rose suggested that Eveline needed to talk to someone that might know more about the box and what might be in it. Eveline looked at her and asked, "Who might that be? I'm not sure who to trust when it comes to Wallace and what he did when he was alive." Just then the telephone rang. Sable left the room to answer the call. Everyone could hear Sable responding to the person that was calling. Eveline made a face when she heard Sable say, "Yes Miss Lounsberry, Eveline she here."

Eveline went to the telephone and her mother was inquiring if anything had been done with the estate. Eveline thought that was a strange question coming from her. She had not heard anything from her parents since the day of the funeral. Eveline wanted to know why she was so interested. Her mother wanted to know if Eveline was planning to get out of that awful city and move back to Canada. Eveline told her she had no intention of moving out of Geneva or much less the country. Mrs. Lounsberry told her she might have no choice when she found out what Wallace was into all those years. Eveline wanted to know why she thought there was anything wrong. Mrs. Lounsberry explained that her father was having lunch at the hotel the other day when someone was inquiring as to how to get in contact with anyone associated with the owner of an import and export company. The person knew that the owner of the hotel was involved with something called TOE&TIC. Eveline told her mother she had no idea about any of those things. Mrs. Lounsberry ended the conversation warning her that if the law was after any wrong doing now she was considered the owner and might need to run to Canada to be free of all the problems. Eveline replied in a disgusted tone, "Good bye Mother."

Eveline returned to the library and found Rose, Sable, and Olitha sitting on the sofa staring at the box. No one was saying a word. Eveline walked over to the women and snapped her fingers at them and said, "Wake up, Wallace is not in the box. The things in the box probably have little to do with any of his work—related issues." Rose suggested that Eveline get in touch with Rudolph since he had the most knowledge of Wallace's business affairs. Eveline told her that Rudolph was probably as manipulative as Wallace. Rose shook her head and said, "I did what Samuel wanted me to do. Whatever you do with the box is your business." Eveline thanked her for the box as Rose was getting ready to go home. While they were at the front door, Eveline asked Rose if she thought Samuel knew more about Wallace than he let on. Rose shook her head and said, "I think he may know a few things but Mrs. Preston is the one I have doubts about." Eveline wanted to know what that meant. Rose explained how Mrs. Preston lectured her about not to trust husbands because they never tell the truth. She explained how Mrs. Preston was careful of how much she told her about the domestic servants. Sable and Olitha were in the other room listening to the conversation. When they heard about the domestic servants Olitha said to Sable in a soft tone, "I hopes they never finds out why weez got to works for Miss Eveline." Sable put her finger to her lips and shook her head. Olitha stopped talking. Rose told Eveline again to get in touch with Rudolph to see if he knew anything about these mysterious things.

Eveline decided to take matters in her own hands. She asked Sable if there were any tools in the house. Sable asked, "Whys you want toos?" Eveline directed her to go to James and ask him for a hammer and a screwdriver. Olitha told Eveline that those things were not for such a lady as herself. Eveline reminded them that right now she was not interested in being a lady. She wanted to get into the damn box and find out what was inside. Sable went to the garage where she found James cleaning the car and said, "Yous never gonna believe what Miss Eveline gonna do." James looked quizzical as Sable said, "She wants a hammer and screwdriver to smash open a tin box." James laughed and said, "I want to see her do that." Sable said, "Well let's go and watch her take her madness out on the box." They went upstairs and found Eveline sitting at the table with the box facing her. James and Sable walked into the room and asked Eveline if she was expecting something to jump out at her. She pursed her lips then told him to give her the tools. He handed them to her and she began hitting the top of the box. The first thing the hammer hit was the word Paine. Eveline looked at the word, which now spelled "Pain" and said, "That's more like what he was." After she kept hitting the box, it fell on the floor. James asked her if he could try. She sat down and watched him pry the side open with the screwdriver. Olitha and Sable said nothing as they stood watching Eveline go mad over the box and then James working hard to try to open it. Eveline grabbed the hammer and began hitting the hinges that held the box together. Then she used the screwdriver and hammer to pry open the side. She took the hammer and with one swing hit the box on the side and it flew open. Sable and Olitha screamed as James stared at Eveline beating the tin box like she was trying to kill it. Eveline looked at them and told them that it always takes a woman to get things done. She handed James the tools and with a sweet smile told them they needed to give her some time to look things over. She informed Olitha and Sable that she would call them if she needed any help.

The contents of the box were all over the floor and the table. The first thing she saw was a small metal bracelet. When she read the name on it she looked up and said, "Patrick Paine." The date of April 1, 1915 was written next to the name. Eveline tried to think back to that date. She knew that date was Wallace's birthday and the birth of their son. That was almost five years ago. It seemed as if it was identification for an infant that was leaving the hospital rather than death identification. She thought this strange and had a feeling she needed to investigate this more. As she was putting the papers in a pile she came upon an envelope. The writing was strange and looked like it came from the Orient. She opened the letter. It was to Wallace from Mr. Ling. Eveline was not sure who Mr. Ling was. She tried to remember something about him as she began reading the letter.

Dear Wallace,

I am very proud to be involved with a wonderful company named Occidental I&E. You have organized an amazing operation. There were reasons to eliminate some people who were originally involved in the company. I needed to find out who was most trustworthy and loyal. I tested their character. The first was Bill Foote who attempted blackmail; not good for trustworthiness. Mr. Booth and Mr. Harmon threatened to go to the authorities when they found out about the possibilities of human transfers. A tactic such as this would put everyone in prison. The last person to be tested and who failed was Mr. Jackson because he wanted to get rid of me! Instead, I had him disposed of. Winston and you were never suspects to dishonesty or undercutting the company. I admit you must have been scared but you never spoke a word about what you found out or knew. As far as where the bodies went or who committed the crimes, it was Ho. He would do whatever he was told to do. Ho took the scarf to your room at the hotel. As you know, he is a small man and can go into places most cannot. He crawled through the transom window to leave the scarf on your bed. That is where he went after you met him. Ho was in Buffalo to dispose of Mr. Jackson the day you approached him about what happened to Mr. Booth and Mr. Harmon. Ho put their bodies in the shipping boxes that Mr. Jackson thought were soap and oatmeal for shipment. Their bodies were shipped to Singapore, their tongues placed on their desks at the H.O. Company in Buffalo. As for Mr. Jackson, Ho decided to leave him for the newspapers to report on but brought his tongue to New York so we could make sure you held strict quiet even though you are the owner of the company. I realize all these crimes would be very difficult to prove, given the methods and places in which they occurred. Even if anyone tried to report the murders, there is not enough evidence to pinpoint any one person. Ho is not registered in New York or anywhere. He is a transfer and not a relative. I own Ho. Since you have been so good at keeping quiet and maintaining good business practices you are welcomed into the New York circle of businessmen. I am remaining in Hong Kong and will do business from there and Ho will do his work in New York. I will be directing him from afar. I hope you can relax now and enjoy the profits and business possibilities in New York.

Regards,
Mr. Ling

Below the letter Wallace wrote a note about the trial. It read: Mr. Burbank told everyone while under oath that he committed the murders not Ho. Burbank murdered Mr. Ling. The letter from Mr. Ling above was a series of lies. I am angry with myself for being too easy when dealing with people and business.

After Eveline finished the letter she wondered if what her mother just told her might be true. The company names did not match. Then she thought about the trial that was mentioned. She remembered how uncomfortable Wallace was and Winston for that matter during that time. Now it was making sense to her. How was Rudolph involved with all of this? Before she asked any questions she decided to call Alice. She remembered some reference to a remark Alice made about telling Wallace he needed to be honest with Eveline. She called Alice and while she was being connected, thought how good it was that Alice finally convinced Frank to get a telephone. She heard Alice answer and was happy it was Eveline. She wanted to know how she was doing and that she missed her. Eveline wanted to know how life was with Frank. Alice told her he was still miserable but she was getting a job and did not care what he did. Eveline congratulated her and invited her to consider coming to Geneva. Then Eveline asked if Wallace ever had a reason to keep things for her. Alice hesitated and told her that there had been a time when registered letters would be delivered to her home for Wallace instead of their apartment on Scio Street. Alice explained that she told Wallace he was being deceitful and needed to tell Eveline everything. She explained that she was not sure of what trouble they might have been in. Eveline told her that she was given a box of things that Rose and Samuel found in their old house that Wallace had hidden. Alice said, "Really, I hope he wasn't a criminal in disguise." Eveline hoped not. She thanked Alice and invited her to join her and her maids for shopping at B. Forman Company in a week. Alice accepted the invitation.

Eveline found a folder with separate compartments with the names of companies that Wallace was involved with. The first was the Weekly Page and the Rochester Post Express. She looked at the contents and found that when the companies merged Wallace received ten times more money than he admitted to. His discretionary fund amounted to $50,000.00. Eveline's eyes went up when she saw that amount of money. Now she remembered the day they got the new car when she asked how he paid for it. No wonder he never wanted to divulge any information to her. The second compartment had information about how Wallace worked with the Larkin Company in Buffalo to invest 1/3 of his income in stocks for that company. Eveline decided she should make a list of all these things so she would have knowledge of this when she met all the company officials. She made a face and thought to herself, I am going to show these men that I am way ahead of them. Now, I might get all that is coming to me. The H.O.Company in Buffalo was included in the compartment with a note that his annual salary was $20,000.00 and there were no investment options involved. There was a note written in red saying he helped them go bankrupt. Eveline shook her head in confusion. The Seneca Powers Hotel folder was larger than the first two. There was a paper that Mr. Helfer and Wallace signed. They agreed the hotel would match equal stocks in the Ford Motor Company from Wallace's salary. As far as she could figure, he had 2000 shares of stock and was considered an owner. There was an envelope with Hilda's name on it. It was the directives of what Wallace was to do with Hilda and that Wallace was named the owner and president of the hotel upon the death of Mr. Helfer. The letter explained that Hilda was a relative but was unstable. She had a son and husband but hated them both. She thought they were too fancy for her. Mr. Helfer included how much he admired Wallace and how Hilda hated him because he over-powered her. There was a list of stocks he had accumulated in Eastman Kodak Company. It looked like the paper was put in that section for no reason. When Eveline saw this she understood why George Eastman was so fond of Wallace. Apparently, Mr. Eastman made a great impression on Wallace from childhood. There was a figure with a question mark of 3000 shares of Eastman Kodak Company stock. Eveline wrote this down.

CHAPTER 10

Eveline thought about what she had read. The first thought she had was that there were many underhanded schemes going on for many years. She wondered how many people were involved in these activities. Was Rudolph one of the major players? Was Winston used in a way that made him look bad so others might not be suspected of any wrongdoing? There was a note written by Wallace about how he had to come to terms with Rudolph. It read: Found out what Rudolph did to us in Buffalo. He was underhanded in his friendship with Eveline, Winston, and me. I should have him eliminated but find him physically attractive and exciting. I will work him to my advantage, but he will never know what is in store for his future. When Eveline finished reading that she shook her head. Not only was Wallace manipulative, he was setting Rudolph up to be a victim and criminal. She wondered if that was the reason Rudolph was made trustee. Throughout the letters and notes there was never anything mentioned about Winston. Eveline thought of all the people in Wallace's life with Winston being the most unique individual. As she was reading, about Shuron Optical Company and its beginnings in Rochester, she found some scratchy information. Wallace had stuffed a paper that he wrote about the times Winston would come to visit him in Geneva. Eveline thought she knew of most of those occasions. She smiled when she remembered how she deliberately confused Winston and Rudolph and the wrong person showed up to see Wallace. She laughed to herself and thought that's what they deserved. Wallace referred to Winston as the companion he always cared for but did not know how to show it. The only way he could do that was to treat Winston as his subservient partner. Little did Wallace realize, until very late, that was what Winston loved about him. Eveline thought of what Winston said at the funeral, that he lost his best friend and the only person he cared about. Eveline pondered the note and said to herself that Wallace had a hard time telling her that too.

The companies in Geneva had a much different description than the other companies Wallace was involved with. The years that Wallace worked at both Shuron and the Safege Company were not as well documented. All Eveline found out was that there was so much income that Wallace had to develop a way to maneuver money so he would not have to pay taxes. It appeared that the Goodwin Printing Company was established as a cover for purposes other than printing. Winston Spaulding's name was clearly written as the manager and he had full knowledge of what the company was all about. The note explained that Winston had good training when he worked in Buffalo for the Occidental Company. The more Eveline read the more she began to think that Winston had all the answers. She realized that he was the only person who knew Wallace from childhood. Even Alice and Frank did not know Wallace like Winston did. Maybe Rudolph felt left out of that relationship and that was why he worked so hard to win Wallace's attention, no matter what he had to do. Eveline was beginning to put the pieces together about the connections the men had with one another. Was she used by Rudolph to get to Wallace with the Women's Rights Movement? She thought about how Rudolph always showed up wherever they went. Things seemed so confusing that Eveline wanted to scream because there was no one she could ask and get an honest answer. She would need to be careful and sly about how she was going to proceed.

The last compartment had notations about businessmen Wallace was involved with. He had listed their names and a brief bit of information, which as he put it was pertinent to their future. Eveline thought it sounded like a set up for trouble. When she thought about it that way she wondered if Wallace purposely hid the box knowing it would be found. The list was mainly the men associated with Geneva and TOE&TIC. When she saw that name she thought about what her mother told her. Rudolph Williams was described as competent and good-looking. He was to be watched for underhanded dealings. The next was Winston Spaulding. He was honest, hardworking, loyal, kept secrets, and loved sex. When Eveline read that she smiled and thought of the night she tied him up. Mr.

Ling's name was scratched out but could still be read as, a strange, mysterious, and devious liar. Mr. Preston's name was listed. The description was a shrewd businessman. His wife was described as a wolf in sheep's clothing. That was not clear to Eveline. Samuel Haynes was listed as the family doctor that knew all about the birth of Patrick. Wallace described him as level headed and careful of what he did and said. A man named Mr. Wellington was listed as the contact in New York City. He was in charge of operations. Eveline wondered what operations those might be. The name of Mike was written. According to Wallace, he was a YMCA boyfriend that he met at Baker and Stark Clothier. As Wallace put it, he made going to the YMCA a pleasurable event, especially in the shower room. Eveline made a face when she read the shower part. She said out loud, "As if I didn't know what the men were doing with each other. Now it's my turn with them." Frank's name was last. All that was written was that Frank never thought he was good enough. He never accepted me. I hope my mother gets away from him before he kills her. Eveline put the folder down and looked up. She wondered why there was not a section about women. It seemed that Wallace had an entire lifetime of people he knew in the box. Eveline looked more closely at the bottom of the box. She thought it was just a black velvet bottom. She looked more closely and found that the fabric could be pulled away. Underneath the fabric was an envelope. Eveline opened it and found a birth certificate, not a death certificate! She screamed, "So where is he?"

Eveline began pacing around the library. It was getting late and she was tired and overwhelmed. She put everything back into the box. She decided that she needed to make a plan for how she would proceed with all the information she had just read. She knew that no one must know about the contents. As she was planning what to do, she realized that all the things in the box were connected. By telling anyone about it might force others to hide things that she needed to know about. The first thing she was going to do was to push Rudolph for the meeting with the companies and anyone associated with Wallace's fiscal affairs. She intended to be quiet and listen to see if what they were going to tell her would be the truth or a partial truth. If she was not satisfied with the information then she would go after the ones that appeared to be covering or avoiding the facts. As she was pacing around Olitha came into the library to remind Eveline of the time. Eveline thanked her and told her that she would take care of herself this evening. Olitha asked if she was all right. Eveline told her that she was okay but was tired and was going to bed. Olitha watched Eveline close the box and take it with her. Eveline knew she must not allow the box to be left in the library. She laughed to herself as she was going upstairs to bed thinking that this must be how Wallace felt when he hid this box. Now, she was doing the same thing but for much different reasons. Eveline spent the rest of the night planning her method for uncovering the past.

CHAPTER 11

The next morning howling winds awakened Eveline. It was December 1 and an early winter storm was sweeping across the Finger Lakes. Olitha knocked on the door to see if there was anything Eveline needed. She told Olitha to bring her some coffee. She had a restless night thinking about all the information she found out about the day before. While she was waiting for her coffee, she called Rudolph to remind him of their appointment the next day in Rochester. As she was speaking on the telephone, Sable came to her and handed her an old looking envelope. Eveline was curt with Rudolph while she explained that she, Olitha, Sable, Rose, and he were going to Rochester. She reminded him that B. Forman Company was having an anniversary sale and it was the beginning of the Christmas season. She told him that James was not driving and to be at her house at 9AM. Since he did not want to go shopping, he could act as their chauffeur tomorrow. She ended the conversation by telling Rudolph to confirm that 11AM was the time she could be available for the meeting at the hotel. After the meeting, the ladies were going to lunch and then have an afternoon of shopping. She hung up the telephone and looked at the envelope that had the word "Women" written on it in Wallace's handwriting. She found Sable cleaning in the library and wanted to know where she found the envelope. Sable told her that it was under the chair near the table. Eveline thanked her and made sure it had not been tampered with and left the room.

While she was having coffee in her bedroom, Eveline opened the envelope. It was the piece of information she wondered about last night. Just like the list of men, the women were listed the same way with a description and some type of foreshadowing. The only difference was the list began many years ago. Eva was the first. He described his grandmother as robust and happy but devious and mentally unstable. She wanted to kill my mother and me but instead killed herself. She was my mother's worry her whole life, until the truth came out. She used arsenic on herself instead of us. Eva was the whore she accused my mother of being. The second name was Alice. She was described in a few short words. She was a saint to put up with my father and could do better on her own. Miss Holleran came next. She did for me what ten people could not do. She respected me and gave me all the advantages I needed to become smart and successful. I can never repay her for that. Eveline's name had a star by it. She is the star of my life. She is bright and fun to be with. I wish I had more time to be with her. She will find out more than she ever thought when she finds this box. She needs to be careful of all the people who are named in here. There are many snakes in the grass and she needs to step carefully. Winston is my beloved friend who will do her well. When Eveline read that part she could not hold back her fear and began screaming and crying. Sable and Olitha came running into the room to find her sitting at the table sobbing with the letter in hand. She looked at them and told them that she had found out so much that she was sorry to upset them. They wanted to know if they could help. She told them to go about their work. She wanted her breakfast upstairs this morning.

Sable and Olitha left the room and closed the door. When they were on the way to the kitchen they talked about what was to happen if Miss Eveline found out about them. Olitha thought it was better to act as if they knew nothing. Sable said, "By the sounds of all dis stuff there is gonna be more than war." Olitha told her to stop saying such things. She reminded Sable that they were invited to go to Rochester tomorrow and they needed to appreciate what Miss Eveline was doing for them. Sable prepared the breakfast tray and started up to Eveline's room. As she was getting closer to the room she heard Eveline saying, "Some year this has been. I lost my husband and now I find out that everyone around me is connected to something bad." Sable knocked on the door and took the tray to the table where Eveline was sitting. She thanked Sable and told her that if she needed anything she would call her. She ate her breakfast as she read the next name on the list.

HILDA was the biggest challenge of my life. She hated me and I hated her. It was a battle from day one. After a while, I began to like the conflict because I knew she was unstable. She tried to undermine me with Mr. Helfer. She taught me a lesson and I didn't even know she did it. It was how to overcome obstacles and she was a big one. I will never forget how much she got away with. She was at her best at the New Year's Eve Burlesque show. She was so drunk that she was a show all her own. She died an unhappy crazy lady. When Eveline read about Hilda she smiled at such an accurate description of her. The next name was Eveline's mother. Catherine Lounsberry thinks she is high class but really is not. She rests on her husband's good fortune. She attempts to be controlling of Eveline. I know she wonders about all that goes on with us and hates my mother for having such a sordid family background. She must hated having a Negro for a grandson. All of a sudden, Eveline felt like everyone knew things but she was in the dark. The more she read the more she wanted to find out what actually happened. The next name in the letter was Rose Haynes. It read: she is Eveline's sidekick. She is good for Eveline because she has a level head and a smart husband. She is good for Rudolph too because she knows how to keep him in line. When Eveline finished reading about Rose she shook her head and wondered how much more she could possibly find out? The last name on the list was Mrs. Preston. Eveline already knew that Wallace thought she was a wolf in sheep's clothing. Mrs. Preston is a high class Geneva woman. She controls many aspects of her husband's companies. The Women's Rights Movement has been good for her. She is a strong woman and will do anything it takes to get her way. She has been instrumental in providing domestic servants for the New York region for many years. She works closely with the TOE&TIC operation. Her husband does not interfere in any of her affairs. When Eveline finished reading the letter she looked at the list and all that was in the box and thought to herself, Wallace knew I would find this. She was certain all this had something to do with making the estate clearer to her and not getting information from other people.

The next day Eveline took a fresh attitude toward all that she had learned. She decided to be shrewd about how she proceeded with all the information. She had lots of time and wanted to take it slow as she watched people react to what she was going to do to find out the truth. She dressed herself in an outfit that was businesslike and suited for a day of shopping. Sable and Olitha wore the only dresses they had; the ones for church. Eveline told them that they were going to the big city and to a fancy store. She was going to dress them up. Eveline told them she would make them into new women. Sable wanted to know why they needed to be new women. Eveline told them that they were going with her when she traveled to New York City and other places. They needed to wear clothes better than maid's outfits. Eveline explained that Winston and Rudolph would be occasionally traveling with them. They laughed and wanted to know if they were going to be staying in a house as big as this one. Eveline told them that they would be in a penthouse wherever they would be traveling.

Rudolph and Rose arrived at 9AM. The weather was cold but sunny. Rudolph asked Eveline if she wanted the top down on the car. Everyone looked and laughed at such a ridiculous thought. She said, "Top down of course." Rose looked at Eveline and told her she was crazy. Eveline looked at the astounded faces and said, "Fooled all of you." They were relieved when the top stayed up. Rudolph liked driving the automobile because it was much larger and more powerful than his vehicle. Eveline sat in the front seat and kept moving her hand up and down Rudolph's legs. Sable, Rose, and Olitha sat in the back seat making faces whenever Eveline turned around to announce how muscular Rudolph was. He did very well driving considering where Eveline's hands were going and what she was doing to him. Rose wanted to know if she could have a turn in the front seat on the way back to Geneva. Eveline told her that she was a married woman and Samuel probably had strong appendages too. As they approached Rochester, Eveline announced that she wanted to learn how to drive the automobile. Rudolph smiled at that statement as he pulled up to the front of the hotel. The doormen helped the women get out of the automobile. Eveline told Rose that they could either wait in the lobby or they could walk around some of the stores. Rose thought it would be more fun to wait for Eveline and go together. Eveline asked Rudolph what he was doing after the meeting. He informed her that he and the manager had some personal things to tend too. Eveline said, "I'll bet. Make sure you save yourself for me."

Eveline led the way into the office. She was beginning to like the attention she was given when she went through the lobby. She deliberately moved her hips from side to side so the men in the lobby would take notice. Rudolph escorted her into the office as the manager stood to greet them. The first thing Eveline asked was, "Do you have a name?" Rudolph looked at him and said, "Of course he does. This is Mike Bennett." Eveline said, "Can't he speak for himself?" She reminded them that they never mentioned his name the first time they met. She further informed him that a nameplate would be in order for his desk. Mr. Bennett said, "I am so sorry Mrs. Paine." She had a questionable smile and a raised eyebrow. They discussed the progress for the bakery and candy shop. The grand opening was scheduled for the week between Christmas and New Year's Day. Eveline told them that would be too late. The shopping season was beginning today and they needed to have the opening the week before Christmas. Rudolph explained that might be too soon. Mr. Bennett agreed. Eveline calmly but sternly told them the opening would be December 18th. She wanted to know if she had to come back to Rochester to follow up on her orders. Mr. Bennett told her that he would do all he could to get the work done. Eveline thanked him and then wanted to see how the new carpeting and draperies looked in the guestrooms. While they were going to the upper floors Eveline noticed how lovely the flowers were at the end of each hallway. Mr. Bennett was eager to announce that the guests noticed the improvements. Eveline saw flowers in each room. She could not remember if that was her idea or not. Mr. Bennett explained that he thought it would be a nice touch. Eveline agreed and complemented him on his work. Rudolph reminded her that he hired him and gave him a thorough training. Eveline made a face when she heard about a thorough training. She thought about the training she was planning for Rudolph at a later date. As they were returning to the office, Mr. Bennett mentioned that an inquiry was made about the owner of the hotel and an operation called TOE&TIC. Eveline acted as if she knew nothing about it. Mr. Bennett continued and told Eveline he asked Rudolph about it but was told that he was not sure about these things. Eveline turned to Rudolph and said, "I thought you knew about all this." He tried to change the subject but Eveline tapped her foot on the floor waiting for an answer. Rudolph explained that it was an import and export company. Mr. Bennett told them that the officials were here the other day looking to find the owner. Mr. Bennett explained that the owner of the hotel had recently died. The only thing they mentioned was about an investigation concerning illegal imports. He told Eveline that they asked for the address of Wallace Paine. Eveline looked at Rudolph and told him that was his first job when they got back to Geneva. He was to meet with these people because she wanted nothing to do with it.

Eveline left the meeting and met the women for lunch. Alice had just arrived and they decided to dine in the hotel. Olitha and Sable were very nervous because they were used to waiting the tables not sitting at the table as a guest. Eveline told them to get used to it. They were going places now. Rose thought it would be fun to go out of town as a women's group now that the law allowed them to. When they finished lunch, Eveline motioned to the waiter. He stood at attention while Eveline signed the bill. She laughed and admitted that it was fun signing her name. Rose reminded Eveline that not too long ago men were only able to sign. Eveline looked at the women and said, "Times are changing aren't they?" They left the hotel and walked up Main Street to B. Forman Company, where they found the store decorated for Christmas. Rose and Eveline directed Sable, Olitha, and Alice to the "Better Dresses" department. Eveline explained that they could have whatever they wanted because this was their holiday present. Eveline went to the hat department. She wanted a fur hat to compliment her fur coat. She reminded everyone that the wind blows hard and cold in the winter. They laughed as she held up a white fur hat. They ended up with boxes of hats and dresses. Eveline insisted Sable and Olitha buy some new shoes. They were like children with new clothes. Alice laughed when she mentioned what Frank would say. Eveline told her to get rid of him and come to Geneva to live. Alice was beginning to think that might be a good idea.

The weather had turned snowy while they rode back to Geneva. Eveline was not as enthralled with Rudolph as she was when they went to Rochester. She was more concerned about his avoidance of the import company that she was not supposed to know about. She needed to discuss that more thoroughly with him. They let Rose out at her home now that she lived further out of town. When they approached 775 South Main Street James had cleared the pavement because the snow was beginning to pile up. Rudolph carried the boxes upstairs. Sable and Olitha told Eveline they felt like they went to heaven today and thanked her for everything. Rudolph told Eveline he was going home. She informed him that he was to be back tomorrow morning bright and early no matter what. She told him in a stern tone that there were things that needed to be discussed. She wanted the date and who was to be present for the meeting regarding the estate. She wanted to know more about the TOE&TIC operation that was mentioned earlier. He froze when she reminded him of those issues. He agreed to be back at 9AM. Eveline smiled and told him they could talk over coffee and breakfast. As Rudolph was leaving, Eveline picked up the mail. Rudolph left and Eveline saw an envelope addressed to Wallace Paine with a return address from the Ford Motor Company. She closed the door and proceeded to open the envelope. The letter was addressed to Wallace Paine Ford Motor Company Stockholder. The letter explained that it had been a record year in automobile manufacturing and 90,000 employees were to receive large bonuses. The shareholders could have their bonuses reinvested in stocks or receive a check. Wallace would be entitled to $70,000.00. Eveline looked at the amount and thought at least this envelope had some good news unlike the ones yesterday. Before she spoke to anyone about this, she needed to think things through. Would this become part of the estate that had to be held for 5 years? Then she thought that maybe she should open her own account for all new income.

CHAPTER 12

It was December 31, 1919 and the Geneva Daily News had a full page article describing the potential problems people might encounter because of the limited supply of alcohol for the evening celebrations. There had been proposals to add an 18th Amendment to the Constitution Prohibiting Alcohol in the United States. Something needed to be done since there were so many people reliant on beverages that contained some form of alcohol. There were warnings that fake whiskeys were being made from deadly substances. As Eveline read the article she thought about what she was going to do to celebrate the New Year. Maybe she would invite Winston to go to dinner and then come back home and celebrate the incoming New Year. She thought about the last time they were together and she was getting a warm sensation in her body. Just as she was pondering her idea, Rudolph was escorted into the library. She turned and said, "Oh, you are prompt this morning. I was just thinking about how I was spending my New Year's Eve. I thought about getting Winston over here for some practice and fun." Rudolph looked at her and said, "I have no plans for this evening either." Eveline said, "Gee, that's too bad. You can sit home and think about us over here." Then she asked if he had any information about the things she requested from him. Rudolph began with the list of companies that would be attending the meeting with regard to Wallace's estate. They would be providing her with the value of each company and how it contributes to the operation that Wallace was so masterful at formulating. Rudolph told her on Monday, January 5, they would hold the meeting at the Seneca Hotel. When Eveline heard that she thought of what Wallace wrote about the Prestons. Eveline shook her index finger at Rudolph and said, "I don't think that is a good idea." Rudolph wanted to know why, since there was a large room for such a meeting in the hotel. She interrupted him, "I want these men to meet me on my ground. The meeting will be held here. This house was big enough for Wallace's funeral; it will do just fine for a business meeting. I will have Sable and Olitha prepare a continental style breakfast and beverages." Rudolph told her he would notify all that were involved of the new place for the meeting.

Rudolph began explaining the TOE&TIC operation. Eveline sat on the couch like a lady with her legs crossed. She tapped the cushion and invited Rudolph to sit with her. He wondered what she might be up to. He was not sure any more of what to expect when it came to dealing with Eveline. He found her intriguing because she could change without warning. He rather liked the unexpected in her. He sat on the couch and crossed his legs. He began telling her that the company was formed when Wallace worked in Buffalo. Eveline told him she knew that because she suggested that Winston be hired as foreman. She made a face and reminded Rudolph that she had been there from the beginning. She thought to herself that she would see if any references were made to his activity in Buffalo. He did refer to the Larkin Company and his termination because of bad attendance. Eveline smiled and said, "That was the time when I met you because of your music and piano ability." He shook his head. Eveline wanted to know what TOE&TIC meant. Rudolph explained that it was a shortened form of The Occidental Export & The Import Company. Rudolph went on to explain that the name had to be changed because the office moved from New York City across the river to New Jersey. Eveline asked, "Why did it move when they were only shipping oatmeal, soaps, fabrics, furniture, and ordinary things to other countries?" Rudolph hesitated. She looked at him and said, "Well?" He explained that there had been a murder on the docks in New York. That was the reason there was a trial. Eveline was curious and waited for more information. Rudolph told her that he had been implicated when he did some underhanded schemes against Wallace, Winston, and her when they were in Buffalo. At that time, he needed money so he got their signatures from a game they were playing one night. Eveline remembered the night that he was there with them. She wanted to know why the signatures? He told her that he did not know at the time why a man from Larkin hired him to get the signatures. He did the work and never was involved with him again. Eveline was beginning to think that his story was not giving her the information she was hoping for. Then Rudolph said, "The things being imported were not always what they appeared to be." Eveline's ears perked up. He went on to tell her that the reason the men were in Rochester looking for the owner was that they had reason to believe that opium was in the shipments. Rudolph hoped that might satisfy her. She wanted to know if it were true. Rudolph told her it was true. Eveline wanted to know if that was the only reason. He told her that was the main reason but there were other minor parts that would not interest her. She wanted to know what the other parts were. Rudolph thought about what Wallace told him the night he died. Was that what she was referring to? Rudolph knew that Winston came back from New York with information about the import and export company but had he told Eveline anything about it? He decided to lie and tell her that a lot of money was made on opiate drugs in the country. That was the reason the authorities were looking to speak with the owner of the company. He assured Eveline that he would speak with them on her behalf. She thanked Rudolph but knew he was lying by omission. She suspected there was more to the imports than he had told her.

The newspaper was open to a page that had an advertisement for a Victrola. It showed a man and woman dressed in high style dancing to the music coming from the music machine. The advertisement was: "Dance any time, the Victrola is always ready!" The Victor Talking Machine Company in New Jersey had just put the machine on sale. If you purchased the machine before the New Year, you received free records. They would include fox trots, waltzes, and one-steps. Eveline thought that might be fun to have for this evening. She called for Olitha to come to the library. She told her to go to the A&P Store for food for the evening's celebration and to go to the piano store and buy the Victrola. She showed Olitha the picture in the newspaper. When Olitha saw it she reminded Eveline of the playerette that she and Sable bought for Wallace and her. Eveline remembered it and explained she left it at 380 Washington Street for Rose and Samuel. Olitha asked if Sable could go with her to buy the machine and the food. Eveline thought that was a good idea because there would be many packages to carry for the meal they would be serving. Olitha wanted to know how many people were invited. Eveline told her three people. She looked at Rudolph and told him he was one of the three. She smiled at him and said, "You don't need to stay home thinking about the evening by yourself." Rudolph wanted to know who else was coming. She looked at him and said, "Winston of course." Olitha called for Sable to get ready to go shopping. Rudolph asked if there was anything more she needed from him. Eveline told him to rest up for the evening because they were going to dance and have a gay old time welcoming in the New Year. Eveline wanted Rudolph to understand that this evening was to be casual and there was no need to look like he was giving a piano concert. He smiled and said, "That is a great idea, no formality." She told Rudolph to be back by 7PM. She asked him to find Winston and invite him for the evening celebration.

Sable and Olitha prepared the list of groceries they needed to buy for the dinner. While they were walking to the A&P Store at 96 Seneca Street, Sable wondered if her friends Hilly and Liza were going to be working at the store. She mentioned it to Olitha and they both hoped so. They had not seen them in a while and hoped there would be time to talk about what they had been doing. Olitha and she had been keeping close contact with the women. Olitha reminisced about how much these women had done for them. She and Sable talked about what a chance they had taken when Eveline's baby was born. Sable said, "Oh, when Miss Eveline find out dat baby never dead she gonna either kill us or thank us." Olitha reminded her that if it were not for Hilly and Liza being there to offer to take Patrick that boy might be long gone to someplace else. Hilly and Liza were happy to help and loved the boy just as their own. The problem was that he was almost five years old and was ready to go to school. Samuel was the one who suggested that local women care for Patrick who were not connected to anyone involved with the Paine family. At the time, Samuel was not sure if the child would live. Wallace never knew about any of it. No one ever thought that Wallace would die and that Patrick would survive Eveline's attack on him. Sable and Olitha went to the cheese department to get appetizers and found Hilly and Liza working. It was the day of a big holiday, so the store was busy with shoppers. They were happy to see one another. Hilly and Liza were forbidden to come near Eveline or the house, with or without Patrick. Sable, Olitha, and Samuel thought it was better to have distance and less familiarity than to take a chance that Eveline or Wallace would find out about Patrick. Even Rose had no idea that Patrick was alive. Hilly told Sable and Olitha that they wanted them to come to their home to see Patrick. It had been a while since they visited him. Liza told them that he was a beautiful boy, very smart, with light brown skin, and dark wavy hair. Sable laughed and said, "Oh boy, when Miss Eveline find out about dis it will be interesting." They laughed and hoped she would be happy. Sable reminded Olitha that they needed to get to the piano store to buy the Victrola. Hilly wanted to know what that was for. Olitha told her that you get free records if you buy it before the end of the day. Everyone wanted to know who was dancing with whom. Sable said, "We all be dancin if Miss Eveline not like what we done. We be dancin from bullets." They made a face as they left the store.

Rudolph found Winston at Goodwin Printing. He was finishing paper work when Rudolph went into the office. Rudolph looked at the ledgers and told Winston it all looked good and that everything had been covered. They would be ending the year with very little evidence of money maneuvering. Winston told him he was only doing what he was told. Rudolph told him, "You will be rewarded in many ways. Maybe you will be rewarded tonight." Winston wanted to know what that meant. Rudolph told him they had been invited to Eveline's house for a New Year's Eve celebration. He thought that might be fun and mentioned the party years ago in Rochester. Winston still remembered as he chuckled about Mr. Horseman. Rudolph was not around when all that happened and was fascinated by what Winston was talking about. Winston said, "You might find out tonight."

Olitha and Sable were preparing the food for the evening. Eveline told them to get some spirits she had stored in the basement. Even though there was threat of bad alcohol they still had a good supply of whiskey and rum. The Victrola was set up in the parlor. It had a big horn coming out of a box. The records were made of glass and were about a foot wide. Eveline looked at all of it and hoped someone knew how to operate it. Sable told her that the salesman in the store showed her how to work it. Eveline hoped for an opportunity to entertain the men and see how they reacted to her especially since Wallace was no longer around. She knew she enjoyed Winston and knew about Rudolph from times past that she would definitely have fun with both of them. While Rudolph and Winston were on their way to Eveline's house they talked about what might happen. Winston, with a devilish look in his eye, showed Rudolph his bottle of Leterbuck aphrodisiac. Rudolph laughed and asked him how much of that stuff he had. Winston told him enough for many years. It gets stronger with time. They knocked on the front door and Sable answered it. Instead of the library, they were ushered into the parlor. Eveline was standing at the Victrola with a glass of whiskey in her hand. Olitha offered each of them a drink. Sable told everyone that dinner would be served in an hour. Winston was excited and looked forward to Sable's good cooking. Little did he know that was not all that was cooking.

Eveline demonstrated her new Victrola. It was like an entire orchestra was in the room. Eveline asked Rudolph if he would like to dance. He was not sure he knew how to dance the one-step. Eveline laughed and told him it was easy. It was only one step back and forth. Winston sat on the couch and watched Rudolph maneuver himself so he would not step on Eveline's feet. He was in hysterics watching the action. Winston offered to dance with Eveline next. She was surprised he knew anything about dancing. He was in his usual attire of revealing pants and a shirt that was open enough for his furry chest to rub on her as they danced. Eveline found that exciting and recognized his musky odor. She felt sexually aggressive as they waltzed around the parlor. Rudolph was surprised that Winston was such a good dancer. When they finished, Winston announced that there was a lot that most people did not know about him. Eveline went up to him and felt his chest and moved her hands further down telling him she was willing to learn all about him. Rudolph watched from the couch as she worked her hands down below Winston's waist. He let her take charge of what she was looking for. At that moment, Sable walked into the parlor to announce that dinner was being served. When she saw Eveline's hand in Winston's pants she stopped short, turned, and left the room shaking her head.

Dinner was served and was tasty as ever. Sable liked the compliments about her cooking. Eveline told her that they would all need to be on a diet in the New Year. Everyone agreed but still kept eating. After dinner, Eveline wanted to try one more record on the new Victrola. It was a tango that required very close contact with your partner. Rudolph was first to try it. He was having no problem with arm movements and the turning and twisting that the dance required. Winston wanted to know where the rose was for Eveline's mouth. She told him there was a bouquet in her bedroom and to go upstairs and get one. He left the room and Rudolph and she kept dancing. It seemed like Winston was gone for a long time. Eveline suggested they go to see what happened to Winston. They went upstairs and found Winston had taken his shirt and shoes off and was standing in the room with his hands on his hips and the rose in his mouth. Both Eveline and Rudolph were surprised but felt like the party was just beginning. Eveline went over to him and whispered something into his ear. He started for the closet. She went to Rudolph and told him it was time to see his muscular legs. She unbuttoned his trousers and they fell to the floor. He took off all the undergarments he was noted for since he dressed like a gentleman. Winston came out of the closet naked with something behind him. He told Rudolph that he remembered how he dressed with all those straps holding up his socks. Eveline asked Winston if he had any of his Leterbuck that he used on her the last time they were together. Winston held it in his hand and Eveline wanted Winston to rub some on his body. Rudolph watched Winston grow to a peak of arousal. While that was happening, Eveline was taking Rudolph's shirt off. Now, both Winston and Rudolph stood face to face examining one another's manhood. Eveline took a hold of the firmness of each man and told them that she wanted to see how men enjoyed themselves. Winston offered Rudolph some of his Leterbuck and Eveline started telling them what she wanted them to do. She wanted to see them embrace. While they were doing that she worked her hands on their buttocks. Each man was different. Winston's was hairy and Rudolph's was smooth. She found it exciting to see them kissing each other while she kissed them behind their ears. While that was happening, she moved her hands to their sweaty groins and could feel the sweat run between their buttocks. Winston looked at Eveline and told her that it was time for more directions. Rudolph's legs were so tight that the muscles were bulging. When Eveline felt this she began to lick his legs until she got to his groin and both she and Winston worked on pleasuring Rudolph. While they tasted Rudolph's sweaty fluids Winston kissed Eveline and then their tongues moved to Rudolph's mouth. By this time, Eveline had removed her garments. In all the sexual excitement, Eveline had positioned herself between Rudolph and Winston. She told them she had never felt so excited and invited them to do whatever they wanted to her. She felt both men work themselves into positions making their manhood disappear. This went on for a while until Eveline motioned to Winston, who was facing her that he needed to do something. Winston moved away and went behind Rudolph and proceeded to do the same to him that he had just done to Eveline. Winston was so aroused when he pressed himself against Rudolph's buttocks that Rudolph received him and moaned with pleasurable pain. Eveline turned to Rudolph and began kissing him over his body until she was on her knees between Rudolph's legs. She pleasured him from the front while Winston worked on him holding tight to his hips from the rear. When Winston took his final whiff of Leterbuck, he exploded with pleasure as Rudolph felt the same explosive pleasure. Eveline stood up and told Winston that he reminded her of Mr. Horseman and how that young woman rode him like a horse at the New Year's Eve Party years ago. Eveline said that they should have more parties like this and maybe invite a few more people. Rudolph was not sure what he thought as he looked at himself and realized what had just happened. She put on her gown and told them she was done. If they wanted to continue to have fun with themselves they could but she would be in the parlor. Dessert was being served soon. As she left the room she turned and looked at both men who were stark naked and said, "Happy New Year."

CHAPTER 13

January 5th was the date for the meeting of associates involved in Wallace's businesses. Rudolph arrived at Eveline's early to help set up the parlor for the meeting. He had not seen her since the New Year's Eve festivities. He was not sure what to say or how to act. When Eveline saw him she was businesslike as usual. He thanked her for the other evening. She looked at him and said, "I should be thanking you. You made my evening what I had hoped for. We need to do that again but with more activities." Rudolph agreed but wondered what else she could possibly want to do. Sable and Olitha came in to the room with the food Eveline requested. There was a large bouquet of flowers on the table where the food was to be served. They were dressed in formal maid outfits. Eveline wanted Rudolph to take notice of how good they looked with their dresses and fancy aprons. Eveline purchased better quality attire for them for occasions such as this one. Rudolph explained that there were about twenty people expected to arrive by 10AM. There were some people coming from New York City, Buffalo, Rochester, and Geneva. He asked Eveline if she wanted to conduct the meeting. She thought for a moment and decided that he could open the meeting with introductions but she would question each group during the meeting. She told Rudolph that she was now the one in charge and they all needed to understand that things were about to change. Rudolph stepped back and accepted her plan.

Men began arriving. It was strange to see so many automobiles parked on Main Street. Not long ago, there would have been only horses and buggies. Most of these businessmen had bought into the Ford Motor Company because Ford's reputation for quality and fair pricing made everyone want one of Ford's automobiles. Eveline and Rudolph greeted people as they entered the parlor. Olitha was positioned at the front door and Sable was at the refreshment table. Eveline nudged Rudolph and told him this reminded her of Wallace's funeral. Rudolph looked at her and smiled but knew this could be a death wish for many in the room this morning. While people were chatting Eveline spotted the Prestons coming to the front door. She asked Rudolph why Mrs. Preston was coming. Rudolph explained that she had a lot to do with one of the businesses here in Geneva. When Eveline greeted them she remembered what Wallace wrote about Mrs. Preston. At that moment, Eveline felt Wallace's presence as if his spirit was in the room. She felt uncomfortable but remembered that Wallace thought she was his star and he had given her warnings about people. She made her mind up that she would be the star and today was to be the beginning.

Eveline invited everyone to have morning refreshments. At 10:30 Rudolph announced that everyone should be seated. Eveline and Rudolph sat at a table at the front of the room. Each person was given a tablet and pencil to write things down. Rudolph took a mental attendance to make sure everyone who was invited was present. He explained that Mrs. Paine was now the one in charge and was going to be conducting the meeting. The men in the room could be heard grumbling, but what choice did they have. She was the boss. Eveline stood and thanked everyone for being present. Eveline explained that society was changing and women had more rights than ever before. As she put it, the new woman of the 1920's was less invested in social services but more interested in fiscal and personal fulfillment. As she spoke, she walked back and forth discussing the things that she had learned since Wallace's passing. No one quite knew what she was working up to until she told them that she would call each company by name and they would report what the company did and give a fiscal report. She explained that since Rudolph was the trustee for the estate he would record the information. Eveline laughed as she looked at Rudolph and said, "You are now my secretary." Eveline caught Mrs. Preston's eye and realized she appeared to be impressed with the presentation. Eveline kept reminding herself that she only had one time to make this first impression. She sat down at the table and pulled up a list of people and companies. When Rudolph saw the list his eyes flew wide open as he wondered how she had come up with all the information.

The Rochester Post Express was first to be called. The current owner reported that since the time Wallace sold his interest in the paper, the company had acquired yet another newspaper company. Profits had doubled. The owner complimented the late Mr. Paine on his ability to start an enterprise such as his and continue it with huge profits. There were 1850 shares of stock in Wallace's name. Eveline made no facial expressions as information was being presented. According to the latest stock rating, each share was selling for $3.19. Rudolph noted the figures. Eveline thanked him and the owner sat down. Just as Eveline was ready to call the second group, a woman entered and sat in the back of the room. Eveline continued and called Eunice Jacobs to report about the H.O. Company in Buffalo. Eunice stood and apologized for her tardiness. She explained that the train was late leaving Buffalo. Eveline told her it was fine because she was on time for her report. Eunice was the only person that could be located since the closing of the company. She had been the secretary to Mr. Booth and Mr. Harmon. She explained that Wallace was always nice to her. She reported that the owners were wasteful when it came to money. She mentioned the differences of opinion they had with Mr. Paine but that they had still allowed him to maneuver funds as he wished. After the murders of Mr. Booth and Mr. Harmon, the company closed and she went to work at Hengerer's Department Store. There was no money left from the H.O. Company but she found a ledger that gave a full analysis of Mr. Paine's accounts. It was noted that he manipulated funds so the company would go bankrupt. There was movement and coughing in the room when people heard that information. Mr. Paine had an account with the Buffalo Savings Bank that had a balance of $168,000.00. Eunice presented Eveline with the statement. Rudolph was called next to report about the Seneca Powers Hotel. He explained how Wallace had an agreement with Mr. Helfer who was now deceased. The agreement was to match equal funds from Wallace's salary, as advertising manager, to buy stocks in the Ford Motor Company. At last record, there were 10,000 shares in Wallace's name. In addition to that he was named owner of the hotel and the recipient of Mr. Helfer's estate, which included stocks and savings accounts. The total without the value of the hotel was about $500,000.00. Eveline interrupted Rudolph and explained how important it was to be exact. She wanted the amount not an estimation of the value. Rudolph cleared his throat and gave the account as $498,890.74. She smiled and said, "That's more like it." No one made a sound. After that statement, people could be seen checking their facts and figures. Eveline made it clear that she wanted the truth and exact figures. Eveline called Miss Holleran's name next. She was not present. Eveline thought this was strange because she spoke to her on the telephone about the meeting. Instead, she asked for Shuron Optical's information. The company originated in Rochester when Wallace was hired. There were no "buy ins" to the company but Wallace negotiated half of his salary to go to the Larkin Company Stocks. The person reported that there were 1800 shares of stock. He knew Mr. Paine was earning $20,000.00 annually until the company moved to Geneva and became the Standard Optical Company. The salary increased to $32,000.00. While Eveline listened to the money being discussed, she wondered why Wallace did not live in a higher style. He never seemed to have any money. Now, she realized it was a cover so others would not know the facts, including her.

Miss Holleran arrived an hour late. She explained that she missed the train from Rochester. Eveline told her in front of everyone that no matter when she arrived she was always welcome. Miss Holleran graciously thanked her and began her report. She explained to everyone that she was Wallace's teacher and advisor through school and knew he would be a success in whatever he set out to do. As she put it, "I was the one who was glad to be a part of Wallace and his success." She continued that she was the bookkeeper for his first newspaper, The Weekly Page. He was the recipient of a scholarship to college. The profits from his business were invested in Eastman Kodak Company. She did not have the exact total but suggested notifying the company for the information. She concluded her part saying, "There will never be another Wallace. He will be missed." Eveline thought Miss Holleran was correct based on what Wallace wrote in the letter. Mr. Preston was called to give information regarding the Safege Company. He explained that a patent had been granted for a razor that would be safer than ever before. Wallace was asked to be an owner and in charge of the advertising department. He was noted for his unique and catchy advertising that made profits soar. Mr. Preston commented on how well Wallace worked at both Standard Optical and Safege at the same time and created two highly successful companies. He had 500 shares of Safege stocks; they were selling for $4.16 a share. The Wire Wheel Company representative was next to report. Wallace was the primary owner with Rudolph and Mr. Preston as co-owners. He discussed how well the company had supplied better wheels for the newest automobiles. The Geneva Motor Company was producing Ford automobiles so both companies worked hand in hand. Mr. Preston did mention that the operation might be moved to a southern state. If that were to happen, he suggested that this branch should be sold. The current annual profit for the company was 1.5 million dollars. After Mr. Preston finished, Eveline suggested a break and announced that they would reconvene in twenty minutes.

Rudolph called the meeting to order. While people were taking their seats, Winston arrived. Eveline went to him and said something. Rudolph did not invite him and wondered why he was there. He hoped it was not to reveal whatever he found out in New York City. Eveline announced that Winston Spaulding had some information that may shed some light on fiscal matters regarding Wallace's estate. Winston had just arrived from the Goodwin Printing Company and was not well groomed for the meeting. Eveline thought to herself, as he spoke, that he looked good with nothing on. She tried to focus on the discussion. He explained that he was hired years ago in Buffalo to be foreman for an import and export company that Wallace created. Wallace trained him to do exactly what he was told. He was never to discuss or question anything he saw. He worked for the Occidental Company for two years until the Buffalo office closed. He moved back to Rochester and remained very close to Wallace and Eveline. When Wallace moved to Geneva, The Goodwin Printing Company was established. Winston was hired to oversee the business and was told to remain quiet about whatever he saw at the shop. When Mr. Preston and other businessmen heard this they became uneasy. Winston continued to tell about the maneuvering of large sums of money. Printing was a cover for the operation that was designed to move funds around so that it would be difficult to track down investor's money. He went on to tell that the company was formed after the income tax laws went into effect. Wallace was clever enough to figure out how to work the system to wealthy people's advantage. Winston explained that Wallace used to be proud of the phrase "It is a good win for all of us." Rudolph put the pencil down and looked at Eveline who was turning a brighter shade of red. She asked Winston, "So what you are saying is that most of the people in this room may be criminals and thieves when it comes to money and taxes." Winston replied, "I'm not sure about that but I know a lot of money is hidden in places you would not believe." Eveline thanked him and looked at Rudolph and said, "We have a lot to discuss." Eveline did not expect that information but the last company to report became more upsetting to her. She called Mr. Wellington. Rudolph and the others did not recognize him when he arrived. It had been some time since Rudolph had seen Mr. Wellington. He was thinner and he had lost all his hair. Eveline thanked him for coming from New Jersey. She told the group that she was grateful to her friend Winston for giving her Mr. Wellington's address and telephone number. She looked at Rudolph and said, "I'm not sure Mr. Wellington would have been invited if it had not been for Winston." Mr. Wellington explained that he was the fourth person involved in the import and export company. He mentioned that he met Rudolph and Winston when they were at the trial in New York City. Eveline asked him to discuss more about the trial. The tension in the room heightened when he was asked to elaborate. He explained that Mr. Ling, who he never knew, was murdered along with four or five other people. The only evidence left by the murderer was their tongues. Winston was a suspect in the multiple murders. He was accused of Mr. Ling's murder because his signature appeared on the ledger at the Waldorf Astoria the same time Mr. Ling was there. As it turned out, Rudolph Williams was instrumental in providing the killer with signatures so he could forge the names of Winston Spaulding, Wallace Paine, and Eveline Paine. In this way, the killer would never be suspected, but the others would be implicated. The people at the meeting felt like they were at a trial as Mr. Wellington continued. It was a stroke of luck the murderer was identified at the last minute. It was Mr. Burbank and he went crazy on the stand and admitted he was the one that killed all the people and explained in graphic detail how he did it and what he did to the bodies. The trial ended and Wallace, Winston, and Rudolph were free to go. Eveline interrupted and mentioned that she remembered how strange everyone was acting then. Mr. Wellington had been in charge of operations since the trial. Eveline asked Mr. Wellington to tell about the company. He explained that it was originally an import and export company of ordinary items. As time went on Mr. Ling from Hong Kong became involved and wanted to expand the commodities. The new imports Mr. Ling encouraged were mainly directed toward less fortunate individuals. He mentioned how furniture became the carrier of these people. Eveline looked at Rudolph and then those seated and asked, "What individuals?" Mr. Wellington explained that a system was devised by her late husband and Mr. Ling to transport children from the Orient to the United States. To insure the safety of the children, there were Negro women used as surrogate mothers as they were shipped in furniture to the United States. Mr. Wellington explained that the transfers and monetary exchanges happened in New York City behind a high-class restaurant. Eveline turned to Rudolph and asked, "Do you know of this and is there anyone else in this room that knows all these things?" Eveline asked, "Well?" Rudolph ignored her question. Mr. Wellington explained that people paid large sums of money for children. He knew some were well cared for but others were used for prostitution and abused. Eveline shook her head and asked, "What about the women involved with bringing these children from far off places?" Mr. Wellington explained that there was a boss woman in every state who was in charge of placing the women as domestic servants after the children were sold. Eveline wanted to know if he knew who it was in New York State. He told the group that New York State had two boss women because of the size of New York City and the rest of the state. Mr. Wellington went on to explain about the time Winston showed up in New York City to verify that human trafficking was occurring. It was the same time Wallace was ill. Rudolph telephoned me about the possibility that Winston might show up. It was too late because Winston had figured out what was happening and who was involved. Mr. Wellington explained that he kept telling Lucille to stop doing business so near to Geneva. He went on and explained that Geneva was central to larger areas where domestic servants were needed. Eveline asked, "Who is Lucille?" When she asked the question Mrs. Preston stood up and in a haughty way said, "I am." When Eveline heard that, all she could think about was what Wallace's letter revealed about so many people in the room. Sable and Olitha were in shock because they were two of the women used as surrogates before Eveline hired them. Mr. Wellington finished with an apology for not having any monetary information. All he said was, "There have been millions of dollars transacted in the company and not for just children."

Mr. Wellington sat down and Eveline stood up and said, "I am not sure what needs to be done next. I am in shock that so many of you who appeared to be honest are not. The idea of making money on little children is sickening. The corruption that I have listened to today is all about greed and dishonesty. I am glad I have found out most of the truth, there is probably much more to uncover. Some of you should be commended for being honest throughout Wallace's life. Now, I'm not sure how honest my husband was. I guess my friend Rose was right when she told me about a women who told her that husbands lie." Eveline looked directly at Lucille Preston and said, "Isn't that right Lucille?" Eveline called the meeting to a close. She reminded them that now she was the boss and things were about to change. There was very little discussion as people began to leave the meeting. Lucille Preston made a point of speaking to Eveline and said, "You and I need to talk. You will be amazed at what really goes on." Eveline told her that she was not afraid of any underhanded people. She told Mrs. Preston that her father and mother were just like the people she had heard about today.

CHAPTER 14

The next morning, Eveline decided to find out about the human transfers. She ordered Sable and Olitha to bring her coffee with no breakfast because she had lost her appetite after all the things she discovered yesterday. When they entered the library Eveline told them to be seated at the table. They were not sure if they were going to be fired. Eveline looked at them straight in the eye. The women did not dare move as she said, "I have my parents to thank for my name now it seems appropriate that I feel evil. I want to get back at all the people who have lied to me." She asked each woman to tell about their experiences as a surrogate to children. Sable explained that it was a way to make money and find work in a good home. She talked about how terrible the ride on the ship was in the cabinet. There were a few holes for air and no light. There was a pot for them to use and very little food. Most of the time when the children were scared and cried they had to be gagged so no one would suspect anything or that anyone was in the containers. The infants had to be breast-fed and usually the surrogates were able to provide enough nourishment and keep them quiet during the trip. Then Eveline wanted to hear from Olitha. She spoke of how scared and dirty they were by the time they arrived in the United States. Sometimes the people in the furniture were so sick they died before they could be helped. The odor was worse than the fear of darkness. No one would come by to see if things were okay. They realized that the ship's crew did not know people were stowaways in the furniture. That was why the women were told never to say anything or they would be killed when they got to America. Eveline thought about how strong Sable and Olitha were as they explained their life before working for her.

After they gave the best description possible of how horrible their lives were Eveline wanted to know how they arrived in Geneva. Sable told about being blindfolded so they could not see where they were being taken. Once they were out of the big city, they were told that they had a new home which was Geneva. Olitha spoke up and explained that they were treated like prisoners but were told they were being placed in well to do homes as domestic servants. For them it was a good thing because they had no life before they were surrogates. Sable talked about how poor her family was and that she never saw them after she was a little girl. She did not know if her mother or father were even alive. Olitha shook her head and said the same thing. Eveline wanted to know if they ever met Mrs. Preston. Neither of them was familiar with her and only knew her as a woman who had servants. Until yesterday they never knew about Lucille Preston. They mentioned that when they arrived by train, they were taken to a place near the train station. A man gave them better clothing and they were able to clean themselves. Across from where they were was a huge room where men were talking about money and how much was transferred that day. Sable said she heard that thousands of dollars were being stored there every day. Eveline shook her head and said, "I can't believe you women survived all that you have told me today. I am not angry with you because you are survivors and have been wonderful to have in my home here and at 380 Washington Street." Sable spoke up and said, "Weez afraid you were puttin us out on the street. Weez so happy you are our boss Miss Eveline."

Just before they were ready to leave the library, Eveline asked them if they had any recollection of her having her baby about five years ago. Sable was first to speak, "Miss Eveline, weez knows more about dat baby than you ever did." Olitha said, "Yes even Wallace did not know." Eveline wanted to know what they were talking about. They moved back into the library and sat down only this time on the edge of their chairs. Sable and Olitha were more nervous about this discussion than the first one. Olitha began by explaining how much trouble Eveline had delivering the baby. Sable said, "When you saw dat da baby was brown like a Negro you thought there was a mistake." Eveline remembered the event. Sable went on and explained how upset she was and that she tried to hurt the baby during the night. Eveline had a fair recognition of that. Doctor Haynes had given you a potion to settle you down. The baby nearly died because he could not breathe. Wallace and Samuel decided you needed to rest, so you went to Willard State Hospital. Eveline admitted she tried to kill the baby and that she felt like she was out of her mind. Sable said, "Oh poor Mr. Paine missed you so bad. He was not himself when you was gone. When you treated Mr. Paine as if he was dead, dat made him even more upset. He would have dood anything for you." Eveline felt like she wanted to cry. Sable handed her a handkerchief. Olitha began to explain more about the baby. Dr. Haynes asked us if we could somehow try to save the baby without anyone knowing. He told them that Wallace did not want his wife to be put on trial for murdering their baby. That was the reason they sent Eveline to Willard State Hospital. They hoped you would have time to rest and forget everything. Eveline asked, "So what did you two do?" They explained that Samuel paid them to find people that would care for Patrick without anyone finding out he was alive. Eveline wanted to know when they planned on telling her all this. Olitha explained that the doctor was the one in charge. Eveline looked at them and said, "Guess what? I am in charge now." Sable told Eveline that Miss Haynes did not know either. Eveline laughed and said, "Another man with secrets." Olitha described where Patrick lived and who had been caring for him. Sable explained they knew two women that work at the A&P Store on Seneca Street. They had been friends for years. Their names were Hilly and Liza. They never were given a job as a maid. Olitha knew that they were smarter than most women. They had enough money to pay off the boss lady and live in their own apartment. That was the reason they worked at the A&P Store. Eveline found the story fascinating. She wanted to know if many women could have paid their way out of domestic service. Sable explained that they could have, but they liked working for her. Olitha asked if she wanted to meet Patrick. Eveline seemed unsure, but knew this was her son. Her mind was racing about Samuel and another underhanded plan that involved a person she thought was dead. She told them she wanted to meet Patrick and see what happened. Before they left the room Eveline wanted to make sure that only Samuel and they knew her son was alive. Sable said, "That's right not even the people in Rochester."

January 16, 1920, Attorney General Palmer stated that there was to be no liquor in the United States. Prohibition had begun. Andrew John Volstead had gotten his wish. He was associated with the National Prohibition Act that was now the 18th Amendment to the Constitution of the United States. Bars throughout the country were closing their doors. There was talk of battling against the amendment. How was that going to happen? When Rudolph spoke with Eveline about the hotel he assured her that they were well on their way with the candy and pastry shop instead of the Hunting Bar. While he was discussing other items of business she wanted to know more about the money she heard about a few weeks ago. He explained that it was in a trust for five years. She told him she was aware of that but wanted to know how she would be able to afford the mansion and have money for herself. He gave her a sarcastic answer that she could consider going to work. She glared at him and told him that was not going to happen. She instructed Rudolph to begin to dismantle the horrific import and export company. She would not allow the company to continue under any circumstances. She emphasized that if it was not sold she would notify the authorities and let them dismantle it, along with him and anyone involved. Rudolph looked her straight in the eye and said, "You will be the first the authorities go to because you are the owner." Eveline was waiting to hear that from him. She came back at him and said, "I have already consulted Mr. Keyes and the authorities in New York City and New Jersey about who would be responsible for past actions after the death of the owner. They reassured me that I would not be implicated if there was no record of me signing and accepting transactions. I asked Mr. Wellington who had been signing for the business. It was Wallace, Mr. Ling, Rudolph Williams, and in an emergency Lucille Preston. Rudolph's mouth dropped open when he heard this. He wanted to know how Lucille Preston was involved. She reminded him that she was the boss lady. She signed for the women who were transferred to her region which implicated her in the criminal affairs of TOE&TIC. She said, "I think we are finished for now. You have a lot of work cut out for you. You have 60 days to get it done." Sable tried to open the door but he pushed her aside as he stormed out, slamming the door. Eveline smiled and told Sable that she had just clipped his wings.

Rose telephoned Eveline to invite her to go to lunch. Eveline was delighted and they planned to meet at Pulteney Park. Eveline dressed up in her fur coat and new white fur hat since it was a cold winter day. As she walked down Main Street, she saw Winston. He had not seen Eveline since the day of the business meeting. He was eager to tell her how he was doing and that some people in town were avoiding him. She told him not to worry. Soon he might be moving into the mansion. She had been thinking about needing a man other than James to help with things. He thought she was joking. She explained that he could keep working in town but live at 775 and be on duty for whatever needed doing. She winked at him as she walked away telling him it could happen very soon. She met Rose and they went to a small restaurant on Seneca Street. Eveline did not tell her why, but suggested they walk through the A&P. Rose was curious since Sable and Olitha did all the marketing. Eveline made up a story about wanting to find some new things for them to buy. Rose told her that she had just employed a domestic servant. She mentioned how helpful Mrs. Preston was. Eveline turned and said, "Oh you mean Lucille?" Rose was surprised she even had a first name. Eveline explained that she had more than a first name. Rose was confused but did not push the conversation. During lunch Eveline made a point of letting Rose know how important it was not to tell anyone about the black box. She wanted Rose to tell Samuel to be quiet. Rose wanted to know why so much secrecy. Eveline told her she did not need any more information. Rose told Eveline that Samuel was getting an assistant for the city health department. Her name was Elma Dilber and she was organizing the fight against the influenza epidemic that was spreading throughout the country. Eveline shook her head and told Rose that no one should die from such things. Rose was uneasy with how much Eveline seemed to change since finding the black tin box. As they passed the A&P, Eveline told Rose to run along because she was going to shop for some things in the store. Rose gave her a look of confusion but went about her business. Eveline spotted Hilly and Liza and wanted to shop in the cheese department hoping to converse with these women. They seemed like the type of women you could be friends with.

CHAPTER 15

Eveline decided it was time to have a meeting with Mr. Keyes. It became apparent to her that there were many unscrupulous individuals that were a part of the fiscal affairs of Wallace's estate. Since there was five year holds on the stocks and bonds Eveline needed to know what she could do to survive financially until the estate was settled. While she was pondering the issue, she received a call from Lucille Preston. She called to invite Eveline for lunch the next day. She wanted to discuss her involvement with the domestic servant aspect of the import business. Eveline thought it was a strange way Lucille presented her position in the company. She obviously thought Eveline did not know her involvement in the business. Maybe Rudolph filled her in on what he was told about who would be held guilty for the corrupt dealings of human transfers. Eveline accepted her invitation and they were to meet at the Seneca Hotel the next day. Eveline called Mr. Keyes who was happy to meet at 10A.M. before her lunch date. Eveline thought about what her approach was going to be with Lucille. She did not want to alienate Lucille but wanted her to understand what measures she was going to take to dismantle the underhanded dealings of the TOE&TIC Company.

Eveline telephoned Rudolph informing him that she wanted to meet to discuss the progress of the estate and her findings. The first thing she wanted to remind him of was the two month deadline she gave him for the dismantling of the TOE&TIC Company. She wanted to review the status of the hotel and its financials and its remodeling of the main lobby and shops. She explained to him that she was displeased with Mike Bennett's attitude during her last visit at Christmas time. Rudolph became uneasy when she requested his presence. After some hesitation, he agreed to see her later that day. When the conversation ended she shook her head and thought that everyone is so uneasy and evasive with her. She felt like there was a conspiracy being planned against her. Then she reminded herself of Wallace's letter and his warnings about people and their personalities. She stood tall and knew she must be the one in charge. Rudolph was to arrive in a few hours so Eveline decided it was time to formally meet Hilly and Liza. She called Sable and Olitha and told them they were taking a walk. Sable wanted to know where and why. Eveline explained that it was time to have them introduce her to her son's caregivers. Sable wanted to know if she was sure she wanted to meet the women. Eveline looked at both of them and said, "Everything has its time and this is it." It was early spring and the air was cool. Eveline wore a jacket and her bloomer style pants. Instead of a fur hat, she wore a cloche cap that looked like a helmet. She bought it because it was the latest style the women of the 20s were wearing. Sable looked at Eveline and said, "Oh Miss Eveline, you look like a man." Eveline smiled and explained that the twenties were going to be like that. As she put it, "Everyone will look like whatever they want." Olitha shook her head as she put on her old coat and an old lady style hat. As they were leaving the house, they looked at one another and burst into laughter. Sable asked if it was Halloween yet because of the way they looked.

Sable kept asking Eveline if meeting Hilly and Liza was what she wanted to do. Eveline stopped them in the middle of the street and told them to quit being so worried. She knew what she was doing and it was about time she got this over with. They came to the A&P and walked into the store. Everyone who worked there knew Sable and Olitha but only had heard about Mrs. Paine. Rumors were that she was a dominating woman who liked men and became very wealthy after her husband's death. She was referred to as the "sophisticated woman in the mansion." All eyes followed the three women as they made their way to the cheese department. Sable appeared to be the most confident while Olitha stayed by Eveline's side. Olitha whispered in Eveline's ear that they looked like they were there to rob the place. Eveline laughed at that remark as she casually strolled behind Sable. When Hilly caught sight of the three women coming down the aisle she darted into the back room. She went to warn Liza about what was about to happen. They came from the backroom wringing their hands in their aprons waiting to be introduced to Eveline. Sable explained to them that this was Eveline Paine and she wanted to meet the women who had been caring for Patrick. When Eveline heard it put in those words she realized how much she had missed. Eveline thought she may not like the boy or wondered how she would feel if he acted strange towards her. While she was worrying about those things she remembered the day he was born and now felt the meeting may have been a mistake. Now, five years later it was happening. She began to feel nervous and felt a cold sweat on her skin. Maybe this was not a good idea? It was too late. Hilly and Liza were as nervous as she. What if they did not do the right things for the boy or maybe they would be in trouble for harboring a small child. Olitha changed the atmosphere when she said, "That boy is the luckiest one. He had five women who wanted to be his mother." They all realized how tense they were and laughed at the same time. Liza suggested they go in the stock room where they could have some privacy. As they walked into the back room, Eveline told them she never thought she would see how people work to make a living. They looked at her and explained that if it were not for them she would not have the nice things she has. Eveline knew she had yet another set of circumstances to deal with along with Wallace's past.

The meeting with Hilly and Liza turned out to be pleasant and informative. They explained that Doctor Haynes offered them the chance to care for Patrick and financed everything. Eveline wanted to know who was in charge of Patrick while they were at work. Liza spoke up and explained that her mother stayed with him while they worked. They explained how they arrived in America and that her mother had come from Europe. She was not a surrogate. While they were telling about the home situation, Eveline remembered Wallace's story of his grandmother caring for him and how she wanted to kill Alice and him with arsenic. Eveline was thinking of that while she was listening to them. She hoped this would not be history repeating itself. Then, she wondered what would happen when the families found out that Patrick was alive and well. These thoughts were beginning to complicate Eveline's thinking. She decided that it was her business and she did not care what others would think. Eveline thanked them for being so caring and asked when she could see Patrick. Liza said she was welcome whenever she felt like meeting him. Eveline suggested the weekend. Hilly thought that was fine because they did not work on the weekends. Sunday afternoon was when they would visit and meet Patrick. Sable explained that Hilly and Liza lived on Genesee Street and she knew where it was because they had been there before. Eveline thanked them and the three women left the stockroom. It was strange for Eveline to see what life was like from a different perspective. While they were leaving the store, Eveline saw Lucille Preston and explained to Sable and Olitha that she was going to have lunch with her. They went on their way back to 775.

Lunch with Lucille was another eye opener for Eveline. Nothing seemed ordinary to her anymore. Everywhere she went and everyone she spoke to had a version of situations that were revealing things to Eveline that she never expected. Lucille was direct and explained that if Eveline were to survive in a man's world she must do two things. The first was to support the Women's Rights Movement and to take responsibility in an area that was risky but profitable. Lucille wanted to be her own woman not her husband's woman. Eveline realized Lucille had been protecting herself by being a strong and tough business woman. She wanted to know how Mr. Preston dealt with her independent attitude. Lucille was quick to tell Eveline that she threatened him with exposure to the law about his fiscal dealings with the businesses. Eveline wondered why she was telling her these things when she could be held along with her husband. She listened and did not push the subject. Eveline wanted to know what involvement she had with the placement of domestic servants. Lucille explained that was easy because the women just needed to be cleaned up and placed. It was easy money. There were people in Hong Kong and Singapore who were working with the office in the United States that found and trained the surrogates. The biggest reason the women were so easy to convince was the idea of freedom and a job in America after they did their work on the ships. Eveline was sickened by the thought of the treatment these women and children were forced to endure. While she listened, she thought of Wallace and what a monster he must have been to develop such a trade business. She wanted to believe he was not the mastermind to such things. Maybe it was Mr. Ling everyone spoke about who might have had a different view of human life. Eveline was less hostile toward Lucille after hearing her story. She realized that maybe Lucille had to survive her independence by being a threat to her husband who was holding her back from her freedom. When the bill came for the lunch Lucille waved to the host who came to the table. She politely told him to charge the bill to her husband. When the host left, Lucille laughed and told Eveline that these men will pay.

Mr. Keyes greeted Eveline when she arrived at his office. She explained what her concerns were about financing her life and the property. He understood why she might be concerned about her financial position. He had the will available and reviewed the exact wording of it. As he read the part about the five year hold, he realized that was for only items that were in joint ownership with Rudolph Williams. Eveline asked if that was a large sum of money and was this the only money in Wallace's estate? Mr. Keyes cleared his throat and began with a story that was not in writing. Wallace wanted Rudolph to be his financial partner. They purchased many stocks, companies, and bonds together. It was important to have two names on everything so if one died the other can take over. Wives were eliminated as the second in line for business dealings. While he was talking Eveline thought of what Lucille had just told her at lunch. Wallace told Mr. Keyes that because of Rudolph's past reputation, only a portion of the estate was to be held for five years. Wallace never trusted Rudolph after what happened in Buffalo. Mr. Keyes admitted he was not sure of what happened. All Wallace told him was by doing this with his estate Rudolph was imprisoned, so to speak, for his dishonest behavior years ago. Mr. Keyes admitted that Wallace told him that his wife would take charge of Rudolph when she found out the truth. Eveline sat in the chair and was overwhelmed that Wallace would think so far ahead and punish Rudolph for his actions years ago. Mr. Keyes assured Eveline that she had every right to open new accounts for everything that happened from the day of Wallace's death. This would free her and allow her to begin a new fiscal life. He further advised her to not let Rudolph know about new accounts and why Wallace set up the estate in the way he did. Eveline assured him she would not include him in any of the new business. She thanked him and told him to take what she owed him for his services. She smiled at him and said, "There is a woman running the show now." While Eveline was walking home she thought of all the things she had found out today. She was proud of herself for asking for Mr. Keyes' advice. Now, she was able to better understand Rudolph's behavior and actions. Better than that, she was now able to deal with Rudolph in her own way. She was determined to make Rudolph pay for his dishonest and manipulative behavior over the years.

When Eveline arrived home Sable told her that Rose had telephoned. She was upset and needed to speak with her. Eveline thanked her and called Rose. Rose began by telling Eveline that Samuel received a call that had upset him. All she could hear was something about being in charge of a situation that no one knew about. When she asked him about it all he said was that the damn black box is going to ruin everyone. Eveline acted as surprised as Rose. Rose wanted to know why the box was so important. Eveline began by explaining that no one should know about the box. They were the only ones who knew it existed. Rose agreed not to say anything. Then she told Eveline that Samuel had to change their plans for Sunday. He told her he had a medical meeting and she was not included. Eveline knew what the story was but was not ready to explain about Patrick and Samuel's involvement with him. Eveline told her to relax and that Samuel was probably telling her the truth. After that Rose wanted to know why she was seen going into the store room at the A&P. Eveline wanted to know how she knew. Rose had been in the store with her new domestic servant showing her the store. They saw Sable, Olitha and her speaking with the "cheese ladies". Eveline wanted to laugh when she heard them referred to as cheese ladies. Again she was not free to explain but told her that she had ordered a foreign cheese and they wanted her to approve it before it was out for sale. Rose sounded like she did not believe any of the story. All she said was, "Oh really."

Sunday arrived and Eveline was nervous about what the day might bring. She felt like she was going to meet someone that she should know but had no feeling for. She was the mother but how was she supposed to feel when all she did was try to choke her child. She began to think this meeting was a bad idea and wished she never found out about him. Sable asked what was wrong and Eveline told her. Sable said, "Miss Eveline dat boy is like a little Wallace. He smart as Wallace was. When you see him you gonna know what I says." The weather was nice enough to walk to Genesee Street. Eveline did not want to have James drive them because it might raise questions for anyone who might see them. They arrived at the apartment and Eveline took a deep breath as Hedy opened the door. Liza was in the kitchen and a child was heard singing. Eveline's heart began to beat faster. She did not think she would be so nervous. After all, it was only a five year old boy. They stood in the living room that was much less grand than where Eveline lived. While they were waiting, someone knocked on the door. Hilly opened it and it was Samuel. No one was surprised. He said very little. Liza came into the room with Patrick. Eveline looked at him and realized Sable was right. Patrick was a small version of his father. Patrick looked at Eveline and said, "Hi, my name is Patrick." Eveline wanted to cry when she saw him and thought how she tried to choke such a cute little child. She looked at his face. It was dark as if he had a sun tan. He was not like most Negroes. His hair was wavy, not curly as she thought it might be. He had brown eyes that matched hers. She kept thinking she was dreaming and would wake up soon. Patrick shook Samuel's hand and Sable and Olitha hugged him. He was familiar with them because they would visit from time to time. Everyone sat down for the meal. Samuel began to explain why this happened five years ago. There were so many things wrong at the time and when Patrick was having trouble staying alive Samuel felt it best for Eveline and the family to have the baby cared for in a private environment. Wallace never wanted his family to have to deal with a Negro, nor did he ever think Eveline's parents could accept it. While Samuel was telling the story, Eveline was trying to remember anything about that time. Now she understood her mother's bad behavior toward Alice. Samuel explained that Wallace saw all types of resistance from the families and how they were trying to divide everyone. Samuel did explain that there was a moment when the baby stopped breathing. At that point, he thought he was dead and took him away. Wallace did not want any more to do with it. That was why he wanted nothing more than a cremation and putting the ashes in the lake. Samuel admitted he was taking a chance but found Hilly and Liza and paid them to be the caregiver to the very ill infant. As time went on, Patrick improved and then Wallace became ill. Prior to his illness, Samuel was going to present the story but Wallace died so everything was left as it was. Eveline wanted to know when he was planning on telling her. He told her that he wanted to see how she was handling Wallace's death and the aftermath of all that might occur. Patrick smiled at Eveline and she noticed he had the same grin that his father had. She could not believe this was her child. She never thought anything like this would happen. She asked, "So now what happens?" Samuel told her it was all up to her. He needed to go to school soon. Was she ready to have a young boy living with her? How were the grandparents going to react? Eveline asked if they could keep things as they were until autumn. She could better prepare herself for him moving and starting school. Samuel mentioned a private school. Eveline had not thought about that. There were too many new things to consider. Samuel agreed to continue the financial arrangement until the fall. Eveline was welcome to visit whenever she wanted. The dinner was finished and it was time to go home. Patrick wanted to shake Eveline's hand all the time. It began to be funny and helped to lessen the tension with a little humor.

While they walked home Samuel apologized for being so secretive about Patrick. Eveline was not sure she understood his intention but was glad Patrick was healthy and appeared happy. She explained that she was not sure what to do just yet and needed time to figure it out. Samuel admitted Rose did not know and asked permission to tell her unless she wanted to discuss it with her. Eveline thought he should do it since it was his idea. He agreed he would tell her this evening. He admitted she was very inquisitive about where he had to go today. As Eveline, Sable, and Olitha came to the house Winston was sitting on the front step. Eveline laughed and said he looked like a lost puppy. He was out for a walk and thought he would stop. She invited him in and they sat in the library while Sable and Olitha prepared some refreshments. Winston wanted to know if she was serious when she told him he could move into the house and be a groundskeeper. Eveline wanted to have a man around to care for things James could not do. Winston agreed and laughed when he told Eveline that it was like living at 380. She smiled and told him, not exactly. Wallace would not be there as his play thing. Winston blushed when Eveline told him that he was her play thing now. Winston's eyes lit up with the thought of what the job might entail.

The next morning at 6 AM the telephone rang and Sable answered it. It was Rudolph calling to speak with Eveline. Sable wanted to know if Rudolph had any idea of what time it was. He told her he did not care but he needed to speak with that woman who was making his life miserable. Sable made a face and her eyebrows went up when she heard the tone of his voice and what he said. She told him she would try to wake Miss Eveline but she may not be too pleasant this time of day. Rudolph snapped back that he was not worried about her attitude, just that he needed to speak with her. Sable went up to Eveline's room and knocked on the door. To her surprise Winston answered the door. Sable looked at him from head to toe and said, "Boy you look good neked but worn out." Eveline heard the conversation and came to the door to see why Sable was knocking so early. She explained that Mr. Williams wanted to speak with her and explained how nasty he sounded. Eveline told her to get rid of him because he was probably drunk on hooch. Sable turned her head and looked confused. Eveline said, "Yes hooch. It is cheap alcohol that makes people nasty." Sable agreed to tell him not to call so early. Eveline looked at Winston and told him they had some work to do in bed. He shook his head as he crawled under the covers. Eveline had forbid him to wear clothing when they were together. Winston liked the idea but wondered how he was going to feel during the winter.

Within a half hour, there was banging on the front door. This time Olitha answered it. She told Rudolph he looked terrible. He barged past her and demanded Eveline come downstairs. He had very important business with her. While Rudolph was yelling, Winston came downstairs. Rudolph looked at his naked body and asked if he had forgotten something. Winston told him that he did not forget anything. He explained that Eveline liked to see his body this way. It was obvious with Rudolph's reaction that he was a bit jealous. Then, Eveline appeared in her gown. Rudolph went up to her and accused her of getting him fired from the Geneva Chamber of Commerce. It was announced in the Geneva Daily News that on April 17, 1920 Mr. P. Rice was to be in charge of the Chamber. It further reported that Mr. Rudolph Williams was released from his duties because of underhanded business dealings. Eveline had no idea that was happening. She wanted to know why he thought she had anything to do with his dismissal. He looked at her and said, "You have made my life miserable and have me in your control. I want to know why?" Eveline was in no mood to explain all she had found out from Mr. Keyes and thought it was not for him to know anyway. She liked having him crawl for things. She looked at him and said, "I had nothing to do with your job at the Chamber of Commerce. If you don't get out of here and sober up I'll have you tied up and held in jail for making such accusations. Now get out!" Winston stood frozen and naked while Sable and Olitha opened the front door. Eveline moved toward Rudolph forcing him to back off. She slammed the door nearly hitting him as he left. She turned and saw the three of them stunned by her behavior. She smiled at them and said calmly, "I told you I was in charge now."

Winston finished moving into 775 South Main Street. He was given the room next to Eveline's bedroom. She wanted him to have a place where he could rest but wanted him near enough to her when she wanted him for her sexual pleasures. Winston agreed to the set up and liked the idea of maintaining the property. Eveline told him he was allowed to have guests of the male persuasion but she was the only woman allowed in the house. Winston seemed satisfied with that rule. He had met Mike from Baker and Stark Clothier the other day. He told him that he was moving into help Eveline Paine with the maintenance of the property. Mike always had an eye for Wallace and had a difficult time when he died. Winston told him that he could come over to see where he was living. He told Mike that Eveline financed his YMCA membership because she wanted to have him stay in good shape for all the activities she had planned for him. Mike's eyes went up and asked what the activities were? Winston compared it to when he lived with Eveline and Wallace at 380 Washington Street. Mike smiled and wanted to know if there was a bungalow in the back of the property. Winston told him there was not and that Eveline wanted him as her play thing since Wallace was no longer around. Mike asked if he could stop by sometime. Winston looked at him with a suggestive grin and told him that Eveline's rule was they had to be naked in the house. Mike blushed at that statement but began feeling aroused by the thought of what might happen when he visited.

It was August 26, 1920 and every newspaper had in the headlines that the 19th Amendment to the Constitution of the United States was passed giving women the right to vote. There were celebrations in cities everywhere. The men were not as happy. There were threats of action against women that would try to vote. There was tension among radical groups of businessmen who were fearful that women were taking over. Eveline, Rose, and Lucille went to a rally in downtown Geneva to celebrate the victory. There were thousands of banners and women singing and celebrating in the streets. The police department was out in full force to protect them. The only woman on the police force gave a speech about how the amendment would strengthen the population and create equality. Not many men dared to heckle her because she was an officer of the law. Winston was in the crowd with Mike. They had just come from the YMCA and joined the three women. Rose wanted to know how many men Eveline was planning on inviting to her home. Eveline laughed and told them that only Winston, but that he could have visitors of the male persuasion. Rose shook her head and said, "Eveline you have really changed." Eveline shook her head and told them that she was waiting for the right time to have lots of men and fun.

Samuel took longer to tell Rose about Patrick. One day, Samuel saw Eveline and she asked when he was planning on telling Rose about Patrick. She knew she still did not know because she would have mentioned it to her. Eveline gave him one more day or she would tell her. Samuel knew he needed to deal with Rose on this matter because Eveline was getting the reputation as being tough. He would rather stay on her good side. She thanked him for getting it done. Eveline told Samuel that she had decided to have Patrick placed in a private school in Rochester. She felt that more time was needed for her to adjust to being a mother and that Patrick could begin formal training in school. She was inquiring about a private school that had a good reputation and was credited with high success in academics. She would visit him from time to time and have him come to her house for holidays. Samuel sensed that Eveline was not connected to Patrick. He feared that might happen. He wanted to know what the cost was for the school. Eveline told him that was her business and that the estate was paying for that. Samuel said no more. Eveline reminded him of his responsibility to Rose about Patrick.

Rudolph had been staying away from Eveline as much as he could. He was feeling pressured whenever she would inquire about the businesses in town. Since he was no longer with the Chamber, she felt he was better able to monitor the Wire Wheel Company, Shuron Company, Safege Company, and the Goodwin Company. She required that he report to her the facts and figures every two weeks. She reminded him that he had only three weeks left before the deadline for the dismantling of TOE&TIC. He assured her he was working on it. In reality, Rudolph was becoming vindictive and set out to ruin Eveline. He thought it was his turn to demolish her since she was trying to ruin him. He had no intention of ending the transfer program. He had arranged to change the name but the activities were still operating as usual. In order to accomplish this, Mr. Wellington was given a raise and sworn to secrecy or he would die. The name of the business was changed to The Foreign Exchange Program. The name made it sound like it was an academic program for students. No one would question such an operation, especially when it involved children of all ages. The transfers were extended to older individuals. No longer was it just for young infants and preschool children. In doing that the need for surrogates lessened. The plan was fool proof. In addition to Rudolph's plan to ruin Eveline, he resorted to his old method. He kept the signatures of Wallace, Winston, and Eveline from Buffalo days. He thought he might need them again. As it turned out, the time was coming for Eveline to be the signee to the financial aspects of The Foreign Exchange Program. Rudolph would slowly introduce her signature on small items so as not to tip off anyone. When the signature was familiar to the banks in New York City, he would increase the checks to higher amounts. When it was the right time, he would notify the officials that there was illegal human transfers occurring and the owner must be liable for such activity. Rudolph decided to streamline things by having rubber stamps made of Eveline's signature so that he and Mr. Wellington would not need to worry about signing things in person. Rudolph felt he had regained the upper hand.

Samuel told Rose about Patrick. Rose was furious when he explained what had occurred. She thought he should be arrested for such actions. He explained that he felt it was for everyone's best interests based on what was happening at that time. Rose was so angry that she was left out of the scheme that she called Eveline to discuss the matter. Eveline was calm when Rose screamed into the telephone about fraud and secretive behavior. Rose told Eveline that Samuel was right. The black box was going to ruin everyone. Eveline tried to explain that she was not upset about it. It was a strange set of circumstances but Patrick was a healthy boy and he looked like Wallace with a sun tan. Rose sort of laughed when she heard Eveline's description of Patrick. She told Rose that they could visit him and that she was planning on enrolling him in a private school in Rochester. Rose started screaming again when she heard the private school idea. Eveline explained her reasoning and Rose could not believe she did not want to be involved in her only child's life. Rose told Eveline that they could never have children and would never put their child in a school so far away. Eveline assured her that he would be part of her life and theirs. After Rose settled down, she realized that Eveline may be right about needing time to adjust to all that she was finding out.

President Wilson had been suffering from poor health. It was November and the presidential elections were upon the country. Warren G. Harding and Calvin Coolidge were elected President and Vice President. Harding's philosophy was one of a laid back attitude. He did not travel far for his campaign and only used a front porch and neighborly attitude during his campaign. Wilson was not so sure of that philosophy. The country was booming with business and money being made everywhere. Wilson warned that a watchful eye on business was necessary to avoid over spending and careless policies. In his last speech on December 20, 1920 before leaving office, President Wilson said, "America must be champions of rights and justice in all world affairs." He warned the people of the need to be careful and show strength and courage in a new world of inventions and progress. The 1920's were beginning to show signs of greater speed and activities in economic and social movements. It was a time of new expectations and equality for all.

CHAPTER 16

In 1921, the economy saw tremendous advancements due to the increase in advertising multitudes of products. The idea of buying things without paying full price allowed the consumer to buy now and pay later. Any item that was sold required a small down payment and the remainder could be paid off in monthly installments. Everyone took advantage of the system and soon it was possible for even the poorest people to have the best of everything. The rise of "chain stores" was expanding to not only major department stores but food stores, such as the A&P Store. As more people took advantage of the rapid speed of the economy, there was more money available for entertainment. Ragtime music was changing to jazz that had its origins in music played at black folks funerals in New Orleans. Jazz was a blend of African-American work songs and West Indian rhythms, combined with a variety of ethnic music from Protestant hymns and Creole melodies. The individual musicians added their own style, making new groups popular.

Eveline discussed the new age of music with Olitha and Sable. They were more aware of it than she was because of their background. A man named Louis Armstrong was an up and coming jazz trumpeter. Eveline wanted to know what a "Satchmo" was. Sable laughed and explained that was Louis Armstrong's name used during his performances. He was working with King Oliver's Creole Jazz Band at the time. Eveline told Sable to buy some of the recordings of the new music. She had begun to change her wardrobe to match the newest styles women were wearing so why not the music she listened to. Eveline and Rose went to a fashion fair and were introduced to flapper wear. It was a carefree boyish style. Eveline remembered telling everyone that the 1920's were going to see a change in attitude and fashion. No longer did men need to dress a certain way nor did the women. According to the master of ceremony, a flapper raised her hemline to scandalous new heights, bobbed her hair and wrapped her chest to make it flat. The women of the 20's were wearing a slim drop wasted dress. The announcer for the show made a point of having everyone look at the woman in the audience that was wearing a bell-shaped hat. She pointed to Eveline and asked her to stand so all could see her up to the minute hat. Eveline was delighted to model her hat as she swirled around to show everyone the front and back of the hat that was called a cloche. Rose was impressed that Eveline was the only woman in the audience that had such a hat. She said to Eveline, "I can't wait to tell Samuel about the new wardrobe. He'll probably forbid me to wear an outfit like that." Eveline told her to remember that these were the days for women to have rights. Rose made a face like she did not believe what Eveline said.

After an intermission, the second half of the show had a new focus. Baker and Stark Clothiers used male models to show the latest in men's fashions. Mike was the announcer from Baker and Stark. When he saw Eveline he went to her and shook her hand. He told her how happy he was to be a member of the first store to have a place in a fashion show. Eveline congratulated him as Rose stared at him. She wondered why he seemed so different than most men. After he left to begin the show, Eveline explained to Rose that he was good at what he did. Rose had a questionable look on her face and asked what that meant. Eveline told her that he liked to be well dressed and he was one of Winston's visitors. When Rose heard it put that way she smiled and shook her head in agreement. Men's fashions took on the look of famous moving picture stars. According to Mike, the fashion-conscious man chose roomy "oxford bags" for trousers. Saddle shoes and a loose fitting sweater complimented the look. Men's hair was now called "Patent-leather hair" because it was slicked back and parted in the center. Eveline whispered to Rose, "Winston will not like that when I tell him to wear baggy trousers." Rose asked why. Eveline said, "He likes to show his manhood when he wears tight work clothes." Rose just shook her head. At the end of the show, Mike announced that there was a new event coming later in the year. The promoters of shows in Atlantic City, New Jersey were having a Miss America contest. It was to focus on the beauty and talents of women. It was a scheme to make money and promote the city. Eveline laughed when she heard this. The city was becoming a vacation destination by the sea. Eveline told Rose that she was going to take her men friends with her. Rose asked why. Eveline told her she wanted to see how they would act. As she put it, "Everyone acts differently when on vacation." At the end of the show, Eveline and Rose spoke with Mike. Eveline told him that he did a fine job and that the fashions were appropriate for some men. He smiled and wanted to know who could not wear these things. Eveline told him that she was not going to allow Winston to wear baggy pants. Mike laughed and agreed that Winston looked better in tight pants or nothing. Rose's eyes went up when she heard that and the reaction from others around them was one of disgust. Eveline winked at him and asked him when he was coming for a visit. Mike told her sooner than she thought.

When Eveline arrived home she told Sable and Olitha about the new fashions for women and men. They were surprised that men had a part in the show. When Eveline told them about the baggy pants style they laughed. They both spoke at the same time and said, "Winston will never be seen in those things." Eveline agreed and continued about the Miss America event in Atlantic City. They were not familiar with where that was. Eveline explained that she was taking them there with Winston, Rudolph, and Mike. When they heard this they wanted to know how many men she needed. She explained they were not all for her. Sable said, "Oh Miss Eveline I don't need no white boy." Olitha agreed. Eveline smiled with a sassy look and said, "They are all for me and they can do whatever they want to each other if I allow it." While the women were discussing the trip and the fashions the telephone rang. Sable answered it and directed the call to Eveline. It was

Rudolph calling her to set up an appointment regarding the termination of the TOE&TIC operation. Eveline was surprised that he had accomplished his work without her being too demanding. She agreed to have him arrive around 4PM. She put the receiver down and thought how different Rudolph was about the company. Maybe she was making progress with him after all? She told Olitha to prepare some refreshments for her meeting with Rudolph.

Rudolph arrived promptly at 4PM. The last time he saw Eveline was the morning of his drunken outburst. When he saw Eveline he apologized for his poor behavior. He admitted that he realized afterward that she had nothing to do with his dismissal from the Chamber. Eveline accepted his apology but warned him to be more careful with his accusations toward her. She smiled and said, "I have my ways with you and it will be more fun if you are careful what you say to me." Rudolph was not sure what that meant because he did not know that Eveline found out why Wallace set the will up the way he did. Ironically, they both thought they had the upper hand. Rudolph told her that the operation had changed and that only material items were being imported to the United States. They would still be exporting the same items as before. Eveline wanted to know what amounts of money were involved in the finalization of the TOE&TIC operation. He explained that he had transferred the money to the trust account that Wallace had set up in his will. Eveline liked the sound of that because she was in charge of that now, but Rudolph was not privileged to that information. She made a mental note to transfer that money after the meeting. She asked him what the amount was. He explained it was around $200,000.00. Eveline reminded him she liked things exact. He looked at her and said, "Sorry, $199,345.00." She thanked him. Eveline wanted to know if he could set up an appointment with Mike Bennett at the Seneca Powers Hotel. Rudolph asked why. She explained that she wanted to discuss the hotel and the possibilities of selling it. Rudolph said that was preposterous. She told him she was the one to decide on what was preposterous or not. She requested a meeting next week. The last thing she wanted to discuss was the possibility that he would teach her how to drive the automobile. Rudolph was so surprised he coughed when he heard this. She wanted to know if he was scared of the idea. He smiled and told her he was not scared but most women do not drive. Eveline reminded him that he and she were always first at things as far back as the Women's Rights Movement. She told him she wanted to drive to show people what a woman could do and wanted to be first to do it. Rudolph agreed to teach her the next week. Eveline thanked him and told him her first lesson would be on the way to Rochester. His eyebrows went up when he heard that. When he left Eveline, he thought that he had accomplished his goal. She was still in charge of a company that was supposed to be closed. Little does he know that Eveline could not wait to go to Mr. Keyes to discuss transferring nearly $200,000.00 to her account.

The time had come for Rudolph and Eveline to go to Rochester for their meeting with Mike Bennett. Rudolph called Eveline before he came over to make sure she was still interested in learning how to drive. When Eveline answered the telephone she smiled when she heard the sound of the uncertainty in his voice. She explained to him that he needed to have a better attitude toward her judgments and desires. Eveline dressed in the latest style to make an impression in Rochester. It just so happened that B.Forman Company was having an exposition of fashions in the Ladies Reception Room at the Seneca Powers Hotel. Eveline saw the article in the Geneva Daily Times. She wondered why Rudolph had not informed her of such an event at her hotel. She would take that up with Mike Bennett and Rudolph during their meeting. Before they left for Rochester, Eveline decided it was time to tell both sets of parents about Patrick. She telephoned them to see if they could meet Rudolph and her at the hotel lobby to have lunch. Eveline was surprised at how quickly they both accepted her invitation.

When Rudolph arrived Eveline requested that James bring the automobile from the garage. James smiled at Eveline when she stood like a queen waiting to take the driver's side. She stood propped on the door with one hand on her hip with her head up to the side. When Rudolph saw that he said, "All you need is a cigarette holder with a lit one in your hand." Eveline smiled and told him it was time for her first lesson. He opened the door and she sat down and held the wheel. He sat on the passenger side and asked her again if she was ready for the lesson. Eveline looked at him and nodded her head up and down. Sable, Olitha, and James stood at the curb and watched them. They were shaking their heads and laughing when Eveline started the engine and hit the accelerator a little too hard. Down the street they went with Eveline screaming just as she had when Wallace took her for her first ride in Buffalo. Sable said, "I hopes they gets home in one piece. Lord have mercy on those two." The others laughed. Rudolph was patient with Eveline while she acted is if she had driven before. She raced down the street and took the corner at Main and Washington Street too fast causing the car to swerve from left to right, nearly going into a tree. Rudolph finally lost his patience and told her that if she did not slow it down he was getting out. Eveline slammed on the brakes and looked at Rudolph and told him, "Then get out and walk to Rochester." He said nothing and she sped up Washington Street. Rose was in the front yard as they passed 380. Eveline honked the horn and waved madly as they went by. She took both hands off the wheel nearly running into Rose. Rudolph took a hold of the wheel and screamed at her to hold on to the steering wheel. This time Eveline realized she nearly killed her best friend so she listened to the instructions with more care. While she was driving, she told Rudolph she wanted a sportier vehicle than this big thing. He asked if she knew what she wanted. She did not know the name of it but that it had only two seats and the top could be taken off. It was designed for speed and flash. Rudolph admitted she was a fast learner as they approached Rochester. She pulled up to the front of the hotel and the valet took the automobile to a parking place.

Eveline walked with a deliberate stroll through the lobby as the employees and guests watched her arm in arm with Rudolph. She told Rudolph he was still good for something. He made a face as they went into Mr. Bennett's office. He stood and greeted Eveline and complimented her about her outfit. Eveline informed them that the tables were turning today. In a businesslike manner she told Mike and Rudolph they were sitting in front of the desk and she was sitting behind the desk. She was conducting the question and answer time. The two men sat like school boys waiting for their lesson. Eveline positioned herself with her hands folded and said, "So Mike, tell me about the hotel." He asked what she wanted to know. She told him not to be silly. She wanted facts and figures and asked why she was not informed of all the events in the hotel. He looked surprised that she knew so much about the happenings in the hotel. Rudolph spoke up and explained that she did not always need to know every single thing that was going on and that was why they hired people like Mike to do those things. Eveline rose from the chair and looked them in the eyes and said, "Don't ever let me find out about things from someone else. I will have both of you tied and tanned." She gave them the example of the fashion extravaganza in the hotel that day put on by B. Forman Company. Mike apologized for the lack of communication. Eveline was not letting him off the hook that easily when she asked him how long it was going to take to get his name plate on his desk. She said, "Do you want me to fire you so you won't have to have one made?" He walked around to the drawer and pulled it out. When Eveline saw that she asked why he was hiding it. He told her he did not think that it was necessary because only people that knew him were in the office. Eveline looked at Rudolph and then Mike and said, "I see that you boys think I am fooling around when I give suggestions." She moved from the desk and began walking to the door. She turned and told them to get the appraisal for the hotel because she was selling it. She said, "I am making plans for the future and this is not part of it." She motioned to Rudolph that it was time to meet the parents.

Eveline strolled through the lobby to the restaurant. Rudolph asked why she invited the parents for lunch. She explained that there had been some new developments that the family needed to know about. Rudolph had no idea what she was talking about. He was as confused as the family. Maybe he did not know as much as he thought. Alice and Frank were seated. When Alice saw Eveline she jumped up and admired her outfit from the cloche to the dress that showed much more leg than she ever thought could be allowed. The waistline was low and Frank wanted to know if she was losing her dress. Alice said, "Oh Frank, wait until I start wearing things like that." Frank laughed and asked if they were applying to the circus as a side show. No one commented on his remarks. Mr. and Mrs. Lounsberry arrived and Eveline greeted them. They chitchatted while they waited for the server. Eveline explained that the hotel was paying for lunch. Alice wanted to know if everything was okay because they were surprised when she called. Eveline's mother was cold to Alice and had never apologized for her actions before Wallace died. She asked her mother, "So how did Alice take to your apology about you attempting to intervene in my recovery and accusing Alice of being the problem because of having a Negro for a father?" No one moved and finally her mother admitted she had never discussed it with Alice and was sorry for her bad behavior. Alice sat motionless and felt like her past was coming forward again. Was she ever going to be able to bury this? Then Eveline began to explain the reason for the lunch meeting. She came right to the point and told everyone that her baby was alive and well. They were stunned and speechless. She explained what happened and how Samuel found and financed two women to care for the baby until he was better. He was five years old and looked like Wallace only with a sun tan and wavy hair. Alice said she was kidding.

Mrs. Lounsberry wanted to know why she was playing a joke on them because they had been through enough. Rudolph was as stunned as the rest because he was sure the baby was cremated. Eveline explained that she had seen Patrick and that she was deciding on what she wanted to do with him. Her mother thought she should bring her son home and care for him as a mother should. Eveline told them that she was not sure how she was handling it and she may put him in a boarding school. They were aghast at the idea of a mother not caring for her son. The fathers were not so vocal about what should be done but did want to know if they could visit Patrick. Eveline thought that might be a good idea but she needed to make decisions first. Lunch was not as appetizing as everyone thought it might be. After hearing this news, they were happy when it was time to go. They agreed they needed time to absorb the news.

Rudolph escorted Eveline to the front of the hotel without saying a word. Mike Bennett stopped them before they got in the automobile. He wanted to know if Eveline was sure about selling the hotel. She snapped at him and told him that he and Rudolph had a week to get her the estimate of the hotel's worth. She would make her decision about the price and the details for the sale. Mike agreed to have it done and Rudolph would give her the details. She reminded them that she liked things exact. Rudolph remarked in a sarcastic tone, "We have found that out the hard way." Eveline told Rudolph that she was tired and that he needed to drive to Geneva. While driving Rudolph wanted to know how Eveline felt about her son. She explained that she was not sure she knew what to do. She found it difficult to understand because she remembered very little about Patrick's birth and what happened after that. Rudolph explained what he thought he knew and that she was admitted to Willard State Hospital for rest and recovery. She told him that she knew all that, but was unclear of her attempt to choke the baby. She told Rudolph that she wanted to put it all in the past and that a private school might be the best. She knew that no one thought very much of that idea but she did not want Patrick around all the time. She was just beginning to enjoy herself and a child would not be welcome in her home.

The next day Eveline began inquiring about private schools in Rochester. She made calls to schools and found that what she wanted was not available in Rochester. Private schools were not boarding schools. A person at Columbia Allendale School referred her to a school near Syracuse named Manlius Pebble Hill School. She made an appointment to meet with the administrator the next day. She decided that she was doing this on her own and would tell everyone after she completed what she set out to do. Sable and Olitha were called to the library. Eveline explained that she needed to go to a small town south of Syracuse. She wanted only them to know and that no one else was to know where she was going. Sable was surprised that after only one time behind the wheel she was going to do it by herself. Olitha said, "You sure Miss Eveline that yous can do dat." Sable suggested she take Winston because he would be good for her and he could be away and no one would find out. Eveline thought for a moment and realized that might be a good idea.

When Winston arrived at home, Eveline invited him to sit with her in the library. He wanted to know if he needed to stay in his work clothes. Eveline smiled and told him that he could because the outline in his pants was showing what she was going to get later. He smiled as she began to explain that she wanted him to go to Syracuse with her. He agreed and thought they would have a great time and maybe could stop along the roadside so she could have her way with him. While he was saying that he felt a pleasant feeling in his groin. Eveline noticed this and told him it was time to go upstairs and deal with his urges. She suggested he get his Leter Buck because they both needed some of it. Winston raced upstairs and Eveline told Sable to hold dinner for a few hours. Sable smiled and shook her head and asked if Winston was coming to dinner naked. Eveline did not answer her, only walked upstairs toward the bedroom. As she walked in the bedroom, Winston was nowhere to be seen. She looked around and found him behind the door. He took a hold of her and tore her dress off. She moaned with pleasure as Winston fondled her breasts. She wanted a whiff of LeterBuck and he gave it to her. She turned her body so her back side was rubbing against Winston's hairy chest. She could feel him rubbing up and down and side to side. While she was against the wall Winston maneuvered her into position. The more he moved his body around the more she pleaded and told him that was what she wanted from all her men and he was always going to be the first to satisfy her sexual needs. She smirked and said, "At least this way, I can't get pregnant. I already have one kid I don't want." Winston said, "That is fine with me."

The next day, Eveline had James bring the automobile to the front of the house. She was deliberate in the way she took the driver's seat with an air of confidence while

Winston sat in the passenger seat. James wanted to know if he should at least ride in the back seat. Eveline told him that was not necessary. She turned the key and the engine hummed. Winston asked if she was going to drive fast like an amusement park ride. She told him she needed to be careful because she was the only one who knew how to drive. Winston agreed that he had no idea what she was doing. Away they went down the street, only this time Winston was screaming because she was swerving trying to avoid people and vehicles on the road. Finally, they neared Syracuse and were on the road to the Manlius Pebble Hill School. Winston asked if the school made less of a man out of kids by the name Manlius. Eveline explained that it was a military school for boys led by Episcopalians and focused on high academic standards and often students went on to West Point. She told Winston that she wanted her son to be wealthy and strong. She hoped that he would be a leader someday and then she could be proud that she was his mother. They entered the main building and saw students dressed in uniforms marching from class to class. The administrator informed her that the boys needed to be trained at an early age. Winston sat and said nothing as he wondered what he might have turned into if he had gone to a school like this. After discussing courses of study and physical training, the issue of money came up. Eveline told the administrator that whatever it cost she was willing to pay. She wanted to know about visitation and time for students to go home. An appointment would be necessary for a visit but they went home for holidays if the parent wanted the child to visit. Eveline liked the sound of the operation and enrolled Patrick immediately. He would start in September. Eveline would have time to get the family together to spend time with him. She told Winston that Patrick would have to stay with her for a while so he would need to behave himself. Winston agreed but told her that he had many visitors of the male persuasion that would be coming to visit. On the drive home, Eveline wanted Winston to understand that his friends were welcome but they needed to be more discreet about why they were all visiting at the same time. She smiled and said, "I'm going to be jealous when that goes on." Winston smiled and said, "Too bad." Eveline was feeling quite competent driving. She realized how much she was able to do without the help of everyone else and their ideas. She was beginning to enjoy the freedom she had so waited for.

CHAPTER 17

The Geneva Daily Times featured the grand opening on August 17 of a restaurant called The Hob-n-Nob Tea Room. Lucille Preston telephoned Eveline to invite her to go to lunch to be one of the first customers. Eveline thought that would be a grand idea and wanted to know if Rose could be included. Lucille told Eveline that she had already invited her. Eveline was miffed but decided it was not worth the time to worry about who was invited first. Lucille had been low keyed since their last social occasion. Eveline agreed to meet them at the new tea room on 63 Seneca Street. When she put the receiver down she made a face and thought about how she would dress. She wanted to upstage anyone else who may be there. Eveline looked in the newspaper to read the information about the tea room. It had an a la carte menu and music for lunch and dinner time. The advertisement showed a table decorated with Martha Washington candleholders and a fashionable woman seated smoking a cigarette with a gentleman conversing with her. Eveline looked up from the paper and she knew this was her type of environment.

The newspaper had another article that caught Eveline's eye. The Miss America Pageant was featured in the travel section. It described the event and that Margaret Gorman had been the first winner and held the title of Miss Washington, D.C. in 1921. She was going to be the guest of honor for the second pageant being held in Atlantic City, New Jersey on September 7, 1922. The contestants were judged on their personality, appearance, musical ability, and how they appeared in a bathing suit on the Boardwalk. Eveline wanted to go to Atlantic City for that event with her friends. She would make reservations in the classiest hotel and they would go by train to Atlantic City. She would tell them it was an early Christmas present. As she read more about the pageant, she discovered there were hotels advertising package deals. The hotels were listed by their location to the Million Dollar Pier where the pageant was being held and from the most expensive to the least expensive resort hotels. She telephoned the first one which was Park Place Hotel, but there were no rooms available. She skipped to the third one, the Shelburn Hotel located on Michigan Avenue and Boardwalk. The penthouse was available with four bedrooms and a veranda overlooking the ocean, boardwalk, gardens, and swimming pool. Without hesitation, Eveline reserved the penthouse for five nights for $2000.00. After she finished her conversation, she realized she only had a month before they were going. In the meantime, she had to invite everyone. She felt guilty about her feelings about

Patrick and needed to invite him to stay for a few days with her before he went off to Manlius and she wanted to shop for a new automobile. She yelled for Sable and Olitha to come to the library. They appeared in a scramble thinking something terrible had happened. Eveline put her hands up in the air and said, "We're going to Atlantic City in one month." Sable wanted to know why they needed to come so fast. Eveline told them they were going with her. It was their early Christmas present. Neither of them was sure where that place was or why Miss Eveline wanted them to go. Eveline explained about the Miss America Pageant and that Atlantic City was the famous playground by the sea. She told them about the hotel and that the two of them would have to stay in the same room. Eveline finished by telling them that they would have time to have fun but they would be there to assist her. Sable shook her head and said, "So weez just movin our work to Atlantic City." Olitha laughed and said, "At least weez gonna see the beautiful peoples and the sea." Eveline smiled and told them they would have a great time and she was glad to take them even though they were servants. Both women stood silent after that statement.

Eveline telephoned Rose to invite her and Samuel to go to Atlantic City. When Rose heard the details, she accepted the invitation. Rose told Eveline that she was telling Samuel they were going and there would be no need to discuss it further. Eveline laughed and told Rose that she was proud of her new attitude. Eveline asked Rose about the invitation to the new restaurant. Rose laughed and said, "That Lucille is so conniving when she called me first instead of you." Eveline wanted to know what else was said. Rose continued, "Lucille wanted to see if she could upset you and make you wonder why you were not first to be included." When Eveline heard that, she was happy she did not respond to her thoughts of who was first. Rose asked Eveline if she cared how Lucille behaved. Eveline said, "I had a feeling that was her intention and that she might be trying to make me jealous." Eveline finished saying, "Lucille will be so left out when she finds out we are going to Atlantic City and staying in the best hotel on the Boardwalk." Eveline got ready to go to the train station to purchase the tickets to Atlantic City. While she was going out the door she looked in her purse and found she was short on cash for the tickets. She hurried upstairs to the bedroom and pulled out her private cash box. She had started that many months ago when she feared not having enough money to survive. She opened the box and pulled out a roll of hundred dollar bills. She grabbed six of them and rolled her eyes and said to herself in a low tone, "Thank you Wallace, it's my turn for fun." She raced out the front door leaving it ajar. Sable came running and saw Eveline drive down the street as if she were going to a fire. Sable smiled and shook her head as she closed the door. On her way down the street, Eveline saw Rudolph. She slammed on the brakes and rolled down the window to tell him about the trip. He went up to the window where Eveline had her head hanging out and asked what was going on. She told him he was going to Atlantic City for five nights to see the Miss America Pageant. She gave him the dates and explained it was his early Christmas present. At first Rudolph thought it was just for the two of them until Eveline told him who else was going. He wanted to know why Mike was included. She told Rudolph with a sweet smile, "I want more men to be around me and you boys can have fun with each other." Rudolph gave her a suspicious look. He told her he was not sure he could go because of other engagements. Eveline snapped back and said, "You have no choice. I'm taking you." Rudolph was surprised that she was paying for the trip. Eveline told Rudolph he would be sharing a room with Winston and Mike. He shook his head as he watched her drive down the street avoiding pedestrians and other vehicles. She arrived at the train station and purchased seven tickets to Atlantic City. She explained to the agent that she was taking her friends for their early Christmas present. The man in the window remembered Eveline from other trips and complimented her on how stylish she was whenever she took the train. She smiled and thanked the man as she strolled out of the train station.

Winston was on his way to work after lunch when he saw Eveline speeding down Main Street. He waved and she slammed on the brakes. She had her head hanging out of the window as Winston approached her. She told him that he would need to go to Baker and Stark and get some new clothes. She told him that they were going to Atlantic City to see the Miss America Pageant. He was as excited as a kid at Christmas when he heard she was paying for it. She wanted him to be fitted for a suit and all the accessories he would need for that type of place. While Eveline was telling Winston about the arrangements she casually mentioned that Mike was included in the plans. Winston was surprised, but happy to know he would be sharing the room with Rudolph and Mike. He jokingly said, "This will be like the time we stayed together with you and Wallace." Eveline reminded him that Wallace was dead and that Mike was nothing like Wallace. Winston smiled and told her that Mike was not as well-endowed as Wallace was.

With that remark Eveline said, "I guess we will find out in Atlantic City." Winston rolled his eyes with a smile on his face. As she started to leave, she reminded him to tell Mike he was included and to be ready to go on September 5th. He stood for a moment and thought that date was the same date that President McKinley was shot in Buffalo at the Pan-American Exposition twenty one years ago. He hoped that was not a premonition of something bad happening again.

When Eveline arrived home from the train station, Sable gave Eveline the mail. There was a letter from Eastman Kodak Company. She studied the front and realized it was addressed to her personally not as shareholder. George Eastman had personally written the letter inviting her to the grand opening of the Eastman Theater in Rochester. There were opening ceremonies with the orchestra and entertainers on September 4. He explained that he understood that Wallace was deceased but wanted her to be a guest along with Rudolph Williams. He remarked at how impressed he was with them when he first met them at his soirée years ago. There were two tickets included in the letter and another sealed envelope. She opened the second enclosure and found a check for $39,875.00 for shareholder earnings for the last quarter of the financial year. Until now the dividend checks were deposited in Wallace's trust accounts. Eveline smiled and thought that Mr. Keyes had been doing his work and all the money was coming to her. She put the check in the envelope and knew that her first stop was the bank before the luncheon. Then she realized that the grand opening was the day before they were leaving for Atlantic City. She called Rudolph to invite him to go to Rochester. When

Rudolph heard about the grand opening he said, "I told you I might not be able to go with you." Eveline realized from Rudolph's remark he knew about the Eastman Theater opening. He told Eveline he received a letter a few days ago about the opening. Eveline interrupted and said, "Now you are officially invited and you will be going to everything. We have enough time to go to Rochester and get back for the train the next morning." Rudolph asked if they were staying at the Seneca Powers for the night. Eveline told him no, but she wanted to confer with Mike Bennett about the sale of the hotel before they went to the theater. Rudolph knew that nothing had been done about the sale of the hotel because there were other plans for its use.

The next morning Eveline was rushing around figuring out what she was going to wear to the grand opening of the Hob-N-Nob Tearoom. She settled on a dress with a low waist and high uneven hemline. She had a variety of hats but decided on a cloche hat. Since it was late summer, she wore a summer weight scarf to wrap around her shoulders instead of a fur. She carried a small purse that held her check from Eastman Kodak. She would stuff a few hundred dollar bills in it in case she wanted to buy something at the dress shop. She purchased a cigarette holder recently. This was the latest fad for women who enjoyed the attention a device such as that might attract. It was designed to keep the smoke away from the face and hair. She liked the image it created as if she were a star. When she came down the staircase Olitha and Sable commented on how different she appeared. Sable said, "Oh Miss Eveline you looks like a actress goin off to a show." Eveline smiled and thanked her for the compliment.

Eveline slowly moved her hips from side to side as she left the house. James had the car waiting at the curb. He helped her into the back seat and away they went. This time there was no swerving to avoid people and vehicles in the street. Eveline wanted to know why he was going so slowly. She told him she needed to go to the Geneva Savings Bank and she did not want to be late for her appearance. James stepped on the gas and they jolted forward. Eveline's hat nearly fell off as they turned the corner at 40mph. Eveline, a bit dazed, went into the bank. She was greeted by the same bank officer that had assisted Wallace and her when they had signed for 380 Washington Street, years ago. He gave Eveline a strange look as he studied her demeanor and shifty movements toward the teller. She placed the check on the counter and the teller motioned for the officer to come over. He looked at the amount, then looked at Eveline as smoke wafted from her cigarette holder and said, "Oh my dear Mrs. Paine, anything you need, we will be at your service." Eveline smiled sweetly and said, "It's Miss Eveline to you. I am no longer going by Mrs. Paine." He accepted her request and handed her a receipt. Eveline turned and blew some smoke in the air as she left the bank. James stood waiting by the open door and into the back seat she went. James was instructed to remain parked at the front of the restaurant until she was finished.

Lucille and Rose were waiting at the front door of the restaurant when Eveline made her way out of the car with James' assistance. She walked slowly toward the two women. Lucille was speechless, while Rose knew what Eveline was up to. Eveline had accomplished her goal of being the most up to the minute in fashion and mannerisms. During the wait to be seated, Rose was talking about going to Atlantic City as Eveline carefully used her cigarette holder. Smoke would occasionally puff out at Lucille. It was evident early on in the conversation that Lucille was not as important as she tried to be with her dealings with Eveline and Rose. While they were being polite to one another, Rudolph was announced as the piano player for the grand opening of the Hob-N-Nob Tearoom. Eveline asked Rose if she knew this. Rose shook her head no but Lucille was quick to announce that she knew quite a while ago. She explained that Rudolph had a meeting with her about some business dealings from New Jersey. Eveline continued to act as if she knew nothing. Lucille told her that the name of the import company had been changed and the commodities were not the same anymore. When Eveline heard that all she said was, "Oh." At least Rudolph told Lucille the correct information and now she was certain that Rudolph was doing as she instructed him to do. Lucille was thinking, as she spoke, that little did Eveline know that illegal commodities were being imported with her signature on the orders. Her hotel in Rochester was the stop off point for some of those items. Lucille had become the informant for rum runners that were smuggling alcohol into the country as well as children. They were using the older children to carry the shipments in their carriers as they came from the Caribbean and Europe. Yes, the commodities and stop off points had changed but not the operation that was now more profitable than ever. Lucille was proud of herself and knew she would get Eveline in the best way possible; her purse and reputation. The luncheon was pleasurable and the food was presented in a classy way. Rudolph was superb as he played many familiar arrangements. One of them was the music that Eveline played on her Victrola on New Year's

Eve. She wondered if he was playing just for her after what happened in her bedroom after the music stopped. After the luncheon, Eveline stopped at the A&P to see Hedy and Liza. When she walked into the store the workers stared as she made her way to the cheese department. It seemed that every time she went to the store the people stopped whatever they were doing to watch as if she was there is rob the place. The cheese department was in the back corner of the store so she had to go through the entire store to get to the cheese ladies. When they saw Eveline, they smiled and chatted about Patrick. Eveline told them his grandparents knew the story and were coming to visit him. Eveline was inviting them to come to her home for the day of the meeting. She reminded them that Patrick was ready for school and that he would be at her place for the last week of August. After that, he was going to a private boarding school in Syracuse. They looked like they were going to cry and Hedy said, "That means Patrick will be leaving all of us." Eveline explained that he would be home for vacations and they could visit him. She knew this was going to be more difficult than she thought. She reassured them it would work out and that it was time for Patrick to leave them. James helped her get into the back seat and while they were at the corner Eveline told James to pull around to the Lincoln Motor Car Dealer. He asked why. She told him she was interested in a sportier car than this big thing. She had seen advertisements for a two passenger roadster. It was a higher class car than a Ford. Even though she was a major shareholder of Ford Motor Company, she wanted to be a step above the rest and own something that might suit her better. She walked into the dealer with James and looked at the options. She found the Roadster and studied the details while James explained it was a very expensive fast moving vehicle. Eveline said, "That's exactly what I want." The price was $3,300.00. Eveline asked the salesman if there was a need for extras. He smiled and said, "Madame, if you can afford this car, it has all the extras." Eveline said, "Sold, I'll have my driver bring the money to you and he can bring the car home." She did the necessary paperwork and walked out with James who was shaking his head as he followed her to the car.

Eveline telephoned Alice and Frank and her mother and father to invite them to Geneva to meet Patrick. They were delighted. Mrs Lounsberry was being much more civil with Alice now that the past had been resolved. Mr. Lounsberry offered to be the driver, Alice and Frank accepted. They would arrive on Sunday and spend the day. Eveline realized that would be the first day she would have Patrick for the week before he went off to Manlius School. Sable and Olitha were instructed to plan a picnic style meal so they could spend most of the time outside. While they were at the store they could tell Hedy and Liza what time to bring Patrick, packed and ready, for his stay in his new home. Sable asked where Patrick was sleeping. Eveline had not thought about that and told them to go to the furniture store and get something that a boy would like. He could sleep in one of the bedrooms at the far end of the house, not to close to her bedroom. She did not want Patrick to hear or see anything coming from her bedroom. Olitha made a face and Sable said, "Miss Eveline dat you flesh and blood. Make sure you make him likes you." Eveline said nothing. She was more concerned with the trip to Atlantic City after Patrick was off to school. Eveline called Rose and invited them for the picnic on Sunday. Rose was excited that they were included and wanted to know what she could do. Eveline told her to bring something that a five year old boy would like. When Sable and Olitha returned from the A&P, they reported to Eveline that Hedy, Liza, and Patrick would be there at noon. Now all Eveline had to do was get through the day and hope that Patrick would like staying with her.

James went to the Lincoln Motor Car Dealer with thirty three one hundred dollar bills in his hand. The salesman had never seen so many bills in one spot. After a little chit chat about Eveline, the car was brought out to the front of the building. James was nervous about driving such a sporty and fast machine. The dealer told him to be careful with its power. It could go from zero to fifty mph in a few seconds. James laughed and wondered if Eveline was going into racing. When the car started to move James was afraid to step on the gas pedal. As he stepped on the pedal, it raced forward and he could not put the brake on fast enough. When he did, the car screeched to a stop. He was embarrassed as pedestrians laughed at the quickness of such a small vehicle. James tooted the horn as he drove into the driveway. Eveline, Sable, and Olitha came out to see the sporty vehicle. Eveline loved the midnight blue color. Now, she owned two automobiles; one for big groups and the other for herself and maybe another person. Olitha whispered to Sable, "Miss Eveline gone crazy spendin all Mr. Paine's moneys." Sable agreed and told Olitha to be quiet that they were living better than most Negra folk. Winston arrived while the car was being parked in the garage. He had no idea what Eveline had bought. She showed him the new addition to the garage. He thought it looked like a ride in a circus. Eveline made a face but did agree it was built for speed not show. Winston asked when they were going to see how it worked. Eveline explained that the weekend was filled with a picnic and Patrick was coming to stay with her until he goes to Manlius School on September 1st. Winston asked what he could do. Eveline reminded him of his behavior with his friends of the male persuasion. He made a face at her and asked if it would be different if he invited her to be included in their get togethers. Eveline moved closer to Winston and felt his groin and wanted to know what he was going to do with that thing. Sable shook her head and went into the house. Winston told Eveline that he saw Mike and he had an appointment to have some clothes fitted. Winston laughed when he told Eveline that the tailor was told to make certain that Winston's clothes fit perfectly to keep Miss Eveline happy. She listened and then told Winston the clothes were only for public events. The rest of the time she wanted to see all her men in little or nothing. She took a hold of Winston and felt his chest and recognized the LeterBuck scent. She asked when he had time to use that stuff. Winston smiled and said, "I just left Mike in the stockroom at the clothing store." Eveline stepped back and slapped Winston's chest and walked away. Winston yelled, "Sorry."

Patrick's furniture arrived on Saturday and Winston helped arrange it in the bedroom. Sable bought some curtains and toys for the room. Winston was as excited as if it were his son coming to stay. He went to the store and bought a heavy rope and found an old tire and made a swing in the back yard from a branch of a tree. Eveline watched him shimmy up the tree and tie the knot around the branch. She found this exciting to see Winston without his shirt with sweat glistening from his chest hairs.

She remembered the times he would appear like that on Washington Street when he was gardening. The pants he wore were torn in the knees and the crotch had ripped open. She went outside to have a closer look as she found the dirty and torn look stimulating, especially when he started to swing back and forth in the tire. Winston was acting like a kid when Eveline caught sight of what his ripped crotch was displaying from the swinging back and forth. She told him that Patrick might not understand his appearance and behavior. Eveline told him to keep those pants for a time when they could appreciate what pants like that could do for those watching him on a swing. Winston got off the tire and told Eveline they should learn how to use this in the house. They agreed it could be fun after Patrick was gone. Eveline smiled and told Winston that could be something to use for New Year's Eve activities. Winston said, "I can't wait for the year to be over."

Sunday arrived with the anticipation of what the day would bring. Sable was busy making her famous Southern fried chicken, potato salad, corn on the cob, and lemonade. She told Eveline, "Children like doz greezee things to eat. I likes to see all dat food on their faces and hands." Eveline corrected Sable and told her that Patrick was being raised to be a proper boy not a slob. Just as Eveline finished her speech to Sable about manners and proper upbringing, Olitha came into the room. She announced that the table was set in the yard and the lake was picture perfect. Nothing was going to ruin Patrick's meeting his family. When Eveline heard this she panicked with the thought that this was really happening and her son was arriving at her home. Somehow it seemed scarier than before. Now she wished Wallace was still alive to be a part of the day.

Sable sensed she was panicking. She said, "Miss Eveline you gonna be alright, Patrick a sweet boy. It is the beginnin of a new life for yous." Eveline still was not feeling good about her new responsibility. Maybe she should have had Patrick live with her and not ship him off in a week. Maybe Hedy and Liza would want to keep him since they knew more about him than she did. After a few minutes, Eveline felt better but was still uneasy about everything. Winston came into the room and asked why all the women in the place acted like the world was coming to an end. Sable piped up and said, "For some of us it may feel like it comin to an end or maybe just startin." Winston had a confused look on his face as he turned and left the room. Rose and Samuel arrived a few minutes before noon. Samuel sensed Eveline's mood and asked if she was going to be alright. She explained how she was feeling about what she was doing. Samuel offered to explain to the families more about how it all came about and why the lapse in years about knowing about Patrick. She thanked him just as Olitha was opening the door for Hedy, Liza, and Patrick. Patrick ran into the house and went directly to Eveline and said, "Hi, I'm Patrick." Eveline smiled and told him she knew that and hoped he liked being at her house for a picnic. At that moment, she was not sure if that was the right thing to do or say. Then, Winston walked in and said, "Hey bud, I'm Winston what's your name?" Patrick looked at Winston and smiled and told him he was Patrick. The women were all quiet as they were watching Patrick interact with the men and not so much with the women. Sable came into the room with a big chocolate cookie that had just come from the oven. He looked at her and said, "Hi Sable, is that my favorite cookie?" She handed it to him and he was happy and quiet. While all the introductions were happening Hedy, Liz, and Olitha were taking Patrick's belongings to his bedroom. They were surprised at how large the house was. Liza told them that Patrick would have a great time running around this big place and sliding down the banister to the front door. Olitha quietly said, "Miss Eveline in for a big surprise with the boy doin all those boy things." They laughed.

It was noon when the doorbell rang. Sable ran to the door and there stood the four grandparents. Sable laughed and said, "You all look like scared rabbits. Git youselfs in here and meet you grandbaby." They moved slowly into the vestibule all holding a stuffed animal. Eveline came into the foyer and welcomed them to her home. She kissed her father and mother. She went to Alice first and kissed her while Frank stood holding a huge elephant. Then Eveline went to Frank and wiggled her nose and kissed his cheek. He actually laughed and told everyone that nothing had changed with Eveline. While they were getting used to the idea of why they were standing in the house that was used for their son's funeral, Eveline asked if they would like to meet Patrick. Alice in her usual manner was teary eyed thinking of what he would look like and Mrs. Lounsberry was doing her usual quick fanning of herself. Mr. Lounsberry was disgusted with her and told her to slow it down. Frank was in a soldier stance. They followed Eveline as she called Patrick from wherever he had wandered off to. When he heard his name he ran from behind a curtain to scare everyone with half the cookie in his mouth. Everyone laughed when they saw him. Alice said, "Oh my God, he does look like a little Wallace, only with a suntan." Frank agreed, adding that Patrick had more curls than Wallace ever did. The Lounsberrys were in shock seeing a person so cute and little. It was difficult to believe he was part of the family. Patrick walked over and put his hand out and said, "Hi, I'm Patrick." They shook hands. Alice said she wanted to kiss him. Frank piped up and told everyone that was all she wanted to do with Wallace. She looked at Frank and sucked her teeth. Hedy and Liza came down from upstairs and were introduced by Samuel as the wonderful women that saved Patrick's life. He continued to explain why things evolved the way they had and why they were secretly caring for Patrick. For the first time, Eveline admitted that she appreciated all that had been done to help Patrick. She would not have been able to handle all that was going on five years ago. Then Sable walked into the room and said, "Are all yous gonna stand around talkin about old stuff? Dat dinner is waitin in the backyard." They laughed as they followed Sable to the table. Eveline thought that things were progressing better than she expected. While they were having dinner everyone watched Patrick in amazement realizing that he was their flesh and blood. Patrick was being a perfect little boy while eating. Then the questions began.

Mrs. Lounsberry wanted to know what plans were being made now that Patrick was with his mother. Before Eveline could respond conversations from others began. The Rochester group all wanted equal time with him and he was coming to stay with them whenever he wanted. Hedy and Liza were quiet and Eveline thought it was time to take control of the questions. She told everyone that Patrick was staying with her now and that he could go to Hedy and Liza's to see them whenever he wanted. Rose stared at Eveline because she knew where Patrick was being shipped off to. There was a pause and she told them she had investigated schools in Rochester for Patrick to enable him to be closer to his grandparents. No one seemed bothered by the news yet. Eveline went on to say that there were no boarding schools in Rochester. Upon hearing this, Mrs. Lounsberry assumed he could live with them. Alice looked at her and asked why with them. Before any more conversation occurred a conflict had begun and then Eveline told them he was going to a private boarding school outside of Syracuse. It was as if a bomb went off at the table. Winston kept on eating because he already knew the story and so did Rose. Everyone started talking at once and wanted to know how she could do such a thing after all the child had been through. Then Mrs. Lounsberry's colors showed when she said, "After those women raised him and now you are shipping him off to more strangers, how could you be so heartless?" Eveline glared at her mother and said, "I had a good teacher. You shipped me off to a girl's school. You were too busy for me and I'm too busy for Patrick." There was no remark made. Alice asked about the conditions of his education. Eveline thanked Alice for always being level headed. Frank grunted and Eveline glared at him. Alice was happy to know he would have a superior education and would be able to be home for vacations. She laughed and said, "Now we have a place to visit. We will be here for all the holidays." Eveline smiled and told everyone that time would work all the issues out. The dinner was tasty but the atmosphere was tense. Patrick and Winston had left the table and were playing on the rope and tire swing. Patrick liked it more than any stuffed animals or toys anyone had brought. Winston had more fun when Patrick would push him so he could go higher. Then it was Patrick's turn and he had as much fun as Winston. Meanwhile, the women were all in a tither about how dangerous it was for Patrick to be swinging on such a contraption.

The day was coming to a close and the ride back to Rochester was over an hour. Mr. Lounsberry told everyone they were leaving. Alice and Mrs. Lounsberry said they felt like they did not have time to get to know Patrick. Eveline assured them that they would see him again. Maybe they could go to Syracuse to visit him at school. The idea seemed to make the ending less difficult. Hedy and Liza were the first to go and told Patrick he was staying with Miss Eveline for a few days. They used the excuse that they were going on a vacation. Patrick was agreeable and ran around jumping on the furniture and being a typical child. Hedy and Liza were teary eyed as they kissed him good bye, but took comfort in knowing he was just down the street. Alice and Mrs. Lounsberry were more in shock about leaving and said that there was no telling when they may see him again. Eveline's mother went to her and said, "I thought you had grown up but some mother you are making." Eveline looked at her and said, "Goodbye mother, you must feel like you are looking at yourself in a mirror." No one said another word. They waved goodbye as they left the front of 775.

The next week turned out to be much more enjoyable than Eveline thought it would be. Patrick liked the big house and especially the tire swing. He would wait at the front door every night to watch for Winston. He knew Winston was his "bud" and would play with him. Eveline began reading him stories in the morning when he woke up and at night before going to sleep. Sable and Olitha filled the spot that Hedy and Liza left behind. Patrick knew Sable and Olitha from infancy so he felt at home. Eveline took Patrick to a clothing shop for children and dressed him up like he was a model in the store front window. He wore knee high socks with buckled shoes and shorts that had suspenders. He thought it was funny snapping them at Eveline when she walked by. Sable made everything he liked to eat and Olitha would take him for walks. Winston was crazy about him and treated him like the son he wished he had. Winston kept thinking that Patrick was his best friend's son. He made a promise to himself that he would stand by Patrick for Wallace. Eveline sat and wondered what next week would bring when they had to take him to Manlius Pebble Hill School.

CHAPTER 18

It was September 1, 1922 and the day had a frosty hint of autumn. As the sun rose over Seneca Lake, Eveline stood in front of the circular library windows and thought about what it was going to be like now that Patrick was in her life. Was she going to handle his life and hers so they would not interfere with one another? Was she dealing with the families correctly or should she have allowed them to be the caregivers to Patrick? She hated her mother's behavior and despised her for that and the nerve of her accusing her of being an unfit mother. While these thoughts raced through her head Patrick snuck around the corner and hid behind the chair. He peered out from the corner while Eveline moved closer to it to sit down. Just as she was seated, he jumped over the arm and landed in Eveline's lap. She screamed and Sable and Olitha ran to see what the matter was. As they entered the library, they found Patrick kissing Eveline's face giggling uncontrollably. Sable clapped her hands and said, "Hallelujah thank you Jesus theys lovin each other." Eveline made a face as if she was more stunned than anything else.

During breakfast, Eveline explained what they were doing today. Winston came into the room just as she was telling Patrick about what the school would be like. Patrick had a confused look on his face since school had no meaning to him. Winston interrupted as he sat next to Patrick with his arm around him and said, "Now bud, you have to go to a place where there will be lots of boys to play with and learn together. Miss Eveline and I are taking you to that school today. It will be like going on a vacation. We will come to visit you and bring you back here often." Patrick stared with his huge brown eyes that twinkled when he heard that Winston was going too. Patrick smiled and said, "Ok." Winston told them that he had a surprise. He had enough rope and found another tire that he was going to take to Patrick's new school so all the boys could use it. When Patrick heard this he went to his room with Olitha chasing after him. When they left Eveline made a face at Winston and said, "How do you know they will allow such a crude play thing at such a fancy school?" Winston explained that he would speak to the person in charge and show him how much fun it could be. Then Eveline said, "I hope you don't give your demonstrations in your crotch less pants." Winston said, "Only for you."

The luggage was packed with some of Patrick's toys and stuffed animals. James had the automobile parked in the front of the house. Eveline made a point of mentioning that she would be driving. James made a face and reminded her that she had a young and innocent five year old in the backseat. Eveline wanted to know what he was referring to. James only said to keep her hands on the wheel, not on Winston, and to be careful with how fast she drove. Eveline smirked at him as they took their seats. Sable and Olitha had their handkerchiefs wiping their teary eyes as the car went down the street. Before they were out of sight, the car swerved to avoid slow moving pedestrians and vehicles. Eveline, Winston, and Patrick arrived at the school in time for lunch. The chief administrator invited them to be seated with the boys that were Patrick's age. Eveline felt foolish dressed in her outfit. It looked like she was going to a dance or party. She sat down on one side of Patrick with Winston on the other. Winston helped Patrick and talked to him like they had been friends forever. One of the other boys asked if Winston was Patrick's father. Winston smiled as he looked at Patrick and said, "No, but I wish I was." Patrick smiled and Eveline thought about how good it would be if he were. After lunch, they went on a tour of the school and the grounds. It was on a creek side plot of land that looked like a postcard setting. Winston said he wished he could stay there too. The administrator smiled and told him that many parents felt that way. Winston felt proud that the administrator mentioned parents to him as if he were one. Eveline strolled behind the rest observing how Patrick was handling the new environment. Next, they were taken to the dormitory. Patrick would be sharing a room with a boy from New York City. He was unhappy because his parents sent him by train. He was stooped over his bed when Patrick and the others came into the room. Patrick went to the boy and said, "Hi, I'm Patrick." The boy looked up with tears in his eyes and said nothing. Patrick told the boy that his bud, Winston and Miss Eveline were with him. The boy said, "That's nice and started crying." Eveline felt horrible and hoped Patrick was not going to feel that bad after they left. Winston went to the boy and asked if he would like to help Patrick and him set up a swing. The administrator's face made a variety of movements when he listened to the type of project being proposed. Winston sat next to the boy and asked him his name. Between sniffles he said Andrew. By this time, Winston, Patrick, and Andrew were seated on the bed. Winston assured him that Patrick would be his good friend while Patrick sat with his hand on Winston's knee. Eveline wished she could be that good and understanding. Maybe it was good for the boys to have a man taking interest instead of the mother. The administrator asked Winston what the swing entailed. Winston stood up and told him that Patrick would show him and explain how it worked. The administrator turned to Eveline and asked, "How old is your son? He seems very advanced for a child that you claim is five years old." Eveline assured him he was five and that many people had helped in his early training. Patrick now led the group to the automobile to get the items for the swing. By now Andrew had forgotten about his sadness and helped Patrick roll the tire to a big tree near the back of the building. Winston carried the rope over his shoulder like a woodsman. Eveline and a nervous administrator walked behind. Patrick pointed to the largest branch and Winston shimmied up the tree. The administrator asked Eveline if he was an acrobat. She smiled and told him that he was a longtime friend of the family who worked in her printing company in Geneva. By this time, Winston was high in the tree tying the rope around the branch. Eveline smiled when she thought about what Winston was not showing this time while in the tree. It was not the time or place for one of his swinging demonstrations. Many of the boys were hanging out of the windows of the dormitory watching this fascinating thing being made. Winston tied the tire around the end of the rope. He was the first to try it out with Patrick pushing him. Andrew watched carefully so he could be next. Patrick asked Andrew if he wanted to try it. Andrew jumped up and down and went to Winston as he lifted him into the tire. Winston started slowly so Andrew would not be afraid. Before long he was laughing as the swing went higher. Patrick was next and wanted to show Andrew how to do it without any help. Winston was cheering them on like they were in a contest. Soon, most of the boys who were in the windows were running to the tree in hopes for a ride. The administrator's face looked like he feared a revolt. Everyone was surprised when Eveline told Patrick that she wanted to try the swing. Winston could not believe she would ever do such a thing. Patrick jumped up and down when Eveline sat in the tire and went back and forth. Her dress started blowing up to her waist and the administrator was mortified to see so much of a woman. Winston thought it was funny and told her it was good she was getting some practice in. Only she knew what he was referring to. During all the fun Patrick yelled, "Look everybody, that's my mother swinging." Eveline stopped short and could not believe her ears when he called her mother.

When it was time to leave, Eveline explained to Patrick that they would be back to see him. He smiled and kissed her and gave Winston a big "bud hug" as he put it. Patrick giggled when Winston tickled him. Andrew stood watching and Winston asked him if he wanted a "bud hug". Andrew smiled and shook his head yes. On the way back to Geneva, they discussed the day and Eveline thanked Winston for being so good to the boys. They laughed about how the administrator was so nervous about anything that might be different. Eveline said, "He would die if he knew how different we are." Winston asked why Eveline wanted to try the swing. She told him she wanted Patrick to see her in a different way. Her mother never would have acted like that and she wanted Patrick to see her as fun, but was surprised when the word "mother" came out of his mouth. Winston told her he thought that was good. Eveline was not sure "mother" was what she wanted to hear just yet. It seemed too permanent.

CHAPTER 19

The next day Eveline telephoned Rudolph to remind him of their date for the Eastman Theater opening and the meeting at the hotel with Mike Bennett. Rudolph was looking forward to the opening ceremonies at the theater but had some troubling news about Mike Bennett. Rudolph was not able to be in contact with him in the last few days. Eveline wanted to know what might have happened. All Rudolph knew was that the last time he saw him he was not behaving in his usual fashion. Rudolph told her that he was evasive when he questioned Mike about the sale of the hotel. When Eveline heard this she knew something was not right. Rudolph assured her that the appraisal of the hotel was done. When he told her that, he knew he was lying, but hoped that might calm some of Eveline's worries. When they ended the conversation, he told her he would be at her home by 10AM so they would have ample time to get to Rochester.

When Eveline put the receiver down she had a strange feeling the story she just heard was not true.

Rudolph arrived at 10 AM. Eveline was dressed in her usual flapper attire giving her the feeling of freedom. Rudolph remarked at how different she had been lately. He remarked about her outfit as Sable and Olitha stood next to her in their dowdy maid's outfits. Eveline wanted to know if Rudolph knew why they were referred to as flappers. He did not know but knew it had to do with women and the way a liberated woman was acting these days. Eveline corrected him and said, "Flapper my dear, means we are considered a new breed of woman flapping our arms for all to see and hear." She continued to give her description of what she thought a flapper might be like. She propped herself on the bannister with one foot on the higher step and one hand on her hip and said, "Flappers are women who wear excessive makeup, like to drink, treat sex in a casual manner, smoke, and drive fast cars." When Sable heard that she said, "Amen we duz have a flapper in dis house. She like a bird flappin her wings." Eveline smiled at them and reminded them that she was the one in charge of everything now. At that, she motioned to Rudolph that it was time to go. They went to the sidewalk where James had parked her new Lincoln. Rudolph had not seen it yet. Eveline walked promptly to the driver's side and told Rudolph that he was in for the ride of his life.

They were in Rochester in record time. They flew through small towns with the dust flying behind them as if a wind storm had blown through. Eveline made a point of coming to an abrupt stop when they were in front of the hotel. The valet attendants could not believe it was

Mrs. Paine driving in such a car with such speed. She got out of the automobile and instructed the attendant to get the automobile washed and cleaned inside before she returned. She reminded them that she was no longer being referred to as Mrs. Paine and that it was now Miss Eveline. Rudolph stood motionless when he listened to her directions and demands. She lit up a cigarette in her fancy holder and strolled into the lobby with her white fur wrap thrown over her shoulder. This time Rudolph was following her not at her side. She went to Mike Bennett's office. Rudolph kept telling her that he was not going to be there. When she opened the door he was there, but DEAD. She screamed and Rudolph called for help. He went to the desk where Mike was face down in a pool of blood. There was a pile of papers on the desk with blood splashed on the top one. Rudolph picked them up to find the evaluation of the hotel. Eveline did not seem overly upset about the crime but asked Rudolph if he knew who might have wanted him killed. He told her that crimes such as this were occurring because of black market business. Eveline asked, "Was Mike involved in this type of activity?" Rudolph said he did not know but wondered to himself if there might have been a connection to the new Foreign Exchange Program he established. The police and a doctor came to investigate and thought Mike had been dead for about six hours. When Rudolph heard this he wondered if Bennett's murder had anything to do with the sale of the hotel. Maybe he was killed so Eveline would not deal with the sale now. Who would know enough about this to have arranged his death?

Rudolph and Eveline went to another office to study the facts while the body was taken away. Rudolph wiped the blood off the first page while Eveline made sickening faces at the paper. Rudolph pointed out that the hotel was worth $225,000.00 not including the furnishings, which would be a negotiable item. Eveline pondered the idea while Rudolph pointed out that she could earn $50,000.00 more if she waited a few years to sell. Rudolph hoped she would dismiss any idea of a sale at this time. While she looked at the figures an investigator came into the office asking for Rudolph Williams. Eveline looked puzzled as the man asked what association he had with the late Mr. Bennett. Rudolph explained that he was his boss and Eveline was the owner of the hotel. Then he said, "Oh you must be Mrs. Paine. We have been advised to watch for questionable TOE&TIC dealings." Rudolph's face turned red and Eveline replied, "Oh that company you are referring to has been dissolved when I found out what the company was doing." The investigator seemed relatively satisfied but asked Rudolph if the hotel was being used for anything other than for guest purposes. Rudolph paused and took a deep breath and denied any other operations in the hotel except for the shops on the main floor. The investigator thanked them and before he left he explained that there were places in town that were being watched for transferring illegal substances from Canada. Since Rochester was 45 miles across Lake Ontario to Canada and a closed port, things could be smuggled into the country more easily than other cities. He left and Eveline wanted to know what that was all about. Rudolph acted like he knew nothing of what the investigator was referring too. Eveline told him she believed him but played it cool waiting to see what was going to happen next. Rudolph, on the other hand, was sweating in his shoes when the word transfer was mentioned. This was part of his plan to destroy

Eveline. She decided to play along with the story and told Rudolph that the hotel would not go on the market. She told him, "When we return from Atlantic City you are being transferred here as manager of my hotel. Now that you no longer work for the Chamber of Commerce you have no reason to be in Geneva. I will be in charge of your responsibilities to all the companies." Rudolph told her she could not do that to him because he was trustee to Wallace's estate. Eveline turned saying, "I just did. If you don't want to do as you are instructed you will be fired for insubordination. Remember who the boss is now. Wallace is dead."

It was time to go to the Eastman Theater. Eveline drove to the front of the theater and the valet parked the automobile while Eveline and Rudolph were ushered to the main foyer. Eveline's tickets were for the best seats in the theater. She was in her glory as she paraded through to the main entrance. The decorations and lighting were exquisite and as they found their seats they could see how the walls were painted with various scenes. When they sat down and looked up, there was a huge crystal chandelier that was similar to the one in Mr. Eastman's music room only this one was gigantic compared to the one in his home. The program explained that the theater could hold over 3000 people and was constructed by George Eastman for various occasions. The primary purpose was to be a moving picture house with a piano player that would play music to the action on the screen. The theater could be used as a music hall and there would be a performance by an orchestra that evening. It was truly an impressive environment and one that was sure to please everyone. When the theater was full, the lights dimmed as people looked around to see what was about to happen. When the lights came up again, Mr. Eastman appeared on stage and welcomed his guests to his new theater. He explained it would be a part of the Eastman School of Music and the University of Rochester. Mr. Eastman gave a short speech about why he built the theater and why he wanted to offer arts and music to the community long after he was gone. He had his mother stand so she could be recognized for her strong support of him throughout his life. An orchestra was ready to give a concert and a reception was being held at the conclusion. The lights dimmed again as the music began. Afterward, Mr. Eastman received guests in the lobby. When Eveline and Rudolph moved closer to him, he recognized Rudolph first. He came to them and was delighted to see them. The first thing he did was express his sorrow for Wallace's death. He remarked about how much of an impression they made on him many years ago at his soirée. Eveline's eyes lit up when she heard this and thanked him for remembering her for the grand opening of the theater. Before he moved on he said he would love to have them come for another soirée at his home because Mrs. Paine was one of his best investors. She accepted. It was getting late and the ride back to Geneva would take more time because it was dark. Eveline admitted she would not be able to drive as fast as she did earlier. Rudolph had very little to say during the ride home. Eveline was determined not to encourage him. She knew why he was quiet and did not care because this was part of her plan to put Rudolph in his place.

CHAPTER 20

I t was September 5th and everyone was to be at the train
station at noon to go to Atlantic City. While they were
packing luggage and making last minute arrangements,
the telephone rang and Olitha answered it. She directed
the call to Eveline. It was the chief administrator from
Manlius School calling to give her some news. Eveline
thought something had happened to Patrick. The news
was about Andrew. Eveline asked why she needed to know
about Andrew. He told Eveline that Andrew's parents
were killed in a speakeasy in New York City. Eveline's face
turned red as she asked what was happening to Andrew.
The administrator wanted her to know Andrew had no
other family and that he was to remain at the school under
their care until he was old enough to go to West Point.
By this time, Winston was standing there with Sable and
Olitha, thinking something was wrong with Patrick. She
thanked him and set the receiver down. She told them the

news about the shooting. The minute Winston heard that he said, "I had a feeling something would happen today. It was 21 years ago that President McKinley was shot and now we know someone whose parents were killed." Eveline said, "I feel so bad for sweet little Andrew. What will happen to him in school when no one comes to see or love him?" Winston piped up and said, "We can take care of him and bring him here with Patrick." Sable said, "I am used to havin loads of youngins runnin around and the more the merrier." Eveline smiled and said, "Well, the house is big enough to have two boys. Maybe they will let us bring Andrew home for vacations and holidays." Winston was ecstatic over the idea of having his two "buds" to play with and care for. It was almost noon and time to go to the train station.

As everyone gathered at the station there was conversation about what it was going to be like in Atlantic City. Eveline told everyone the news about Patrick's roommate and how she might take care of him when Patrick was home. Rose was the most surprised with the news because Eveline was not sure she even wanted Patrick. Eveline explained it would be only for times when Patrick was home. Winston was quick to tell about how excited he was to have two "buds" to care for. Sable shook her head and said, "My, my, sounds like Miss Eveline fillin up da big house." Rudolph remained the quietest of all because he was feeling left out and the thought of moving back to Rochester was bothering him. Eveline noticed his mood but did not address it and no one else seemed to notice. It took 8 hours to get to Atlantic City but when the train pulled into the station it was like a city of light and action. They got their luggage and hailed a driver to take them to the Shelburn Hotel on the corner of Michigan Avenue and Boardwalk. The driver told them they were staying in one of the finest hotels in town. Eveline explained that she liked the sound of Michigan Avenue because it reminded her of Chicago. When they walked into the lobby, they were greeted by a staff member that was part of the amenities of penthouse living. Sable and Olitha were the most stunned because they thought that was why they were coming along for the vacation. Eveline mentioned that she had told a white lie. If she told them about the staff, they would not have come. Sable and Olitha both said, "We news you was up to sumpin when you told us we was servants. We thought weez your friend too." Eveline said, "I have lots of tricks up my sleeve that none of you know about." They entered the penthouse to find fresh flowers in every room and were escorted to the balcony to see the lights of the Boardwalk and the amusements below. Winston said he felt like he was back at the Pan-American Exposition. Samuel asked him what he was talking about. Winston said, "You, Wallace, and I were at the Pan-Am. President McKinley got shot then and now Andrew's parents. I feel like I am reliving the past but in a different place and time." Eveline discussed the sleeping arrangements. Sable and Olitha were in one room. Winston, Rudolph, and Mike were in another room. Winston's eyes went up when he heard this. He could not wait to be in the same room with Rudolph and remembered the things he had done to him in the past. Rose and Samuel were together and Eveline jokingly asked them if they wanted to go to a different room with someone else. Winston spoke up and said, "Come on Samuel, we will make room for you." Rose told them he was hers and was not sharing him. Eveline had the best room with an ocean view and a private balcony.

Eveline told the men that they could come to her room if they were too cramped. She would love to share her bed with each of them or all at once. The women's eyes rolled up as they went to their rooms to unpack.

During breakfast on the veranda overlooking the Boardwalk, everyone was a buzz about what they had planned for the day. It was their free day before the Miss America Pageant. The women were going shopping. The men were going to the amusements and the Ferris Wheel they saw off in the distance. When they appeared in the lobby it was hilarious to see Winston in a bathing suit. It looked like full body underwear with his genitals flopping around as he walked. Samuel was more reserved and wore trousers and a shirt with a panama hat. Rudolph as usual, was overdressed in a summer suit and straw hat. Mike wanted to be just like Winston so he wore the same bathing suit only his genital were not nearly as noticeable. Eveline wore a flowery dress with a huge brimmed hat. Rose had on a similar dress, only with a scarf around her head and a pair of Shuron Sunwear glasses. Eveline surprised Rose when she pulled out a pair just like it for herself. Sable and Olitha decided to stay back and relax on the beach and pretend they were wealthy travelers. As a gift to Sable and Olitha, Eveline gave them each a pair of Sunwear glasses with white frames. Sable laughed and said to Olitha, "Oh girl, weez lookin fine like important girls now. Maybe weez gonna find a real man out there." Everyone was in hysterics when they realized how much fun they were about to have. They agreed to meet at 4PM to rest and get ready for the evening. Eveline reminded them that they were going to a dancehall after dinner.

Winston and Mike spent most of the day at the amusement park and swimming in the ocean. Each time they got out of the water they looked at how their bathing suits clung to their bodies outlining the size of their muscles. Mike told Winston he wished he was as well-endowed as he was. Winston told him that he did not need to worry about that. Mike knew why. Samuel and Rudolph were not as adventurous; they went to a restaurant with their newspapers and magazines. They spent most of the day people watching and enjoying the warm ocean breezes. Rose and Eveline were being pushed along the Boardwalk in a roller chair built for two. They saw Samuel and Rudolph and stopped to brag about how the wealthy people got around in Atlantic City. The buggy style chairs were full of their purchases. Eveline remarked at how much fun they were having spending Wallace's money. Neither man thought that was very funny but knew there was no changing her mind. Olitha and Sable were having the time of their life being waited on by handsome men that worked for the hotel. They brought them anything they wanted to eat or drink to their beach chairs. Olitha spotted a Negro man and made eyes at him and he came over to chat. Sable watched Olitha make the move on him and before she knew it they were off somewhere. Sable was amazed at how quickly Olitha caught a man. She wondered if Olitha was ever coming back. Sable said to herself, "This place is makin wild peoples and Lord knows what theys all doin to each other."

Everyone arrived at the hotel except Olitha. Sable said very little. Everyone had to tell their story of buying things and people watching. Winston and Mike told about their over active enjoyment of the amusement park. Sable sat quietly and told them about how nice the beach was and that there were servants at the beach. Rose asked what happened to Olitha. Sable in a coy way smiled and told them Olitha found a man. Laughter broke out and Eveline said, "Good for her. I hope she gets all the things I like to get out of a man as she looked at Winston and Rudolph." Mike sat quietly, because he had no contact with anyone except Winston. Just as they were discussing Olitha, she came in. She realized that she must have been the topic of conversation because it all stopped when she arrived. She had flushed cheeks and was a bit messed up. Sable asked, "So how was your man?" Olitha said, "Perfect, he gave me drinks in his cabana house. He made me feel like a real lady. He made love to me in a way I jest never knew could happen and touched me in places I know nothin about. I think he musta come from another country because he had a thing so big I wasn't sure if I could take it" No one knew what to ask or say next about her encounter. Then Winston, in a smart tone said, "Now you can be just like Eveline. She likes it anyway she can get it." No one said a word.

After a scrumptious dinner on the veranda, it was time to go to a dance hall. The men were not as eager to go until Rudolph and Winston told the group about the New Year's party Eveline had a year ago. Rose wanted to know why it had anything to do with tonight. Eveline watched the two men tell about the music Eveline played on her Victrola and how she danced with both of them. Rudolph was most interesting with his description of the tango using a rose in his teeth as part of the dance. While they were being escorted in the roller chairs, Eveline asked the driver operating it, where a good place might be to go for dancing.

He knew exactly where to take them and pulled up in front of a restaurant. Eveline told him he must be mistaken because she wanted to dance. He had all of them get in a group and began to whisper. He explained as everyone was straining to hear him that they were going into a place that had dancing and other things. Samuel wanted to know what other things he was referring to. The man told them it was called a "speakeasy" and you needed to speak softly so you could not be heard when ordering a drink. He gave the evil eye and then they understood that alcohol was served in a quiet private way. It was Prohibition and illegal to serve alcohol. The man explained that the dancing was the best in town. Rudolph gave the man a large tip for his work and information. All the women except Eveline were reluctant to go inside. Eveline told them they could go back to the hotel and sit like old ladies but she had four men at her side, so in they walked. The women followed too. As they were going in to the dance hall Mike mentioned the word "moonshine". Rudolph told him to be quiet because a place such as this would never serve such cheap stuff. Mike told him that was more powerful than anything that could be bought in a place like this. Eveline reminded Rudolph of his drunken behavior when he had too much "hooch." He was embarrassed when she told everyone how she threw him out of her house because he was drunk on it. They moved in closer and found a lively environment. One of the groups was telling how music and dance had changed. The Foxtrot, Waltz, and Tango were the latest craze in dancing. The more radical and eccentric dances were the Breakaway and Charleston. The dances were based on Negro musical styles and beats. Sable and Olitha were having a great time because the beat of music had been part of their background and it took no time for them to start moving around the floor looking for dance partners. Winston went to Eveline and started to kick up his feet. Eveline had practiced the Charleston and had learned how to kick backward, shake, and shimmy around the floor. She wore long beads around her neck and a loose fitting dress so everything flapped around as she kicked up her heels and waved her arms around. They were the show on the dance floor. Eventually they were all shimmying and kicking up their heels.

It was closing time and no one wanted to leave but were told they had to be out in ten minutes. They arrived at the hotel and took their respective bedrooms. Eveline invited Rudolph to spend the night with her. The others wondered why him and no one else. They were too tired to question anything Eveline wanted to do. Winston had other ideas for Mike after spending the day with him. When he got him in the bedroom he told him, "Now I'm going to show you why I'm more interested in your back side than your front." Mike gave Winston a devilish smile. Rudolph on the other hand was at Eveline's mercy. She helped Rudolph unfasten his clothing. She maneuvered her hands in his trousers to tantalize him. He kept thinking how pleasurable it was and wondered what he might be allowed to do with her. When she had his clothes off and was stroking his body she told him to get in bed and that she would be out of the bathroom in a minute. He did as she instructed and waited. His eyes were closed and he felt his body was ready to explode with pleasure. Eveline came out and found that Rudolph had dozed off. She took a cloth and stuffed it in his mouth and quickly tied his hands before he knew what had happened. She put her finger to his lips and told him to be quiet or he would not have any fun. Then she tied his ankles. There he lay stark naked, on his back. She took a feather from her hat and began moving it across his body using quick movements on the most sensitive areas. He could not speak, only moan. She took a few pins from her hat and touched his nipples with the points as she moved the feather that was in her mouth. She wore a black hooded cape and made suggestive remarks as she moved her head to his groin to tantalize him. Rudolph's eyes stayed closed because Eveline threatened that the pins would do more than tease his body if he lost control or disobeyed her. After she had finished pleasing herself, she told him he could get out, but not to tell anyone what she did with him. If he breathed a word of this, she would do more than use pins on him. Rudolph enjoyed her sexual dominance better than her behavior with him in business.

CHAPTER 21

September 7, 1922, Atlantic City was a buzz about the Miss America Pageant being held at the Million Dollar Pier. Eveline was the first to be at breakfast and wondered why it was taking everyone so long to get downstairs. Rose and Samuel were next to arrive. Samuel was dressed casual compared to Rose who was dressed as if she were in the Miss America Pageant. She wore a sundress that opened when untied to show a fancy bathing suit. She informed Eveline that the daytime events were being held along the Boardwalk. Eveline wanted to know how she knew about the day. She smiled and told Eveline that she had the paper delivered to the room early that morning. After that, Eveline decided that she needed a more appropriate outfit for the day. As she was leaving the table, Olitha and Sable appeared. They seemed uneasy. Eveline stopped them and inquired about how they were doing. Sable mentioned that she slept well but she looked at Olitha and shook her head and said, "This girl can't get enough of her new man. She gone out after weez got back last night and she just came to the room." Olitha looked like she was ready to drop. Eveline asked if she needed to stay in and rest. Olitha shook her head no and said, "I can't get enough of dat new man. He more than I can handle it but I keeps tryin." She told Eveline she was not going to the events today but had to get back to her man's cabana. Eveline warned her to be careful because they were in a resort town and everyone was out to have a good time and no one cared what happened. Olitha went on her way and Sable sat with Samuel and Rose. The three men were leaving the penthouse as Eveline came to the door. They too looked like they had been out all night. Eveline asked if they rested well. Winston spoke up and told her they had but all in the same bed. Rudolph was walking in a strange way like he had been horseback riding. Eveline smiled and told them he needed to take it like a man. He made a face at her as she closed the door.

A fashion show given by the contestants was held on the beach near the pier. Tables and umbrellas were set around an enclosed area and a platform was constructed for the contestants to walk on instead of the sand. Eveline had reserved a table for lunch but now that Olitha had better things to do they would have one seat open. Eveline was not happy about Olitha's sudden change of behavior. The men decided to do the same things they did yesterday because they were not as interested as the women were about a beauty contest. Everyone went their separate ways. The women enjoyed their breakfast in the breezy warm sunshine. Just as they were leaving the restaurant, a roller chair came toward them on the Boardwalk. It was Margaret

Gorman who was the first Miss Washington, D.C. in 1921. She waved to everyone as her roller chair passed by. She was dressed in a fashionable outfit and wore a huge brimmed sun hat with white sunglasses. Eveline noticed that they were Shuron sun wear glasses that she, Rose, and Sable were wearing. When Miss Gorman spotted the women she told the man to stop the chair. She stepped off and went to them and admired their stylish glasses. They giggled and Eveline said, "Yes, I am the owner of the company that manufactures them." Miss Gorman was impressed and inquired where they came from. Eveline told her Geneva, NY. Miss Gorman was not sure where that was but was happy to have met someone who knew about the glasses. Eveline told Miss Gorman that her late husband began advertising these glasses a few years ago. Miss Gorman asked about the company and what it was like to be the owner. Rose and Sable watched Eveline go into her discussion about how important it was for women to move into management positions whenever possible. Rose could not stand to listen to anymore of Eveline trying to impress the women. She spoke up and reminded Eveline that if her husband did not die she would not be in a position to manage a company. Eveline looked at Rose with a writhing look and stopped. Miss Gorman politely left the group and resumed her ride on the Boardwalk waving to the people. Eveline asked why Rose said such things. Rose said, "You were acting like a spoiled woman taking advantage of her dead husband." Eveline admitted she did not handle the conversation very well.

While Winston and Mike were swimming in the ocean and having fun on the roller coaster they heard a song being played. It was a man singing to a woman about being by the sea and there were children around them. Winston thought it was a catchy tune so he went to see where it was coming from. He listened so he could memorize it and sing it to Eveline. The words were: *By the sea, By the sea, By the beautiful sea, You and me, You and me, Oh how happy we will be.* There was a women and man dancing as they sang the song. Mike wanted to know why Winston was so excited about the song. He told Mike he thought it would be fun to dress in his bathing suit and sing it to her. The entertainers were dressed in swim wear so that gave Winston the idea. Mike thought he was crazy but Winston told him he now had a new responsibility at home. Mike asked what that might be. Winston told him he was in charge of being Patrick and Andrew's new "bud" and wanted them to see him as an important part of the family. Mike wanted to know if Winston was falling for Eveline. Winston shook his head no but explained that they had a long time friendship and now she had a family. Mike turned and went in the other direction.

The afternoon events included a luncheon served by handsome and virile waiters. Even Rose noticed how accommodating they were to the women. Every now and then one of the men would escort a woman away from the tables. Rose mentioned that to Eveline, who wondered about that herself. While they were speaking about that Sable explained that she had worked a long time ago for an event like this when she first came to the United States. She told Eveline and Rose that those men were not just serving food they were serving themselves to the wealthy women that wanted some action. When they heard that Rose wanted to know which one they would take. Eveline explained she had enough action at home and if Rose wanted to go she should because her life seemed boring. Rose was offended at first but did say she wanted to try out the muscular blond that was eyeing her. Eveline encouraged her to attract his attention. Rose in a shy way looked and caught his eye and he was at the table in a flash. Eveline told her that Atlantic City was a place to have fun and she would never tell. Sable shook her head and said, "Girl, you go for it. Now it just Miss Eveline and me." When the man heard that he offered himself to all of them at once. Eveline was even taken back by the suggestion. She refused and told Rose to have a good time. The man winked and said she was in for the ride of her life. The Bather's Review contest began. The contestants were judged on their charm and the way they walked on high heels in a bathing suit. The colors were grand and the music was perfect for the parade of beauties. Eveline jokingly told Sable that they should have entered. Sable laughed hysterically and said, "Oh my Lord, my thighs would be shakin all over the beach in an outfit like that." Eveline laughed and thought it would be quite amusing. After the parade, Miss Gorman appeared on the stage and announced the winner of the Bather's Review who was a young woman from New York. Miss Gorman gave her a pair of white Shuron sun wear glasses. When she placed them on the woman's face she announced that there were other stylish women in the audience that wore the same glasses. She asked Eveline and Sable to stand and wanted Eveline to explain where and how they were developed. Miss Gorman wanted to know where the other woman was. Sable spoke up first and said, "That girl off with a blond muscle man for a ride of her life." The audience roared with laughter and Miss Gorman responded, "Good for her." Eveline explained where the glasses came from and how her late husband developed the advertisement for them. The audience applauded when Eveline finished. She turned to Sable and said, "Oh I wish that Rose was here to have heard all that after what she told me earlier about being overdone." Miss Gorman announced that there were 300,000 people in Atlantic City for the event. She explained about the evening events that were to be held inside the Million Dollar Pier at 8PM.

It was the last night in Atlantic City. On the way back to the hotel Eveline thought about some fun things she could do after the pageant. She thought it might be fun to have a Mr. America Pageant in the penthouse. When Sable heard that she wanted to know who were going to be the judges and what the men were supposed to do. Eveline smiled with a sly look and did not answer her questions. When they walked into the penthouse Rudolph and Samuel were the only ones there. Samuel wanted to know where Rose was. Eveline hesitated and told him that she was shopping for something big. Sable's eyes opened so large they looked like saucers when she heard that answer. Samuel did not ask anymore. Olitha, Winston, and Mike were not there yet. Eveline went into her room to rest until dinner time as she thought about the little pageant she was planning for that evening. Winston and Mike arrived shortly after Eveline left the room. They paraded in their wet suits and Rudolph asked, "So, did you two have enough fun in the ocean?" Winston was happy to announce that he got Mike's suit off in the water and had his way with him and would not give his suit back. Mike said he was beginning to worry about what might happen if Winston left him naked in the water. Samuel said, "I'm sure a mermaid might come to rescue you." Mike made a face as he left the room. Shortly after that Olitha came in. She was more disheveled than the last time. The men did not know she went out by herself that day. Samuel wanted to know if she was okay. She did not say too much except she had a lot of work to do to get ready for the evening. Rudolph shook his head and said, "These women are so unpredictable." Samuel looked at his watch, it was 6PM. There was no sign of Rose. At 6:15 Rose hurried into the penthouse. Samuel asked her if she got what she was looking for. Not knowing what Eveline had said about her shopping for something big, she blurted out, "How did you find out?" Then she tried to cover her tracks and said, "I was looking for something and I lost track of time." Just as she finished Eveline walked out and asked the same question, "Did you get something big?" Rose's face turned scarlet and she said, "I should have never left because I ended up on a ride of my life." Sable heard that and said, "Oh girl you do looks like you been on a bumpy ride for sure. You best go soak that behind in a tub and gets ready for this evening. Miss Eveline got a surprise for us tonight."

The finale of the pageant began with a lavish dinner at the Million Dollar Pier. Miss Margaret Gorman began the evening explaining what the contestants would be judged on. They had to sing, dance, and tell a story. They were dressed in evening gowns and would be judged on poise and personality. While she was explaining these things, Winston told everyone that he was glad he did not have to perform that night. Eveline smiled and devilishly said, "What makes you think you won't have to perform tonight?" No one dared continue to question her. Lately, Eveline was unpredictable and usually had a reason for everything she said. After the contestants performed their acts, the judges took a few moments before the winner was announced. You could hear the women all saying, "It's about time women are being recognized for more than staying home." When Eveline heard that she told her table that those women had not been as involved as we were about Women's Rights and voting issues. Rose laughed and said, "We were lucky we were free to do what we wanted." Samuel shook his head and looked at Rose and still wondered what she had been up to all afternoon. Margaret Gorman called for attention as she began reading the name of the winner of the Miss America Pageant 1922. It was given to 17 year old Katherine Campbell from Columbus, Ohio. The audience applauded for minutes as she was given a white fur cape and huge bouquet of red roses. Some people were heard saying that she was too young and inexperienced to know what to do with the title. She gave an acceptance speech and thanked the audience for attending. There was dancing afterward but Eveline suggested they return to the penthouse.

No one knew what to expect when Eveline was so eager to get back to the penthouse. When they arrived the door opened and there was one of the muscular and well-endowed waiters from the afternoon's luncheon. Eveline had arranged for him to be on duty for the evening. She said as he stood in a loin cloth that he was in charge of the Mr. America Pageant. Sable and Olitha could only stare and Rose was too busy worrying about who Eveline may have hired for the rest of the night. Winston and Mike were so excited they wanted to know if he brought the same outfits for the men. He told them yes and that they were going to part of the contest. Sable said, "I suppose weez women gonna be the judges." He told her she was correct and the women could have a seat. Eveline referred to the man as Mr. Loins. He sensed Rudolph's uneasiness. He went to him and asked if he wanted to be the first to demonstrate how his outfit would look on him. Rudolph refused but Winston was half undressed while Rudolph made excuses why he could not be first. Winston knew why because of all the undergarments Rudolph wore. It would take him half the night to get ready. Mr. Loins told Rudolph he could be last. Samuel looked at Rose and she said, "You accused me of looking for something big so let them see what you have." Mr. Loins smiled at Samuel as he handed him the outfit. Mike was as anxious as Winston to model their loin cloths. The women were seated as Mr. Loins served some drinks and said as he gave it to them, "Speakeasy girls." They giggled and waited for what was to happen next. Just as they were waiting for the private show, there was a knock on the door. Eveline answered the door and there stood a huge Negro man and another muscular white man. Eveline thought they looked like salt and pepper standing next to each other. They walked in and went to Mr. Loins. They acted like they were going to wrestle with him but instead picked him up and swung him in the air. While that was happening his loin cloth fell off and there was nothing left to the imagination. He was bounced up and down and then dropped on the women's laps. All that could be seen now was skin, no loin cloth. The other men were trying to get themselves ready when all this was happening. Eveline knew this was going to happen because she arranged it earlier with Mr. Loins. The men posed for the women who were beginning to feel aroused by the men's gyrations. They walked around and felt themselves and offered for the women to do the same to them. Eveline was the first to make the move. Sable decided it was her last night so she moved in on the Negro who had muscles and just the right amount of manhood she liked. Rose was still trying to settle down from her afternoon escapade and now more of the same thing was being offered to her. Olitha was standing by the door where Winston, Samuel, Mike, and Rudolph were trying to get ready to appear in loincloths. She opened the door and Samuel came out first. Eveline was surprised at his physique and looked at Rose and said, "So what's your problem, he's got enough for you and someone else." Then Mike came out and he was the shyest one. According to Rose he was the most ordinary one of all. Eveline made a smart remark and said, "Now I can see why Winston likes your backside." Mike smiled and turned around to show off his firm buttocks and told everyone that is all he needs to offer. Winston came out in his loincloth that could hardly be seen because of all the dark hair around his legs and back. Olitha looked at him and said, "Oh Winston honey, weez seen that thing so much it makes no matter where it is or how big it is." Winston was proud to have such a reputation. Then out came Rudolph. When Mr. Loins saw Rudolph's physique and manly features he went to him and said, "I think you should stay in Atlantic City so you and I can do shows for women and men." While he was saying that he was fondling Rudolph to see how excited he could make him. Eveline thought that staying in Atlantic City might be a good idea and a way to get rid of him.

After the men were lined up, Mr. Loins explained that Atlantic City was a playground for people and anything was possible. There were lots of crime, drugs, murders, and sex of all types. He explained he liked the entertaining part along with the sex that resulted in good entertainment. The women began to stir in their seats. Olitha was thinking about all of her action in the last days and thought she could take no more. Sable was beginning to think more seriously about the Negro who was there. Rose knew she had to behave after her experience that afternoon. Eveline, on the other hand, was ready for all of them. She had no problem explaining that to the group. Winston spoke up and told them, "That's our Miss Eveline." They laughed as the men were lined up for the first contest. They were to pose like it was a muscle contest. This was not too demanding or so they thought. The next was to flex any part of their body. Most did their legs or biceps. Mr. Loins demonstrated by flexing his entire anatomy and twitched his manhood. While this was happening Olitha told them that he was as big as her man. Sable said, "Lucky you girl." The other two men proceeded to do the same as Mr. Loins. Winston was next and flexed his body just as the others were doing while he watched Eveline take pleasure in his performance. Rudolph was next and was as good as the other guys. Mr. Loins still had his eye on Rudolph's abilities. The last part was the touching event. Mr. Loins explained that women were allowed to touch and work any part of the men's bodies. They could tease the men to see how long it would take before they lost control of themselves. That was the part the women were waiting for. They had the best time feeling, massaging, and fondling the men. The hired men were given the most attention from the women except Rudolph was manipulated mostly by Eveline as she continually pulled and yanked on him. Winston had a great time allowing the women work on his front and backside. He had taught himself lots of self-control in activities such as this. The others had to stop long before Winston. The Negro became so excited he was eliminated within the first few seconds. Mr. Loins asked Winston if he gave lessons on sexual self-control. He laughed and admitted he did have lots of practice. Mr. Loins told Winston maybe he should stay and work with him. Eveline reminded Winston and Mr. Loins that he had a job in New York. The contest ended with Winston being the winner and most in control. After the contests, Olitha went for the white muscle man; Sable finally got what she wanted from the Negro muscle man. Rose went with Samuel but fantasized about her man from the afternoon. Eveline went for Mr. Loins because part of his pay was to attend to her every need and desire for the entire evening. Winston and Mike continued with their activities into the night. Mike told Winston he was glad he had lots of self-control. Winston laughed and admitted he was proud of it too. Rudolph was left alone as everyone went off to satisfy their sexual hungers. He was beginning to see a pattern in what Eveline was attempting to do with him. Maybe he should stay in Atlantic City.

CHAPTER 22

The train was scheduled to leave Atlantic City at 8AM. Everyone was ready to go except Olitha who was exhausted from her man friend. Eveline was so angry with her that she threatened to fire her if she did not get ready to go. The train was to stop in New York City where they would transfer to the Hudson River Line to Albany and west to Geneva. Rose asked if they would have time to go shopping in New York City. Samuel told her that she had had enough time to shop and did not need to look for something big in New York. Every time he would say that Rose tensed up thinking he might know more about her escapades than he was letting on. The front desk clerk called for a taxi cab and while they waited in the lobby Mr. Loins appeared in a smartly tailored suit. He came to ask Rudolph again if he wanted to stay in Atlantic City to be a performer with him. When Eveline heard this she watched Rudolph explain why he could not stay. Then she said, "He works for me and I determine what he can and cannot do." Mr. Loins was surprised that a woman could have such control over a man. She went on to say, "If Mr. Williams continues to make mistakes involving my businesses he may have no choice but to come crawling to you." Rudolph said nothing but took the contact information from Mr. Loins. He said, "I may need this offer after hearing that remark." The rest of the group felt uncomfortable but said nothing.

When the train arrived in Grand Central Station they disembarked and found the train for Albany. There were shops and newspaper stands around the station. The women looked at cheap trinkets but bought nothing. Samuel and Rudolph went to the newsstands and bought newspapers. They boarded the train to Albany with its final stop in Buffalo. When the train stopped in Syracuse Eveline thought about Patrick and what was happening with Andrew now that his parents were dead. She wanted to get off and visit them but she would have to take a train the next day and wondered where she would stay. Winston assured her that she would find out everything when they got back to Geneva. Samuel handed Eveline the New York Times and told her that there was an article she might find interesting. She looked in the fashion section and there was an article about Coco Chanel. Eveline had heard about her but was surprised to find out that she was born a month earlier than her in 1883. Coco was born in France to an unwed mother who was a laundry woman in the charity hospital run by the Sisters of Providence in Samumur, France. She was named Gabrielle Bonheur Chanel. In 1895, when she was 12 years old, her mother died. Gabrielle was sent to the Correze in central France to a convent of Aubazine that was founded to care for the poor and rejected. It was a stark and demanding life with strict discipline. At 17, Gabrielle was sent to live in a boarding house in the town of Moulins. She learned the art of sewing while living at Aubazine and found employment as a seamstress. When not sewing, she sang in a cabaret frequented by cavalry officers. She made her stage debut singing at a café-concert which was a popular entertainment locale of the time at a Moulins pavilion called La Rotonde. She was among many young singers and made minimal money by passing the hat. This was where she acquired the name Coco from a song "KoKoRiKo" and "Qui qu'a vu Coco". It was a reference to the French word for a "kept" woman, cocotte. She learned to maneuver her way among the wealthy of Paris. Having many relationships, Coco met Arthur Edward Capel in 1908, a wealthy member of English upper class. She was torn between two wealthy gentlemen that were bidding for her hot little body, as the article stated. Capel set Chanel up in an apartment in Paris and financed her first shop. In 1918, Chanel was able to acquire the entire building at 31 rue Cambon, which was in one of the most fashionable districts of Paris. In 1921, she opened one of the first fashion boutiques featuring clothing, hats, jewelry, and fragrances. Early in 1922, Chanel was introduced to Pierre Wertheimer who wanted to introduce her Parfum Chanel No.5. When Eveline read about the life of Coco Chanel, she was dazzled by her style. Coco was the designer that was credited with liberating women from the constraints of the "corseted silhouette" and popularized the acceptance of a sporty and casual feminine standard in post-World War I era. Another of the newest looks for women was to have a tanned body. Until now, women were looked at as a peasant if they had a suntan. Coco popularized the bronzed look as a healthy glow for women now something only the wealthy did. She wanted to make sunbathing fashionable so she advertised women lounging on the beach without a hat to shield the sun's rays. Eveline showed Rose the article and said, "See we were ahead of our time when Wallace advertised sun wear and showed wealthy people having fun in the sun." Rose shook her head and agreed but said that it was too bad Wallace could not be here to appreciate all he did. Eveline said nothing about that statement. Instead she told Rose she needed to find out where to buy some of the Parfum Chanel No.5. She wanted to be up to the minute with everything and fragrances were a major part of fashion. Rose said, "Sometimes Eveline you are beginning to behave like a tart." Eveline turned her head upward and away from that remark.

It was late in the evening when they arrived in Geneva. Eveline went to bed and told Sable they could unpack the next day. No one was concerned about anything but rest. It had been an exhausting weekend but they had new experiences and many stories to share. The next morning, Winston was up and at work long before Eveline arose. Sable was preparing breakfast when the doorbell rang. It was the postman. He asked for Mrs. Eveline Paine. Sable explained that she was still in bed and that she could take the letter for her. He hesitated but allowed Sable to take it. He told her that because Mrs. Paine was so well known around Geneva he did not need her to sign the registered letter. Sable thanked him and closed the door. While she was walking to the library to put the letter on the table Olitha came into the room. She was better able to read than Sable so she looked at the envelope. It came from the Manlius Pebble School administrative office. Olitha looked at Sable and said, "I hope our Patrick okay." Just then Eveline came into the room because she awoke when the doorbell rang. Sable handed the letter to her and explained what the postman had said about everyone knowing her. She smiled and said, "All the men in town will eventually know me for something." She opened the letter. It was from the chief administrator explaining that Patrick was doing very well and was a good match for his roommate Andrew. The second part of the letter explained that the school would be closing for the Christmas holiday from December 23 through January 2. Eveline was asked if she would consider inviting Andrew to stay with her family for the holiday. Since Andrew's parents were deceased and Patrick was such a good influence on him, would she mind having him as a guest? If he was not invited he would need to go to a home for wayward children during the time school was closed. When Eveline read this she told Sable and Olitha that they would have to prepare for two little boys for Christmas. Eveline was not going to have a little boy be placed in a home or with people he did not know. It was sad enough about his parents and he would always be welcome with Patrick. She went to the telephone and rang the operator to connect her to the Manlius School. The administrator answered and after a little chit chat Eveline told him that Andrew would be welcome. They would come to school to see them before the holiday and would invite him then. The conversation ended and Eveline thought to herself about how different her Christmas would be this year with the boys there. Then she thought about her New Year's Eve celebrations and made a face and thought they could have fun some other time.

When Winston arrived home Eveline explained about the holiday. He was excited to think about a Christmas he never had as a child. Eveline laughed and told him now she would have three kids in the house. She told him they would go to visit them in a few weeks and tell the boys about the holiday. Eveline thought about it a bit more and decided it was time to get everyone together. She would invite her parents and Alice and Frank. She thought the more the merrier. Eveline telephoned Rose to tell her what was happening for the holidays. She was happy to hear about the boys coming but felt sad for Andrew. Rose suggested Eveline invite Hedy and Liza. Eveline asked Rose if they could go the A&P to invite them. It would be more fun to see their faces as they were invited. Then they could go to the Hob-N-Nob Restaurant for lunch and discuss the trip to Atlantic City.

The next morning Rose and Eveline strolled down Main Street to Seneca Street. It was a warm autumn day. They discussed the upcoming Christmas holiday and Eveline made sure Rose and Samuel knew they were included. They walked in to the A&P and received the same reaction as on previous visits. Eveline jokingly told Rose that they should pretend they were there for a hold up to see what would really happen. They went to the cheese department and only Hedy was working. Eveline inquired about Liza and was told that her mother was near death. Rose asked if there was anything they could do but Hedy told them no. She explained about the upcoming Christmas holiday and invited them for Christmas Day. Hedy was delighted and would relay the information to Liza. By that time, they would both need a celebration to look forward to. Eveline explained about Andrew and his being left without any family. Hedy thought that was too bad but Patrick could enjoy his friend at home. They left the store in a deliberate stroll just to spark a gossipy conversation among those in the store. They walked into the Hob-N-Nob Restaurant to hear Rudolph playing the piano. Eveline went up to him and asked, "Don't you have more important things to attend to in town with my companies?" He continued to play and said not one word to her. Eveline was furious when he gave her the cold shoulder. She decided then that he was in for an even rougher ride with her. They enjoyed the lunch and Rudolph's music even though Eveline would not tell him so. Rose sensed something was wrong but did not attempt to discuss it.

The day Eveline and Winston went to Manlius it was warm enough to drive her Lincoln with the top down. Winston appeared wearing a Panama hat and a casual outfit with slacks that were baggy instead of his usual revealing attire. Eveline acted as if she did not recognize him. He told her that he wanted to impress the administrator so he would allow Andrew to come to Geneva whenever Patrick was there. He admitted he borrowed Samuel's hat that he wore in Atlantic City. Eveline was happy he did not buy it because she told him she liked him in his own outfits, they were more fun. Eveline wore a more appropriate dress this time now that she knew the importance of making the right impression on the administrator. James parked the Lincoln at the front of the mansion and lowered the top. Eveline strolled out with Winston at her side. Off they went like a bullet being shot from a gun. They were speeding along at record rates and arrived at the Manlius School in an hour. Eveline slammed on the brakes and looked at Winston who seemed a bit dazed. She shook her head and readjusted her hair and hat and walked to the main office. The administrator greeted them and discussed the decision about Andrew. They went to the dormitory where they found the boys in an activity room. They were being instructed on proper dressing procedures. They were working on buckles and shoes by putting a lace through holes in a card. It was funny to watch little boys work their tiny fingers trying to lace up a piece of cardboard. The administrator explained that an activity like this helped their dexterity. Winston was not sure what this meant but knew it was good for learning something. When Patrick saw them he came over to them and politely said, "Hi Mother and Bud." Eveline was still not used to being referred to as mother; it reminded her of her tone toward her mother. Winston, on the other hand, picked up Patrick and hugged him while Andrew stood waiting for his turn. Winston picked up Andrew while he still held Patrick and hugged them both. The administrator told them that he never saw any of the parents hold two children at the same time. Eveline told him that Winston was as strong as a bull. The administrator made a face like he feared Winston's strength. Winston asked how they liked school. The boys were happy about all the things they were doing. Andrew did mention he did not like the lacing on a board. They laughed when he said that. Eveline sat down and the two boys sat on either side of her. She told Andrew she was sorry about his mother and father. Andrew shook his head and stared at her like he was waiting to be told something else. She asked him if he would like to come with Patrick for the Christmas holiday. Both boys started jumping up and down and the administrator knew he had made the right choice by asking Eveline about the holiday visit. Winston told them he would have the house ready for a whole week of fun. The administrator mentioned how much fun all the students were having on the swing he made. Winston offered to make a few more in the springtime. They had lunch with Patrick and Andrew. All they could talk about was how much they liked the school and that they were learning lots of new things. They showed off their art work. Eveline showed Winston and they complimented them but could not tell what was colored or scribbled. The compliments made them so proud that they offered the pictures to Winston and Eveline. Winston told them he would hang them in the window for Christmas. While they were walking back to the car the administrator mentioned that there was a will found from Andrew's parents. There were no relatives and the money in their estate was to go to Andrew for his care. The administrator wanted Eveline to think about the options of Andrew's care and possible guardianship. When she heard this, she told him she would need time to consider the idea. Winston knew he would love the idea but could not say anything because he was not included in the conversation. The boys hugged Winston but kissed Eveline on the cheek when they said their goodbyes. On the ride back to Geneva, Eveline thought about the guardianship and the little boys kissing her, which was something her mother never did. Winston was quiet and thinking of what possibilities the future might bring if Eveline took on yet another child.

Eveline wrote letters to her parents along with Frank and Alice, inviting them for the Christmas holiday. She encouraged them to stay for a few days. She explained who would be there and that there was another young boy coming with Patrick. She hoped they would consider it a new tradition. She mailed the letters and figured they would respond within a week. The letters went out on Monday and on Wednesday morning the telephone was ringing from both sets of parents. Her mother was excited that they were invited because they had nowhere else to go. Alice was as excited as the children were when she read the invitation. They were all surprised that there was to be another boy in the group. They thought it was a fine idea and planned to arrive on Christmas Eve.

Eveline decided it was time for a business meeting with Rudolph. She wanted to see financial reports and discuss his moving to Rochester to manage the hotel. She telephoned him and he was agreeable to a meeting the following week. She informed him that the hotel was the first topic and she wanted to see evidence of the import export company's title and finances. When he hung up the phone he looked at the Shuron, Safege, Wire Wheel Works, and Goodwin Printing Company paperwork. Everything was in order and making large sums of money. He deliberately eliminated the reserves of cash being stored in the basement of the printing company. He was doing the same thing Wallace had done with a discretionary fund, only this was money skimmed off from profits from all the companies including the Seneca Powers Hotel. The only other person that knew was Lucille Preston but Rudolph did not know that Hedy and Liza saw the money storage years ago when they first arrived in Geneva. He needed to speak with Lucille about his moving and how they would conduct business and money movement when he was in Rochester. The transfer of humans had changed since they were not selling babies and young children. Because of Prohibition an older teenager was more valuable because they were carrying alcoholic beverages in the shipping containers and were used as rum runners when docking in cities like New York and now Rochester. Rudolph began to think that living away from Eveline might work to his advantage. She may never find out about the import business that she was owner of. He had a devious smile when he thought of those possibilities.

Eveline had been planning for the holidays which were only a few weeks away. Sable and Olitha were given many lists of things to do and buy for the occasion. They were having a great time planning for decorations and Winston agreed to do all the decorations inside and outside. Eveline made a point of instructing them to tell Winston he was to wear his ripped trousers when he did the high work. All three women laughed and agreed they had seen Winston in all types of positions. The doorbell rang and Olitha answered it and directed Rudolph to the library. Eveline welcomed him and began by telling him that they had just finished discussing Winston's revealing work outfits and how much they liked to watch him when he was in high places. All Rudolph said was, "I'll bet you like to look up his pants." Eveline said, "You're jealous." He told her that he was not interested in that. He wanted to get on with the meeting. For once, he felt he took the upper hand while she was trying to prolong the meeting. He was going to be businesslike and make it quick. He was ready for her and needed to be careful how much he divulged. Eveline sat politely with her legs crossed, smoking a cigarette from her fancy holder. Rudolph went over the finances related to the companies in Geneva. Eveline was pleased that there was money coming in on a large basis. She was more interested in the hotel. He showed her the balance sheets and profits were rising. He reminded her that selling the hotel was not in her best interests. She did agree that he gave her sound advice. When he heard this he thought the advice was sound to keep her from selling the hotel. Now, he would be free to set up underworld businesses and operate them through the hotel. Eveline reminded him that he would be relocated to Rochester as of December 31, 1922. She asked if he had found a place to live. He told her he could stay in one of the larger suites in the hotel. Eveline agreed that was a grand idea because she would not need to finance his living accommodations. He thought to himself that it would be easier to conduct underworld business while living on the premise. The meeting was civil and Eveline wondered why Rudolph had such an agreeable attitude. She still did not trust him after all these years. She had a nagging feeling something was awry.

Early in December, Olitha began acting strange. Eveline noticed it and confronted her about her behavior. She denied that anything was wrong. Eveline asked Olitha if she remembered the day she threatened to fire her in Atlantic City for her behavior and slowness. Olitha was apologetic and grateful Eveline forgave her. Eveline still knew something was not right. She waited for a few more days and asked Sable what might be wrong with Olitha. Sable said, "I knows that girl is in a bad way. She don't says nothing to me either. Weez be together for you Miss Eveline for years and she has no family but usins." Eveline thanked her but still wondered what was wrong. That same day, Sable and Olitha were going to the A&P to begin shopping for the holiday food. They had James take them in the big automobile because there would be too much to carry on foot. While they were shopping they saw Hedy and Liza and discussed the passing of Liza's mother. They were sympathetic but Liza was relieved because her mother was almost too sick to be home. During the conversation Olitha felt dizzy and fell to the floor and the manager came to see what had happened. Sable got some cold water and threw it on her face. Hedy bent over and whispered something in Olitha's ear. Sable asked what was so secret. Olitha was still seated on the floor when she told Sable that she had done something bad. She was afraid to tell anyone and was considering running away. She was crying and told Sable that she was with child. Sable stood with her hands on her hips and said, "Oh girl you done got youself knocked up by that big Negro in the cabana in Atlantic City. You couldn't get enough of all that and now look." Olitha nodded her head in agreement. Olitha, still on the floor, knew she was in trouble and was afraid Miss Eveline would throw her to the street. She remembered how terrible living on the street was years ago. Sable and Hedy helped her up and straightened her hat and left the store. The store clerk saw the incident and carried the groceries to the waiting automobile. Olitha walked slowly with Sable holding her arm. Liza said, "If that doesn't look like something is wrong nothing will. You best let her go on her own or there will be more questions."

When they arrived at 775, Eveline asked what had taken so long for the shopping. Sable made an excuse about the store being very busy with long lines at the cash registers. Olitha went downstairs to the kitchen and started dinner. Eveline reviewed the list and explained what type of decorations she wanted Winston to put up. All along Eveline knew something had happened. She went downstairs to the kitchen, something she had never done, to find Olitha crying as she was cooking. Eveline approached her and said, "I need to know what is going on around here. You have been acting strange for a long time." Olitha looked at Eveline and told her she was with child. Eveline watched Olitha as she moved around the kitchen trying to avoid eye contact. She was afraid she would be fired and reminded Eveline of her threat when they were in Atlantic City. Eveline explained that she was upset seeing her be so lazy and slow when everyone was always waiting for her. Eveline looked her straight in the eye and said, "Look at me when you are talking to me. I don't care if you are pregnant. We have enough room here for you to care for the child and continue your responsibilities to this house. If you can't understand that then you are fired." Olitha was shocked that Eveline was so forceful yet gave her the choice to stay. She looked at Eveline and told her she wanted her to be happy for her even though she was not married to the Negro. Then, Eveline laughed and told her about all the things and men she had been involved with. Olitha smiled and realized things were not that bad. Eveline turned and said, "It seems like we are filling up the house with lots of children from many backgrounds. I never thought we'd even have one and now there will be three."

CHAPTER 23

Christmas was a week away. The weather had been frigid and blustery. Winston had decorated the outside of 775 with wreaths and boughs of holly. For a spark of fun he bought a large sprig of mistletoe and hung it in the entrance way. He made it high enough so no one could take it down. He wanted to see how many people would spend time kissing under it. Sable and Olitha were baking and preparing snacks for the holiday celebration. They had been to the A&P more often than usual for food. While they were there they would speak to Hedy and Liza. They wanted to know what they could bring on Christmas Day. The only request Eveline made was for everyone to bring presents for Patrick and Andrew. Eveline was planning the activities for the holiday. She wanted to see if she could manage to get the parents to be more excited about life in general. She placed the names on the doors of who was sleeping in which bedrooms.

She had Winston get another bed for the boy's room. She had a feeling he might be spending the same amount of time that Patrick would be spending at her home. While she was thinking about the possibility of having children around, she still worried about her personal life. Now that Olitha was pregnant, that meant a baby in the house all the time. After thinking about the future, she dismissed the worry and thought about the holiday and hoped this might be the start of a new tradition.

Severe weather was predicted for the end of December. The chief administrator telephoned Eveline to discuss when and how she was planning to come to the school for Patrick and Andrew. He offered to send the boys by train if she approved of it. She hesitated at first thinking of the way Andrew was delivered to the Manlius School because his parents were too busy to take him themselves. She discussed her thoughts with the administrator and he thought it was good of her to remember that. After they considered how much better Andrew was doing, they thought that as long as Patrick was with him it would be fine. Eveline would not need to drive to Syracuse in such treacherous weather. The administrator would make sure the boys were safely on the train and the conductor would watch over them. Eveline and Winston would be at the station when they arrived. Now she thought about the Rochester people and how they were planning on getting to Geneva. She telephoned her father. While he was speaking with her she could hear her mother in the background yelling at Mr. Lounsberry about things she was trying to understand from their conversation. After a few minutes Mr. Lounsberry excused himself and put the telephone down and Eveline could hear him lecturing her mother on how rude she was for acting like a crazy woman. Eveline asked her father if things were okay. He explained that her mother was extremely demanding, wanting decisions to be passed by her before they were made. Eveline laughed and said, "She hasn't changed much has she?" Her father admitted she had been difficult since they moved from Canada years ago. Mr. Lounsberry had offered to drive to Geneva for the holiday with Alice and Frank. When he heard about the weather and the possibility of taking the train he decided that would be safer. Eveline told him that James would be at the train station with the roadster.

Winston and Eveline were at the train station early. Eveline wore a large fur hat with a fur coat that went nearly to the ground and a fur muff for her hands. She instructed James to keep the automobile heated while they waited at the station. Winston wore a long wool coat and had a stocking cap on his head. Eveline laughed and told him he looked like an elf. When she said that, Winston pulled out two more caps from his pocket for Andrew and Patrick. Eveline laughed and told him now there would be three elves in the house. They saw the train coming through the blizzard. Eveline told Winston the weather reminded her of the time she and Wallace moved to Buffalo in 1904 in the same type of weather. Winston told her he remembered that time because he was the one who missed them the most. The train came to a stop and the conductor was in the window with Patrick and Andrew. They were waving as they jumped off the train. Winston picked them up and gave each a hug. They both felt his cap and told him he looked like he was going to bed. Winston laughed as he put the boys down. They went to Eveline and as she bent over they each kissed her. She felt awkward. She still felt uncomfortable about being called mother and being kissed by two sweet little boys. On the way back to 775, Eveline inquired about the train ride. Patrick was eager to tell her about how much fun it was while all the people watched them and talked with them. Andrew told them the ride was more fun than the last time he was on a train. No one said anything about his trip from New York City to Syracuse. Winston explained to Andrew that he would never have to be alone again. Eveline smiled, but wondered, as James pulled in front of 775, how will all this turn out? Before they got out of the back seat, Winston pulled out the two caps. He put them on Andrew and Patrick's heads and they laughed when he said, "We can't let our heads be cold. Now we look alike."

Sable and Olitha were waiting at the front door waving as they approached the door. When they were inside they took their belongings and their little suitcases that the school gave them for their first trip. Each of their names were written on the side. Upstairs, they found the bedroom decorated for Christmas with two large stuffed panda bears on their beds. Winston was sure to let them know he bought them and realized the boys were the same size as the pandas. It was strange to have children at the dinner table that evening. Eveline was surprised with the table manners the boys had. Patrick explained that was what they were told to do in school. Eveline knew then that her money was being put to good use. During dinner, Winston told the boys that he had something for them to do together. After dinner Winston took them to his room and showed them his bathing suit from Atlantic City. He showed them two smaller suits that were for them. They laughed when they saw them because it looked like their underwear or night clothes. Patrick wanted to know why they needed bathing suits. Winston told them it was too cold to go swimming but they were going to surprise Miss Eveline with a little show on Christmas Day. He told them about a song he heard when he was on the beach. The next day they would practice the song and give everyone a show around the Christmas tree.

James went to the train station to meet the guests from Rochester. The weather had not improved and was getting worse. The train arrived covered in snow. The engineer had only a small spot to see out of the train. The windows were frosted and as people got off the train they mentioned that there was no heat on the train. James hugged Alice and Frank but Mr. and Mrs. Lounsberry politely shook his hand. They got into the warm automobile and thanked him for such comfort. Alice was chattering about the holiday and asked James about the boys. He explained that the house had taken on a completely different atmosphere. He laughed when he told them about Miss Eveline's attitude. Mrs. Lounsberry smirked when she heard this and asked if she was still sick from a bad attitude. Mr. Lounsberry told her if she could not improve her own attitude toward Eveline that he was sending her back on the icy train to Rochester. When James stopped in front of the mansion Alice spotted two little faces in the front window. She poked Frank and told him to look at them waving. Sable and Olitha hugged all of them and Eveline came downstairs in a festive holiday gown. Alice complimented her but her mother remarked that she must be spending all of Wallace's money to look that good. Mr. Lounsberry nudged her and told her that was not a good way to say hello. Everyone was squeezing and hugging

Patrick and Andrew. It seemed like Andrew was already part of the family. Patrick and he stood together like they were twins but with different skin tones. After the luggage was put in to the bedrooms, Sable served drinks and there was conversation about school and what was happening for the next few days. Alice talked about her new job in Rochester. She was returning to the Women's Club as their event's organizer. Frank was his usual disconnected self but no one seemed to care. He sat enjoying his cocktail. Mrs. Lounsberry was surprised about Alice's job and mentioned she was considering going to work. Mr. Lounsberry looked surprised because he did not have any knowledge of this intent. He asked her what type of work she was interested in. She told everyone that she would be working from home as a consultant. Frank wanted to know what she was consulting about. She gave him a disgusted look but told him it would be for products coming from Canada. Everyone was surprised she had any intent on working. Mr. Lounsberry was suspicious of her conversation. Eveline spoke up and said, "Why mother it may be good for you to have more to do at home rather than sitting around." Her mother snapped at her and said, "I told you I would be working at home and I do much more than just sit around." This ended the conversation and it was time for dinner.

Christmas Day arrived very early because Patrick and Andrew were anxious to see what was under the tree for them. They ran downstairs and met Sable and Olitha preparing breakfast. There were piles of presents in the parlor. The fireplace glowed and Patrick stared at it. Finally, he asked Olitha why there was a fire in there. She said, "Why boy, it is warming us." He shook his head and asked, "How could Santa get down through there with a fire going?" Winston heard the question and before Olitha could answer he said, "Santa just left and I started the fire so we could be warm." That was the end of the questioning. The boys had their caps on that Winston had given them and were still in their nightclothes. They looked like midgets on either side of Winston. Eveline walked into the room and saw how they looked. She went over to Winston and whispered in his ear that he still looked like he just got out of the water. His manhood was clinging to his suit. She wiggled her nose at him and wanted to know when they were going to use the mistletoe. Winston took her arm and the two boys followed them to where the mistletoe was hanging. He kissed Eveline and then Patrick wanted to know if he could do that. Winston told him he could. Thinking he meant Eveline, he moved away but Patrick pulled on his leg and told him he wanted to kiss him. Winston was surprised but picked him up and Patrick gave him a kiss. While this was happening Andrew asked Eveline if he could kiss her. She felt frozen but picked him up and he kissed her. Then, Winston told them he thought they should switch. Eveline made a face at him but agreed. Winston felt the happiest he had in a long time when he felt his little buddies giving him genuine affection. The rest of the family came downstairs. Alice was in a chenille bathrobe that dragged the floor. Frank was dressed in his usual blue shirt and slacks. Mrs. Lounsberry had her hair in pin curls and wore a silk bathrobe. Her slippers were small with puffs on the tops. Mr. Lounsberry had on a corduroy smoking jacket and silk pants. Patrick went to him and rolled his hands around his large stomach. Eveline told him that was not polite. Patrick apologized but Mrs. Lounsberry remarked at the size of his stomach. She said, "I keep telling him it is too big." Again no remarks were made. Alice wanted to know when she could stand under the mistletoe. She motioned to Frank and he slowly moved to the spot. Alice grabbed him and kissed him longer than she could remember. Patrick and Andrew jumped up and down and wanted to be next. Alice knelt down to be at eye level and kissed them all over their faces and tickled them while they giggled and kissed her back. Mrs. Lounsberry stared at them with her hands on her hips. Eveline watched the action and thought about how life was changing. The doorbell rang and Sable went to see who was arriving. It was Hedy and Liza. They walked from downtown in the blizzard with handfuls of packages. Everyone was cordial as they sat in the parlor. Patrick ran to them and kissed them. They were happy to see how well he was. The presents were distributed and everyone opened theirs for all to see. The boys received so many presents and clothes that it looked like a department store. Eveline presented her staff with a present but reminded them the real one was Atlantic City. Olitha spoke up and said, "I'll never forget that place. I got pregnant there." After some questioning about how she got pregnant especially from Mrs. Lounsberry she said, "So, Eveline is turning this property into a home for wayward children." When she said this Frank spoke up and said, "You have nothing good to say about anything. So what if she turns this place into a playground what business is it of yours?" She was speechless that Frank dared speak up to her. Eveline then said, "Mother you are jealous that you don't know how to open up and offer more to people." Her mother sucked her teeth. Alice said nothing after she heard Frank say such pointed things to Eveline's mother. For the first time, she felt some amount of pride in him. Maybe his age was mellowing him.

After the gifts were opened Winston stood in his bathing suit and cap. Everyone in the room watched as he paraded around with Patrick and Andrew dressed in the same outfit. Eveline was hysterical when the three of them were marching around the parlor. Winston explained that his buddies and he had been rehearsing a skit for them. The women were laughing and the men were staring at Winston wondering how he could appear in such an outfit exposing so much. Winston told the story of seeing some people singing a happy song on the beach in Atlantic City. He taught Andrew and Patrick the words and they started dancing together in a circle singing: *By the Sea, By the Sea, By the beautiful Sea, You and Me, You and Me, Oh How happy we will be.* They sang it a couple of times and skipped around the parlor. They started bouncing up and down. The women were roaring with laughter as the men only continued to stare. Alice piped up and said, "This is almost as good as the burlesque show many years ago." Winston, in a smug way said, "At least this time I am the entertainment not those men from the burlesque show." After the performance, Patrick and Andrew put their arms around Winston and told him that he was their best buddy. For the first time in his life, he felt like he was the best. When the laughter subsided, Sable announced, "You all get your behinds in the dining room. I haven't be fixin all dis good food for it to get cold." The two boys were like race horses getting to the chairs first. It was the first time since living at 775 that the house was full of life for the holiday festivities. As Alice sat she thought about what life would have been like if Wallace were still alive. Little did she know what went on when he was alive.

January 1, 1923 arrived with very little fanfare for the New Year. Winston and Eveline prepared the luggage and some of the gifts to go back to Manlius Pebble School. Patrick and Andrew were leaving the next day on the train. It was the same day that Rudolph was moving back to Rochester to be manager of the Seneca Powers Hotel. He felt he was being demoted but Eveline had a different view of the move. He was scheduled to meet with Eveline early in the morning to discuss the future of the businesses in Geneva and the hotel. It was the time of year that she would be receiving annual meeting invitations to Ford Motor Company, Eastman Kodak Company, and the companies in Geneva. On the front page of the Geneva Daily News was an announcement by the State of New York. It was a decree that all operators of motor vehicles would be required to have a license to drive. Eveline shook her head as she read it. Just as she finished Sable came into the room and inquired why she was shaking her head. Eveline explained about the new requirement. Sable laughed and said, "You Miss Eveline better be the first one at the office. The way you drives you needs more than a license. Oh girl the roads will never be safe until you slow down." Eveline laughed and shook her head pretending to ignore what Sable said.

Rudolph arrived promptly and Eveline received him in the library. He and she conversed about the holidays and Eveline made a point of telling him about the boys and all the people that were invited. Rudolph spent the week packing for his move to Rochester. He tried to act as if he was not bothered but Eveline could see in his eyes he was unhappy. The financial papers were turned over to her because now she was handling all the local businesses. The larger companies like Ford Motor Company and Eastman Kodak Company would be handled as they had been. Rudolph would still be answering to her about the hotel and The Foreign Import and Export Company. Eveline explained that she would be making trips to Rochester to monitor the hotel and keep in touch with the latest fashions. Rudolph studied her demeanor and knew she was not going to be easy to deal with. The meeting ended. At the door, Eveline made a point of hugging Rudolph and reminded him she was still in charge. He smiled and shook her hand. As he was leaving, he thought if she only knew what was going to happen. Eveline went back to the library to read the newspaper. The telephone rang and it was Rose asking if she could come to visit. Eveline wondered what so important that she wanted to come to visit in the middle of the week. She would have rather gone out to have a meal instead of sitting there. Rose arrived acting as if she had a secret. Rose began by asking if she knew anything about why the man who was her manager in the Seneca Powers Hotel was killed. Eveline explained that she saw him the day he was found dead. The police explained to her that there was underhanded business dealing going on in Rochester. Rose continued to tell her that she overheard a woman in Samuel's office talking about Lucille Preston. Eveline was confused about the connection to the discussion. Rose explained that Lucille had been working with domestic servants long ago. Eveline was still waiting for a clue. Lucille had been seen with Rudolph. They were exchanging papers and a bag. Lucille opened the bag and the woman saw rolled up money. Rudolph took the money and they agreed she would be in Rochester after he was settled in the hotel. Eveline began to wonder why Lucille Preston would have anything to do with Rudolph's affairs in Rochester. She asked Rose who the woman was that spoke about this. Rose would not tell her because Samuel would not approve of her passing office talk around town. Eveline decided it did not matter who it was only that she needed to look into this matter.

Eveline asked Rose if she had read about the sexual movement for woman. Rose said she had not so Eveline began reading an article to her. It explained that women had begun staking claim to their own bodies. Many of the ideas that fueled this change in sexual attitudes were thought to have come from the New York intellectual circles prior to World War I. Sigmund Freud, who was a leader in the new field of psychology, believed that women were sexual beings with human impulses and desires just like men and restraining these impulses was self-destructive. It was now fashionable to maintain a feminine mystique and be out in the world. No longer was the modern woman of the 1920's conforming to what men wanted. Equality in sex and appearance was making life more fun for women. Rose was squirming in her seat as she listened to Eveline. Eveline told her she needed to break out and tell Samuel what she was going to start doing. Rose was not sure she could do that. Eveline lectured her on all she had done with her 10 years ago when they attended the Women's Rights rallies. The article continued about the mixing of whites and minorities and socializing in nightclubs. Rose spoke up and said, "Not nightclubs but speakeasies." Eveline went on about the new social acceptance of homosexuality. There was a song entitled "Masculine Women, Feminine Men." A piece of sheet music was pictured and poked fun at the masculine traits women were taking on. It was called: *We Men Must Grow*

A Mustache Because This Is The Only Thing A Girl Cannot Do. Eveline admitted that she was happy to see equality for both men and women in sexual matters. There was a cartoon added to the end of the article showing a young woman draped over a chair asking her dowdy looking mother a question. It was, "Mother, when you were a girl, didn't you find it a bore to be a virgin?" Rose was aghast but Eveline laughed and said, "I should ask my mother that question. I think the only time my father had sex with her was when she got pregnant with me." Rose told her she was being mean and should not say such things. Eveline turned her head upward and puffed on her cigarette. CoCo Chanel was mentioned in the article that told that she was exerting influence from Paris on the women in America. She was appealing to women to take charge and show themselves through her use of simple ensembles, scarves, and jewelry. She advertised in Vogue and Harper's Bazaar magazine which American women adored for the latest fashions. Eveline reminded Rose that she needed to take more charge of herself. After Rose left, Eveline thought about the information about Lucille. She knew she was not to be trusted. She decided to wait awhile and then make an unannounced visit to the Seneca Powers Hotel to see what business was like when a meeting was not scheduled.

CHAPTER 24

L ife had settled down as the winter was coming to an end. Eveline invited her parents along with Alice and Frank to come to Geneva to take an afternoon trip to see Patrick and Andrew. Mr. Lounsberry agreed to drive from Rochester. Eveline would not consider having her father drive to Syracuse. She informed them that she was driving the roadster because there was enough room for everyone. When Winston heard this he laughed and said, "I can't wait to see your parents and Alice and Frank's reaction to your driving." Eveline smiled and said, "That's my intention to scare them a little. They haven't had a thrill like the one they are going to get when I'm driving." Before they set off for Manlius, Eveline made a stop at the Seneca Hotel. She was hungry so they had lunch in the restaurant before driving to Syracuse. When they walked in Eveline spotted Lucille Preston having lunch with her husband. Eveline introduced everyone to the Prestons. While everyone was chit chatting Eveline noticed that her mother was talking with Lucille as if they knew one another. The gestures they made looked like they had agreed on something. Eveline thought about Rose's information. How was her mother involved with Lucille? The group sat down for lunch and Eveline asked her mother about the conversation she had with Lucille Preston. Her mother quietly told her that Rudolph had put her in touch with Lucille regarding the consultant position in Rochester. Eveline did not ask any more questions. It was all becoming a mystery. Mr. Lounsberry offered to pay for lunch. Eveline asked if he had come into some money. He laughed and said, "Actually I have." No one pushed for more information.

After lunch, they took their seats in the roadster. Eveline was driving with Winston in the middle and her father on the passenger side. Frank was in the middle with Alice on one side and Mrs. Lounsberry on the other in the backseat. Eveline was careful to take it slow until they got out of Geneva. She looked at Winston and threw the automobile into high gear and pushed the accelerator to the floor. They were traveling so fast that dust was flying behind them for almost a mile. Alice was having a grand time but Frank yelled at Eveline to slow the damn thing down. Her mother was screaming and Mr. Lounsberry turned and told her to shut up. She was shocked at his lack of concern for their safety and his daughter's crazy behavior. Eveline turned to her mother and said, "If you don't like my driving then get out." Just as she finished with her mother, a cow had wandered into the road and Eveline swerved to avoid hitting it. Even Winston looked frightened but the rest screamed. They arrived at Manlius promptly at 2PM. The chief administrator greeted them and looked at them and asked, "What in the world has happened to you. You look like you are nearly dead." Frank told him that they had been on the ride from hell. Eveline smiled and explained that these people were from Rochester and they were afraid to go too fast but she liked to speed; according to Eveline that was their problem not hers. The administrator appeared confused by the conversation but began explaining to the group about how well Patrick was doing and Andrew was taking after him. Alice told Frank she was happy for the boys. Frank made no gesture of approval either way. Mrs. Lounsberry said under her breath, "Anything goes in a school for wayward boys." Mr. Lounsberry looked at her with pursed lips and she knew she better stop the remarks.

Patrick spotted them from his window and was in the yard with Andrew in a flash. They ran full speed toward Winston and jumped up to him. He caught both of them and pulled them up to his waist and they kissed him and told him they were happy their buddy was back. Eveline watched and so did the rest all wondering why Winston was liked so much and not them. Patrick went to Eveline and she bent over and he kissed her and then went to Mr. Lounsberry and felt his stomach and asked if he could call him Grampa Lounsberry. He was so taken he asked Mrs. Lounsberry and she said she was not sure. She explained that would make them old. Alice spoke up and said, "You boys can call me Gramma Alice and Grampy Frank. Andrew and Patrick both said at the same time, "Ok Grumpy Frank." Laughter erupted from everyone because even though it was a slip of the tongue, it was true. Alice blurted out, "Oh Frank they have your number." He looked like he was stunned. Patrick wanted to show the family the swing that Winston made for them. Andrew was excited to explain how Miss Eveline's dress was over her head when she tried it. Her mother made a scornful face when she heard about the swinging. Eveline spoke up and said, "Oh Mother, you should see how Winston looks when he is in the tire." Winston's face turned red, and then he laughed and realized that only he knew what she was talking about. The day was coming to an end and the boys had to go for dormitory training on how to shine shoes and dress appropriately. On the way back to Geneva, Eveline drove the same way as she did on the way to Syracuse. Her father reminded her never to offer to take them anywhere again. She laughed and said, "Ok, that was my intention." Her mother made a disgusted face at Alice in disapproval of her daughter's attitude. Alice giggled and told her to stop worrying about everything.

Eveline took Olitha to see Samuel for a checkup. He reminded Eveline of how she was during her pregnancy. Eveline thought about the event and told him she was still in shock that she had a son and he was doing very well. Olitha was having a healthy pregnancy and Samuel told her she had only a few weeks until the baby would be born. Eveline jokingly said, "I hope it is a Negro and not a white baby." Olitha laughed and told them she was sure it would be a Negro. She would never forget what that Negro did to her in his cabana. On the way back to 775, they saw Rose and she asked them if they wanted to go for a cup of coffee. Olitha refused but Eveline was always ready for entertainment. They stopped in a coffee shop near the A&P where they ran into Lucille. Eveline deliberately asked her if they could share the table. Lucille appeared infringed upon but Eveline had a motive for her actions. While they were having coffee and pastries Eveline inquired about her affiliation to Rudolph and her mother. Lucille made light of the question by saying, "Rudolph asked me to contact your mother to see if she was interested in a consulting position in Rochester. It would be work that she could do from home." The story matched what she heard from her mother. Rose sat and listened and watched Eveline pursue her line of questions. Eveline wanted to know what type of work she was offered. Lucille hesitated but termed it like being an interviewer. Eveline wanted to know who would be interviewed. Lucille explained that her mother would interview and place students coming from the Foreign Exchange Program in Rochester. She continued to tell Eveline that Rudolph was directed to change what the import company was doing. There were younger people needing placement in schools. Eveline shook her head and agreed that Rochester had many good schools. Rose still said nothing but was eager to speak to Eveline about the conversation. Eveline thanked Lucille and felt a bit better about what Rose had told her. Everything had a reason so maybe she was being too cautious. Then Eveline had one last question. She asked Lucille, "Why was a bag of money exchanged between you and Rudolph?" Lucille was taken back and asked, "What do you mean?" Eveline told her that someone saw Rudolph and her passing a bag with lots of rolled money in it. Lucille in a casual but off handed way said, "Oh that is money for the students so they can buy things they need after they were placed in institutions." Eveline said nothing and thought the word institution might not have been a good choice of words. She still needed to visit Rochester to see how everyone was connected to the import company and the Seneca Powers Hotel.

When Rose and Eveline were strolling home, Rose asked Eveline if she believed what Lucille told her. Eveline looked at Rose with a sly grin and explained that the story made sense but she was not going to believe a word she heard until she made a visit to Rochester. Rose shook her head and told Eveline, "You have become a strong and cautious business women." Eveline said, "You haven't seen anything yet." Rose told her that she wished she had her nerve. Eveline arrived at 775 to a stack of mail. Olitha handed it to her as she walked into the foyer. Eveline was surprised that there was so much to look at. Most of the envelopes came from companies addressed to the owner or president. She was stunned when she saw the words owner and president. The names were changed after Eveline repositioned Rudolph back to Rochester. She laughed when she thought of the word repositioned because it was perfect for what she did to his job position. Most of enclosures were profit and loss statements except the statement from The Foreign Exchange Company. It listed very little loss and huge profits. Mr. Wellington enclosed a letter explaining that since they changed the items being imported, money was coming in at record rates. The next part explained that she would now be the signer to all transactions for the company. Mr. Wellington and Rudolph felt that as the owner she should be the signer. He requested her signature so he could have a rubber stamp made for all transactions. Eveline thought this was good that she forced the change in the company and all seemed to be working more effectively. She signed the paper and had Sable take it to the mailbox to be sent back to Mr. Wellington. There was an invitation to a soirée at Mr. Eastman's home and she was asked to bring an escort. When Eveline finished reading the program, she thought it might be fun to invite Winston. She hoped that Rudolph might be hired to play the piano. She and Winston could surprise him just as she and Wallace had 10 years ago.

Eveline told Winston that evening that she wanted him to go to a soirée. He had no idea what she was talking about. She explained what it was and where it was being held. He wanted to know why Rudolph was not asked. Eveline told him she wanted to make him uncomfortable seeing her with him. Winston agreed to go and was glad he had a proper suit for the evening. Winston told Eveline that Lucille stopped at the Goodwin Printing Company to get money from the vault in the basement. Eveline wanted to know if he asked her what she was doing with the money. All Lucille told him was that it was money for the import company expenses. Eveline heard about that earlier but wondered why so much was needed. Winston told her she rolled hundred dollar bills into small sizes. Eveline asked how the money was getting to Rochester. Winston told her that Lucille was sending it on the train and Rudolph would be there to receive it.

It was a warm and balmy evening, so Eveline had the top down on the Lincoln on the way to the Eastman soiree. She drove with her foot to the floor. Winston sat with his hair flying in all directions. She told him how handsome and exciting he was to her. He explained that he liked being with her and was happy he could help her with Patrick and Andrew. She agreed, but made it clear they were only close friends and she did not want him to stop seeing his friend Mike. Winston assured her he had no intention of stopping Mike from coming over for a visit. He wondered why she brought Mike up but decided not to question her. They arrived right on time for the soirée and the same butler from 10 years ago showed them to the conservatory where there was music and food served. Mr. Eastman was pleased that Winston was her escort. Eveline inquired about who was going to play the piano. Mr. Eastman mentioned a name that was not Rudolph's. He told them he had to release his former pianist because he was involved in some underworld business affairs. Mr. Eastman said, "I have no use for people like that." He explained that the last time they were at the opening of his theater someone pointed out Mr. Williams and divulged what he was up to. The next day, Rudolph was eliminated from Mr. Eastman's payroll. He suggested that Eveline be careful of him. Winston said, "Lately no one seems to like Rudolph." As Mr. Eastman walked away he said, "And for good reason." The evening was as delightful as the first time. On the way back to Geneva, Winston thought about the night 10 years ago. That was the night that Wallace dropped Eveline and Rudolph off at the hotel so they could spend time catching up while Wallace and he got together in Wallace's apartment on Scio Street. When they arrived at 775 all the lights were on. When they walked in Sable met them and explained that Dr. Haynes was upstairs tending to Olitha. Sable said, "That girl about ready to burst. She havin her baby." Eveline went into the bedroom and saw Olitha delivering a baby boy. She went to Olitha and told her there were now three boys in the house. Olitha said, "Praise the lord he is okay." Then the baby began to cry as Samuel cleaned him off and put him on Olitha's chest. She looked at the baby and said, "I'm namin him Chester." Samuel laughed and Eveline made a face thinking of a name like Chester.

CHAPTER 25

Samuel had a patient in his office that was a representative for Safege Razor Company. He was hired to promote a new patent. On November 6, 1923 Jacob Schick received the patent for the first electric razor. Samuel called Eveline to tell her what he had found out. When Eveline answered the telephone she was surprised it was Samuel because he never called her. Eveline listened to the news and said, "This may be the beginning of the end of Safege." Samuel was not sure of that but thought she might like to know for her future plans. When she hung up the receiver she thought about the future and what she was willing to do to maintain her position with so many companies. Maybe it was time to sell some of them. Mr. Schick was clearly a threat to Safege Razor Company. The newspaper had a featured article about how electricity had changed the world at the end of 1923. The White House had the first electrically lit Christmas tree on the lawn that was being turned on December 25. Eveline knew then that the day of simple living was changing. Between Samuel's information and the newspaper she knew it was time to look into possibilities of liquidating her companies. There was a local advertisement to electrify homes and it could be paid for on installment plans. The Reuter Electric Company on 91 Castle Street was offering a $10 down payment and $5 per month installment plan. The advertisement stated, "Be able to see at night and pay for the installation of electricity on a payment plan." Eveline put the paper down and thought how lucky she had been to be able to live in the first home at 380 Washington Street with electricity and Wallace had 775 electrified before they moved into the mansion. While she was thinking about the past she thought about the black box. She had not looked in it for some time. She may have missed some information about the Prestons. After all that had occurred with Lucille and Rudolph and now her mother, maybe she missed some of Wallace's warnings. She went to the bedroom closet and pulled the black box out of a hatbox where she had hidden it. She laughed and thought no one would think to put it in a hatbox. Eveline sat on the side of the bed to read what Wallace wrote about Lucille. She did remember he thought she was a wolf in sheep's clothing to be careful of. She gets whatever she wants at any price and her husband does not interfere. Eveline knew that from what Lucille told her about blackmailing and the money involved in placing domestic servants. She put the letters back in the box and said out loud, "I need to find out what is happening in Rochester with Lucille, Rudolph, and my mother."

The latest figures for automobile sales showed that the Ford Touring Car was selling faster than it could be manufactured. It was still the cheapest selling for $295 and a Chevrolet was second place at $605. Eveline smiled when she read about how well Ford Motor Company was doing. She gloated over the idea that she was driving one of the most expensive automobiles in town. She loved being seen in her Lincoln two seater, especially on a nice day when the top could be down. There was an article about how the government was cracking down on smuggling illegal cargo from foreign countries and Canada was one of them. A whiskey and rum laden ship was fired upon as it attempted to dock. Upon investigation of the ship, $250,000.00 worth of alcohol was uncovered and young people were being used to deliver these shipments to places selling alcoholic beverages. Eveline made a face as she read about the methods used for shipping and delivering the illegal products. Something was not setting well when she thought more about what may be happening in New York and now Rochester.

Winston saw a sign that a circus was coming to town. He asked Eveline if she wanted to go and if Patrick and Andrew might come for a visit then. She called Manlius and arranged for the boys to come on the train. In the meantime, she had business to attend to. She was concerned about the smuggling that was happening and wanted to find out if there was any wrongdoing in her companies. The next day she would take a trip to Rochester. She would not tell anyone where she was going. She decided to go to her mother's house first and would invite her out to lunch. She wanted to keep her in sight so she could not warn others about what was happening.

Eveline went to the train station to be on the first train to Rochester. While she was waiting she saw an advertisement for the new Forman's Store being dedicated on Clinton Avenue South that day. Being interested in shopping for new things, she knew she must go there first. When the train arrived it was almost 9AM. She would have enough time to be at the store when it opened. She went directly to the fragrance department. Eveline wanted to find CoCo Chanel's #5 Parfum. There was large display of it and was featured as the most luxurious fragrance made. Eveline bought the first bottle sold at Forman's. As she was walking around she spotted her mother and Lucille. Now she was even more curious about why Lucille was in Rochester. She approached them from behind and said, "Fancy meeting you here Lucille." When they turned around and saw Eveline they were red faced and stuttered something about shopping. Eveline did not let up on her questioning. She wanted to know why Lucille was in town. She made another excuse about shopping. Eveline looked at her mother and wanted to know why they were together. Her mother told her she had just met her a few minutes ago. Eveline looked at them with a questioning eye and said, "I hope you have a good time." She turned and walked out of the store and headed for the Seneca Powers Hotel. While she was walking, she thought it was good she saw them in the store. Now she did not need to worry about someone warning people that she was seen in town. She walked into the lobby without having a doorman open the door, hoping to be less noticeable. As she approached the office, there were a few young men waiting in chairs as if they were waiting their turn for something. She smiled as she walked by. They watched her hips move side to side as she sashayed down the hallway. She approached the door and put her hand on the knob to go in, when one of the young men said, "Maybe you should not go in there." Eveline asked why. She was told that there was something big going on in there. Eveline asked why they were all seated. No one said a word. She turned the knob and in she went to find Rudolph, her father, and a few cigar smoking men around a table with stacks of money being counted. She stopped with her hands on her hips and said, "So have I caught you boys at the wrong time? Someone better have some good answers for me." She looked at the stunned group of men and said, "Daddy, why are you here?" He grumbled and said, "I was helping your mother with her consulting job." Eveline said nothing as she walked to the table and saw stacks of hundred dollar bills. Rudolph asked why she was there. Eveline curtly said, "To see what happens when I'm not supposed to be here." She wanted to know why there were so many young men in the hallway. One of the cigar smoking men told her they were the carriers for merchandise. All Eveline could think about was the article about smuggling. As everyone was trying to smooth things over, Lucille and Mrs. Lounsberry walked in. Eveline stood with everyone around her and said, "I have the whole lot of you here and I want answers." Rudolph began by explaining that the men in the hall were being placed in institutions because of the Foreign Exchange Company. She stared and waited for more. Her mother spoke up to explain that she had just finished interviewing them for placement. Her father tried to convince Eveline that he walked over to the hotel with the young men. While this was going on, the men in the hall were listening because the door was ajar. Eveline threatened to ask some of them to come in for their side of the story. Rudolph told her that would not be necessary.

She looked at the group and said, "I've had enough of this and I am selling this place. I have an idea there is more going on than I want to be responsible for." She glared at Rudolph and then looked at the rest and told him to get it sold as fast as possible. She turned and walked out. One of the young men followed her to the street. He told her he had overheard the conversation. Eveline asked where he was from. He told her Puerto Rico. She looked confused and asked how he got here. He said he was a carrier on the ships that were delivering things to places like the hotel. He was not sure what the stuff was. He explained that there were hundreds of people like him going all over the country with containers from Canada and Puerto Rico.

When Eveline returned to Geneva she promised herself she was not discussing any of what she suspected with anyone. Sable met her at the door and wanted to know if she was okay. Eveline said, "Never better." She showed Sable the Chanel#5 and told her she went to Rochester for a new store opening. Eveline went to her room and rested. Winston left a note for her about the circus. She smiled when she saw what it was. He drew a picture of himself with Patrick and Andrew on either side wearing clown hats. It was a reminder that the circus was tomorrow and to be ready for company. She was not in a festive mood but knew she should be looking forward to seeing the boys have fun at a circus. The mail was on the table so she sat down to read it. There was a letter from Mr. Preston asking Eveline if she had any intention of selling the Seneca Powers Hotel. He would like to have first right of refusal whenever she decided to sell it. He explained how much he would like to have a chain of hotels. Since the Rochester Hotel was so much like the Seneca Hotel in Geneva, he would not need to change the names. Eveline smiled and thought she should take him up on it immediately. Then he could untangle whatever was going on in Rochester. Then she wondered if the same thing may be going on in Geneva and having two places might be a cover. Without further thought, she wrote a response to Mr. Preston. She told him she would entertain an offer as soon as he was ready. She called for Sable to take the letter to the post box. Sable said, "Boy Miss Eveline, you sure is in a mood. You sure you only went to Rochester and not a fight?" Eveline said, "It was worse than a fight but I will win no matter what." Sable left shaking her head.

It was April 26 and the circus was in town. Winston was ready to go to the train station early. Eveline was not as eager to go to the circus because of the odor. She told Winston, "I hate smelling all that animal manure and seeing how nasty the people are who work in a circus." He told her she was too high class acting and that she should try to come down to earth. She pretended she did not hear a word he said as they left for the station. When they got there the boys were standing alone. They had arrived an hour ago. Winston asked at the ticket booth about the time change. The man nicely explained that this was the first year for daylight savings time and he probably did not reset his clock. Embarrassed for blaming the station, he apologized and went to the boys. They hugged and kissed both of them. They told the boys why they were late. Winston laughed and told them they were not used to the new rules for time changes. Eveline admitted she never knew about it. She would take that up with Sable and Olitha.

They approached the circus and the tent could be seen
from everywhere. Winston had circus hats for all of them,
including Eveline. They laughed when she put it on her
head. Winston told her she looked like she should sit in
the corner with that cone hat on her head. She smirked but
held hands as they walked to the show. While they were
passing by the sideshows Patrick eyed Jolly Irene and Baby
Bunny Smith. The sign read that together they weighed
over 1000 pounds. They were 23 years old. Andrew stared
at them and asked, "Why are they so fat?" Jolly Irene
yelled and told him she liked to eat tons of food. Eveline
was disgusted at the size of them. She did not see Colonel
Culver come behind her. He was twice as tall as her. He
had a sign that read 8feet 4inches printed on it. He came
over to the boys and stood in the middle. Eveline burst
into laughter when she saw how short they were next to
an enormously tall man. Even with their cone hats on,
they looked like midgets. They sat on the bleachers just
as the show began. The Ringmaster introduced the act
as a beautiful woman in full costume rode an elephant
into the ring. Patrick screamed and said, "Mother, you
should be doing that because you are as beautiful as she
is." Eveline kissed him on the cheek and thanked him for
the compliment. She thought circus work would not be
for her. Winston piped up and told her he wanted to be a
tight rope walker with tight pants on. Eveline made a face
at him. When the lions came out Andrew started crying
and shaking from fear, so Winston held him. Patrick held
his hand and told him he would take care of him. It was
a sight to see with Winston holding both of them with
cone hats on. When the popcorn man came along Eveline
bought a bag for each of them. She and Winston shared
one and the boys devoured theirs in minutes. Winston

told Eveline how nice it was that she thought to buy the popcorn. She looked at Winston and said, "I'm not as nasty as some people would like to think." On the way out of the circus, there were pony rides. Winston bought each boy a ticket. The ponies were the right size for the boys. Andrew commented that the pony was the right size for him but Colonel Culver could never ride one this small.

They got back to 775 late in the afternoon. Everyone was tired so they took naps while dinner was being prepared. Winston went into the boy's room and the three of them snuggled up together under a big blanket. When Eveline came into the room they had put the blanket over their heads with the point of the hats sticking up. Eveline went to get Sable and Olitha so they could see how they looked. Sable blurted out, "Oh, I hopes theys not the Ku Klux Klan cumin in here." At that, everyone laughed and they threw back the blanket and said, "Boo!" Olitha showed Andrew and Patrick her new baby. They stared at Chester as Andrew said, "There are three boys in three colors. I am white, Patrick is brown, and Chester is real black." Eveline's eyes went up and she laughed when she realized what was just said. Winston told them they lived in a house that welcomed all colors. Olitha said, "Amen." Sable made the boys favorite chocolate cookies which were huge. They were put to bed with smiles on their faces as Winston tucked them in and gave them a hug.

The next morning Eveline went to see Mr. Keyes regarding the financial aspect of selling the hotel in Rochester. He was surprised she was interested in such a transaction. He advised her to take as much as she could get for it and that she should be tough when an offer was made. He advised her to negotiate with Mr. Preston alone and not involve Lucille. Eveline assured him she would be careful. She discussed her thoughts about reducing the number of companies she was involved with. He thought she was wise for that consideration but advised her to keep stock option high so she had the majority of the votes but would not be responsible for the operations. She assured him she would confer with him on those matters. When she got home she found the boys and Winston at the lake. He was teaching them how to fish. Eveline yelled to them from the top of the bank. They waved at her and asked her to come down to see the fish. She was not into hiking down the embankment but managed to slide down instead of walking. By the time she got down to them she was dirty from head to toe with her hat half off her head. Winston and the boys burst into laughter at the site of her. Andrew waved a flopping fish at her making her scream while everyone laughed. Winston told her they were having fried fish for dinner. Patrick spoke up and said, "I asked Sable if she knew how to cook fish." As if on cue, Sable yelled from above asking if the fish were ready for the frying pan. Eveline made a face and asked herself how she got into all of this stuff.

Winston got the boys ready to go back to Manlius the next morning. They told him how much fun they had and wanted to know when they could come back. Eveline heard that and told them they could come home for part of the summer. When Winston heard this, he promised he would make a tire swing that would go out over the lake so they could fall into the water from it. Eveline looked at Winston and inquired about what he was planning on wearing for that occasion. He smiled and told her she would have to wait to see. When they went to the train station, the ticket agent complimented them on being on time. Winston went to work and Eveline went downtown to shop. She stopped into the A&P to see Hedy and Liza to tell them about the baby and the circus. They were their usual careful selves and took Miss Eveline into the storeroom for privacy. Each time she was stared at when she left the store. She thought that by now everyone should know why she was visiting Hedy and Liza. As she walked up the street, she passed by the Brevoort Hotel on 407 Exchange Street. Lately, hotels had been on her mind but this one had signs posted that it was closed for 30 days. The owners had been selling illegal substances that were against the Volstead Act. All the business was being sent to the Seneca Hotel. Underneath the sign was written "Speakeasy Shut Down." Eveline had the strange feeling that this might be what was going on in Rochester. Was that why Lucille had been so involved with people in both areas?

Eveline stopped at the Goodwin Printing Company. After seeing all the money in Rochester and hearing about where it was stored, she wanted to investigate this matter. She walked into the office and asked where Winston was. She was told he had taken the day off. Eveline was surprised because he never mentioned this when they took the boys to the train station. Winston left a message explaining he was going with Mike to the YMCA to relax for the rest of the day. She proceeded to the vault in the lower level of the building. She could hear the machines printing above her head. While she walked around she thought about Wallace and his first printing press and how antiquated it would be now. She worked at the combination to the safe until the door opened. When her eyes adjusted, she found nothing but papers. Why was it empty and where did the money go? She went upstairs and inquired if anyone had been downstairs. She was told that Mr. and Mrs. Preston had been there yesterday. Eveline thought that was very strange. She wondered if this had anything to do with her being approached by Mr. Preston about selling the hotel in Rochester. She left and on her way home considered the idea of selling the company in New York City. There seemed to be connections to both operations. Her next job was to find out more about The Foreign Exchange Company.

CHAPTER 26

March 4, 1925, Eveline was reading the travel section of the newspaper, while listening to the first radio broadcast of Calvin Coolidge's inauguration. The weather had been gloomy and cold, so the article about travel to the tropics caught her eye. An ocean liner was shown with an advertisement encouraging people to get away from the bleak wintry days. Southern destinations were listed as the land of perpetual summer. The ships sailed daily from New York City and made stops in Florida and Texas. Eveline heard that Miami was growing in popularity and that thousands of people spent the winter there. She thought about how convenient it would be to go to New York City a few days before the cruise. It would give her a chance to investigate the New York Foreign Exchange office. She might be able to find answers to her questions and meet Mr. Wellington in his environment. The only person she could rely on would be

Winston. He would know where to go and what to expect, but the trip had to be a secret.

When Winston arrived home, Eveline invited him into the library. She avoided telling him the whole story as to why she wanted him to go to New York City. While they were discussing his work in Geneva and what he had revealed to her about hiding money, she swore him to secrecy about the trip to New York City. She explained that she had questions about what was happening in Rochester with anyone connected to the Seneca Powers Hotel. Winston asked what his involvement was going to be in New York City. Eveline said that he was familiar with the locations and what the company had been doing and that he could assist her in investigating the operation. Winston was uneasy during the conversation because he had flashbacks of the trial and the events that led up to the arrest of the killer. Eveline assured him she would not allow him to do this on his own. She wanted to go to the offices and docks to see for herself how the imports were handled and what they consisted of. After she promised him all would be okay, Winston agreed to go with her. He said, "I am the only one, other than Rudolph, who knows about the operation." Eveline smiled and told him he was in for a surprise when they finished in New York City.

Eveline telephoned the travel agent. The gentleman assisting her was eager to explain that Miami was comfortably and conveniently reached by oil burning luxuriously equipped passenger steamers. If she wanted a larger stateroom there would be an additional cost, so she reserved two of the best staterooms from New York City to Miami. The trip would take two days. They would return to New York the following week. They would be staying in the Hotel Halcyon which was the largest hotel in Miami, located on the corner of East Flagler Street and 2nd Avenue. Its motto was "Where Winter Spends the Summer." She reserved the penthouse facing the ocean. According to the travel agent, a large sandbar could be seen in the distance from the hotel that was soon to be developed as ocean front properties. When she finished, she felt like she had just made plans for the next step in her life. First, she had to unravel and conclude some business affairs.

The next few days were spent organizing the trip and buying clothing to wear in Florida. As Eveline was shopping, she ran into Lucille Preston. Whenever they met Eveline sensed Lucille was nervous. This never happened until Eveline put pressure on the group in Rochester. Lucille asked Eveline why she was buying summery outfits in the early part of March. She explained that it was time for her to go to the sunny south for a while to get out of the bleak winter weather. Lucille changed the subject and told Eveline she should stay in town and tend to her businesses. Eveline asked what she meant. According to Lucille, her husband was preparing a purchase offer for the Seneca Powers Hotel. Eveline did not want Lucille to know she had received the letter regarding the offer from Mr. Preston. She was never sure who knew what or what the purpose was for information. Lucille implied as if it were a done deal. When Eveline heard this she thanked Lucille and began walking out of the store. Lucille followed her and asked why she did not have a better attitude about her information. Eveline turned and said, "The offer will be there when I return if I don't get it before I go away."

Eveline telephoned Mr. Keyes and inquired about any news from the Prestons regarding the sale of the hotel. He had not received any offers. When Eveline heard this she decided to stall any response to the offer. She had a feeling Lucille had tested her to see how anxious she might be to get rid of the hotel. Eveline had better plans for those people in Rochester. Winston arrived home from work while Eveline was packing. She told him that they were leaving in two days. She explained about the arrangements and what she wanted to accomplish in New York City. As he was listening, he wondered what Eveline would do if she found out things were not as she expected and asked her about it. Eveline paused and told him she had been in contact with the New York Port Authorities. Winston became nervous about this information. She sensed that and asked him what was wrong. He explained that he had been there with Wallace when there had been discussion of shipments from the Orient. As a result of that conversation, the office and docks were transferred to New Jersey where the rules were less strict about cargo. After he left, Eveline made another telephone call to a gentleman that had been helpful in New York City. She asked if he could be with her and Winston when they visited the shipping docks and office. Eveline explained what she sensed about some trouble and that she now owned the import company because of the death of her husband. He admitted he heard about an ownership change. When Eveline heard this she wondered why he knew about it. They agreed to meet at the Waldorf Astoria Hotel in two days.

Mr. Keyes sent a messenger to 775 with a letter that contained the offer for the Seneca Powers Hotel. He telephoned Eveline to explain what it consisted of and urged her to read it carefully. He felt sending it to her would give her a chance to think about it and then they could confer if there were any questions. An hour later a messenger was at the door and Sable answered it. He asked for Mrs. Wallace Paine. Sable was startled because she thought he said Mr. Wallace Paine. Eveline heard the conversation and came to the door and reminded him that she was no longer referred to as Mrs. Paine, much less Mrs. Wallace Paine. Sable's eyes went up as she backed away from the door. When Eveline closed the door she winked at Sable and said, "I love letting people know about my new identity." Sable smiled and said, "You doin a good job with that one." Eveline took the envelope to the library and studied it before opening it. She wondered what the future held and if this was the beginning of a new life. The offer was very simple. Mr. Preston offered $750,000.00 cash for the hotel which would include the building, contents, staff, ledgers, and monies involved in the hotel's operation. All she would need to do was to sign the agreement and set a date to transfer ownership. After she finished reading the letter, she thought it seemed too concise and quick. She telephoned Mr. Keyes for his opinion. When he heard her voice he laughed and told her that he knew she would be calling because of the type of agreement it was. Eveline wanted to know if there was any reason to counter the offer. Without any hesitation, he told her if she could be paid cash there should be no hesitation. She thanked him and explained about her trip to Florida. He told her to wait until she returned to sign anything. She had fourteen days to respond. She hung up and thought that was fair enough and they could just wait. She wanted the upper hand with the Prestons.

The day arrived for Eveline and Winston to go to New York City. She told Sable and Olitha that she and Winston were going on a business trip to see how things were in New York City. After they left for the train station, Sable told Olitha that she was worried Miss Eveline would find out more than she wanted to know. Olitha had the same bad feeling. While Eveline and Winston were on the train they discussed how uncomfortable it had been when Wallace and he went to New York City. Eveline tried to understand but thought about how much fun Wallace and he used to have with each other when they went on those trips. Then she patted him on the knee and said, "Now we can have some fun." Winston wondered how she knew that they had fun when in New York City. Winston was beginning to feel like Eveline knew everything all along. He told Eveline about how helpful the bellhop used to be in the Waldorf Astoria. Eveline told him he probably wanted to have fun with the two of you. Eveline admitted she had never been to New York City and hoped it would be a thrill for her. When they arrived at the Waldorf Astoria the same bellhop still worked there. He recognized Winston. Winston was surprised he had such a good memory. When Eveline saw the gilded lobby and its grandeur she said, "Now this is my type of living." The bellhop smiled and asked Winston where his partner was. Eveline looked at him and said, "I am the dead partner's wife." Winston stood speechless as the bellhop said nothing, looking in a confused way at Winston. He escorted them to the front desk. The mystery of the forgery and murder were still heavy on Winston's mind as he watched Eveline sign for the rooms. While in the elevator, Eveline deliberately told Winston she wanted her own room. The bellhop listened and stared at Winston with excitement in his eyes.

Eveline was shown to her room. She told Winston he was free to do what he wanted and that she would see him at 8PM in the lobby. She tipped the bellhop and explained it was for Winston too. He escorted Winston to his room at the end of the hall. While they were going to the room the bellhop told Winston that the woman he was with ordered the rooms to be far apart. Winston wondered why she did that. The bellhop opened the door and took the luggage into the room. Winston followed and closed the door. The bellhop turned to him and said, "I never thought I would see you again. I knew a few years ago that you and your friend were more than buddies. I was jealous." He asked the bellhop what his name was. He told him that did not matter because he could be fired for having anything to do with the guests. Winston found that to be even more exciting as he began to unbutton his shirt. The bellhop moved closer and studied Winston's movements as his hairy chest was in full view. The bellhop asked what Winston wanted from him. Bellhops are to be at the guest's service was all he said. Winston asked how much time he had. The bellhop's day was finished so he had all night. By this time, Winston had removed his clothes. The bellhop admitted he wanted to have this opportunity the last time. It was as if Wallace returned from the dead as he watched the bellhop undress. He was hairless but firm like Wallace had been. He was like a snake when he wrapped himself around Winston's waist as Winston carried him to the bed. Winston was on top pinning the bellhop down with his hands and feet. The bellhop allowed Winston to be the dominant one. For Winston, this was how he liked it to be. After a few hours of intense physical contact, the bellhop needed a rest from Winston's continuous domination. Winston invited him to return the next day.

Eveline knocked on Winston's door at 8PM. He was not ready and answered the door with only his trousers on. She walked in and asked why it was taking him so long to get ready. He hesitated and before he said anything Eveline said, "You probably ruined the bellhop." Eveline admitted she came to the door earlier and heard sounds of ecstasy coming from the room. She told him she thought that might happen being familiar with Winston's aggressive ways. They went to the dining room that overlooked the street. It was the same location that he and Wallace sat in the night before the trial. Only this time there was no man watching them from across the street. Eveline discussed what she had done with the investigator. When Winston heard this he was more comfortable having an authority with them. He was not sure Eveline knew the measures these people would take to eliminate anyone who may cause trouble.

The next morning the investigator met them in the lobby and told them that he had been surveilling the operation. He was pleased that he was asked to assist Mrs. Paine during her visit. Eveline wanted to correct him on the title he used for her but thought it best she not be too demanding. They took a taxicab to the New Jersey docks but were let out of the vehicle a block from the office. They walked to the area that had a sign that read The Foreign Exchange Company. So far it seemed okay. There was a bell that Eveline rang. A man appeared through a small window and asked what the reason was for the visit. Winston told him they were looking for Mr. Wellington. The window closed and the door opened. It was a damp, chilly, and dimly lit area. The investigator followed as Eveline asked if she could speak with Mr. Wellington about some products she ordered that had not been delivered. The little man held his hands up and went into an office. A man appeared that wore a nametag of Mr. Wellington but he did not look like Mr. Wellington. He asked what the matter was. Eveline asked where Mr. Wellington was. He was emphatic that he was Mr. Wellington. Without telling him why she was there, she had a feeling that the man who appeared in Geneva may not have been the right person. Eveline had enough confusion and this put her in a mood that it did not matter what she said. She looked at him and said, "Look, whoever you are, I am the owner of this dreadful place and I am here to see what is going on. Now if you are Mr. Wellington, who came to Geneva for the meeting of Mr. Paine's business associates?" He hesitated and stepped back and invited her into his office. Eveline said, "No way, unless my friends come too." Eveline wore a large brimmed hat that got caught on a nail that held a drape back. She was furious when it fell to the floor. Winston thought it was funny until he saw Eveline's pursed lips.

The supposed Mr. Wellington began to explain that there had been some confusion when the authorities came to see about the company and its imports. Eveline knew that and asked to hear more. He stuttered when he became nervous. The investigator knew of this but never let on to her when he agreed to come along. As the explanation continued, the imposter told them about an investigation about checks and who was signing for money and expenses. As he was finishing about the bank issue, the investigator stood up and said, "Eveline Paine and Winston Spaulding, you are under arrest in connection to an illegal import and export company." Eveline demanded more explanation. He told her it was not the exports but the imports that were illegal. She was the signer of all transactions related to the smuggling of alcohol, transferring, and selling of children coming from various parts of the world. Winston spoke up but was told he was still implicated because he was living with and travelling with the person owning and conducting such operations. Eveline asked where Mr. Wellington was. She was told that he had been dead for many years from a mysterious poisoning. The imposter was a set up by the investigator. She was told that they had a tip off from an unknown informant about rubber-stamping all checks by the owner, who was Eveline. Now, she knew that Rudolph had never closed the company but merely changed the name and made rubber stamps of her signature. She would be blamed for everything. Eveline explained that to the investigator and he agreed he received that tip. Until they found out who the culprit was she and Winston were under arrest. Handcuffs were placed on them and they were escorted to the police vehicle. While they were being transported, the investigator told her the place had been raided and closed. They found children restrained and illegal substances that violated the 18th Amendment to the United States Constitution. He told them that the courts could place a $50,000.00 bail on each of them. Eveline was so angry that she could not say a word. When the bellhop saw them coming into the lobby with handcuffs on he winked at Winston. Security guards were placed in front of their doors that were locked from the outside for the night. They were to appear in court the next morning.

The investigator arrived at the Waldorf Astoria Hotel in the morning with additional officers who would escort Eveline and Winston to the courthouse. They were fed breakfast in a private room to avoid unnecessary attention.

During the meal, Eveline explained why she was in New York City. She did not expect this treatment since she came to unravel the underhanded business. The investigator listened and asked how they expected to make bail. Eveline requested that she make a call to her friend in Geneva. She would tell Rose where the money was and she and Samuel could come to New York City with the bail. The investigator was not certain the judge would grant that to them. They would need better guarantees about who was responsible for them until the investigation was settled. The investigator offered to travel with them to inquire about the operation in Rochester, since he knew they were connected. During the conversation, he told Eveline that he had been tracking her whereabouts and had a secret service person following her the day she went to Rochester and confronted the people in the hotel office. Eveline tried to remember if anyone seemed suspicious, but then that day was full of suspicious people. He smiled and asked her if she remembered the young man who claimed he was from Puerto Rico. Eveline was stunned and remembered that the young man seemed concerned but did not offer too much information. Winston listened to everything and finally asked the investigator if he had a name. He smiled and said, "I thought you would never ask. My name is Thaddeus Cooper." He explained that he would speak on their behalf when the judge asked questions. They left the hotel through a back door to a waiting police car.

Mr. Cooper introduced the complainants to the judge and explained why they were in New York City. The judge did not seem concerned about the bail issue and agreed that Mr. Cooper and one other officer should accompany Eveline and Winston to Geneva and then to Rochester.

As the judge put it, "Then you boys can arrest the right culprits. We have been tracking this company for a number of years." The judge apologized to Eveline explaining that she had been set up. She was the only person that could walk in and have reason to question everyone who was connected with this company and its various names. The judge decided that because there were law enforcement officers accompanying them, he would not place bail on them. Eveline was relieved when she heard there would be no bail. Now, she knew she was going to go after the right people. Winston thought about all the times he was in New York City and that each time it turned into criminal involvements and courtrooms. The plan was to leave the city immediately so that they could surprise people in Rochester when they arrived earlier than expected. Eveline spoke up and told the judge they were planning to go to Florida on a ship the next day. The judge with a devilish smile said, "I guess you will miss the boat." Winston having been so tense from all the events burst out laughing when he heard it put that way. He recovered from his outburst as Mr. Cooper told Eveline to cancel the trip. They were escorted to the hotel trying to cover the handcuffs as they walked to the elevators. The bellhop approached them and asked if they were leaving and needed assistance with their luggage. Winston looked at the bellhop and knew what he was thinking. The second officer appeared as they were going into the elevator. Mr. Cooper went with Eveline and the other officer with Winston. The bellhop waited in Winston's room for the luggage to be prepared. He asked Winston if he liked to be cuffed. Winston said, "I do not like to be handcuffed but if there is another time here, I should cuff you and gag you. You would probably enjoy it more." The officer said nothing as he rolled his eyes.

They traveled in a special section on the train that transported criminals that was separate from other passengers. Eveline made a face at Winston like they were in a cattle car. She was still not happy with the way things were turning out. She could not imagine what Sable and Olitha would think when they arrived home in handcuffs. During the train ride Mr. Cooper briefed the officer on the plan. The first target was the holding room in the Goodwin Printing Company. Mr. Cooper informed Winston that he knew about his work and his orders to remain quiet and was aware of the amounts of money coming and going from that company. Mr. Cooper apologized to Eveline and explained that he was familiar with her late husband's shifty business dealings. She sat and wondered how much more she would find out before it all ended. Winston told Mr. Cooper he had been sworn to secrecy or he would be eliminated. Mr. Cooper reminded him of the activities with the people years ago that had their tongues cut out for saying too much. Eveline thought of the black box and the letter she found about Mr. Ling and the killings. She decided not to mention the box. She had a feeling she may need it as evidence at a trial. Mr. Cooper explained that any money they found in the basement of the printing company would be taken away. Then, they would take a trip to the Seneca Powers Hotel. Mr. Cooper had contacted the Rochester Police Department to have them ready when it was time to move in on the operation. If they planned it correctly, they would be there when a shipment arrived from Canada. The Puerto Rican informant had been reporting the activities to the New York Port Authorities and tipped off the Port of Rochester office. Eveline would arrive by herself as she did last time. The other officer would follow her into the hotel, not Mr. Cooper. He had been spotted in Rochester previously and would stay back until the end. Winston was expected to be with them because he was still considered part of the case. He would be in a Rochester policeman uniform. When Eveline heard this she said, "That's just what he needs is to be in uniform. He will want to wear it all the time."

Eveline had no choice but to invite the officers to stay overnight. They accepted, to avoid staying in a hotel. When the taxicab pulled in front of 775 South Main Street, Mr. Cooper told them that he had been by this place many times. Eveline told him she always felt like she was being watched. When Sable answered the door and saw Winston and Eveline handcuffed she screamed, "Olitha, come quick Miss Eveline and Winston are in trouble. Oh my Lord, what did you two do?" Olitha appeared and said, "Yous look likes criminals." Eveline told them to settle down that it was not as bad as it looked. Sable shook her head and said, "Anyones in cuffs is in big troubles." While they were in the library waiting for dinner to be served, they finished discussing the next day. The last thing Mr. Cooper explained was about finding out how Mike Bennett died. Eveline told him she was there the day he was found hunched over the desk in a pool of blood. Mr. Cooper interrupted and asked if she knew who did it or how it was done? She shrugged her shoulders. The cuffs were removed before dinner.

After breakfast, they went to the Goodwin Printing Company before any of the workers arrived. When they entered the basement room, they found a barrel full of money that smelled of alcohol. Eveline looked at the money and asked how much there was in the barrel. Mr.

Cooper took a fistful and held it up and said, "More money than can be counted by the four of us." How were they going to get the money out of the basement? Winston told them about a trunk that was upstairs in the office. They stuffed the money in it and put it in the trunk of the roadster. Eveline threatened James with losing his job if he mentioned anything about this day to anyone. Eveline made a point of telling everyone in the car that she threatened Sable and Olitha with the same thing. They did tell Mr. Cooper about their days as surrogate mothers on the ships coming from the Orient. Mr. Cooper did not know about this and said they would be good witnesses when there was a trial. Eveline shook her head and said, "That's all they will need is to be on trial." When they were close to the hotel, Mr. Cooper had Winston dropped off with the policemen that had his uniform. Mr. Cooper, Eveline, and the other investigator walked to the hotel but separated just before she turned the corner. The men would wait a few minutes and then act as if they were checking in. Everything was timed in hopes that the delivery would arrive as they were told it would.

Eveline walked through the lobby with her usual stroll, only this time no cigarette holder. She spotted the Puerto Rican and he motioned for her to go to the next door. She acknowledged him in a disinterested way as she went further down the hall. The door was ajar but no one was in the room. She went in and listened. She heard voices coming from the next office. At that point Mr. Cooper joined her. There was yelling and then a low voice was heard. It sounded like Eveline's mother explaining something about Mike Bennett. Mr. Lounsberry told her to shut up because they needed to keep that quiet. Then he said it was time to go to the dock for the arrivals. Eveline shook her head when she heard her parent's voices in the midst of such criminal activity. There were more than two people leaving the office through a back stairway. Mr. Cooper told Eveline to wait a few minutes to follow them to the dock. They went into the office that smelled of stale cigars and alcohol. When they left through the doorway the other investigator came into the office to keep guard. The hallway had been crudely built between the walls and was difficult to get through. Eveline nearly fell because of the type of shoes she wore. When they reached the end, they saw young boys and girls unloading containers. Mr. Lounsberry signed a paper for the delivery that had just come from Kingston, Ontario. Eveline whispered to Mr. Cooper that they used to live near there years ago. Lucille Preston came in from the dock area and was handed a list of names and a bag of money. She told everyone that the money was from the people who had purchased their new servants or sexual slaves. Eveline shook her head thinking that everyone she knew was a criminal. Where was Rudolph in all this? Mr. Cooper nudged Eveline and told her it was her turn to drop in on the group. She took a deep breath and opened the door. She walked in with an air of authority and said, "So, we meet again in a suspicious way." Who would like to tell me what is happening in my hotel?" Just as her mother started speaking, Mr. Preston rushed in and was surprised to see Eveline standing there. She sarcastically invited him to come into the meeting. She told them she was not used to conducting business on a shipping dock but seemed like the right place for such dealings. Mr. Preston was so taken back and said, "I thought you were on a ship to Florida." She smiled and told him she liked to surprise people because she finds out much more this way. She asked if he was still waiting for her signature for the sale of this hotel. Then she said, "And speaking of signatures, I found out that some of you have been using a rubber stamp of my signature on transactions in New York City." She looked at Mr. Preston and asked why he was in such a hurry to buy the hotel. He told her he wanted to get it over with, but may not be able to buy it now. She asked why. He told her he lost the money he was going to use to buy the hotel. Then Lucille screamed at him, "Where the hell did it go?" At that moment, Eveline knew where it went; it was in the trunk of the roadster.

During Eveline's questioning, another officer came in and whispered something in Mr. Cooper's ear. Eveline thought something might have happened to Winston in all the confusion. Mr. Cooper told Eveline to continue with her meeting. She looked at him and said, "I've just begun to work on these people." She looked at her mother and asked, "So Mommy, why are you involved with these people? I thought you didn't like to go out of the apartment." Her mother glared at her and told her she was the interviewer for the Exchange Program. Eveline smirked and said, "So, you do your interviewing on the docks." Her mother yelled at her and told her she was like all the rest and that she had hated Eveline since she was born. Mr. Lounsberry told her to stop but she went on to say that Eveline was too smart for her own good and that was why she put her in a boarding school. She reminded Eveline that she was just like her and that was why Patrick and that little orphan kid were thrown in Manlius. She smiled at Eveline and said, "You are just like me, you bitch." Mr. Cooper told her to be quiet. Eveline was finally seeing what she thought was true after all these years. Mr. Cooper wanted to know if any of these people knew how Mike Bennett died. Lucille cleared her throat and looked at Mrs. Lounsberry and in a shaky voice admitted Mike was turning against any authority. Rudolph instructed Mike to defy Eveline's authority in the hotel. Mrs. Lounsberry was the one who kept telling Mike to make Eveline feel like he was listening to her but to do as he pleased in the hotel business. He stood up to me one too many times, so Lucille and I gave him what he wanted. Eveline asked, "What was that?" Lucille shouted, "We killed him so he would not need to take sides." Lucille went on to say that he was such a nice boy but too innocent to do such work. Eveline looked at her father and asked what his place was in all the corruption. He admitted he needed to be more active, so he organized an office in Canada and at the hotel for deliveries. He knew people in Canada that were against Prohibition and were happy to assist in smuggling and transporting alcohol through Canada into the United States. When he finished, Mr. Cooper called the Rochester police officers to enter and handcuff everyone. Winston came in with the officers and when Lucille saw him she said, "Oh my God, you knew about the money all the time in the basement." He smiled and agreed and then Eveline said, "Yes, it's all in my trunk." Mr. Preston then knew were the money went that he would have used to buy the hotel. Eveline wished everyone well and told them she would be happy to see them in court. Mr. Cooper added that these were federal offenses that would require a much larger trial than usual. The paddy wagon was waiting at the door as they were all ushered into the back of it.

Mr. Cooper told Eveline he had something else to do and would be back in the office as soon as he had finished. Winston would stay with her and the other investigator.

Winston liked wearing the uniform because it made him feel important. Eveline commented about how good he looked dressed like a police officer. She told him he could dress up and they could play police games. After all that she had been through, she still had the flare for adventures with Winston. While they waited for Mr. Cooper, they discussed what would happen next. Eveline had not had time to fully understand how long all this had been going on. What was even more upsetting was that her family, friends, and her dead husband were the worst offenders. It was all done to make big money at the expense of poor people. Mr. Cooper came back and asked Eveline to sit down because he had more news for her. She looked at him and said, "Now what?" He explained that Rudolph Williams had hung himself. There was a note left for her. She looked at it and thought about the black box and all she had learned from it. She opened the envelope and read:

Dear Eveline, I had no choice but to end my life. We have been friends for years, but now enemies. You took over in a way that Wallace never would have. You are too honest and good for this type of work. Wallace pleaded with me on his deathbed to not let you know of all these wrongs that he started many years ago. After you began to uncover things, you found out too much. You are a very astute woman and I knew you were getting to the bottom of everything. Instead of letting you put me in prison and having the last laugh, I eliminated myself from your control. I am in my own control now. Signed, Her Ruddy

When Mr. Cooper heard the "Her Ruddy" part he questioned what that meant. She explained it was a nickname she had given him along with her late husband, being "Her Wallace." Mr. Cooper said, "It sounds like you had a lot of control over them." Winston piped up and said, "She sure did." They left the hotel and walked back to the Roadster where James was waiting. Eveline told him to get her home as fast as he could because she had had enough for one day. Winston was still in the uniform and Mr. Cooper told him it was a donation for all the trouble he went through. Winston was as happy as a kid at Christmas with his new outfit. Mr. Cooper explained that all were arrested on federal charges and the trial date would be set. He told them not to go too far because they would be called as witnesses along with her servants and friends. Eveline wondered what she was going to tell Rose and Samuel. How were they going to take the news or were they also involved in some way?

CHAPTER 27

Thaddeus Cooper contacted Eveline to tell her that her mother and father were incarcerated as criminals of foreign countries. Eveline never knew that her parents remained Canadian citizens because she had become a United States citizen a year after she arrived in Rochester. Mr. Cooper told her that during the interrogation both of her parents admitted they were still loyal to Canada. When Eveline thought about this news, she realized they may have been involved in other criminal activities. Mr. Cooper asked Eveline if there was any information she may have about the past and how these people became involved with one another. She told him that the people that bought the home her husband built found a black metal box in the crawlspace. She told him that it contained various letters about everyone her late husband had been involved with. Mr. Cooper was fascinated that her husband would be so organized to have done something of this nature. He suggested that her lawyer sit with them when he read the contents. Eveline agreed to speak with Mr. Keyes about his request.

Mr. Keyes telephoned Eveline to ask her to stop at his office for a conference regarding Wallace's estate. He explained that the five year hold on all assets, stocks, and money had expired. She went to his office and was informed that, since Rudolph was dead and had no family, she was entitled to the entire estate, including his assets that were part of Wallace's businesses. Mr. Keyes asked Eveline if she had any idea of the total from all the investments Wallace had been involved with. Eveline said, "Shall I stay seated or do I have to stand for this?" Mr. Keyes told her she may want to remain seated because she may faint when she heard the next sentence. Wallace's total assets were calculated to be close to 10 million dollars. Mr. Keyes said, "I know how you like exact numbers but it is impossible to determine because of the constant fluctuation of money from interest and splitting of stocks." Eveline took a deep breath and said, "I thought there was more than I knew about." Mr. Keyes explained that she should continue with the companies that were growing but to consider getting rid of other less productive companies. Eveline smiled and told him she was selling the hotel to a different group now that Mr. Preston was in jail. The import and export company had already been closed and the Goodwin Printing Company was a cover for underhanded business and was also being closed. Mr. Keyes offered to take care of the legalities of those closings but advised that she secure a lawyer in Rochester who was qualified in federal court cases.

The next item was the black box and its contents. Mr. Keyes thought it was okay for the contents to be read, but only in his presence. Thaddeus was invited to listen to Eveline as she read the letters that pertained to those individuals who were in jail on criminal charges. He was amazed that Wallace wrote so much about everyone and was either warning Eveline or trying to make himself appear guilt free. As Mr. Keyes listened, he too was surprised that someone would spend their life writing about the things people did, with Wallace being the mastermind to all of it. Eveline felt like she was being dragged through her life with Wallace again as she listened to herself reading the letters. Mr. Cooper suggested they keep the box in a safe place. Mr. Keyes offered to keep it in his safe. When Eveline heard the word trials she made a face and asked, "How many trials?" Mr. Keyes explained that her parent's trial might be the easiest because they were Canadians. They could be deported as criminals and dealt with in Canada. Lucille and Mr. Preston could be individual trials. Mr. Cooper told them it could take months for all this to be finished.

While Thaddeus and Eveline were walking back to 775, she told him about Patrick's life and his background. He told her that he never married. He was married to his work and never wanted to be responsible for all that marriage entailed. Eveline told him how much she liked her new identity and enjoyed her freedom. She told him that Patrick had just turned 10 years old and Andrew was an orphan that she had overseen for a few years. She mentioned that they were coming for a visit to celebrate their birthdays. Eveline invited Thaddeus to the party and he accepted. The topic of Samuel and Rose came up as they were walking into the house. Thaddeus thought meeting them might give a better light as to how they fit in to all that had transpired. Eveline said she would include them for the celebration. Mr. Cooper excused himself and said he had meetings in Rochester but would be back for the party.

Winston asked how many people were coming for the celebration. Eveline wanted to know what he was up to. He was a bit hesitant to tell her but wanted to know if he could have a parade for the boys. Sable laughed when she heard this and Eveline rolled her eyes with the thought of a parade. She wanted to know how he was planning such an event. He told her he would need her permission and some money for it. Eveline wanted to know more about the money part. Winston explained that he wanted to invite Patrick's classmates. They would arrive by train and become part of the parade along Main Street that ended at 775. He would rent ponies, employ some clowns, and he would be the policeman leading the event. Eveline knew she would need to discuss it with the school and probably have to invite the old stuffy administrator. Eveline thought about it and agreed to telephone the school in the morning. Winston wanted the party to be a sleep over. Sable started laughing and said, "Weez cookin for a camp then." Olitha overheard the camp part and told them she had been in a camp for girls a long time ago. Eveline asked what happened. Olitha explained it was for young girls that were afraid to be brought to America. Eveline interrupted and told her it was not going to be like that ever again. The party would be for boys in Patrick and Andrew's class. Sable said, "The whole city gonna turn out to see what the rich lady in the mansion is doin now."

When Eveline heard it put that way, she knew it was a good idea.

The next morning, Eveline telephoned Manlius School. After some discussion with the administrator, he agreed to allow the boys to come to Geneva. He would need to chaperone them and they would need reliable people to care for the students while they were in town. They were only allowed in the parade and would have to stay at 775. Eveline assured him she would employ extra help for the two day event. There would be 20 boys. Eveline paid for the transportation and any costs the school might have for this occasion. The administrator would get permission from the parents. When she finished her conversation, she made a list of chaperones making sure Rose and Samuel were included, thinking a doctor might be good to have on the property for emergencies. She thought about Alice and Frank since they were the only people left in the family that were not in jail. There would be Winston, Mr. Cooper, and James could be the delivery person if Sable and Olitha needed party supplies. She made up her mind she was spending as much money as she wanted to now that it was all hers to spend. Eveline called Rose, who thought she was crazy, but agreed to be there with Samuel. Hedy and Liza were more excited than anyone because they feared less communication as Patrick got older. Winston rented 20 ponies. He knew a horse farmer outside of town that would bring the ponies to the train station. Sable spoke up and said, "Sounds like weez havin a circus not a party." Winston wanted Samuel and Frank to be clowns. Eveline went into hysterics when she heard this and agreed they both would make great clowns. She said, "I know Frank has had loads of practice at being a clown. I'm sorry my father couldn't be in it as the fat man." No one laughed at that remark as Eveline sucked her teeth.

Winston asked about the sleeping arrangements. There was enough room for the boys to sleep in sleeping bags and pretend they were camping. The adults could share the extra rooms and use the parlor and library. Eveline had been paying Winston a salary to assist her along with being in charge of the party and the groundskeeper. The property never looked so good now that his full attentions were on 775. He decided to build a dock on the shore. He would have a few boats the day of the party for boat rides. He ordered the lumber which would be delivered the next day by horse and wagon. He thought how things had changed, when only a few short years ago this was the only means of transportation.

Hedy and Liza were excited about the idea of the parade and party. They offered to dress up and be in the parade and walk with the ponies. When Eveline heard this she decided she would have James drive her Lincoln with the top down and she would sit on the back dressed up like a queen. Patrick and Andrew would ride the first two ponies in the lineup. When Sable heard this she said, "Oh my Lord weez got a fairy tale coming down the street. Weez better have the newspaper covering this parade." Olitha said, "I hope the townspeople don't run you out of town after all this." Eveline said, "I hope they do. I'm ready to go."

There was a special delivery from the United States Federal Court in Rochester. The man at the door insisted he give it to Mrs. Wallace Paine. When Eveline heard

Sable explaining the name issue she went to the door. Eveline looked at the man and asked, "Do I look like a Wallace?" He shook his head and admitted he had to say that because it was on the envelope. Eveline signed for the letter and the man said, "Thank you, Miss Paine." She shook her head and slammed the door. She went to the library to read the letter. She was subpoenaed to appear as a witness in the murder trial of Mike Bennett. There was an addendum requesting Mr. Keyes to deliver the black box to the law office for review. This would be used as evidence against the accused individuals in her companies. Eveline telephoned Mr. Keyes to verify the request. He had received the request also. She suggested they deliver it together then they could meet about the specifics of the trial. Mr. Keyes informed her that many people received the letter requesting their appearance in court. Shortly after the conversation, the telephone rang and Olitha directed it to Eveline. It was Samuel, in a fury of anger, wanting to know what was in the black box to implicate him in a trial. Eveline took an immediate offense to the attitude and asked him why he was being so suspicious. He had no answer except he had a feeling that box was going to be the end of many people.

The next morning there was a knock on the door and Olitha answered it. The same delivery man had a letter for her, Sable, and Winston. She called them to the door so they could sign for the registered post. Sable did not know how to read and Olitha was limited in reading, so Winston read the letters to them as Eveline was coming down the stairs. They were required to appear in court under penalty of the law. Eveline told them all to settle down because she had received the same letter. She did wonder why the tone of their letters was so direct, when hers was more businesslike. Sable spoke up and admitted that she was at the A&P and Hedy and Liza got the letters yesterday. Winston said, "It seems like the whole city will be in the courtroom." Eveline told them that Dr. Haynes would be there too. Rose was the only person who was not requested to appear in court.

Eveline received a letter from Patrick. It was the first time he had ever written to her. When she saw the envelope addressed to Mrs. Eveline Paine, she stared at it. She could tell it was not the writing of an adult because it was written in a childlike way. Patrick was writing to let her know how excited he was to bring his friends home for the party. There was a list of boy's names that were allowed to come to Geneva. Patrick told her about how much he was learning and that he and Andrew had become the leaders in their class. Patrick wanted to know if Eveline liked Andrew enough to have him be part of the family. He signed the letter, Your son, Love, Patrick. Eveline sat quietly and thought about how much she appreciated what Patrick said. She was still having trouble with the idea of being a mother. Part of her wanted more than one child but the fear of any responsibility to children made her uneasy. Was she still trying to be young at 40 years of age?

It was the day of the first trial. No one except Winston had been at a trial before. He acted like a pro when they got in the car and told them about the trial in New York City years ago. He forgot most people did not know about that incident and they were surprised about his part in the trial. They arrived at the courthouse where they saw the front page of the newspaper featuring the entire story of the murders, suicide, human transfers, and company closings. There was reference to Wallace Paine's empires being crushed and associates being tried for crimes against the Constitution of the United States. Eveline perused the newspaper to see if her name appeared. The only reference was that the late Wallace Paine's wife was the recipient to his empire. Her mother and father were named but only as possible deportees to Canada. Thaddeus was waiting in the court chambers with the lawyer who was defending the group from Geneva. Just before they entered the chambers, Eveline spotted Alice running into the building. She stopped Eveline and told her she would be in the courtroom to support her. Alice told Eveline she was embarrassed and angry that her son had done so many underhanded and dishonest things to her and the family. For the first time, Eveline broke down and wept when she saw how pained Alice was over the situation. Eveline and she sat and consoled one another for a few minutes. Alice wept while Eveline explained that she was feeling betrayed by the family and that Alice was the only person she trusted. Eveline was called to the chamber for a pretrial briefing.

The lawyer explained how they would proceed with the trial. There would be a presentation to the jury about the case and the process for the trial. The judge explained that many times the accused confess long before going to jury deliberations. Thaddeus sat next to Eveline and clarified the legal terms that were used. The hope for the trial was that the accused would confess to their crime without calling many witnesses. When the judge finished his introduction Eveline, Thaddeus, and the lawyer were taken to the courtroom, where the witnesses were seated in the back of the room. Eveline, the lawyer, and Thaddeus sat near the front of the courtroom. All were requested to rise as the judge took his chair and the proceedings began. Lucille was brought out in handcuffs, making everyone realize the severity of the crime. Introductions about the murder of Mike Bennett were explained to the jury. After the lawyer finished, Lucille Preston was called to the stand and sworn in under oath. The questions began about the intent of Mike Bennett and his threat to expose the operations at the Seneca Powers Hotel. Lucille admitted she and Mrs. Lounsberry attempted to quiet Bennett. He threatened to tell the owner of the hotel about the smuggling of alcohol from Canada to Rochester. The lawyer asked who the owner was of the hotel. Lucille pointed to Eveline and said, "That fancy women who overpowered all of us." Lucille was reminded to keep her personal judgments to herself. She was then asked who murdered Mr. Bennett. Lucille admitted that Mrs. Lounsberry did it because she knew she would be sent back to Canada and could possibly be set free. Lucille explained that she approached him to gag him, while Mrs. Lounsberry stuck the knife into his chest. Lucille told the jury she used a handkerchief so no prints could be found. The judge asked if there was any more information for the court. Lucille continue saying, "As long as I am going to prison, I am telling the whole story. My husband Mr. Preston was running a speakeasy in Geneva. He wanted to buy the Seneca Powers Hotel in Rochester to be used as a cover and a speakeasy. The hotel was the classiest one in town and might never be found out as being an illegal operation. He was going to pay, that Eveline, $750,000.00 cash for the hotel. He hoped she would go away then. When he found the money was gone he panicked. Mr. Lounsberry had been working in the underworld since he arrived in the United States about 20 years ago. When the Volstead Act became law, he hated the legalities of this country and developed a system of smuggling alcohol from Canada. As for myself, I became involved many years ago when I was assigned to be the placement officer for domestic servants, after they we used as surrogate mothers for children being smuggled into the country from the Orient. I helped operate the program her late husband was so good at starting. I knew of all the murders in New York, including the people who had their tongues cut out for talking too much. I should have thought about that with Bennett but realized that would have been too obvious. As far as my husband is concerned, I don't care if he likes me telling the truth now, because we are all going to be put away."

The judge cleared his throat and asked the stenographer if she got all that information. She proceeded to reread the confession. The people in the courtroom were aghast at such a conspiracy. Lucille sat in the front of the court with a smile on her face. The judge wanted to know what made her smile about such a story. She answered, "I think it is funny that we got away with this for years. Rudolph was told on Wallace's deathbed not to let his wife ever find out because she would tear everyone apart. As you all have seen, over the years, she has accomplished her goal. She is a wicked woman but she had a good teacher. Her mother always told me to beware of Eveline because she could uncover anything. I admired such a woman because I was able to do the same thing." The judge thanked her and she stepped down. Eveline was motionless while Lucille told her story. The group from Geneva was equally as stunned by the confession. The women who were surrogates agreed they felt relieved that they did not have to tell about their lives as surrogates. Winston remembered how nervous he was at the trial in New York City. Alice was beyond comment. She thought about how her son could do such things and never be accused of any of it. He must have been good at getting others to do the dirty work, while he sat back and watched his empire unfold.

The judge dismissed the jury and thanked them for their brief, but interesting time in the court. The four people mentioned were to be brought to the court for sentencing. They had been separated until after Lucille's questioning because the lawyers and the judge felt she would tell all. There was to be a recess and the court would resume at 1PM. At that time, the judge would determine the punishments for the four individuals. Eveline looked at Thaddeus and said, "I need to go to the hotel for lunch. I want to see it for the last time." She got up and invited everyone to walk there for lunch. Sable, Olitha, Hedy, and Liza were the most impressed that they were invited. They were usually the servants but now they were being served. Sable told them, "You girls better get used to Miss Eveline. She a good soul and treats us like weez important." Alice walked next to Eveline apologizing for Wallace's ways. Eveline told her not to worry because it was over. She reminded Alice of how her mother and father undermined her for her whole life. Alice was still in shock about the family history from her mother's affair with the Negro Civil War soldier right up to today's story. Eveline whispered in Alice's ear that she was preparing to sell everything and get out of town. They arrived at the hotel and were seated for lunch. There was very little conversation because people were trying to unravel the information they had heard.

Lunch was served in the usual elegant fashion. Eveline commented on what the hotel would be like when she was not in charge. Winston spoke up and said, "It's good you are letting it go. We have had many good times here but now we better leave before things change." Everyone laughed, but agreed it was time to go. Eveline left the hotel with the check unpaid. While they walked back to the court, Thaddeus wanted to know what Winston was referring to about good times in the hotel. Eveline said, "It is such a long story you will have to let him tell you. It goes back to 1900 when Wallace was advertising manager for the hotel." Still confused, Thaddeus let it go with no more questions.

The court came to order at 1PM. The judge had the stenographer read the confession to the court and to Mr. and Mrs. Lounsberry and Mr. and Mrs. Preston. There was no sound in the court as the information was given. The judge asked the accused if they had anything to add. Eveline stared at her mother, with fire in her eyes, when Mrs. Lounsberry said, "The only thing I want to say is that I never want to see my daughter again. I hate her." There were gasps heard in the courtroom and the judge said, "Don't worry, you are being deported." He continued with his sentencing. Mr. and Mrs. Lounsberry were to be escorted to the Canadian border. The authorities in Canada had already been informed and investigations were underway about the reason why they left Canada years ago. Eveline wondered why they came to America in the first place. Their apartment was to be locked and everything auctioned and given to children in orphanages. Lucille Preston was sentenced to life in prison for being the accomplice to murder and the transporting and distribution of children for illegal purposes. She was to be sent to Auburn State Prison. He warned Lucille to watch herself because when the female inmates found out what she had done they would have a heyday with her. Mr. Preston was sentenced to 25 years in a prison in Pennsylvania far from civilization. The Seneca Hotel in Geneva was to be closed until sold and proceeds would go to assist organizations that help homeless women and children in that part of the state. The judge told Eveline she was free to do as she pleased with her hotel. She asked to speak. The judge said it was highly irregular but under such circumstances he would allow it. Eveline stood and said, "I have just been to the hotel with my friends. I have said my good byes to the past, both good and bad. I will have my lawyer be in charge of its sale and the proceeds will go to the Manlius Pebble School in Syracuse where my son and his friend attend. I want my mother to hear that I am not as terrible as she thinks I am." The judge asked her if she was finished. She said, "One last thing, Mother, I hope you rot in hell along with Daddy. You deserve everything you get." As they were leaving the courtroom, the judge motioned to Eveline and said, "You were terrific. You said all the things I wanted to say but I am not able to give my opinions." Eveline smiled and said while the others listened, "Now you know why I'm glad they are being sent away."

CHAPTER 28

After the trial, Eveline and Winston made final plans for the birthday celebration. Winston had arranged for the twenty ponies to be at the train station. Sable and Olitha reminded Hedy and Liza they were helping them during the birthday weekend. Samuel prepared a medical bag with things he might need for injuries. Rose was the only person without a job, so Eveline assigned her to keep the peace if anyone became rowdy. James decorated and polished the Lincoln. Eveline found a gown in a costume shop that looked like something an actress might wear in a show. Winston wanted to know if she had a wand so she could wave it at everyone. She laughed and told him she had one she used for fun that was not magic. Winston finished building the dock and had two boats available for rides or fishing. Eveline made it clear; she was not getting into any boat for either activity. Sable overheard her and said, "You's gonna have enough trouble with your circus on Main Street. No need to worry about boat rides." Eveline asked what kind of trouble. Sable continued, "I done heard the gossip about the lady in the mansion bringin orphans to town on ponies. All the domestics were a buzzin about it at the A&P Store." Eveline asked how everyone knew about the party. Winston spoke up and told them he mentioned it to the farmer when he rented the ponies. Eveline said, "Good, I hope the whole town comes to Main Street. I'll show them how a decent party should be conducted." Olitha shook her head as she left the room saying, "You sure are a brave woman. Weez glad we work for you, ain't nobody we'd rather be with."

The train was scheduled to arrive in Geneva at noon. Winston went early, dressed in his police uniform, to make sure the farmer had delivered the ponies. Eveline planned to arrive a few minutes before noon so as not to create a scene. Rose had called Alice and Frank to invite them to the party. Rose hoped Eveline would appreciate their presence since they were the only relatives left who would be able to attend. When Alice accepted the invitation she offered for Frank to play the drum for the parade. When Rose told Eveline that she invited Alice and Frank, she did not respond. When she heard about the drum she said, "I never knew Frank could play a drum. Thank you for thinking of them." Rose was surprised Eveline was so agreeable because she usually liked ideas to come from herself. It was sure to be the most unique birthday party ever.

Winston bought party hats for the ponies. The people at the train station looked in amazement when Winston, dressed like a police officer, was decorating the ponies. Along came James, driving with Eveline in the back seat dressed like a queen. Frank found an old high school uniform he had worn in the band. Alice saw a side of Frank she never knew existed. He appeared the happiest she had seen him. The engineer had been told ahead of time why so many young boys were going to be on the train. As a surprise, the engineer blew the horn a mile away and made intermittent horn sounds like a song. As the train pulled into the station, the boys were hanging out of the windows waving and cheering. Then they saw Winston, the ponies, and Eveline dressed like a queen. Patrick and Andrew were the first ones off the train and ran to Winston and Eveline. Patrick hugged and kissed Eveline and thanked her for being such a good mother. Andrew hugged Eveline, but looked at her as if he hoped for a kiss and Winston got the usual buddy hugs. He said, "You boys are getting too big to pick up. I could never do that anymore." They laughed and told him they would soon be picking him up. Eveline said, "How things change, they are almost as tall as me." By now the rest of the boys were around them and the administrator was impressed with what he saw. Samuel introduced him to Rose, Alice, and Frank. While they were chatting, Winston explained to the boys about the technique for riding on a pony. They mounted the ponies and looked like an army. Eveline took her place in the Lincoln that would follow the ponies. Winston and Frank were leading the parade. Winston had a whistle and blew it as they approached busy areas. Sable was right. There were crowds of people waiting to see what was coming down the street. Some people cheered and clapped while others just stared. Children could be heard asking why they could not be in the parade. By the time they reached Pulteney

Park, Frank was beating the drum in a rhythmic way. A few people were standing by the fountain playing trumpets. It was turning into a city event. The newspaper photographer was taking pictures as they went by the park. The boys were waving to the people on the street. When the women saw Eveline sitting in the back of the Lincoln, heads were shaking back and forth. Eveline only smiled as she waved her wand.

Sable and Olitha had banners printed with "Happy Birthday Patrick and Andrew" on them. The banners could be seen in the front yard as the parade approached the driveway. The neighbors asked what in the world was she doing now. When the parade ended, the farmer was there to put the ponies on the truck. Patrick wanted to know if they could keep a few ponies. Winston told him they were only rented and they were getting too big to ride a pony. Eveline walked around the yard as the boys surrounded her. Winston blew the whistle and quieted everyone. When all was quiet, he wished the boys a fun weekend and announced that the party was about to begin. During the festivities, presents were given to all the boys, not just Patrick and Andrew. The administrator was speechless because of how well organized the party was. He said, "Mrs. Paine, I think you are a marvelous woman. You have shown me a side of you I did not see when I first met you." Eveline smiled and replied, "I have changed quite a bit in five years." Everyone was having a grand time in the boats and on the tire swing. Winston made a point of warning the boys not to fall into the water. He told them there were serpents waiting for boys. The adults were mortified he would say such things. The boys thought it was funny and played along with his story, acting terrified every time one of them jumped into the water.

Eveline spoke with Patrick and Andrew while they sat on either side of her. Winston and Alice were walking around and spotted the three of them. They approached Eveline and Alice said, "You remind me of Mother Goose speaking with her children." Eveline smiled and said, "Andrew, tell them what Patrick and I have just asked you." Andrew said, "Miss Eveline wants to adopt me. She asked me if I wanted her to be my mother." Winston was speechless and Alice's mouth was wide open. Patrick beamed and Eveline smiled. Andrew said, "I told Miss Eveline that was my birthday wish." Eveline hugged them as Winston and Alice clapped their hands. Eveline told the boys that she was going to announce the news in a few moments to the guests. Eveline explained to Winston and Alice that she had made all the necessary legal arrangements and needed to sign the paperwork. As they were walking toward the guests, Thaddeus Cooper arrived. Eveline greeted him and reminded everyone of who he was. Eveline had forgotten he was invited in all the confusion of party planning and adopting Andrew. Thaddeus looked at Eveline in her queen's outfit and asked, "Do you always dress like this?" She gave him a smart look and said, "Only when I'm entertaining." Winston spoke up and said, "She likes to wear different outfits when she entertains." No one dared question his remark.

Eveline called for attention. She thanked everyone who helped organize the day. She thanked the school administrator for his help in allowing the classmates to be together. She explained how she came upon the Manlius

Pebble School and how much she appreciated it and how much Patrick had grown. She winked at Patrick and said, "We have an announcement." Patrick stood up and said, "My mother is adopting Andrew." Everyone cheered. Frank said, "She should be dressed like the Old Lady in the Shoe. She is going to have so many children she won't know what to do." Everyone around them laughed when they heard this. Rose and Samuel thought it was a joke. Sable nudged Rose and said, "Miss Eveline not kiddin, she's serious. She got Olitha's kid livin here and now Andrew. Weez living in the house of many colors." The administrator went to Eveline and admitted he hoped she would adopt Andrew. He told her that was all he talked about at school. The administrator thanked her and offered to do anything he needed for the transfer. Eveline told him that her lawyer had started the paperwork and the courts would finalize whatever was required for the adoption.

The party weekend ended with everyone having had a wonderful time. As Patrick and Andrew got on the train they said, "Goodbye mother." Each boy waved and grinned from ear to ear as the train left for Syracuse on Sunday afternoon. The remaining guests left shortly afterward and the house seemed as if nothing had happened. Winston sat on the porch thinking of the parade and party and was amazed at how well it had all turned out. He thought about Eveline with the many sides of her personality. Winston was the only person who had knowledge of what she was capable of being and doing. While he sat on the porch, Thaddeus Cooper was inside speaking with Eveline. Winston wondered about his intent and to what degree he would be involved, since the investigation and trials were finished. The door opened and Thaddeus said his goodbyes to Eveline. When he saw Winston he said, "Take good care of my girl." Eveline smiled, but Winston frowned at his remark. Thaddeus tipped his hat and walked to the taxicab. Winston asked Eveline what his remark meant. Eveline shook her and said, "He has the idea he wants to know more about me." Winston made no further comment but wondered what Thaddeus' intentions were.

Eveline decided it was time to call the travel agent. She wanted to reschedule the trip to Florida. It had been nearly a year since she missed the cruise to Miami. When she telephoned the agent, he remembered her and reminded her that she had a credit toward the trip. She explained that she wanted to take the trip just as she had planned a year ago. The weather was gloomy, so a trip to the land of perpetual sun would be perfect. The agent was able to offer the same deal. She and Winston would be sailing on a ship that had all amenities included. Eveline reserved two top level staterooms. The penthouse at Hotel Halcyon on East Flagler Street and Second Avenue was available. The agent told Eveline that the best view was the east side because it had a view of the ocean and the sandbar. He reminded her that a sales office was in the lobby of the hotel. Many people living in the cold northeast would come to Florida and buy land on the sandbar. As the agent said, "It is a gold mine not a sandbar." When Eveline heard this, she thought she might take a look and maybe invest in land. The agent would send Eveline the travel packet, along with newspaper articles about Miami and the surrounding area.

When Winston arrived, Eveline told him she had made reservations to go to Florida. She explained the details and told him all he had to do was be ready to go. Winston liked the idea of going to Florida and a warm climate. He told her he hoped they made it this time. Winston told Eveline he would need more clothes so he would go to Baker and Stark for a fitting. Eveline gave him a questionable look when he said that. Winston knew what she was thinking until he said, "I found out that Mike decided to get married. He told me that he was tired of being alone. He is marrying a high school sweetheart. Her family lived in Philadelphia and her father owned Wannamaker's Department Store and Mike will be working there." Eveline was shocked after what she knew about Mike and Winston. Winston told her, "A lot of men do that. It is a way of covering things up." Eveline thought that seemed to be what most of the men she associated with were like. The news surprised Eveline but made her ask herself why she went for men like that. Thaddeus Cooper's name came to mind. Why did he want to get to know her better?

The travel packet arrived and the agent included the information about Miami. The first headline was "Wild Dreams of Romancers." It told about how people bought land in the Everglades called a tropical swampland. Land purchases in this area were not encouraged but land purchases were abounding toward the ocean. The article stated that the population of Miami was over 300,000 with more than 1,000,000 winter visitors. Construction of hotels would be a way to invest money and make large profits. The automobile was making it possible to go from Miami to the new Miami Beach at a rate of 180 cars per hour. When Eveline read this, she could see herself driving around Miami in her Lincoln, especially with the top down. The possibilities of building a small hotel on Miami Beach gave Eveline ideas for using Wallace's money. The article ended with photos of the skyscrapers and traffic congestion around Miami. She looked up from the paper and said, "This is my kind of place." She showed Winston the articles and as he read them he agreed it would make for a great adventure.

The Geneva Daily News featured articles about how people could get everything they wanted. The new slogans were to buy today and pay tomorrow. There was a joke in the newspaper showing a new born baby leaving the hospital with the mother and the caption read: "The baby only cost $2. We can take the rest of the baby's life to pay the hospital bill." There were articles about buying on speculation. Investors would take a chance on everything in the hopes to make huge profits. There was mention of land speculation in Miami. When Eveline read it, she thought it was the thing to do, even though President Coolidge warned the public of such spending. This was the new and improved era and people were not worried about the future. The only thing to worry about was how to get enough money for a down payment. President Coolidge wrote in an article for the country to beware of buying on credit because it was the foreshadowing of an out of control economic devastation. The President said that people read articles of that type with a blind eye and listened to warnings with a deaf ear. Eveline put the newspaper down and thought that did not apply to her. She had all of Wallace's money and would pay cash for everything.

CHAPTER 29

During the train ride to New York, Eveline and Winston talked about the events when they were there before. Winston told Eveline that he did not want to spend much time there because every time he had been there he was in trouble. She spoke about the possibilities of living in a warmer climate. She remembered the weather in Canada and knew going south would be a better plan. They would not need to stay overnight because the ship was scheduled to leave at 5PM and the train arrived at 3PM. Winston asked Eveline what her plans would be for Patrick and Andrew if she moved to Florida. She told him that they would stay at Manlius until they graduated and then she hoped they would go to West Point. They would come to Florida for holidays and she would travel to Syracuse to see them. While Winston was asking these questions he wondered where he fit into the plan. Eveline sensed his discomfort and said,

"You will of course be with me wherever I go." Winston decided to address the issue of Thaddeus Cooper. Eveline explained that she thought he was a nice man but she was not interested in him. She told Winston that she made it clear to Thaddeus that she was happy not being married. Eveline said that Thaddeus had never been married because he was married to his work. Winston had a feeling Thaddeus was more interested in the relationship between he and Eveline. Was he going to be another Rudolph?

They arrived in New York City at 3PM and took a taxicab to the ship. Passengers were boarding and the luggage delivered to the staterooms. The ship was enormous having three smoke stakes. They were told as they boarded that the more stacks the more power. As they waited in line, Winston overheard a woman telling her group that she hoped the ship was not going to be like the Titanic. Gasps of breath were heard and Eveline told Winston that if the ship went down they would be first on the lifeboats. Eveline winked at Winston and told him he could wear one of her dresses and pretend he was a woman but hoped that did not happen. When they arrived in their staterooms, they found a luxurious environment. There were crystal glasses for every use. As part of the top level, each stateroom had an attendant. Eveline was assigned with a stylish maid. Winston found a suave male attendant in his stateroom. They would assist the passengers in any way they could. Winston thought of the bellhop at the Waldorf Astoria and wondered if this attendant was going to be as accommodating. Eveline requested a massage for herself and would see Winston for dinner at 8PM. Winston thought a massage might be fun and his attendant explained that he would be ready after

Winston had showered. Winston unpacked and went to the bathroom and found a room as big as a bedroom. The attendant followed him and asked if he needed anything for his shower. He explained that the massage table would be set up in the bath area and that there was no need for clothing.

Eveline's attendant offered to style her hair and offered to give her a pedicure and a manicure. After her bath, Eveline found the massage table set in the bathroom. The attendant was very professional and made Eveline feel like she was floating in air, not on the ocean. She used a colored nail polish for both her fingers and toes. During the treatment, Eveline was told CoCo Chanel products were used for the passengers on this level. In keeping with Chanel's policy, a private sun tan area was available for tanning. After a two hour make over Eveline could hardly find energy to dress for dinner. She wore a fancy ruffled dress with matching gloves. She carried a small purse that matched her shoes. When she saw herself in the mirror she thought how much better she looked and felt.

Winston finished showering and appeared, as instructed, at the massage table. The attendant was waiting with a small towel wrapped around his waist. Winston reclined on the table and the attendant began oiling his legs. As he was lying on the table he asked, "Where are you from." The attendant told him he was from Havana, Cuba and had worked for the cruise line for two years. Winston commented on his skin being so tan and perfect. The attendant told him that if he lived in Florida he too would have skin tones like his. Winston was confused when the attendant massaged his groin and hips. He tried to relax but he became aroused as the attendant moved his fingers around Winston's body. The attendant told Winston to turn over on his stomach and was told to close his eyes. During that time, oil was applied and the attendant complimented Winston's backside. He said, "You are a real man in every way." He moved his hands on Winston's shoulders and down the center of the back. When he reached the buttocks he stopped as Winston's muscles tightened. The attendant massaged the buttocks separately then moved his fingers through the center of them massaging deep into them. While he was finishing the legs, the attendant admitted that Winston reminded him of a close friend. Winston, still confused about the attendant's intent, decided to do nothing. After the massage, a tuxedo was handed to Winston. The attendant tied the tie and adjusted his sleeves and made sure the trousers fit perfectly. He was not sure if the attendant was doing his job or was trying to be in control in a passive way.

Eveline was surprised at how handsome Winston was and called him a beauty. He blushed when he heard her say this. She had never seen Winston so well put together. They were seated at the captain's table with the rest of the passengers on their stateroom level. Eveline nudged Winston and said, "I sure am glad I paid for the top shelf." The atmosphere was elegant and music could be heard from an orchestra across the way. It was like royalty seated in the front and the ordinary people down below. The service and food were exquisite. The orchestra played music for dancing after dinner. Eveline and Winston danced to a few familiar arrangements. Then Winston spotted his attendant who was dressed in a tuxedo. He went to women and offered to be their dance partner.

Eveline was impressed with his style and how smooth the attendant danced with the women. Winston told her that was his attendant. Eveline's eyes went up and then asked, "So what did you do to him?" Winston said, "It's not what I did to him but what he did not do to me." Eveline looked confused and Winston explained that during the massage nothing happened. Winston told Eveline that he let him do what he wanted, which was nothing. Still confused, Eveline waited for her turn to dance with him.

The attendant approached Eveline and offered to dance with her. When she was getting up from her chair, the attendant winked at Winston. Eveline did not see this because she was taken by the man's good looks and stature. He was very smooth on the dance floor. Winston studied his movements trying not to think of what he might be like in a sexual environment. It was clear that the attendant wanted to be the one in charge but was Winston willing to go along with him? As Eveline and the attendant returned to the table, Winston studied the man's dark and appealing face. Winston asked himself why he always admired men that were handsome and appealing. It would make his life easier if they were fat and ugly. After Eveline thanked him for the dance, the attendant told Winston that he would be in his stateroom to assist him when he went to bed. Eveline listened to him and looked at Winston and said, "We have never been treated like this." The attendant said, "My dear, you are getting closer to Miami. Everyone is treated like this in a hot climate." Winston looked at Eveline as the attendant left and said, "I'm not sure I have ever felt like this." Eveline told Winston that they better get to their staterooms. She wondered what her attendant would do when it was time for bed. Eveline sensed her treatment would not be as hot as what the Cuban's treatment might be. Eveline went to her stateroom and found a nicely arranged bed and flowers at her bedside. Her attendant wished her a good sleep and said she would see her in the morning. Winston went into his stateroom and found the attendant with only a towel around his waist. He offered to assist Winston with his tuxedo. He carefully and deliberately removed each item. When he was down to the underclothing he told Winston he wanted to watch him take the rest of his garments off. Winston did what he was told and when he had his clothes off the attendant told Winston there was a bath ready for him. The attendant stood at attention with his hands on his hips staring as Winston fondled and washed himself. The attendant told him that he should not do that. Winston asked why. He told Winston that he should save himself for better things. The attendant deliberately rubbed the towel around Winston's body to tantalize him. He then told Winston to get in bed for his last treatment. Winston was still aroused as he walked across the room to the bed. The attendant then took his towel off and began powdering Winston. There was so much happening in Winston's mind that he realized this man had him in his control. For the first time, he liked that control. It was different than ever before. The attendant said very little and told Winston he was a good follower. He promised Winston more the next day.

The next morning, breakfast was served on the balcony of the stateroom. Eveline and Winston had breakfast together while both attendants served them. Winston wished the women were not there, but knew he would get his time later. After a leisurely meal, Eveline was taken to the private sun deck. She was pampered with

Chanel fragrances and moisturizers for her skin while in the sun. Winston had the opportunity to do the same thing in a separate area for men. Some men preferred a woman attendant for pampering and some wanted a male attendant. Winston wanted his attendant. When they arrived, there were a number of men enjoying the feeling of sun tanning in the nude. Attendants were applying lotion and offering covers or shades when the sun became too warm. Winston's attendant was dressed in a white gauze outfit and his body could be seen through the fabric. Lotion was applied to Winston's body and periodically a water spray could be felt cooling the skin. When the sun became too warm, there was a pool to swim in. The attendant stayed with Winston all the time as other men came to Winston making suggestive remarks about his physique. The attendant made sure they knew Winston was his territory. Winston heard other men bragging that their wives were coming on to handsome men. It was their time to be pampered by a woman or a man which ever they chose. One man told his friend he hoped his wife got what he could not give her. It was time to be free and not tell. Winston questioned this and his attendant explained that people paid lots of money to have sexual favors while on vacation that they do not get at home. He wondered if his attendant thought he and Eveline were married and that was why he was being treated a particular way. After a few hours, Winston decided to go to his stateroom. He told the attendant he did not need his assistance. The attendant was surprised and wanted to know why. Winston told him he wanted private time. He implied he may be having a guest. Winston walked away fully knowing he had no guest coming. He wanted to see what would happen.

Winston went to the stateroom and waited. After about half an hour, there was a knock on the door. He opened the door and the attendant stood without saying a word. Winston invited him in and the attendant asked if he was alone. He said he was. The attendant told Winston that if he needed special attention he could provide it today. Winston asked him if he treated all of his guests the same way. The attendant admitted he did not, but found Winston playful and workable. Winston did not like what he said because it made him feel like less than a man. Winston told him he wanted to take charge of him instead of the attendant being the dominant one. The attendant stepped back and told him he could do what he pleased but that would cost money. The reason he was being controlling was to see how far he could go until the issue of paying for sexual pleasures were negotiated. When Winston heard this, he decided to allow the attendant to continue his work in his way with no money exchanged. Now, Winston was in control and told him to massage him until he felt fulfilled. The attendant did what he was told and Winston had him massage him in places that even aroused the attendant. Before the attendant lost his control, Winston told him that it was his turn to do the massage. Winston got off the table and told the Cuban to lie on his stomach. Winston was surprised that the Cuban enjoyed what he did to him and there was no money exchanged.

The ship docked in Miami at noon and Winston and Eveline disembarked first. On the way off the ship, their attendants were there to wish them well. When Winston saw the Cuban, he was standing in an unusual way. Winston went to him and thanked him for his time and body. The Cuban smiled and told Winston that if he was his attendant again, there would be no more games. Winston smiled and said, "I don't pay for my fun." When Eveline heard this, she knew Winston was the victor over the Cuban. She smiled and said to Winston, "My attendant was no fun at all." They hired a taxi to take them to the Hotel Halcyon. The temperature was 85 degrees and it was February 1. Eveline shook her head and wondered how this could be, with it snowing in New York. Winston told her he could not wait to get into his bathing suit. Eveline asked him if he had a new one. He told her that he liked the old one because it was very comfortable. She shook her head and said, "It sure is. Everyone can see how free you are with your body." The taxicab pulled up to the hotel and parked under a palm tree. They had never seen one and watched it sway in the warm balmy breeze. The luggage was taken directly to the penthouse. The men at the desk were dressed in tropical shirts and baggy pants but the parking attendants and bellhops wore panama hats to keep the sun off their heads.

The view from the penthouse was what the travel agent said it would be. The sandbar could be seen in the distance. There were a few buildings there and only a rough structure for a bridge across the bay. Eveline called the front desk to have an attendant come upstairs to show them what to look for in all directions. Within minutes, there was a young Cuban girl who wore a flowered dress with little straps holding it up. Eveline complimented her on the dress and she explained that they were for sale in the dress shop on the main floor. The young girl was helpful in showing the different areas around Miami. She thought Eveline and Winston would better enjoy the ocean and the southern side of Miami. There was a town called Coral

Gables that would be a fun trip. When she was finished, Eveline went with her to see what dresses were available in the shop. Winston unpacked and found his bathing suit. He went to the pool and found high class people seated around the pool. The men wore bathing suits, jackets, and panama hats. They were smoking fat Cuban cigars and most of them were as fat as the cigars. The women wore fancy bathing suits and were using cigarette holders as they lounged around the swimming pool. When Winston walked in the area all eyes were on him. He knew why and decided to use it to his advantage. He dove in the water and let his suit fall to his knees. Before he got out of the water he pulled it up and made sure it clung to his body. He used the steps to come out of the water and went by the crowd that watched his body as he walked past them. Some of the women winked at him and one woman wanted to know if he was staying in the hotel. Winston told her that he was in the penthouse. He heard another woman say, "He must be a hustler. No man I know has that much to offer his wife." Winston took a place on a chaise and smiled as he listened to the comments. He thought that if those fat guys were their husbands, no wonder they had nothing to offer. Shortly after that, Eveline appeared in a new dress. She walked over to Winston, as all the women watched her. She poked him and said, "Look at my new dress." The design of the fabric had oranges, limes, pineapples, and lemons with green leaves on it. Winston told her she looked like a fruit basket. She sucked her teeth and walked away. As she went by the women, one asked if Winston was her husband. Eveline turned and said, "He is my dead husband's boyfriend." Winston laughed when he heard what she said, since she did not hear their comments earlier. The faces on the women and men were priceless. No one could figure out how such a thing could happen.

Early the next morning, Eveline went to the land sales office in the hotel. She made an appointment to discuss buying land either on the mainland or Miami Beach. The young woman who showed Eveline Miami worked in the sales office and told the agent about her. Eveline figured that was how they spiked people's interest by having such a pretty young girl start the sale. Eveline had a choice of viewing land from the roof of the hotel or a sales site on Miami Beach. She was warned it was rough there because the area was mosquito and snake infested with tangled mangrove trees. Eveline decided to be adventurous and go to the land being sold. She was advised to wear a hat and have a full cover of clothing. Eveline left the office and found Winston by the swimming pool. She explained what she had done and that he needed to get ready to go land shopping. When she told him he would need to cover up or he would get bitten because they were going to the sandbar, he perked up. He thought he might get a chance to go swimming in the ocean.

While they were waiting for the beach vehicle to arrive, they looked at the information about things to do in Miami. They made a reservation to take a tour of Coral Gables. The young woman that assisted them the other day would be the tour guide. Eveline liked her and told Winston that she would know about shopping in fancy dress shops. Winston was not nearly as excited as Eveline about such shopping. He saw an article about a trip to the Everglades, with an alligator pictured and a tourist hugging it. Winston told Eveline he was going with or without her. She agreed to go but was not interested in wrestling an alligator. The lobby of the Halcyon had a tropical atmosphere with wicker furniture and ceiling fans with palm fronds used as paddles. While they had lunch and waited for the beach vehicle there was a poster in the restaurant about a show in Miami. Eveline read about the actress doing the show. She had a reputation as a sex symbol that was known for her bawdy performances. The show was to be held in the new Biltmore Hotel in Coral Gables. Eveline told Winston they would go to the hotel to purchase tickets when they were there.

The vehicle used for the trip to the beach was more like a buggy than an automobile. Winston reminded Eveline that this car was not her Lincoln. The dust flew by as they approached the bridge to the sandbar. It was a wooden bridge with very little room for a vehicle to pass coming in the other direction. It was built on stilts with wooden planks. Eveline could not understand how the land was so valuable because the closer they got the rougher the road. Finally, they arrived at an unpaved sand road. There were some buildings and inhabitants. The sun was blazing hot and the air had a heavy feel of humidity. The sales office looked like an old building that could blow away in a breeze. They went inside and saw a large map of the proposed land plots with a street plan. The agent explained that Miami Beach would someday be a gold mine. As they stood in the office, hundreds of people were doing the same thing. They could see one tall building in the distance. Eveline asked about that building. The agent explained it was a hotel and the fifth floor was the sales level. From that point a prospective buyer could see the land they were interested in buying. He told Eveline that she needed to select a plot from the map and then they would go to the fifth floor to see where it was located. Winston asked why they could not go to the actual plot. The sales agent explained that the roads did not go to all the areas. As Eveline looked at the map, she thought of the article in the newspaper about speculative buying. She told Winston, "If this isn't speculative buying nothing is. I feel like I am buying into a jungle." The agent laughed and told them he heard that every day.

Eveline studied the map and the names of the proposed streets. The south part of the beach was the only area being developed and there were five north-south streets with numerical side streets going toward the ocean. A sign read, "The closer to the ocean the more expensive the land." Eveline decided to look at the middle street named Palm Avenue. The agent told her that the streets would be renamed as the beach developed. They went to the top of the hotel to see where the land was located. When they walked into the lobby it was surprisingly nice, compared to the wilderness they had just left. The agent told them there was nothing to do because only guests that enjoyed wilderness were staying there. Winston asked how far the ocean was from where they were. When they got to the rooftop, the ocean was about a half a mile away and looked like an uninhabited area where not many people adventured for a swim. The agent had a pair of binoculars so Eveline could see the general area of her land choice. He pointed south to the plot which was in the middle of the area being developed. Eveline studied the area and liked it because it was moderately priced. She asked the agent what the terms of the sale would be. He explained they would do the paperwork and she would have a month to have her lawyer examine the papers and transfer the funds. Winston asked her if she was sure about what she was doing. She looked at him and said, "I think it is taking a chance, but my whole life has been like that. I want to do this on my own terms not Wallace's." Winston tried to calm her down and the agent asked, "Who is Wallace? I thought Winston was your husband." Eveline laughed and said, "Everyone in Florida thinks he is my husband. Winston is my dead husband's boyfriend." The agent was speechless but gave Winston a sly look. They went back to the beach vehicle and took the shaky bridge back to the main land.

Time had been going by fast and they only had two days before the ship set sail for New York City. While they were waiting for the tour bus to Coral Gables, Eveline discussed her anxiety about the land purchase on a sandbar. Winston told her that she was smart for not buying the most expensive land available. He reminded her she had a habit of always buying the best. Eveline made a face when he said this and agreed she did not want to lose all her money in the sand. Winston said he thought she was too smart to gamble on only one thing. She said, "I can always depend on you for support." While they were riding on the open air bus they passed by buildings that were taller than they had seen since New York City and there was hustle and bustle in the streets of Miami. The young girl who was pointing out places said that the Biltmore Hotel had just opened in January. They were building a canal that would have gondolas taking people to the ocean from the hotel and there was a Venetian pool at the hotel for swimming. She passed a poster around that showed the hotel with the title "Florida's Perfect Kingdom of Beauty, Pleasure, and Play." The girl read, "The hotel will attract the right kinds of people to the land. People with money will find comfort and style at the Biltmore." Eveline nudged Winston and said, "I wish we had stayed at the Biltmore." Winston was interested in the Venetian pool but he had no bathing suit. Eveline reminded him they were only stopping to buy tickets for the show. The guide told the group they would have an hour to tour the grounds and lobby of the hotel. Eveline went to the concierge to inquire about tickets but they were sold out for the next three evenings for the show called "Sex." Mae West wrote the play and was playing the part of Margie La Mont.

Eveline was not happy about missing out on a play written by a woman who had a reputation for being on the edge with her behavior. Winston was sorry he was not going to see what type of sex she was going to have in the show. They went to the gardens and the pool area and saw lush tropical vegetation everywhere. The pool was huge with flamingoes surrounding the area. It was like a dream with the colored flowers, birds, and blue water. The tour bus went to Coral Way, which was the main street in Coral Gables. The town was noted for its coral structures and moss laden trees. The tour guide explained about shopping and a walking tour of the town and informed them that the bus would leave in three hours. Winston decided to sit on the bench and watch people. Eveline was interested in the shops. While Winston sat, he observed the slower pace people had because of the heat and hot sun. He felt warm sitting in the shade and it was only February. Eveline returned and sat with him because she was worn out from carrying hat and dress boxes. Winston told her she was going to need to buy a steamer trunk to get her new belongings to Geneva. She ignored what he said. The bus tour returned to the hotel at 6PM. It was a tiring day so they had an early dinner. The ship sailed back to New York at 5PM the next day.

Eveline picked up the paperwork for her land purchase. Winston spent the last hours at the pool entertaining the people with his bathing suit antics. Eveline spent the last hours in the sun with him. The guests still buzzed about them and such a relationship. Winston told Eveline they were all jealous. They laughed because they were glad they were not like the people around them. The taxicab arrived at 3PM. Eveline, being late, ran to the taxicab, which took them to the ship without any time to spare. They were on the ship and in their staterooms before they knew it. Winston looked for his Cuban attendant but he was not working that cruise. He was relieved that he did not have to play games with him again. Winston's attendant was an older gentleman who was proper in every way. Eveline had the same woman as before. It seemed like a dream when they lost sight of Miami.

During the trip back to New York, Eveline discussed, in great detail, her plans for Florida. Winston listened and wondered why she was in such a hurry to go back to Miami. He told her she had a lot to accomplish in the next few years if she wanted to leave Geneva. He asked her if he was included in her planning and she told him she needed him to be in charge of whatever property she owned. When they arrived back to 775 South Main Street, Sable and Olitha were excited to hear about the trip. Eveline told them a little about it but did not tell all. She needed time to plan things before she made any announcements. Her first order of business was to meet with Mr. Keyes about her land purchase and investments.

During breakfast Eveline read the newspaper. The front page featured the Ford Motor Company's profits of $94,560,400.00. Eveline smiled as she calculated how much of the profit would be coming to her. The article continued to say that because Ford was doing well, Henry Ford instituted a 40 hour, 5 day workweek for the company. It was a first for any company, even though there was much labor force unrest. Many companies were not as good to their employees as Henry Ford was. Fear of strikes and walk outs were beginning to happen throughout the country. Another headline read, "Actress arrested in a hotel in Miami." Eveline read that Mae West had been arrested during her opening performance at the Biltmore Hotel. She performed a belly dance and was arrested for indecent exposure. She saw Winston in the hallway and showed him the article which disappointed him that they had missed it.

Rose telephoned Eveline asking her to go to lunch to find out about Miami. Eveline agreed to meet her but explained that she needed to go to Mr. Keyes' office first. Mr. Keyes went over all her transactions and gave her an update on the progress of Andrew's adoption. He told her it could take a few months for the final signing of the adoption papers. Eveline presented the land purchase offer to Mr. Keyes. He studied it and asked, "Why are you leaving?" She explained she was not going anywhere soon. Eveline told him about the sandbar and how untamed it was. He listened and said he heard about the land rush to Florida. She asked him to review the offer and advise her on the financial aspect for payment. Mr. Keyes told her she should only pay the required down payment and have a mortgage on the undeveloped property. He explained how easy it could be to lose it to a flood or natural disaster. He agreed to set up the mortgage with the bank. Eveline met Rose at the restaurant. She told Rose about how beautiful and fun Miami was. Eveline had worn one of her new dresses even though it was cool weather because she wanted to show off the tropical fabric. Rose wore a drab grey suit, black shoes, and carried a black handbag. It was like day and night between Eveline and her. Eveline, in a smart tone told Rose, "It's time you get Samuel to Florida for some fun." Rose told her that would never happen. Eveline did not divulge any information about her sandbar purchase. She and Winston had agreed to remain quiet about it.

Summer arrived with unusual heat and humidity. Eveline felt like she was already living in Miami. Winston enjoyed the hot weather because he enjoyed caring for the grounds and swimming in the lake in only a pair of shorts. He tried to get Eveline to swim in the lake but she did not like the smell of the water and the rocks on the bottom of the lake. He suggested they invite Patrick and Andrew for a visit. Eveline agreed and made arrangements for them to come by train. Olitha and Sable asked if there was a parade this time. Eveline told her it would be a quiet weekend. Sable planned the menu with the food the boys liked. Winston was just as happy because it was the only time he ate food like that too.

The economy had been a topic of much debate in recent months. The buying on credit had escalated, much to the warning of financial analysts. The stores were advertising credit before cash. The new JC Penney Company at 519 Exchange Street was having a grand opening sale on September 3. It would be selling furniture, appliances, clothing, and accessories. The advertisements stated, "Bring very little cash. Everything is on credit." The automobile dealers were selling the newest models for higher prices and charging a percentage for buying on credit. The consumer did not care that it was more costly; they wanted to have it all. President Coolidge sent a message to the American people, that the economy was thriving and stable. When Congress met it decided not to rock the boat. The newspapers had a heyday with the news because so many people feared a collapse because of the frivolous economic policies in the country. The question the newspapers had was credit helping or hindering the economy? Spending and use of credit continued to escalate when people read about prosperity. No one worried if they would ever pay off their bills.

Patrick and Andrew arrived the week before school began. Winston measured them and discovered they had grown 3 inches. At first Eveline thought that was corny but was glad Winston kept the practice of measuring their heights. There were no more buddy hugs. Winston shook their hands instead and Eveline hugged and kissed them. The school provided uniforms for them with sporty caps worn like berets. Eveline liked how they looked and commented that they looked like they were on their way to West Point. Sable greeted the boys with their favorite chocolate cookies. Winston gave them bathing suits to match his. Eveline laughed when she saw how they looked. It was cute when they were young but now the boys were beginning to look like young men and things were not as little as they once were. Winston did not care and the boys were not bothered especially when they used the tire swing and fell into the water. While they were in the water their bathing suits were usually off. Sable said, "Weez got a bunch a neked men on the shore." Eveline would shake her head and let them do what they wanted.

Shortly after the school year began, there were reports of violent weather in Florida. The summer had been warmer than usual, making the ocean temperature higher, intensifying the possibilities of hurricanes. On September 20, a hurricane hit South Florida. According to the reports, "The Magic City of Miami and Miami Beach were leveled." Many people were killed and the Hotel Halcyon was destroyed, as were many other buildings. It was reported that it would take many years to recover from such a disaster. When Eveline heard the news she thought of what Mr. Keyes had warned her about paying cash for something that could be destroyed.

CHAPTER 30

A few months after the hurricane in Florida, Eveline received a letter regarding the land on Palm Avenue. The development of the utilities and underground improvements were delayed for one year because there was extensive work being done to rebuild the existing properties throughout Miami. Eveline telephoned Mr. Keyes to discuss the letter and her mortgage on that land. He told her that she should be happy she did not build anything before the storm because it was difficult to destroy vacant land. When she finished speaking with him she felt better about making her first payment for the Palm Avenue land. The newspapers had continued coverage of the damage in Florida. People would ask why some places were flattened and others withstood the winds and torrential rains. The Biltmore Hotel was featured as a building that had very little damage, compared to the Halcyon, which was a total ruin. The Halcyon was built of wood and the Biltmore was constructed with concrete and iron with a stucco exterior. It withstood winds over 100 mph and all new structures were required to be built with similar materials.

There had been coverage of the economy of the United States. Reports were that the stock market had a disease that had been ruining the health of the economy. The President would say the economy was healthy but the expansion of the stock market increased because of speculation. Mr. Keyes had warned Eveline not to fall for speculators. These were people who offered to assist investors to purchase stocks on a margin all in the hopes of getting rich. Eveline had received offers in the mail from brokers offering these things. Mr. Keyes advised her that buying stocks on a margin was really buying stocks on credit. He used the example of buying $200,000.00 worth of stocks. The investor might pay the broker $10,000.00 still owing $190,000.00. Everyone hoped the stock doubled and then they would sell it, paying the broker his money and still making huge profits. The gamble was, if the market slipped and stocks went down, the investor may not be able to pay the broker. The speculative spending could eventually create an economic disaster. Financial advisors had different views of the tactic. The other factor that was publicized was that United States banks and big investors made huge loans to help foreign governments rebuild after World War I. Many of these countries were experiencing difficulty in repaying the loans. Mr. Keyes warned Eveline to be wary of any offer for such, get rich quick, ideas.

The United States mail was now being transported by air flying companies that had outbid railroads for faster delivery service. The last letter Eveline received from Florida had a stamp with an airplane on it. Charles Lindbergh made news when he flew across the Atlantic Ocean; a feat no one believed could be done. When he reached England, the British government had planes escort Lindbergh as he crossed the English Channel. Charles Lindbergh wanted to prove that by using a new California Anti-Knox gasoline, he could make a Trans-Atlantic flight. He landed in Paris on May 21, 1927 after a 33 hour flight from America. After a week of rest, Charles Lindbergh sailed for the United States on the USS Memphis. He was welcomed in New York City with parades and celebrations. He was the first to prove that air travel could extend across the ocean.

Charles Lindbergh had been scheduled to make air tours. The mayor of Geneva invited Lindbergh to land in Geneva on his tour. The invitation was turned down but Lindbergh would land in Syracuse on July 28 and Rochester, on Friday July 29, 1927. People from everywhere went to these cities to see and hear about Lindbergh's journey across the ocean. Eveline and Winston decided to go to Syracuse to see Lindbergh. They would pick up Patrick and Andrew. During their trip to Syracuse, Eveline talked about buying a new Lincoln. She wanted to have it before she moved to Florida. Winston asked her why she needed a new automobile. She said, "I am selling the touring car and the Lincoln and ordering the best 1928 Lincoln." Winston said nothing because he was just satisfied that he was part of her plan and did not want to upset her. They stopped at Manlius and the boys were ready and anxious to see Lindbergh. They were the only ones going and the administrator asked them to bring back something from Lindbergh because they would be presenting a report to their classmates. When they arrived it was warm and sunny. They had to park in an open field and walk nearly a mile to where Lindbergh would be. Thousands of people stood in the hot sun to see and hear Mr. Lindbergh tell about his trip. A band played until he appeared on a stage, raising his hands to calm the crowds. He told them about how afraid he was during the dark hours over the ocean. He explained how the airplane would go up and down in a wind draft. Many times he lost his bearings and prayed he could get back on his route. His greatest relief was when he was met by the British planes because he knew he had made it to land. After his speech, Lindbergh went from the stage to an airplane that was waiting for him in the field next to the crowd. He got in and took off in front of the crowds on his trip to Rochester. As Lindbergh took off, people were heard saying they could not wait to fly in an airplane. Patrick and Andrew had picked up a flyer about the trip to Europe and a story about Charles Lindbergh for their school report.

On a hot and steamy day, Winston was trimming the shrubbery in the front of 775. He was in usual gardening attire, a scant pair of shorts. He heard a car horn blow and turned to see Thaddeus Cooper being let out of a taxicab. Winston wondered what he wanted and saw that he had a folder in his hand. Thaddeus went to Winston and asked if Eveline was at home. As Thaddeus spoke his eyes wandered over Winston's bare chest. Winston ignored his eye movements but told him she was in the library. Thaddeus tipped his hat and went to the door and rang the bell. Olitha invited him inside. It looked as if he was expected. Did Eveline set up something with Thaddeus?

Winston used an excuse to go inside to see what might be happening. He entered the side service door so as not to be heard or noticed. Sable saw him and said, "That Thaddeus, he a cookin up somethin with Miss Eveline." She and Winston stood behind the drapery to hear what was being discussed. Thaddeus had retired from being an investigator. He was now working as an investment broker. He told Eveline, "I thought of you often and wondered how you were doing." Eveline told him she was very happy and had purchased land for development in Miami Beach. Thaddeus told her she was smart for looking ahead with investments. Eveline asked why. He explained that there were people in the financial world who were speculators just as there were carpetbaggers after the Civil War. Eveline wondered why she needed a history lesson. He explained that he was investigating the financial trickery these underhanded people were so good at accomplishing. While he was talking, Eveline thought of Mr. Keyes' advice about speculators. Thaddeus wanted to know if Eveline was interested in allowing him to be her financial consultant. She asked what he could do that she was not able to do herself. He told her because she was a woman she could be easily swindled. Eveline did not respond to this and only listened. He suggested she needed someone that could manage her money and allow her to be worry free. After a few minutes of his salesman approach, she said, "Thaddeus, my dear, have you forgotten so soon about what I uncovered a few years ago? You really think I need someone taking care of my money? That is what certain people attempted to do for me. As you know, some of them are in prison or dead." Thaddeus sat motionless but insisted she needed help. Sable decided to walk into the library to ask about refreshments. Thaddeus had his back to Sable.

Eveline reminded Sable that she did not call for her. When Eveline was speaking, Sable motioned with her head to go out to the hall. Sable apologized and played the game of the sorry servant. Eveline knew there had to be a reason for her actions. She excused herself and went into the hallway and saw Winston and Sable. She whispered, "What the hell is going on around here?" Winston took Eveline's arm and walked to the parlor. He said, "I know you don't like me to interfere with your business, but Sable and I have listened to Thaddeus. I have an idea he is up to something." Eveline asked him what that might be. Winston asked, "Can you set up a little party for the three of us?" Eveline smiled and told him she could but questioned why. Winston told her that he had a feeling Thaddeus was a lot like Rudolph. Eveline had not compared the two but began to think he might be right. Eveline and Winston would speak later but now Eveline had to deal with Thaddeus. She went into the library and apologized for leaving. She made an excuse that Sable needed some directions. Eveline thanked Thaddeus for his offer and told him she would need time to think about his proposal. She sensed he was not finished so she invited him for dinner that evening. Thaddeus was not expecting her to dismiss him so quickly, which changed his approach with her. He accepted and told her he was staying at the International Hotel on the corner of Seneca and Exchange Street. He would enjoy dinner with her instead of hotel food. Eveline failed to let Thaddeus know Winston would be the other dinner guest. She led Thaddeus to think they would continue their financial conversation during dinner. As she showed Thaddeus to the door, she told him to dress casually because they would be dining on the terrace and to return at 7PM.

After Thaddeus left, Eveline and Winston had a discussion about what happened. Winston compared Rudolph's actions in the past and Eveline could see how Winston thought they may have similar behaviors. Sable and Olitha were instructed to prepare a casual summer dinner. Winston told Eveline that he had an idea that might prove what his intentions were. Eveline wanted to know what Winston had in mind. He asked her if she could wear something light, casual, and provocative for the evening. She laughed and told him that was not a problem. She asked what he was planning. He gave her a sly look and asked her if they had ever had a chance to use the tire swing when children were not around. Eveline said, "Oh my God, I think I know what you are up to." Eveline left the room saying, "It will be an interesting evening." Sable went to the kitchen to tell Olitha what to plan for the evening meal. They agreed there may not be much food eaten at that dinner after the last party Eveline had with men.

Eveline watched from her bedroom window as Winston made sure the swing was tied tight and secure. She looked forward to whatever Winston had in mind. She prepared herself for the evening and wore one of her dresses she had purchased in Florida. She twirled around in front of the mirror and said, "This is provocative enough with only strings holding up the dress." She went downstairs and found Winston wearing his work shorts. She asked him when he was dressing for dinner. He told her that he did not want to eat dinner. He was planning to interrupt them before the meal and would come to the terrace dressed in his shorts. He would begin a conversation to distract Thaddeus. Eveline caught on to what Winston was up to. Winston said, "You will determine for yourself, before the night is over, what Mr. Cooper's intentions are."

Thaddeus arrived promptly at 7PM. Sable told him that Miss Eveline would be receiving him on the terrace. Thaddeus wore a casual shirt with the top buttons undone exposing his chest with a pair of baggy trousers. When Eveline saw him she said, "How dashing you look this evening. I like men who are not afraid to show some of their body." Thaddeus was surprised by her remark. Sable offered drinks. They each chose a whiskey. Thaddeus enjoyed the drink and remarked that drinks were difficult to come by. Eveline was careful how she discussed the details of having such provisions after what happened with her family. Thaddeus did not question the refreshments but began asking about the conversation they had earlier. Eveline made light of it and said she wanted more time to think about a financial consultant. Thaddeus told her that he thought that was the reason for this dinner meeting. As he was speaking, Winston came up the steps to the terrace. Thaddeus spoke to Winston like he was the hired hand. It was clear to Eveline that Thaddeus had an attitude that he was of a higher class than Winston. Eveline caught his tone and said, "Oh Winston, why don't you stay and enjoy our company?" Winston accepted and sat down. Sable was called and took Winston's order for rum. Eveline asked Thaddeus if he liked his new work. Winston asked what type of work he did. Thaddeus explained he investigated people who manipulated rich people and their money. He was open about having approached Eveline about that very issue. He had enough of his drink to admit he would like to oversee her money. Eveline said nothing. While Thaddeus was speaking about his work, Winston stared at Thaddeus' exposed chest. Winston sat in a very relaxed position with his ripped shorts exposing more than his legs. Eveline directed the conversation toward what Thaddeus liked to do other than work. He was more interested in Winston's behavior than her question. She did nothing but watch the two men begin a contest of who was more virile. Eveline enticed them when she asked Thaddeus if he ever used a tire swing. He had not. Eveline told him how much fun they were. She asked if he wanted a demonstration. Winston spoke up and told Thaddeus that he had made one for this house and one for Manlius, where Patrick and Andrew go to school. Eveline stood up and took each man arm in arm to the swing. She asked Winston to demonstrate it. Winston was eager, as he put his legs through the tire and held on with his hands. He started swinging as they watched. He spread his legs open and closed and back and forth to make the swing go higher and faster. By this time, his shorts were inside the tire making it look like he had none on. Eveline told him how good he looked like that. She began coaxing Thaddeus to see if she could excite him. Strangely, there was no sign that she was the one Thaddeus found interesting. Winston got off the swing and Eveline wanted her turn. She acted like she did the first day at Manlius when she used the swing and her dress flew up over head. While this was happening, Thaddeus admitted to Winston in a low voice, that he would like to help Eveline with her finances but could enjoy being around for fun with him. Winston did not respond. Thaddeus took his shirt off and exposed a muscular chest much like Rudolph. Eveline admired his chest and told him she hoped the rest of his body was as nice. She got off the swing and told Thaddeus it was his turn. As he was getting into the tire, Eveline tried to entice him again. Nothing she did worked. Winston stood behind him when he got positioned in the tire. Winston told him he would help him get used to making it go back and forth. Eveline knew what Winston was up to. Whenever the swing came back Winston put his hand down the back of Thaddeus' trousers. Thaddeus did not resist. Eveline went to the front of Thaddeus for one last attempt. When he came forward, she ran her hand up his leg. She was surprised at how well muscled he was. She told Winston they needed to switch. They did and Winston aroused Thaddeus almost immediately. When this happened Winston told Eveline he found something she may enjoy. Thaddeus spoke and admitted he wanted both of them. Eveline smiled and asked, "Where do you want me? I like it all." Winston spoke up, "Me too." By this time, Eveline had Winston's shorts off and fondled him in front of Thaddeus. He was not able to get out of the tire as easily as the others. While he was struggling, Eveline asked, "Why do you really want to be in my business? I train my men to do what I like and what I want. How do you ever think I would allow you to take over my life?" Thaddeus said nothing because he was not sure what Eveline and Winston were going to do. He thought he knew them but maybe not. Before she allowed this activity to end, she enjoyed Winston in her usual manner but left Thaddeus alone, as his eyes savored Winston's body. Dinner was never served. Sable played the game and cooked food Winston and Eveline would normally have for dinner. She understood how Miss Eveline operated. After Thaddeus left, Winston commented about Thaddeus and how he felt about him when he told Winston to take care of my girl. Eveline had not been aware of this remark. They discussed how Thaddeus operated with others when he found out about people and their money. It was a good way to maneuver himself into a person's life, by knowing all about them from his investigations. Winston asked Eveline if she was going to have any more to do with Thaddeus. She said, "I would be better off without someone who would attempt to undermine me as others have done before."

The third quarter of the fiscal year came to a close and the Wall Street Journal printed that Henry Ford was the richest man in the world. His profits, before taxes, exceeded $125,000,000 and after taxes $110,000,000. He had been named the biggest banker in the country; if not the world. The stockholders would be given the choice of a check or to reinvest their dividends in the company. When Eveline received her letter of intentions, she decided to do what Mr. Keyes recommended. She would request half in a check and reinvest the remainder into the company. Between Eastman Kodak and Ford, Eveline was receiving well over $100,000.00. Nothing could compete with Eastman and Ford, so she would maintain those two investments and rid herself of the Wire Wheel Company, Shuron Optical, and Safege stocks. Eveline decided to use part of her check from Ford to order her new Lincoln. There were advertisements about the new and more powerful automobiles and Lincoln was at the top of the list. As a present to Alice and Frank, she would give the roadster to them instead of selling it and hoped Frank would accept the gift. It was the automobile that ultimately ruined his business many years ago. She thought about donating her old Lincoln to the Manlius School instead of selling it too. Eveline grew to appreciate the administrator and thought this might be a good gesture by giving it to him. When she thought about this, she decided it would help his image when seen in a car of that sort.

October 20, Eveline received her dividend check from Ford Motor Company. Every time a check would arrive, she studied the name on the envelope; Miss Eveline Paine, owner. The amount for the quarter was $19,875.00. She called James to get the car ready because she was going to the bank. She dressed in one of her Floridian dresses and wore a wide brimmed hat. She pulled out her cigarette holder and was ready to go. When James pulled up to the front of the bank, he assisted her as she got out from the back seat. She sashayed into the bank, cigarette lit, purse in hand, and asked for the manager. When he saw Eveline he said, "Oh my dear Miss Eveline, how may I help you?" She handed him the check and said, "Sir, I wish you would address me differently. You have used the same greeting every time I come into this bank. You need to have more variety in your conversations." He blinked his eyes like he had been slapped. Eveline smiled as she puffed on her cigarette holder, blowing the smoke in his direction.

From the bank, she instructed James to take her to the Lincoln Motor Car Dealership. The same sales person helped her as the previous time. He remarked about how much more expensive the Lincoln had become since her last purchase. Eveline waved her hand and said, "Money is no object." While she waited to finalize the special order for the Lincoln, she saw a sign hanging in the show room. It read: "Safeguard Your Credit, Pay Promptly. Save Your Self Respect!" Eveline wondered how people could reach such points where they did not pay for things. The salesman discussed the possibility of financing the new vehicle. Eveline reminded him that money was not important. He explained to her that everyone who said that usually meant they had no money and would buy the automobile on an installment plan with low monthly payments. She said, "Take my name off that list. I have the money to pay you." She looked at the cost for her purchase which was $9,999.00. She looked at the salesman and said, "You've got a deal for $9,000.00. Take it or leave it." He accepted her offer.

CHAPTER 31

Prohibition caused corruption and crime throughout the United States. A national campaign with over three million people was formed to fight for the repeal of the 18th Amendment to the Constitution. Eveline signed up to be in a rally being held in Rochester. Even though her family had been involved in the smuggling, bootlegging, and sale of illegal substances, she thought it was a ridiculous law. The officials were beginning to see that gangland crimes were rampant because of Prohibition. Nowhere else in the world were there such regulations against the sale of spirits, but how was such a campaign going to be financed? The rally was being held at the Seneca Powers Hotel. Eveline wondered how she was going to feel when she returned to the hotel. It had been sold and was operating with the same high level of standards. Eveline invited Rose to go to the rally. When Rose heard about the rally, she compared it to the

Women's Rights Movement rallies they used to attend. She reminded Eveline that it might be different now without Rudolph. Eveline mentioned that she had thought about that. Eveline told Rose she would pick her up the next day to go to Rochester.

The mailman came to the front door with registered mail for Eveline. There were two letters she signed for. The first was from the Federal Courts in Rochester. It was the documents for Andrew's adoption. As Eveline read the letter, it finally hit her that she was going to be responsible for two children. She shook her head as she read this. After the papers were signed, he would become Andrew Paine. Mr. Keyes had been assigned the legal work with the school and the courts. Andrew would become her son officially on December 31, 1927. The second letter was from the Ford Motor Company announcing the newest model scheduled to be in showrooms starting January 1, 1928. The shareholders were informed before the general public, as this was something only Henry Ford practiced, that the new model would be more reliable and have a larger engine for greater speed. The basic model would be sold for $395.00 and the Tudor Sedan would be priced at $570.00. When she read the prices of the new models, she thought about how much she paid for her new Lincoln. The two automobile companies were very different. Ford was known for producing inexpensive cars for common people, while the Lincoln Motor Car Company sold only to the well to do.

The Dorchester-Rose Oil and Chemical Corporation had announced the opening of the Super Service Station in Geneva. Eveline picked Rose up in the Lincoln and stopped for gasoline. The service station was featuring eight gallons of gasoline for $1.00. The building was located on Main Street and built in a half-moon design. The servicemen would check the engine oil, wash the windows, and clean the headlights while filling the tank. When Eveline drove up to the pumping station she said to Rose, "Watch this. I am going to play up to the cute guy working on my Lincoln." She tooted the horn and the man came to the car. She said, "Oh sir, would you please brush out the floor of my car." He tipped his hat and winked at her. She got out of the car and stood with her hand on her hip as he bent over to brush the floor. While he was bent over, Eveline rubbed her hand on his behind and said, "Oh you should come over to my house sometime. We could have some fun." He stood up and smiled as she gave him the dollar for gas. Then she flipped him another dollar for being so nice to assist her. Eveline reminded him to stop over sometime. Rose told Eveline that she had enough nerve for two people. Eveline laughed and said, "I like to have as much fun as possible. I knew he would never take me up on my offer but he did have a tight behind." Rose only shook her head.

They arrived in Rochester for the rally at the hotel. Eveline strolled around the property to see how things were. To her surprise, it was similar and the employees still referred to her as Mrs. Paine. Eveline told Rose she feared that it would be awkward coming back to so many memories. Eveline realized it was good for her to return and reinforce the need for closure and letting go of the past. The grand ballroom was open for the rally. There were hundreds of participants. As expected, those attending the rally were encouraged to donate money for the campaign.

Rose said, "I feel like I'm at a presidential rally when money was mentioned." Eveline smiled as she stuffed a number of hundred dollar bills into the donation box. The rally was not nearly as rowdy as the Women's Rights rallies had been. This rally was more about presenting the need for repeal of the amendment that would lessen crime and corruption. The leader spoke about the positive aspects of allowing alcohol to be sold again. While they were standing in the crowd, Eveline felt someone nudge her. She turned and there was Thaddeus Cooper. Eveline asked what he was doing in a place like this. He said he was there to see what type of people favored the repeal. Since so much of his work was investigating corruption, he wanted to see who would show up for the rally. While he was speaking to them, Eveline wondered if he was telling the truth. She spoke up and said, "Don't try to convince me of needing a financial consultant." Rose was unaware of the intent of the conversation. Thaddeus put his hand up and said, "Oh don't worry. You yanked on me enough to know who the boss is in your affairs." Eveline smiled and said, "Good, you learned your lesson." After the rally, Eveline and Rose went shopping at B. Forman Company. The holidays were coming and they bought an outfit for Christmas. On the way home, Eveline told Rose not to be surprised if this might be her last year in Geneva. Rose had no idea that Eveline had purchased property or had any intention of leaving. Rose was quiet for the rest of the trip home.

Patrick and Andrew were coming home for Christmas. Eveline planned a special occasion this year. She was announcing Andrew's adoption and was going to give Frank and Alice her roadster. She wrote the invitations for the holiday to Alice, Rose, Hedy, and Liza. While she was preparing the invitations, she hoped that everyone would be as happy about the holiday as she was. Sable and Olitha were given lists of things to buy and cook. Winston had his usual routine of decorating and making sure the tree was the largest he could find. The chief administrator had spoken to Mr. Keyes and Eveline regarding the adoption completion. He promised not to mention a word to the boys until Eveline had announced the news. While she was writing the invitations, the announcer on the radio interrupted the program with news of a shooting at Baker and Stark. When Eveline heard the name of the store she thought of Mike. The announcer explained that Don Baker was shot at the store. He was the owner and was shot by Charles Green a disgruntled salesman. Don was shot in the abdomen and was in critical condition, according to Dr. Samuel Haynes. Charles Green had been dismissed from the store because of monetary thefts.

Everyone accepted Eveline's invitation for Christmas. Alice and Frank would be staying for the night and would arrive by train. Eveline hoped Frank would be willing to drive the new car home after the celebration. Patrick telephoned Eveline and spoke with her about how he and Andrew could not wait to be home. Eveline thought about what the future might bring after the adoption when she would be moving. While she thought of all the possibilities, she decided to tell everyone during Christmas dinner about Florida. Since the liquidation of the Goodwin Printing Company, Winston finalized the closure of the building and stayed at home to be on duty at the mansion. Eveline watched Winston take pride in the property as if it were his own. She had been thinking of what she could do to repay him for his years of allegiance and friendship to her and the family. The thought occurred to her to buy a nursery in Miami. Winston would be sole proprietor and she would be a silent partner. For his present, she wrapped a small palm tree in a box. For Rose and Samuel, she would ask them to be the godparents to Patrick and Andrew. As for Hedy and Liza, she would give them a trip to Miami to see everyone, after they settled into a new life. Sable and Olitha did not know that they were moving with the family. Eveline thought this would be present enough, for women who never wanted to leave her employ.

Mr. Keyes telephoned Eveline to discuss the last details of the adoption. Everything was complete and he wanted Eveline to know that the stock market had been fluctuating. He wanted to alert her to the stability of her investments. He recommended she unload everything except Ford Motor Company and Eastman Kodak Company. The Wire Wheel Works was being consolidated and would be moving south and he suggested she sell the Shuron and Safege stocks now that she had full control of Wallace's estate. Eveline explained to Mr. Keyes about her recent decisions about moving to Florida. He was surprised she may be doing it sooner than expected. During the conversation, Mr. Keyes asked about the boys and their schooling. Eveline told him they would remain at Manlius until she settled into a home and could find adequate schooling equal to Manlius, or they could remain at Manlius and go to West Point. He offered his assistance in whatever way she needed.

Christmas Eve arrived and the headlines of the Geneva Daily News reported that Don Baker had died and Charles Green pleaded insanity. Patrick and Andrew were arriving by train as was Frank and Alice. The doorbell rang and it was Hedy and Liza. Sable said, "You all can git youself in the kitchen and help us with the food." The doorbell rang again and Olitha answered it and saw Patrick, Andrew, Frank, and Alice standing like frozen statues. Eveline greeted them with a big hug. Sable came to the foyer and said, "Oh my, you boys are huge. They must be feedin you real good at dat scoo." Eveline stood many inches shorter than the three of them. She wondered how she had ever produced such a handsome, dark skinned young man. Alice was her usual self with the kissing and squeezing the cheeks routine. Frank was still the same in his tan slacks and blue shirt, with little reaction. Eveline said, "Frank, you are so predictable. Do you ever wear anything different?" Alice spoke up and said, "He has five of the same outfit and a suit for church." Everyone went to his or her rooms to unpack before dinner. During that time, Winston and Eveline had a conversation about the shooting and Mike's whereabouts. Winston told her that since Mike had moved away, that the store had not been doing well. All indications were that Charles was at the bottom of it. He wanted to get the money and leave town but Don reported Charles to the police and then came the shooting.

Dinner was being served just as Samuel and Rose arrived. They apologized for being late but wanted to show off Samuel's new car. He had just picked up a Hudson-Super-Six. He purchased it at Curtis C. Scofield Motors on 309 Main Street. The Hudson Cars were in close competition to the Lincoln Company. The car was called: "Tomorrow's Vogue as a Custom Landau Sedan." Eveline congratulated him on his purchase. Rose said, "I finally convinced him that we need a nicer car than most others have. Now we are up with Eveline." Samuel was embarrassed with her remarks but Eveline laughed and said, "That makes two flashy groups in town now." Eveline decided that as long as they were discussing cars, she would give Frank and Alice their gift. She invited everyone to the garage where they found the roadster with a huge bow on the top. Alice asked about the bow. Eveline explained to Frank and her that because they had always been on her side, even in bad times, she wanted them to have a better way to travel than by train. Frank's face turned scarlet. Eveline was fearful of what Frank might say or do. She went to Frank and squeezed him and told him she understood how, in the past, automobiles put him out of business. She wanted him to know she was unhappy about that also. She said that Wallace would have done the same thing she was doing. The car was his and Eveline handed him the keys. Frank was speechless and Alice began crying as usual. After what seemed like forever, Sable said, "Well, do you like it or not? My dinner is getting cold." Frank looked at Eveline and then Alice and said, "I can't drive the damn thing." Alice said, "I think I could drive it." Frank laughed and thanked Eveline for being the person she was and told her he was happy to accept the gift. He assured her he would take perfect care of it and learn to drive it. James offered to give him lessons in the morning.

During dinner, Patrick and Andrew monopolized the conversation about school. They were in charge of various clubs. The chief administrator moved them to a larger room so they could conduct meetings about school business. They were turning into leaders. While they were talking, Eveline watched them being so different, yet very close to one another. Winston wanted to know if the swing was still used. They laughed and explained how they made a few new ones for the little boys. They had outgrown the swing. During dinner, Eveline announced the finalization of Andrew's adoption. She had a new certificate of name change and gave it to Andrew. When she handed it to him she kissed and squeezed him. She told him she was very proud of him and glad he was now part of the family. Patrick nudged Andrew and said, "See, I told you she was pretty cool." Everyone cheered and clapped for Andrew. Alice wondered how this might have turned out if Wallace were still alive. Would all this have ever happened? There was no mention of Eveline's parents or any of the past. Frank spoke up, "I can't believe all this is happening. I never thought we would be part of this family after Wallace passed away." Alice cried in her usual fashion until Sable came into the room and said, "This ain't no funeral. Weez celbratin more family and new life."

During dessert Eveline discussed her plans for the future. It appeared that most people thought she was going to remain doing the same thing as she had in Geneva. Winston knew of the land purchase in Miami but did not consider what she was planning to do with it. She talked about how nice Florida was when they visited. She explained how she and Winston found vacant land on Miami Beach and explained how desolate the sandbar was. Winston spoke up and told everyone that she thought she was going to live on the sandbar. Frank mentioned that a hurricane ruined Miami and questioned why she would want to live there. Eveline explained that she was making plans to relocate. She wanted to start a new life, now that things were settled. She handed Hedy and Liza their tickets for the cruise to Miami. They looked at

Eveline with fear. Eveline knew why. She told them not to worry; they were not taking children with them. They were traveling first class to visit them in Miami. Eveline turned to Rose and asked if they would be godparents to Patrick and Andrew. They were delighted and accepted unconditionally. Winston sat quietly. Eveline handed him the wrapped present. He looked at it as if it was not big enough. She told him to open it and he found a palm tree. Winston asked if it was a souvenir. She explained it was his first palm tree for the tropical gardens he was soon to be owner of. She was setting him up in business as The Spaulding Tropical Gardens. He would be the owner and operator of a property that would sell tropical vegetation and offer tours of lush garden environments. Winston was speechless. Eveline called for Sable and Olitha to come from the kitchen. She explained that she felt the best gift she could give her house servants was an invitation to move with her to Miami. They would continue as domestic help in the new residence she was planning to build. They too were speechless. Alice told Frank that now they could go to Florida because they had a car to drive. Andrew asked what was happening to Patrick and him. Eveline explained they would stay at Manlius until things were settled. They could be moving to a similar school in Miami. She clarified that they did not have to leave Manlius unless they wanted to. The decision was up to them.

The next day James gave Frank lessons on how to operate the roadster. Frank found the car to be easier to drive than he expected. After about an hour of practicing, James felt Frank could easily drive to Rochester but would need to get a license to operate a motor vehicle before leaving Geneva. Alice was surprised that Frank accepted the gift and was able to drive the car without too much trouble. Hedy and Liza left still in shock about the cruise to Miami. Rose and Samuel did the appropriate paperwork to be guardians for the boys. Sable and Olitha wanted to know how soon they had to have the house packed up for moving. Eveline assured them it would at least a year before they left for Florida. Winston started planning his new adventure in a tropical environment. He thanked Eveline but had questions about finances and residence. She explained that he had a choice of where he wanted to live. He would be welcome to remain in her home or he may want to venture out on his own when they arrived in Miami. She told him in a smart tone he might want his own place when he met loads of Cubans. She told him they would have a lot more to offer than the men up north. Winston reminded her of his experiences with his Cuban assistant on the ship. He was excited thinking of the new possibilities for the future. Before Patrick and Andrew left to go back to Manlius, they spoke with Eveline about the move to Florida. They told her they were not sure about leaving Manlius and hoped she understood if they chose to stay in New York. Eveline was shocked but hoped they might reconsider when they visited Miami.

CHAPTER 32

January 1928, the economic climate in the United States continued rising with uncontrollable greed. Everyone wanted everything no matter how it was acquired. Advertisements warned of "caveat emptor" where the buyer should beware. Swindlers tried to sell products that were not what they appeared to be. Peddlers were seen in all areas of merchandising and service work. The consumer would get involved with characters that promised the goods or services and would never produce the work or merchandise. The stock market was on a high, but warnings were made about the future. Some financial analysts expressed fear that the economy could not withstand a nation on credit. Eventually, everyone would suffer and possibly lose everything for non-payments. Eveline received a notification that her Lincoln would be delivered in a few weeks. She received offers in the mail about financing her automobile. She discarded any mail that dealt with buying on credit. The latest advertisement featured a family dressed up and ready to go in their new high-powered automobile. The background pictured a shack where they lived. Eveline could not understand how that type of life could be secure.

Rose called Eveline to tell her that Samuel had returned from testifying about the murder at Baker and Stark. He had been the attending physician to the patient who was brought to the hospital, who died from a gunshot to the abdomen. The jury took no time in convicting Charles Green of manslaughter in the first degree. He was sentenced to 10-20 years at Auburn State Prison. When Eveline heard this, she thought about Lucille Preston and how she was being treated at the Auburn Prison. All those events seemed so long ago. She was happy she was on her way out of Geneva to a new life. Rose inquired about the boys and asked if they were excited about moving to Miami. Eveline was hesitant to tell Rose that they were unsure of going with her. Rose was surprised and asked why. Eveline told her that she was not sure either. The only thing she thought of was they might fear not having the same opportunities in Florida as in New York. They had been told that many of the Manlius students go on to the officer training school at West Point. Rose asked how Eveline felt about that. Eveline had no response.

Architectural design was taking on a new look in the United States. A skyscraper was being built in 1928 in New York City called: "The Chrysler Building." The design was Art Deco which had its origination in Paris in the 1920's. It was a modern approach to architecture and design in all facets of the arts. There was extensive use of dramatic lines and designs with heavy use of lighting. The top of the Chrysler Building would have curves and lights to illuminate the building at night. There were 77 floors that made it the tallest building in America. Art Deco had been receiving a fashionable reputation. Eveline thought about Art Deco and saw photos of how it was being used in Miami. She would investigate to see if architects were designing Art Deco buildings. She might want to be one of the first to build one. She read high-end magazines on design and fashion. Collier's and Harper's Bazaar often featured the latest in home and fashion designs. She learned there was a Spanish influence in Miami home designs. She wondered which designs she would actually like for her residence.

Winston studied everything he could find about tropical vegetation. He had little knowledge of what it would take to operate a tropical environment. He decided he might need to go to school for lessons on maintaining a tropical garden when he arrived in Miami. Eveline suggested he hire some natives of Miami to assist him in the development of the property. She had purchased a tropical garden near Coral Gables that had been damaged by the last hurricane. Eveline inquired about private schools for boys. The realtor knew of a few but the best one was Pinecrest Private School. It was north of Miami and considered top notch and was noted for their excellence and quality of school life. When she finished her conversation, she realized how much needed to be accomplished to make such a move possible. Now, all she needed was to convince Andrew and Patrick to transfer to Pinecrest.

The Lincoln dealer notified Eveline that her new automobile had arrived and that she could take delivery anytime. When she heard this she had to figure out how to get the old Lincoln to Manlius. After some thought, she decided to call the administrator at Manlius and have him bring Patrick and Andrew on the train. They could visit and she would transfer ownership of the car to him. The boys could stay and go back to Manlius a few days later. She contacted the administrator, who was agreeable to visit Geneva. He was not aware of the gift of an automobile. They arranged to come at the end of the week. The boys would stay until Sunday afternoon. Eveline requested that James polish the Lincoln and put a bow on it, just as he had done for Frank's roadster.

Eveline made an appointment with a real estate agent to discuss the sale of 775 South Main Street. She thought it might be a good idea to begin selling the mansion early in the spring. The agent was eager to assist her because it would be an easy property to sell. He knew of a few clients who might be interested in a quick transaction. Eveline wanted to relocate to Florida by the beginning of autumn. She had decided to rent a four-bedroom apartment at the Biltmore Hotel until her residence was completed. She had secured an architect and he was designing an Art Deco building. The architect sent Eveline a description of what she should expect when the property was completed. The letter began with the theme of Art Deco being a decorative architectural style with geometric designs and bold colors. The diagram showed eyebrow overhangs above the windows with small circular windows that matched circular designs throughout the walls of the building. There were five bold colors used to show how the completed building would look. When she saw the sketches, she was excited that a new world of color was soon to begin.

Patrick and Andrew arrived on Friday afternoon with the administrator. He was uncertain of the intent of the visit. Usually Patrick and Andrew traveled alone on the train. Eveline knew that the administrator would not be staying overnight but he did not know this. Sable and Eveline talked about all the things that were happening to get ready to move to Florida. After some discussion of the timeline for moving and liquidating everything in New York, Eveline asked the administrator to come to the garage. He said, "Every time I come here there is a different event taking place. Nothing is ever the same." Eveline smiled as she welcomed him into the garage to see the shiny Lincoln. He asked, "Why do you want to show me your car?" Eveline handed him the certificate of ownership that had his name on it. He was stunned until Patrick said, "Wow, my mother is giving everything away." Eveline laughed and told them she was giving things to people who deserve such gifts. The administrator asked why she gave the car to him. Eveline explained that a man in his capacity should be seen driving in a good car. He agreed he needed to improve his image. Eveline told him that he had been a good model for her children and she wanted to thank him in a different way than most people would. He was still stunned as she handed him the keys. He asked what she was going to drive to get around Geneva. She told him her new Lincoln was at the dealership ready to be picked up. He thanked Eveline and told the boys he would see them on Sunday. James opened the garage doors and out the administrator drove.

While Patrick and Andrew were visiting Eveline, she showed them the diagrams and sketches of the property being built in Miami Beach. Winston discussed his tropical gardens and all the work that needed to be done. He asked the boys if they would like to spend some time helping him. Eveline thought this was a good way to entice them to come to Florida. They said it would be fun to help their buddy get his business started. They agreed to visit Miami during their vacation. Eveline hoped that they would like Florida and agree to go to Pinecrest School.

The economic conditions remained top news in the nation. Systematic savings were being encouraged instead of credit. There were millions of people unable to pay their bills. The stock market was booming and Eveline's investments were skyrocketing. She received quarterly statements from the companies she was affiliated with. The latest total of her assets was nearing thirteen million dollars. When she saw the figures she wondered how she would get large sums of money transferred from the bank when she moved. She needed to discuss this with Mr. Keyes. When she sold the mansion she decided to transfer that money to her building fund in Florida. She would transport the Lincoln by train. Sable and Olitha would use their gift of a cruise to Florida after they finished cleaning and packing for the movers to transport her possessions to Florida.

Prohibition continued to be an issue in the United States. People had been receiving threats on their lives from gangsters that were being uncovered because of bootlegging and the smuggling of alcohol into the country. The rally group that had been started was the target for threats and gangland style murders. When Eveline read about the warnings, she thought about her involvement with her family and the hotel being used for a speakeasy and stop off point for trafficking. She decided that it might not be a good idea to continue to support the rally efforts to abolish Prohibition. There were billions of dollars being made from bootlegging, illegal operations, and speakeasies. She told Rose about the letters she received asking if Rose wanted to continue rallying. Rose explained that she only did it because Eveline thought it was a good idea. They decided it would be better to avoid any publicity. Eveline showed Rose the plans for her property in Florida. Rose appeared disinterested in the discussion, so Eveline asked what the problem was. Rose admitted she was missing her already and that Samuel would never consider leaving Geneva. Eveline understood and explained that it was time for her to start a new life because she had been through enough in New York. Rose agreed, but knew their friendship would either change or end. Eveline said, "It will end only if you want it to."

Things began happening in the summer. Patrick and Andrew were looking forward to coming to Florida to help Winston with the tropical garden. Eveline had arranged for them to go to Florida by train at the same time the Lincoln would be transported there. Mr. Keyes conferred with Eveline about how to transfer her money and stocks. The real estate agent received an offer on 775 South Main Street. He explained that it was different than the usual type of offer. When Eveline heard this she said, "What else is new? My life has been different than the usual." She had an appointment the next day to discuss the sale of 775. After the real estate appointment, she would go to the bank to see her manager friend. She hoped he would address her with new enthusiasm. Mr. Keyes offered to accompany her to the bank to assist her in the financial business. Eveline told Sable and Olitha about the possible sale and that they should begin preparing to pack and clean the mansion. Winston had been packing his belongings weeks ago in hopes of getting to Florida to begin his work on the Spaulding Tropical Gardens.

The real estate agent arrived to show Eveline the offer for 775. She listened as he told her that the prospective buyer wanted the contents of the mansion and was offering her more than she listed it for. Eveline was surprised but thought it was perfect. She would not have to hire movers to take the furnishings to Florida. She thought of how much fun it would be to buy new furnishings that were appropriate for a tropical environment. She signed the offer and would be receiving a check for $220,000.00. She telephoned Mr. Keyes while the agent was present to tell him what had transpired. Mr. Keyes had been aware of the offer earlier as the agent and he shared the office building downtown. He congratulated Eveline on such a good sale. She had been very lucky to sell everything with no strings attached. After he left, Eveline prepared to go to the bank. Mr. Keyes would meet her there. As she was on her way, she thought of how many times she went to the bank and was now a multi-millionaire. When she approached the bank, the manager opened the door and invited her in. Eveline was surprised and said, "Oh, you took my advice and changed your way with me." He said, "My dear, anything for you." As Mr. Keyes and she sat down, the manger inquired about how he could help Eveline. Then Mr. Keyes told him about the sale and the need to transfer money from the bank. The manager attempted to discourage transferring such large amounts of money. He explained that some banks had that happen and were left with no funds to operate. Eveline puffed on her cigarette holder and blew the smoke at the manager and said, "I'm very sorry for you, but I am leaving town and need my money." Mr. Keyes handed the manager the address of the Miami Savings and Trust Company. The amount of seven million two hundred sixty five thousand dollars was to be transferred by the end of the bank day. Eveline watched the manager gasp for air when he heard the amount of money. He assured Eveline he would have the transfer done. Before they left he said, "I hope we don't have to close the bank after all this money is transferred." Eveline said, "Make sure you don't close until you are finished with my transaction." When Mr. Keyes and Eveline were outside he said, "You were rough on him." Eveline smiled and said, "He's used to me and how I treat him."

The closing for 775 South Main Street was scheduled for two weeks. Sable and Olitha would stay to finish closing up the property. Eveline made arrangements for her and Winston to cruise to Miami. After they settled into the Biltmore, she would arrange for the boys to come to help Winston with the tropical gardens. She still hoped they would like it enough to want to stay and go to Pinecrest. Eveline telephoned Manlius School to explain when Patrick and Andrew would be taking some time off from school to help in Florida. The administrator understood and agreed to get train accommodations for them. Eveline explained that her Lincoln would be on the same train. The administrator asked if she had the Lincoln put on the train to make the boys feel important, as if they were guards for her car. She said no, but realized they might feel it was their responsibility to watch over the car. Whatever worked, as long as they wanted to live in Florida.

CHAPTER 33

The time came for Eveline to say her farewells to Rose and Samuel. She invited them for lunch and discussed all that had happened over the years. Rose explained how happy they were at 380 Washington Street. She understood that it was not Eveline's favorite place, but it had all worked out. Eveline asked if they were planning to visit Miami. Samuel was less excited about it than Rose. Eveline told Rose she should come by herself. They would have loads of fun. They discussed moving and the hope Eveline had that Patrick and Andrew might want to move to Florida. Rose assured her that they would watch over them as long as they were in New York. Eveline admitted she was nervous about taking a chance such as this. She was happy Winston was going along because they wanted a new adventure. Samuel wished them well and was not sure he could undertake such a drastic move.

Eveline called the school to confirm the schedule for Patrick and Andrew's leaving Manlius to go to Florida. The administrator agreed he would wait until he heard from Eveline and then would get them to the train. Everything was set for her and Winston to leave for New York. Winston had no regrets and was happy to be on a new journey. As they were riding on the train, Eveline made mental notes of things she hoped were done. Winston told her to stop worrying about the Lincoln because nowadays people were transporting their automobiles to Florida for the winter. When they arrived at the dock, the ship was the same one they had cruised on before. Winston, in a smart tone, asked Eveline if she had arranged for the same Cuban assistant as he had before. She told him that she had not and was through with his sexual adventures. Winston told her that he could accomplish that by himself. After that conversation, Eveline settled down and began to enjoy her time on the sea. The cruise was different this time because there were no personal assistants. The cruise line had reduced the services and only offered room service. Eveline did not worry about it very much because she did not plan a trip like this again very soon.

The ship docked in the Miami harbor and Eveline and Winston took a taxicab to the Biltmore. The desk attendant recognized Eveline because he helped her rent the penthouse apartment that could accommodate up to eight people. They were told about a Labor Day party on Monday that included residents and guests of the hotel. When Winston and she saw the apartment, Eveline wondered why she would want to build a home. The apartment was lavish in its decorations and had breathtaking views. The next day she and Winston would go to see the tropical gardens. Winston admitted he was uneasy about what it would take to be successful with his new business. Eveline reminded him that they both were on an adventure.

The next morning the sun was shining and the weather warm. Winston prepared to go to the tropical gardens. Eveline dressed as if she were going on a safari. Winston told her it was not a desert, but a jungle and it was probably very buggy and humid. When the taxicab pulled up to the front of the property, Winston saw vines of yellow flowers that entangled everything. Eveline told the driver to wait until they were finished because it was a remote place and there was no way to call for a ride back to the hotel. She agreed to pay the driver whatever he wanted, but insisted he not leave them in this jungle. They attempted to walk around but there was so much growth that the paths were hard to find. They did come upon a pond with flowers and vegetation of all types. The orchids caught Eveline's eyes because they were huge, unlike the tiny ones in the north from a florist. Winston was thrilled about the possibilities of the gardens and was determined to make it a place where people would want to visit. He mentioned it was going to be a lot of work and told Eveline he was happy Patrick and Andrew were coming to help him. Eveline asked if he had inquired about hiring natives from Miami to help untangle this jungle. Winston was planning on doing that now that he was here to stay. Eveline picked a few orchids for the apartment and stuck one in her hair as they went back to the taxicab.

When they returned from the tropical gardens, Eveline telephoned Manlius School to let them know it was time for the boys to come to Florida. The administrator had confirmed the tickets and the schedule for the train that would have her Lincoln on it, as well as the boys. They would be leaving in three days. Eveline thanked him and asked if he liked his new Lincoln. He admitted it did perk up his life and that he even took a lady friend on a date. Eveline was glad he was happy.

The days went on with Winston spending many hours at his gardens. He would arrive back to the apartment exhausted every evening. He had very little energy to go downstairs for dinner and had it served in the apartment. Eveline used her days conferring with the architect and the builder for her new residence. The weather forecasted a possible hurricane. Eveline hoped the boys would be safe and get to Florida before any bad weather. She knew the Biltmore withstood the last hurricane because of the way it was built. She had no fear of being in that type of building during a storm. She had been advised to spend extra money to have her building reinforced just as the Biltmore was.

It was September 17, when Eveline woke to the sound of howling winds. She looked out the windows and saw palm trees bent to the ground. The rain was pelting against the windows. Winston had been so exhausted that he did not hear the sounds outside. It was true, the hurricane that was predicted was about to happen. Eveline called the front desk about any word on trains arriving because of the weather conditions. The operator said all transportation was still on schedule but there was a special letter delivered for her. Eveline said she would be down to pick it up, thinking how strange it was for a special delivery letter for her because her regular mail was sent to the hotel mailbox.

She woke Winston up and explained about the weather and the letter. He dragged himself out of bed and dressed for breakfast. They went to the lobby and the clerk handed the letter to her. It was not a registered letter. Eveline looked at Winston with a strange look and feeling. She opened it and it read:

Dear Mrs. Wallace Paine,

We regret to inform you that your boys Patrick and Andrew will not be arriving to you at the Biltmore. If you wish to ever see them again, a ransom of two million dollars will cover their return to you. Since you were so determined to undermine the operations in Rochester and New York City, we feel the amount listed above will help to refinance these operations you so happily ended with deaths and imprisonments. You will be receiving further instructions for the delivery of the ransom. Do not attempt to involve the law because we are the underworld lawmakers.

Eveline began screaming and ran to the desk and demanded to know how this letter was delivered. The man explained it was left in the drop box during the night. As he was explaining, the lights went out and the front doors blew open. Winston held Eveline tight, as she sobbed in fear and uncertainty that she may never see Patrick and Andrew again.

ACKNOWLEDGEMENTS

Thanks to the staff of the Geneva Public Library's research department for their assistance in researching 10 years of newspapers on microfilm. Thanks to Marsha Houser, for assisting me with the reading and editing of this manuscript. Special gratitude goes to Shirley Wharton, Donna Gibbs, and Michael J. Hines, M.D. for accepting the challenge to read the drafts and to offer valuable feedback as the book was being written. Cover photo used by permission of Hobart William Smith Colleges.

DISCLAIMER

The places and historical events in the book are real. They were included to enhance the authenticity of the story. The names of the characters have been changed to protect any person who may still be alive.

SOURCES

_____. *Democrat and Chronicle*, Rochester, New York, Local History, January, 2012

Downey, Matthew T. *The Twentieth Century*, the MacMillan Publishing Company

_____. *Geneva Daily Times* 1919-1930

McElvaine, Robert S. *The Great Depression*, Times Books 1993

Shlaes, Amity *Coolidge*, HarperCollins Books 2013

WEBSITES

Andrew Volstead, Wikipedia.com

CoCo Chanel, Wkipedia.com

Columbia Girls' School—<u>www.columbiaallendaleschool.edu</u>

Fashions of the 20's, Wkipedia.com

Flappers, Wikipedia.com

Miami Archives, Biltmore Hotel.com

Mae West, Wkipedia.com

Manlius Pebble Hill School—<u>www.manliuspebblehillschool.edu</u>

Prohibition in the United States, Wikipedia.com

Roaring Twenties, Wikipedia.com

Speakeasies, Wikipedia.com

CPSIA information can be obtained at www.ICGtesting.com
Printed in the USA
BVOW02s1053090913

330682BV00001B/1/P